ABOUT THE AUTHOR

GREG MELLOR is a Canberra-based author with 50 published short
stories. His work has appeared in *Cosmos Magazine*, *Clarkesworld
Magazine*, *Daily Science Fiction*, *Antipodean SF* and *Aurealis*, as
well as small press anthologies in Australia and the United States.

Greg holds degrees in astrophysics and technology management.
He was a finalist in the Aurealis Awards and is a member of the
Science Fiction and Fantasy Writers of America (SFWA).

Wild Chrome is his first collection.

WILD CHROME

WILD CHROME

GREG MELLOR

Ticonderoga
publications

for Cat and Chris

Wild Chrome by Greg Mellor

Published by Ticonderoga Publications

Copyright © 2012 Greg Mellor

Introduction copyright © 2012 Damien Broderick

Cover artwork by Leanne and Jamie Tufrey

Designed and edited by Russell B. Farr
Typeset in Sabon and Franklin Gothic

A Cataloging-in-Publications entry for this title is available from The National Library of Australia.

ISBN 978–1–921857–23–2 (hardcover)
978–1–921857–24–9 (trade paperback)
978–1–921857–25–6 (ebook)

Ticonderoga Publications
PO Box 29 Greenwood
Western Australia 6924

www.ticonderogapublications.com

10 9 8 7 6 5 4 3 2 1

CONTENTS

PREFACE

GREG MELLOR

Men! We get into trouble and we make trouble.

I think most men suffer a silent, inner turmoil that often manifests itself in all the wrong ways. Many of us end up tumbling along life's avenues, searching for the indefinable, lurching from one crisis to another. And of course we expect our loved ones to sacrifice many things along the way, loyal and unquestioning ... yeah, right! Sure, there are some gems among us who are really worth it, and some men can find their destiny or character, while others make a truly positive contribution to the world. But sadly the decisions men make can just as easily send our society into a tailspin, and a small minority can summon ruin to themselves and everyone they hold dear.

So heaven knows how we'll cope in the future when technology finally goes through its singularity, or when consciousness expands beyond the individual into a collective, or when a hungry humanity transforms into something terrifying, or when we encounter something out there far more intelligent than ourselves. We—

men and women alike—will be made of data and algorithms, of nanotech and exotic matter, of cybernetic parts and flowing chrome.

Then, to paraphrase the American poet, Mary Oliver: what the hell will we do with our wild and precious lives?

This theme for the collection emerged as I continued to write and publish more stories during 2011. In part it reflects a lot about me—a man with a science and technology background writing about his hopes and fears. My outlook on life and my training pervade the crazy tales and adventures. However it also reflects the fact that I care deeply about the world, about the impact we are having as a species, and about where society is really heading. In this regard my stories are intended to shock as well as instil hope. I guess I also wanted to explore my emerging writing techniques and have a lot of fun along the way.

So, now that the dust has settled, I would like to thank Russell Farr for his support in bringing this project together. Russell and the team at Ticonderoga are leading the way in keeping speculative fiction alive in Australia.

I am deeply indebted to Damien Broderick, not only for helping me with my first professional sale to *Cosmos* in 2009, but for his kind and generous words in the Introduction. I think most writers suffer doubts and insecurities, and there were many times when I questioned the long hours I've put in, but Damien's words have made me more determined than ever to take my writing to the next level. It's a lot to live up to, and with it goes the sage words of advice behind the scenes: this is just the beginning, and there is still a lot to learn.

I am also incredibly grateful to Leeane and Jamie Tufrey, the quiet achievers of the digital art world in Australia, for their incredible cover illustration. Jamie does some awesome work for *Cosmos* and really got to the heart of the Wild Chrome theme right from the concept stage.

Thanks also to the editors of my published work: Cat Sparks and Wilson da Silva at *Cosmos* for their continued support through 2010 and 2011; Neil Clarke at *Clarkesworld*—this was a major milestone to finally break into the US market with "Signals in the Deep"; Dirk Strasser and Stuart Mayne at *Aurealis*; Ion "Nuke" Newcombe at *Antipodean SF*; and many others. Plus I would also like to extend a special thanks to Gina Wyatt for her insightful editing on several stories during 2011.

Finally, to you—the readers—thank you so much for stepping into the worlds of my imagination. I hope you have enjoyed the experience, and I hope you'll stay with me for the next adventure!

Greg Mellor
Canberra, July 2012

INTRODUCTION

DAMIEN BRODERICK

Forty-five years ago, when I was young and in love with science fiction, and Gregory Mellor was a toddler, the great sf fantasist Theodore Sturgeon faced a tough task, introducing the first collected stories of a quite new writer. Here's how he began:

> There has been nothing like Zelazny in the science fiction field since—
> Thus began the first draft of this introduction and there it stayed for about forty-eight hours while I maundered and chuntered for ways to finish that sentence with justice and precision . . . Suffice it for now to say that you'll be hard put to it to find a writer like Zelazny anywhere.

Suffice it as well to declare that there has indeed been nothing like the meteoric arrival of Mellor in the Australian science fiction field since—Since who? Terry Dowling? Stephen Dedman? Lucy Sussex? Sean Williams? Yes, there are resemblances to all of these, in different ways—the professional competence pretty much right from the start, with a rapidly developed accomplishment, high-energy attack, a poetry blending reflectiveness and kinesis, closely observed detail of surfaces and scrutiny of what lies below the surface.

So I'm not making preposterous claims here. Greg Mellor is a new and remarkable writer of enormous promise. Enjoy these early premonitions of considerable achievement. Mellor pulls you right into realities as vivid as any I've inhabited lately, replete with the fabled sense of wonder. A mother searches from her absconded, angry son, pursuing hints to the far extremes of the outer solar system, and finds him transformed:

> Silhouettes glided languidly across the star field until I could see the sheer, terrifying wonder of him. He was there—at the centre—but the rest of him was strung out in many disconnected parts. What looked like advanced relay panels were stretched over delicate bio-ceramic bones, unfolding over kilometres. Titanium pivots and joints secured critical junctions of the larger pieces. The entire array ebbed and flowed, resonating to Matt's remote commands, a thousand separate parts miraculously working in synch—a dark cybernetic angel gliding down to meet me.
>
> I extended my arms as he approached, the sheer scale of his structure more daunting as he got closer, until I was at his centre, his human body encased in a sleek black bio-alloy skin. His eyes were still the same, that dark brown with green flecks, glazed with a protective covering that blended into his skin.

At its core, Mellor tells us, this is a book about being a man, yearning for completion, buggering things up, trying again, moving into realms we dimly imagine but cannot quite perceive. Some of his men are genuinely monstrous, and abetted in their monstrousness by technology out of control. Other stories share a universe blighted by relic weapon systems able to overwhelm and parasitize men and women alike, in ways that make the horrifying scenes in *Alien* seem cosy:

> The air crackled around her as the entity tunnelled into the nexus. It thrashed over her head and latched onto her collar bone. She screamed as it ripped open her chest.
>
> Blood sprayed across my face and I staggered back. I heard grunting in the distance and realised it was coming from me...

I stepped out into vacuum. The entity was inside Chenzira now, *zipping* her up from crotch to shoulder. Her skin blackened as the spacesuit activated, its amber lenses glowing.

A Scourge cloud sprayed out from the suit, boiling space in a confusion of black on black. It spread in all directions, penetrating my field, cutting through me.

Aliens can be frightful, but there's also a clear-eyed recognition in these stories of how flawed our own species is, even in its most utopian ambitions. This recognition is not cynicism, just brutal and uncompromising honesty, and we need to face such truths if we hope to go beyond them, especially into uploading of minds into machine substrates, or along the screaming upward curve of a technological singularity:

The Enlightened Age lasted a decade, a short-lived, contained tech singularity. For the first time in history, life-changing, global-spanning technology was in the hands of scientists and philanthropists with no agenda other than to provide a lasting vision for humanity. But Old Earth choked on its own vomit before the new memes could get a foothold, and the survivors came clutching at Mars like ghouls.

An alien visiting a slightly future world appraises us sorrowingly:

>*Working hypothesis: the dominant meme has hampered global self-awareness and intellectual capacity.*

She placed her wine glass down, propped her elbows on the table, slipped her shaking hands under her chin, and held me with her gaze.

I'd stared down politicians and dictators alike, brought corporate executives and rogue activists into line, and convened peace talks around the world... but *this*... damn it, I just wasn't prepared. *No* one was prepared.

"I have not seen anything like it," she said. "And trust me when I say I've seen a lot in my time. You've created a slaughterhouse in your own backyard. The environmental degradation and bio-depletion is staggering, but *still* you carry on with your consumption."

It's not all gloom and despair, though; that would smack of adolescent posturing. Indeed, of one story, Greg Mellor notes in an illuminating afterword:

> I really did just want to write a feel-good story set against the backdrop of the solar system. I wasn't trying to break new ground or develop new takes on future science or provide fresh insights into the genre.
>
> It was interesting how the feedback from the reviewers varied from the readers. I think the reviewers see such a volume of material that they are always looking for that needle in the haystack that takes the genre another step forward—"something new". But I think there's a place for heartfelt, traditional themes that don't constantly stretch (and shred) the limits of science (and plausibility), so long as they are entertaining and make readers feel something. Judging by the readers' comments on "Signals in the Deep", I think they felt something.

Mellor has two advantages not all sf writers bring to bear on our play with words: he holds an honours degree in astrophysics (which admits him into the privileged company of such scientifically trained sf experts as Alastair Reynolds, Catherine Asaro, Gregory Benford, Vonda McIntyre, Greg Egan, Joan Slonczewski, Paul McAuley, Charles Stross, not to mention Asimov and Anderson and others of the old guard), and he has worked in industry ("professional service firms") for a decade and a half, so also he knows a thing or two about the non-academic world. He has a wife and son, and aside from a decade-long residency in Britain he's lived in the Australian political and bureaucratic capital, Canberra, all his life. That provides grounding in reality, and a distinctive vantage point such that most readers in the rest of the planet will find his everyday world sufficiently alien to give it a running start into the imaginary.

You'll feel astonishment in most of these pieces, and sometimes your pulse will race; always, there's that very Australian way of looking at, let's say, the end of the world, or a son's relationship with his father. When I opened the submission file of "Defence of the Realm" at *Cosmos* science magazine, where I was fiction editor for its first five years, I had that immediate clutch of delight that grabs you when you find new talent. When I passed over the editorial keyboard to Cat Sparks, the current editor at *Cosmos,* I bequeathed her a truly extraordinary story by Mellor, "Day Break." She added her own touches, honing the piece to a hard gloss. Here was the funny but heartbreaking opening of that terrific story:

> It rained cows on Christmas Eve.
>
> When the world broke, the atmosphere tore in raging cyclones, tornadoes, oceans of air sucked up and flung down, and those poor animals were caught in the turbulence, hurled into the sky. Until they fell back to Earth, crying in terror.
>
> They were Jerseys, all deep tan with white patches. The sight of them rupturing like swollen bladders was terrifying. I had known each of them by name, with their soft brown eyes and flickering ears. Only Jessica had survived, tethered to a fence. I sobbed my heart out in the three days of cold snow that followed, and then again when the snow melted and I found Jessica in a pile of muddy slush with her legs sticking up stupidly.

How many professional writers with years under their belt would have the chutzpah to start with: "It rained cows on Christmas Eve"? It sounds like a shaggy dog story. And yes, the black humour, the gallows comedy, is intended. But the global catastrophe that murdered the terrified animals is of larger than biblical proportion, and is told with exactness and poignancy from the viewpoint of one man moving toward the end of the earth—literally, in several senses. This is a *tour de force,* and by itself is proof that Gregory Mellor is a writer to watch in the way we kept an eye on Ursula K. Le Guin and Brian W. Aldiss and Roger Zelazny when they were setting out, learning to pilot their burning imaginations into the realm of words shaped to ignite the dreams of their readers.

Damien Broderick
May 2012

Tell me, what is it that you plan to do with your one wild and precious life?

—Mary Oliver

A man should look for what is, and not for what he thinks should be.

—Albert Einstein

Sooner or later something seems to call us onto a particular path ... this is what I must do, this is what I've got to have. This is who I am.

—James Hillman

FRAGMENTS

The qualia storm hit our camp during the night.

It was the worst I had felt in years, the oily rain lashing against our tents, the fragments howling like tortured banshees. Such a mournful wail that lingered on and on, grating against my ears, cutting deep into my soul until the clouds slowly swept away. I must have stood in its wake for an hour or more, mesmerised by the lightning along the northern horizon. Even from this distance I could still hear voices, calling.

A grey dawn eventually crept across the sand dunes, forcing its way under my heavy eyelids. I heard something rustle behind me. I spun around and cursed out loud. New vegetation was sprouting, slithering towards us, pale sunlight glinting off lethal metal thorns. The storm had blown in the run-tech seeds and now they were mutating rapidly.

Man turned his chrome face to me, his synthetic voice a close approximation of mine. "We must go, now." He hastily packed up our tents and gear as the vegetation grew closer, twitching at our presence.

As for the slicker, it ambled over to the new growth and began to munch on the thorns. We had picked the creature up at Kalgoorlie— it had been a camel in a previous life, but now it had an array of razor teeth and shaggy metallic fur. I needed some means of traversing the ruined wastes of the outback, and the traders had assured me it was impervious to both the storms and the bizarre flora.

I threw on the packs and saddle bags then reached out and gently took hold of the reins, as there were rules to riding slickers. I firmly planted my foot on its foreleg before stepping up to the saddle— the creatures only prostrate once. Then I fastened the alloy harness around me, avoiding the slicker's face and teeth. I was also careful to avoid its eyes. Its run-tech programs, despite being sequestered, could still drill through my firewall like a plasma lance.

Now that I was in the saddle I patted its flank, more to reassure myself than to give the creature any comfort. It quivered at my touch so I pulled my hand away.

"That's the ugliest thing I've ever seen," Man said. "What were you thinking, Damian?"

I hitched up the reins. "Are you ready?"

"Watch out," he shouted.

My vision spun and I would have fallen out of the saddle were it not for the harness. The slicker had arched its neck back in an attempt to eyeball me, but I had already programmed my optical sensor to deflect my eyes away from its deadly scan. The only side effect was induced vertigo.

"Feisty one, aren't you?"

I felt a rumble deep within its chest. It was hawking up something terrible so I dug my spurs in and it lurched forward across the dunes.

"Are you sure you want to do this again?" Man jogged beside the slicker, the plants brushing harmlessly off his titanium alloy plating.

My silence was confirmation.

The wind had picked up again, and now it was swirling the sand into small spirals. It wouldn't be long before our footprints were erased completely, and the thought brought back memories of Melina. I never strayed far it seemed, clinging to her ghost and to an impossible dream.

I pulled up my collar as we worked our way north, chasing the storm.

Melina watched me through her white veil, her blue eyes radiant. We had waited so long for this day and now my hands were shaking as we exchanged our vows to the sound of Bach's *Arioso*. The celebrant ushered us towards the run-tech node that rose like a chrome spire beneath the roof of the Brisbane chapel—a new shrine under old. Melina let go of my hands and entered the chamber at the base of the node. The celebrant closed the glass door behind her.

It was tradition for brides to be copied first, but it was terrifying for the grooms to watch. Yet the couples still formed long queues into the chapel, all of them caught up in the craze.

Melina waited nervously, but the run-tech quickly activated, scanning into her eyes and across her body, burning like a cleansing fire—slowly copying her, in body, mind and soul. My hands clutched at the air as if I could somehow ease her pain. Then I forced myself to relax and tried to imagine what she could see, on the other side.

A tremor ran through the earth and several people shouted in panic. I grabbed hold of a railing as the windows rattled. An ear piercing sound filled the chapel like the concussive beats of rotor blades then the whole building lurched upwards, the roof was ripped away and I was hurled through a window by the blast wave . . .

The dream faded and I felt hands on my shoulders . . . then a staccato, like distant gun shots . . .

"It's raining."

I woke to the sound of Man's voice and the rain pattering on our makeshift corrugated shelter. The slicker grumbled on its tether.

I peered out into the dark to the ruins of Alice Springs. Water was pooling in the cratered tarmac. Melted buildings cast wax-like silhouettes in the gloom. I could just make out the word "plaza" on a corroded sign. The skeletal remains of towers loomed behind the old hotels. I felt a familiar tension fill the air as the run-tech particles in the rain slowly coalesced, drawn like a magnet to whatever remained of the node deep inside the ruined towers.

"How long do you think I have?"

Man peered over my shoulder, his metallic eyes calculating. "Five minutes, ten at the most."

"That will have to do."

"You don't have to do this, you know."

I glared at him then took a deep breath and held my obsession in check as best I could. "You're right. I don't have to do this at all, but I don't expect you to understand."

"I think I understand well enough. It's very noble, Damian, but foolish."

I felt the anger rise. Not for the first time had I regretted programming my logic and reasoning centres into his old-tech wafers. "Just keep your rational thinking to yourself for a while, okay?"

"Fine." He stepped back into the shadows. "Go find her. I'll watch over our new friend."

"Man—"

"Don't worry about it. I've got your back." He tossed a nano-sheet pack over to me. "Don't forget this."

The pack unfolded and a silver sheet quickened over my skin, covering me from head to foot. I stepped out from the shelter and felt the impacts of the rain drops then a wriggling sensation as the run-tech particles tried to burrow through the sheet. At the same time their software probed my firewall. The fragments had not had time to group around the node with any real force, but I still felt their presence like strangers in the fog.

As always, I let some of them through my firewall.

A man was having breakfast outside a bakehouse. He always loved the smell of apple and cinnamon, but he was on edge this morning. His wife was late. She was never late and now he began to worry. He got up from his table and started to pace up and down the street, calling her name. Then his worry turned to panic and he sat on the pavement and cradled his head in his hands. He took in a deep, shuddering breath and began to sob.

A stray dog barked somewhere and a young girl ran past. She had skipped her lunch and left the house to find the dog. She loved the dog so much and was afraid for it so she ran and ran, but then she tripped and scuffed her knees. The cuts burned and now her dress was dirty. Big tears fell from her cheeks—she couldn't remember the way home.

Dozens more fragments came and I sifted through each of them—broken qualia and memories, pieces of digital personas—caught in the middle of the upload when the bombs fell. As heart wrenching as it was, I had to search through them all—how else would I find Melina?

"Are you there?"

I waited a few seconds, but all I could hear was the wind funnelling through the towers.

The few seconds turned into a minute.

"Melina?"

"She's not here, Damian." Man's data cast sounded far away now. I ignored him and approached the towers.

It was cold along the coast. The ocean was choppy and Melina could hear the tide ebbing down in the bay. She was sitting in front of the fire with the doona wrapped around her, watching me bring more logs in. An orange glow shimmered over her face, dabbing colour to the edges of her hair. She lifted a corner of the doona to reveal bare skin beneath then she pulled me down and wrapped us both up. We were warm and soft and our hands roamed freely, exploring those places that were still new, still exhilarating. Then the exploring took on a new urgency and we made love, cocooned in our private world.

"Melina?"

"Da-ian . . . love . . . dan-s . . . "

Her voice was drowned out by static. The run-tech node continued to draw the fragments in, strengthening their programs. The fragments slipped through my firewall until I could see a crowd through the rain, but the images were patchy and grainy like old sepia photographs. The crowd surged forward, wailing and screaming, their hands clutching at the air, hysteria in their eyes.

I spotted Melina in the pack, reaching out to me. Then she was lost again as the crowd closed in—angry, betrayed, fearful. I shoved my way through the fragments and ran towards her as if by sheer force of will I could bring her back to life, not just a program, but a living, breathing Melina.

My head hit something hard. The towers were on their side and it took me several seconds to realise I had slipped in the mud. I tried to stand up, lost my footing again and lurched across the sodden ground.

Then Man was dragging me away and I fell under the slicker's head. My eyes fluttered and the world spun again. I vomited as Man lifted me up into the saddle and fastened the harness. He pulled savagely on the reins, coaxing the slicker into a trot and then to a gallop.

We escaped the ruins of Alice Springs, south along the trail we had entered, the torment of those lost souls lingering on the breeze.

I swayed back and forth in the saddle, numb and cold. I had ditched the spent nano-sheet sometime during the night and now my mouth was parched and my lips were swollen and cracked. I managed to grunt once and Man threw a filtered water canteen back over his shoulder. I snagged it by the strap and took several swigs.

"It was her," I said.

"You were stupid going so close to the node." He still wouldn't look at me and instead glanced up at the sky. The sun was partially eclipsed by a shape like a small crescent moon.

"What do *they* care?"

"I doubt that they do, but they still watch for anomalous activity. They don't want anything to catch them up—the run-tech never stops."

I hissed through my teeth. I hated the cliché. The entire stagnant world hated those words ever since the post-humans had realised that their precious run-tech was mutating. And their only answer to the problem had been an apocalyptic deluge. Bombs had rained on all the cities of the world, on all the run-tech nodes that had once been their infrastructure, their homes.

I raised my hand against the glare, but couldn't make out any detail. I knew they were all up there, safe in their new heaven—billions, maybe trillions by now—living off the energy of the sun.

I turned on Man. "Give me a break."

"Stay away from the nodes. The last thing we want is for them to send something down to investigate."

"I think that is unlikely." But what did I know? I pulled at the reins and the slicker came to a dead stop, its belly gurgling. "And besides, you know I can't—"

Man turned and I caught my breath. The rain had completely disfigured his face. Deep grooves were gouged into his forehead and cheeks, and the chrome was hanging off in melted chunks and strands.

"I'm sorry." I could replace his face, but I couldn't stop the guilt, knowing that I had created him solely to help me find Melina. "We had better get you some new gear . . . maybe we should try Brisbane."

He sighed. "You're a piece of work."

"And you're beginning to tick me off. You're not supposed to have emotions."

"Yeah, well the logical way to deal with you is to be completely illogical."

We walked on in silence.

Within a week we found the old Birdsville Track. The endless plains were free from run-tech mutations and I thanked our good fortune that some parts of the outback were still unscathed. Soon the open skies felt like an anodyne and I dreamt of Melina on the cold, cloudless nights under the constellations.

On the third morning I picked up a metal flower preserved on the side of the road, its petals perfectly formed. Run-tech could produce disturbing mutations, but it was also capable of recreating true beauty. It was this which had given hope to everyone: that the fleeting wonder we find in our lives could be replicated, etched forever into a post-human existence. But it turned out that hope was a fleeting thing as well.

I placed the flower in the saddle bag.

We rode on, hardly speaking for the better part of two weeks until we reached the wasteland that had been known as the Sunshine Coast. The final run into Brisbane was blessed by an ocean breeze, but no further sign of storms.

The town had grown in two years, the central and surrounding craters sprouting more haphazard shanties like a dirty grey-brown moss. The bigger homes with their rusting corrugated sheets were stacked up on the rim—the high side of the street.

I laughed out loud.

"What is it?" Man asked.

"Nothing."

The murky waters of the Brisbane River still churned around the base of the crater. Fields of crops were growing under filtration nets and a few solar panels glinted underneath crudely constructed shelters. Oil-filled trenches and kilometres of electrified fencing protected the perimeter of the township.

We walked down to a line of stalls along the river bank. The market was much larger than I remembered, as if commerce was starting to get a hold again after all these years. We blended into the crowd, though I soon felt claustrophobic with the constant noise and jostling. Thankfully the slicker allowed us a wide birth, even though I had blinkered its eyes. Man tethered it out of harm's way and went off to play soccer with two children who were being chased by a terrier covered in a metal exoskeleton. Its bent tail wouldn't stop wagging.

I approached a familiar stall stacked high with equipment, clothes and ration packs, filtered water cans, reclaimed cybernetic parts and batteries, hundreds of cannibalised robotic components, laptops and wafer circuits, and a few valuables like the solar panels and nano-sheet packs.

"Damian!"

"Long time, Hector."

He was a lot like me, a freak survivor, but he wasn't quite as gaunt or intense. And now he had a new family. His wife smiled at me as she cradled an infant at the back of the stall.

Hector shook my hand. "I thought I'd never see you again. You look awful."

"We came in off the Track."

His eyes widened. "You are welcome to stay with us if you want. We have a new home."

I glanced up the side of the crater and shook my head. "Thanks, but no. We'll make camp on the outskirts."

"At least come and visit," he persisted. "We've got running water, properly filtered."

I nodded even though I knew I'd try again later to avoid the socialising.

"Now," he said, rubbing his hands together, "are you looking for—"

"Have you had any storms?"

Hector frowned. "Yes, about two weeks ago."

"Damn." But there was something more that fretted at the back of my mind. "Did you finally manage to remove the node remnants?"

"Remove them?" He looked astonished. "Damian, why would we get rid of them, they're our only hope."

"Hope?" I felt my blood pressure rise.

"Yes, one day we will have the node functioning again. Do you think we want to keep living like this?"

I sighed. We were all chasing dreams of a kind . . . but this? Salvation in the arms of the destroyer—now the world really had gone mad.

Despite my protests, Man convinced me to stay at Hector's place on the southern ridge of the central crater. The community had developed a kind of religious zeal since my last visit. According to Hector, they were defying the odds and had made huge efforts to reassemble the remains of one of the buried nodes. A building of metal girders and sheeting had been constructed at the centre of the crater—a new chapel of sorts—where people worked daily to uncover more of the run-tech remains, sequestering it piece by piece with banks of old-tech hardware.

On the second evening in his shanty Hector mentioned there had been an increase in visitations. He wouldn't elaborate, but it seemed that some dialogue was being established with the post-humans. To save whatever dignity I had left in my bruised beliefs, I told him that the post-humans were evil and that he was an idiot, but he just laughed.

The following morning I went to the shed and began packing up our gear next to the sleeping slicker.

"I wondered where you were." Hector walked in and saw my face. "You miss her, don't you?"

I nodded.

"Is there anything you can really do now?"

"You sound like Man."

"I'm only trying to help. You have looked so miserable and lonely since you arrived. You deserve more, my friend."

"You're right, I probably do," I replied, the anger draining away. "But in answer to your question: I can be there for Melina, or whatever is left of her. And that's really all that matters."

But he knew me well enough to pick a lie. "Is that any way to live?"

Man walked in before I could answer. I was still getting used to his new titanium face.

"A storm is approaching." He tossed me a pack.

I peered out the door towards the centre of the crater. Lines of people were walking along the narrow streets towards the new chapel.

"You should all stay in your homes," I said to Hector.

He smiled. "The chapel is safe."

I cautiously followed the crowd, but I did not have the courage to go into the chapel. The sky darkened so I triggered the pack and the nano-sheet covered me. The first rain drops fell on the dusty road that encircled the chapel, and soon sheets of rain were slanting across the crater, transforming the road into brown mud.

The fragments ploughed into my firewall.

I let some through.

A mother searched for her son and daughter. She was confused by her divorce and worried that her kids were growing up too quickly. She never seemed to have enough time for them and now she was driving around aimlessly, recklessly. She smashed the car up against the kerbing then got out and stood in the middle of the street, screaming and tearing at her hair.

A teenage boy was skateboarding down a ramp and his friends laughed at him when he crashed. The taunting brought back his rage and he shoved his friends about until there was a fist fight. He was knocked to the ground and kicked savagely, but somehow managed to get back on his feet. Tears and blood flowed freely as he ran away, overwhelmed by the mixed feelings of shame and guilt since his parents had left him.

On and on they came, hundreds calling for their loved ones, but none of them Melina. They grew stronger, swirling around the run-tech node within the chapel, drawn together by the node and the chanting of Hector and his friends.

I heard Man data casting frantically, but I couldn't understand—

A man-shaped tornado descended from the clouds, a vortex made up of a thousand bright holograms. It watched me all the while with its piercing eyes until it touched the ground. There was something predatory in its stance, a conviction, a purpose.

It began striding towards me.

I spun around and sprinted back up the street, ducking for cover down a narrow alleyway. I ran to the end of the alley and slid to a halt about one hundred metres from Hector's house.

Man was standing at the shed door, waving at me to hurry. His data cast resounded in my head, "It's a trick. Get out of there."

The entity burst into the street behind me, its individual holograms in synch like a flock of birds. It paused here and there as if to sniff the trail. I stepped into an open shanty and hid in the shadows, hoping that the rain would cover the sound of my ragged breathing. The entity glided by and I exited through the back door and made my way round the alleys up to Hector's house.

When I reached the shed I climbed up onto the slicker. Man

shut the door and surveyed the street through the gap in the door frame. The entity appeared in front of our hideaway and the slicker reared up in panic. I grabbed hold of its neck as it smashed through the door, the sheet metal clattering to one side. The entity leapt out of the way. I felt surprise, anger, curiosity from the holograms that whizzed past me in shades of green, yellow and blue.

I clung to the slicker as it galloped down towards the centre of the crater.

Man dashed after us.

The entity launched into the air then flew over us and landed on the road ahead. It stretched out a hand and I felt a tsunami crash along the edge of my firewall. The slicker collapsed beneath me and I was thrown into the mud. Man also slumped to the ground.

I stood up. The entity tilted its head to one side. Was that a smile on its multi-hologram face?

"What do you want?" I had to force the words out.

It didn't answer and just stood there, smiling again.

I had had enough of its games. "If you want to kill me then get it over with."

A single hologram materialised in the air between us. I tried to focus, but it was hard to see through the rain. Then the hologram sharpened and I saw Melina's face. More lines traced into the air, filling out the curves of her body.

"I missed you," she said.

"Are you real?"

"It's me, Damian." She raised her hands in front of her face. "As much of me as there is."

"Why . . . why do the post-humans have you?"

She watched me beneath her fringe. She was in there, behind those baby blues, but not the old Melina I knew. There were gaps, aspects of her former self that had vanished. There was a time I was able to sense her moods and her emotions, but not now, at least not completely. The person before me seemed part lover, part stranger.

"What have they done to you?"

"They are trying, they really are. They know they made a terrible mistake, and they're trying to make things right where they can. But it takes time to rebuild."

"Rebuild? They've done *nothing* to repair the damage here."

She hesitated. "The run-tech fallout is all through the world's weather patterns, integrating more each year into the ecosystem. It can't be undone. There are some things even the post-humans can't repair." But then she smiled and I could see her confidence return. "I'm talking about rebuilding fragments like me. Our complete personalities and memories can be reconstituted, but it's a long process, and there is so much missing, so the post-humans have to improvise, fill in the gaps."

"Ah." My shoulders sagged.

Her eyes pleaded with me. "I can't come back, Damian."

Her image blurred through my tears.

"Did you really think you could make me corporeal again?"

I shrugged. "I would have found a way, somehow."

"You never give in, do you?"

I couldn't tell whether she was cursing or complementing me, maybe both. It brought a smile to my lips in any case.

Man moved on my periphery and managed to lean against the comatose slicker.

"So what does this mean, Melina? Can't the post-humans just copy me?"

"The mutations in the run-tech are too severe; the risk of contamination is too great."

"But I'm fine. The run-tech hasn't changed me." Not that I was aware. "People have survived here for years. Isn't that what the entities are doing now, finding ways to help communities leave the Earth once and for all?"

"Yes, but in small steps, Damian. It may take a lifetime to sort out —time that you don't have." She turned, distracted. "I've got to go."

"No." I reached out, terrified by my next words. "Upload me, here, now. Use the node."

"It's still too soon, too dangerous." She shook her head and stepped away. "You need to stop this, Damian. Let me go."

"Melina . . . please . . . wait."

Her image faded.

I cursed the entity as her hologram was subsumed and the thing started to drift up through the storm.

I ran back to Man and slid to a halt next to the slicker. "Wake it up."

"*Listen* to her, Damian."

"Damn you," I yelled. "Wake it up."

He got up and placed his hands on the slicker. The air hissed and crackled as an arc of electricity surged from his power pack into the creature's chest. The thing let out a blood curdling sound and its hooves dug into the mud as it tried to stand up.

I jumped on its neck and wrestled with its head, but it snapped my hand in its jaw. I screamed as it teeth cut to the bone then I pressed all my weight against the creature's head. I craned my neck forward and held my eyelids open with my free hand.

The slicker's scan found my retina.

"I'm sorry, Man." The words slurred as I felt the run-tech copy and burn into my brain. "Please understand . . . "

"I do Damian, I always have."

We strolled along the bay, content with the sound of the ocean and a few pesky seagulls. The sand was warm between our toes as the tide tugged at our ankles. I picked up a shell and turned it in my hand, its colours bleached away by endless days of erosion. The sun felt like a balm on my face and the wind was making me think clearly for the first time in weeks.

I was going to marry this woman.

I felt those blue eyes searching. "What are you thinking?"

"You know what I'm thinking."

She could always tell . . .

The entity drew us up in a kaleidoscope of holographic light. The muddy street receded away below us.

Melina was crying, but I couldn't understand why.

"Was that our life?" I asked.

"A small part." She paused and held my hands. "Yes. Yes it was."

"Where are we going now?"

"To a new home."

I swallowed hard. More memories surged back, but there seemed to be so much missing. "Do you think we can find what we had again?"

"I hope so," she said.

Far below I could see Man leaning over my body. He reached into the saddle bag then placed the metal flower gently on my chest. Its petals glistened as sunlight broke through and the storm clouds were swept away by a brisk westerly wind.

∞

AFTERWORD TO "FRAGMENTS"

Botched technology singularity: What happens to the people caught in the middle of the upload? How do you save someone caught between this world and the next? You can't bring them back to the real world because they're digital. And they can't be used in the next world because they're like a bad segment on a hard drive.

Ah, never mind the technology. I hope you liked the human story of Damian and Melina, plus the slicker creature, which Russell B. Farr has quaintly named "the medusa camel"!

THE TROUBLE WITH MEMES

>*Effigy status: adorned and stable.*
>*Xeno-qualia interface status: engaged and stable.*
>*Working hypothesis: there is a single, dominant meme.*

I met Sabrina on the beach at Paraggi in Santa Margherita Ligure. It was a perfect day on the Riviera, the sand warm on our feet, the sun painting a chiaroscuro out across the bay. We walked for a while, soaking up the sights and sounds and before I knew it our small talk had turned to a banter laced with anticipation. Perhaps it was the invitation in her deep brown eyes or her husky Italian accent. Whatever it was, I had a strong feeling that the day would end differently.

We left the beach around noon and took a ride in the jet boat out to the Presidential yacht at anchor. Sabrina climbed up on the deck and placed a hand on my shoulder to shuffle her shoes back on her slender feet. She had been carrying the lacy Ferragamos all the while and now she stood a few centimetres taller. There was a classic, understated elegance about the way she moved in her sleeveless black dress. Her dark hair brushed against my cheek as she adjusted her slim strap Gucci purse. She smiled close to my face, her eyes sensuous beneath a fringe of dark curls.

The yacht powered up and Sabrina moved to the prow. I went inside and grabbed my shoes and a dinner jacket. I winked at the skipper as the crew went about their business, seen but not heard. I watched Sabrina through the tinted windows. She knew I was watching but pretended not to notice and leant against the railing. She seemed captivated by the passing scenery of ravines, tree canopies and stretches of inviting sand.

We finally docked at Portofino. The small, sheltered harbour was embraced by rows of three, four or five storey terraced houses in yellow and red, all set against the leafy backdrop of the rugged headland. A few small boats were at dock, but thankfully the larger ones had been cleared for us.

I helped Sabrina down from the yacht and we strolled up the road to Castello Brown. The sounds of the sea and the bustle of the tourist town provided a pleasant background noise. I heard the electric whine of mopeds in the distance, though none were allowed near us. When we finally reached the old fort we stood and took in the panoramic view of the harbour.

As evening encroached we made our way back to town and found a small restaurant overlooking the sea. Candle light filled the room and a turquoise calm descended over the harbour. We ordered a delicious Pollo Compomere and pale yellow Pinot Grigio. The chicken was sautéed to perfection and the wine left a lingering apple taste.

After dinner we stretched our legs, sipped at our wine and watched the stars appear through the velvet spreading in from the east.

"This is the best it gets," I said in Italian. "It's one of the most popular tourist destinations."

Her eyes reflected the subdued light, but at the same time seemed to soak in everything with a consuming inner glow. I must have sounded clumsy, as she gave a knowing smile. Perhaps it was my use of *migliore*, though my mind had thought *prime*, derived from Latin *primus*, but so misused in commercial circles. I had completed the didactic only yesterday. No matter how good the training, you just can't go from speaking American to complete fluency in another language. There were some nuances that no virtual could trick the brain into replicating.

"It's been recreated a few times?" she asked.

"That's true," I replied, unsure where this was going. "The most accurate replica is in Orlando, though there are others in Reston, Chiba, Dubai and a few other resorts."

"And this is not the original location." A statement of fact, brought to life in the way she tilted her head so the candle light caught the plane of her cheek, and in the way her hands weaved a whole new dimension to the conversation.

"The original town was relocated higher up to accommodate the sea rise back in the thirties." I thought about it then added, "Is this important?"

She held my gaze. "Everything is important."

Seconds ticked by. I let out a long, silent breath when she finally looked away.

"This is a beautiful setting, without doubt," she concluded. "But things haven't changed."

"What do you mean?"

"Oh, come on, David." Her hands were doing their Italian magic again, showing enough open frustration and at the same time implying more than I could guess.

"Look, I know it's not perfect . . . " I paused as several bright streaks scrawled across the sky—the re-entry trails of barges carrying asteroid iron-ore, dumping somewhere off the coast of China.

She sat silent, her eyes tracking the lights until they disappeared into the east.

She turned to me, one word on her gorgeous red lips.

"*Merda.*"

>*Conclusion: hypothesis confirmed.*
>*Effigy status: some serotonin fluctuation induced by frustration, some neurotransmitter impairment and minor loss of muscular coordination induced by Pinot Grigio.*
>*Xeno-qualia interface status: stable.*
>*Working hypothesis: the dominant meme has hampered global self-awareness and intellectual capacity.*

She placed her wine glass down, propped her elbows on the table, slipped her shaking hands under her chin, and held me with her gaze.

I'd stared down politicians and dictators alike, brought corporate executives and rogue activists into line, and convened peace talks around the world . . . but *this* . . . damn it, I just wasn't prepared. *No* one was prepared.

"I have not seen anything like it," she said. "And trust me when I say I've seen a lot in my time. You've created a slaughterhouse in your own backyard. The environmental degradation and bio-depletion is staggering, but *still* you carry on with your consumption."

"Now *you* come on," I said, still reeling. "It's a legacy we're trying to work through. You can't fix the over indulgences of generations in a single life time."

"I bet every President before you has said the same thing."

I breathed in through clenched teeth. Shadows crept across the walls as the other patrons were being asked to leave.

"Sabrina, I can understand you being cautious, but you can't judge us like this."

"Why not?" She leant further forward. "You don't seem to be able to work it out yourselves."

This time I matched her stare with my own steely blues.

"We're not some backwater planet. Our global economy has achieved a lot of good and has raised the standard of living for billions of people. Our technology has escalated tenfold in the last generation and we're on the verge of uploading consciousness. We feel we have a lot to offer. But you know all this from previous talks. What's the real problem, Sabrina?"

"Don't you see?" She waved her arms to encompass more than our immediate vicinity. "You're locked into a capitalist meme that has been left to its own devices. You can't keep escaping to havens like this because there won't be any left soon."

"That's not true. We regulate more than ever and we've turned the corner on a lot of legacy infrastructure. Our best corporations are working on sustainability without growth. I'm sure you had to deal with similar issues in your past."

Her eyes flared for an instant, and then her impeccable front descended. "You missed my point. And this is not about us."

"Then what is your point? It all sounds a bit sanctimonious, if you ask me."

"That's just it," she said, her voice turning to vitriol, "No one's asking you now, because it's too late."

"It's easy for you to talk," I said, but the words seemed hollow now. I had thought the day started well, there seemed to be a real spark between us that might lead to a successful negotiation and . . . well, perhaps . . . but it was clear that her mind was already made up. I tried one last appeal by reaching over the table and taking her hand. "I know it must be infuriating, but you don't have to deal with the complexities. It's virtually impossible to see when you're not part of it."

"*See?*"

Damn. She moved her hand away and clutched her purse. What was it with these Italian women? I corrected myself—not Italian at all. Perhaps I'd been falling in to the trap all day, intoxicated by her curves and her smouldering looks.

"Tell me how you see," she said.

"Free market economies need selected regulation—"

"I meant literally."

"I see with my eyes."

"And how do your eyes see?"

"Light through the optic nerve—"

"Yes, yes."

I had been warned about this at the Union briefings in Washington. I knew it was pointless to discuss science with her, but I would be letting everyone down if I didn't try. "It involves a collapse of the wave function. Objects are probabilities until we see them. Observer and the observed, it's a fundamental principle of quantum physics—the Copenhagen interpretation. There is a phenomenal element above this, our perception and consciousness, the way we feel, the qualia of subjective experience. These experiences build up over time and our character emerges, like a tree growing from an acorn."

"Okay." She gave a fleeting smile and her mood seemed to lift a little.

I started to wonder if I was finally getting somewhere. "What is your point, Sabrina?"

"My point is: you don't *see* much at all."

>*Conclusion: hypothesis confirmed.*
>*Effigy status: continued serotonin fluctuation and neurotransmitter impairment, now with reduced social*

inhibition . . . also sexual arousal induced by self (?—legs are so very long!), by other (?—he is very athletic!), by conversation (?—power-dominance interplay!),by xeno-qualia interface feedback (?—unlikely, but mind-reading can be sexy!), or by all stimuli (yes, most likely!).
>Xeno-qualia interface status: stable, but monitor for feedback loops.
>Working hypothesis: The dominant meme presents an immediate danger to both the noosphere and biosphere.

I gritted my teeth.

She ran her hands up and down her long, smooth legs. Her eyes lingered over me as they had done on the beach, only hours ago, but now it seemed like a lifetime away.

"You're doing it again," she said. "You're still not opening your mind. You only look at the world through a sliver in the electromagnetic spectrum, you still don't get quantum reality, you think with only a small portion of your brains, and you have no perception of deep time. No wonder your civilisation is stuck in a rut."

"So now you're going to judge us for our genetic legacy?" Now I was waving my arms. "It's foolish and simply wrong to cast sentence on us for factors outside our control. You can't take the moral high ground in all our negotiations, no matter what the context. Our past is what makes us human. It makes us diverse and strong, determined to strive for a greater good and a better life for everyone. Are we there yet? No. Is there a long way to go? Yes."

I paused, and took a breath. In a calmer voice I said, "You talk about capitalism. Well, call it a meme or whatever you want. When you remove the trappings you'll see there's a collective desire to make it work here."

"I believe you, David, I really do. I admire your tenacity, and you're right, you can't be blamed for the past, no one can."

"Now you're starting to make—"

"But you and those like you can be held accountable for the present and what it augers for the future. And right now your actions speak louder than words." She reached into her purse and pulled out a small ray gun.

Shadows moved behind me. I could hear the soft release of a dozen safety catches, the charging of pulse stunners.

She held the gun loosely in her hand. Alarmed chatter spread around the dark suited figures that now filled the restaurant.

I made a calming gesture to stop a lethal escalation.

"Put the gun down," I said.

She waved it around as if it were a lipstick tube. "It's not a gun."

"Please put it down. Why don't we call it a day? Perhaps we can reconvene."

"What good will it do? How could you think of uplifting into the local network when you're nowhere near ready? Did you think we would let you bring your baggage through? Or did you think it would be fine just to let your wealthy and privileged in while the rest of your world is discarded like trash?"

She squeezed the trigger.

The room erupted into chaos.

>*Conclusion: hypothesis confirmed.*
>*Effigy status: discarded . . . overly impaired, aroused and aggressive (?—but warranted!).*
>*Xeno-qualia interface status: stable, but now switching to mass storage array interface.*
>*Working hypothesis: this species may never be ready for uplift.*

"Mr. President?"

David York, the 55th President of the United States, stood at the podium, alone. "Yes, Richard."

"Do you think it was wise to aggravate her?"

"I think she was already angry, don't you?"

Subdued chuckles spread around the old stadium. There was standing room only, but the night air was still cold and crisp, the floodlights sharp and white.

"Please keep your questions constructive," David said.

As one, a thousand arms waved frantically.

"Yes." David pointed to a red haired reporter.

"Emily Hawkins from *GMP Online*, Mr. President. Why did you choose the Riviera?"

"I wanted something less formal. All previous negotiations had been held in Washington and had achieved nothing. I also wanted to show her some of our heritage, but it was clear that she had either already settled on an outcome or that, at best, the conversation had reinforced their thoughts about us . . . next . . . yes."

"Thank you, Mr. President. Carlos Rodriguez from *Conectado Mundo*. Do you think you might have been a little distracted? Our optical tracking analysis indicates that you looked at her legs 34 times, her breasts 53 times, sized up her buns—"

An unsolicited voice from somewhere in the crowd interrupted, and in an exaggerated southern drawl said, "I did not have sexual relations with that woman."

David held his palms out, but there was a half-smile on his lips. "Look, I don't mind the humour. I know it helps under the circumstances, but there's a reason why I've opened up the classified material. I want people to bring ideas to the table."

He looked towards the middle of the crowd at the Union representative dressed in black and grey.

"Emmanuelle, you must have some thoughts on the matter."

"Yes, we have invoked the Crays again."

The crowd hushed.

"There are no hidden messages in her words," Emmanuelle said, straightening her hair as if suddenly aware that nine billion eyes were watching her every move. "The escalation was clearly borne out of frustration on both sides, plus an obvious communication barrier. And we're not referring to English-Italian. You did fine, by the way."

David hushed urgent appeals from other reporters.

"Go on, Emmanuelle."

"Sabrina was genuinely trying to bridge the gap between us and her kind."

"Yes, I know, but she seemed unable or unwilling to accommodate our views on so many fronts. It's not as if we haven't criticised ourselves enough for our short sightedness over the last century. I thought I got most of what she was saying, but I couldn't understand her constant rebuttals. Maybe it was some test. Whatever it was, we've clearly failed."

"Perhaps," Emmanuelle said. "Would it be easier if we briefed you privately, Mr. President?"

He looked around at the stadium with the representatives from 300 nations, 5,000 online communities and four other qAI unions.

"It's not like we're going anywhere," he said, but no one laughed. He cleared his throat. "We're all in this together. There's no room for secrets anymore."

"Thank you, Mr President. The Crays believe you responded well, but despite the preparations, they now believe it is unlikely Sabrina's species ever intended to grant us immediate access to the local network."

David frowned. "Why? We hardly pose a threat to them, at least not physically. Are you suggesting that we might present an intellectual threat—dumb them down, so to speak?"

"The Crays are still working through the scenarios, but we can't rule out the possibility. We carry a lot of baggage, as Sabrina so quaintly put it. However it's almost certain there are broader cultural issues at play: how we might integrate into their society, how we might cope with such massive change. And of course there is the great unknown—will they ever let us back home?"

"You have a point. Our *baggage* might damn us from going one way or the other."

David paused, reflecting on the conversation that ended the world. "She was right. Our actions speak volumes."

He looked around at the stadium. This was where the Yankees had won their first World Series against the Phillies. Joe DiMaggio had paved the way to four consecutive World Series titles and Don Larsen had thrown a perfect game in 56.

It was a stunning replica.

He turned his gaze upward, through the dome to the blanket of stars, the constellations so etched in his memory—but not real at all. It was all a cocoon, a virtual limbo, a miracle. Such an achievement required patience and control, a tempered power and dominion that he could only dream of.

But there he was, thinking like a human again.

He turned back to the crowd.

"It would be astonishing to see through their eyes."

>*Conclusion: hypothesis not confirmed . . . keep going, David, you're doing well.*

Sabrina closes down the interfaces and slips back through the simul-entity firewall on a wave of encoded photons. There's a lot of interest awaiting her: 600-trillion correlations and counting.

She quells the tsunami, and starts to respond to them, one at a time. She selects a hive intelligence—it looks like a small nova in the local network. It's practical and has been through first contact many times.

>*Your actions were perhaps a little pre-emptive, but necessary.*
She sighs inwardly.

The hive spirals up the question that has plagued her for weeks now.

>*Can the human collective be safely uplifted?*

She confers with the vigilance that monitors and protects the mass storage array and then growls impatiently, rattling off a string of Italian expletives.

>*My apologies* . . . she isolates the residual feelings from the effigy, storing the qualia packets for future analysis . . . *it may take a while to answer that one.*

Another hive, nostalgic for corporeal life.

>*We loved your shoes.*

>*I tried to blend. Brand-obsession is just one aspect of the complex, dominant meme—classification confirmed: power-sex-money self-fulfilment. This is mutated from a narcissistic speciation progenitor meme. All of it, of course, is the cultural chicanery of the underlying competitive-aggressive gene replicator, mutated from some ancient prokaryotic progenitor gene, most likely terrestrial in origin.*

Another hive blossoms, this time more poignant.

>*The meme appears terminally regressive. Is the human noosphere corrupted? Worse, has the deep-time biosphere reached an early terminus?*

The sentient quark computing array embedded in a vacuum flux that is Sabrina recalls David's words, and her response: "I believe you, David, I really do."

>*The noosphere is not corrupted, but needs time. The biosphere mapping is still in progress, but results so far show typical deep geo-strata indicative of prolific complex adaptive biological systems; mature carbon, nitrogen and hydrocarbon cycles; post nuclear, mechanistic-consumer industry triggering non-linear global degradation—thus intervention protocols have been initiated.*

>*And the impact of the meme on the tech-sphere's ability to uplift human consciousness?*

>*The tech-sphere emergence includes first generation nanotech and first generation quasi-artificial intelligence, which seem to be untainted by the meme. Their third generation virtual web connectivity has provided an ideal channel for propagation of the meme, creating weird memetic aberrations (fame-debt-porn self-indulgent); hence the technology singularity problem remains unresolved. There is no evidence of advanced photonic trap, exotic matter technology or major boson or lepton manipulation short of some crude particle accelerators.*

>*Wham, bang!*

600-trillion voices chuckle.

She feels the tension break. Perhaps there is hope for this civilisation. She wishes now she had not sloughed the beautiful effigy, as there was a sexual luxury and primal power that she missed. But she didn't really have a choice. Still, she could reconstitute it later as the discussions weren't over yet . . .

Several more hives overlay, blossoming like a new sun.

>*Their ability to move beyond the meme appears tenuous. What is the consequent threat to the simul-entity if sex-power-money* sine qua non *of homo sapiens is uplifted?*

A collective groan spreads across the simul-entity at the vulgar joke. The hive continues, more serious.

>*Coital health, vitality and happiness are compatible with the simul-entity; power, dominance and subjugation overtones are incompatible. He really wanted to have sex with you, for all the wrong reasons.*

She thinks about it, knows what a double-edged sword a corporeal effigy can be. Despite her frustration, she was attracted to his cool looks and athletic charms. She considers transferring into the array, walking up to him in the middle of the stadium and planting a kiss on his lips. To see the shock of the crowd, feel the attention, jealousy, admiration.

Jitters spread across the simul-entity.

>*Are you compromised?*

She laughs. Memes were fickle things, you could police them but you couldn't quarantine them. That's why first contact was so risky, but the need for diversity was an imperative of the simul-entity, the need itself a progenitor meme of the collective consciousness of the 7,432 species that formed the local network.

She looks out through synchronised satellite interfaces at a beautiful blue-green world now devoid of human life. It looks healthy from the outside, but she knows it's not. Her seed programs are running things for the time being. She urges them to complete the mapping so she can customise the intervention protocols— there's a lot of work to do. Atmosphere scrubbers begin to flower from Earth-based nanotech refineries bootstrapped up to fifth generation by more seed programs.

She reassures the simul-entity.

>*It's just another residual fantasy. Qualia packets have been archived for future reference.*

But wouldn't it feel good, she thinks to herself in those deep, dark energy states of her quark array where not even the simul-entity can reach. It was a primal place, like the human limbic brain, where urges rise.

Or was it? Were her thoughts really her own or were they the collective sentiment of others?

But that was the real trouble: she never knew whether it was her or her memes talking.

AFTERWORD TO "THE TROUBLE WITH MEMES"

Imagine if you were an alien with the job of assessing humanity's potential for uplifting into the local interstellar community? I'd love to have a crack at that job. Tell me you haven't thought about applying for the role!

In "The Trouble with Memes" I wanted the first contact to be with an advanced post-singularity network of civilisations. I reckon Sabrina did the right thing by giving us a good grilling. But watch out for those memes. They are like a nasty flu contagion, spreading exponentially and impossible to quarantine.

TERRA Q

Meeting Tasman Wishart for the first time is like a punch to the solar plexus.

All that stuff you were told about terraformers in your childhood—it soon gets blown away. He's not the mechanised, robot-god of legend. Sure, he does leapfrog through time in his spindle-ship on the frontier of humanity, which makes him as close to immortal as anyone can get, but Tasman is . . . well, I have to keep pinching myself . . . he is *just* a man.

Segue to my second point, as this "just a man" towers over my short stature, assailing my frail ego until I feel kind of insignificant . . . primordial, even. And there's the final segue—this guy is smart, and I don't mean intelligent or streetwise, I mean razor sharp with a sea-blue gaze that holds you, cuts through your social mask, rummages around in your soul and leaves you spinning like a top before you realise what has happened.

"You see those?" He points to some fractal structures flowering up over the glowing crescent of the planet below.

I have to concentrate because I'm still in overload. We're in the nexus of his ship. It's a virtual sensorium of sorts, but I think that's a crude analogy given the spindle-ships were constructed in the Enlightened Age. Whatever the tech origins, the end result is churning my stomach because we're floating above the surface of a world in the Goldilocks Zone of a warm orange star. It's Wishart's latest project and he's in full swing, monitoring an array of avatar AIs that provide instructions for the invisible nanotech, coaxing this lump of rock into a habitable planet.

Images of demigods moulding the fabric of worlds still niggle, so I shove them aside as best I can, suck in the clean air of the nexus, straighten my quivering legs and hazard a guess: "Atmosphere generators?"

His lips turn up at the edges: wrong.

"Cities. They're grafted onto the tectonic bedrock."

I'll be damned. They look like bee-hives from this distance, crystallising outward to the hidden tunes of the avatar algorithms that drive the world-shaping nanotech.

Yes, I did my homework, but it seems I'm not so good with exams. Maybe I rushed the didactics in the excitement leading up to this rare meeting. Only 50 spindle-ships were ever constructed and now they are spread through a bubble of spacetime well over 3,000 light years across.

Tasman catches my slack-jawed look of wonder. "Are you up for this?" he asks. There's mischief in his eyes that makes me feel as if I'm being tossed around on an ocean, a plaything for some predatory sea-mammal that hasn't made up its mind whether to eat me or set me free.

I clear my throat. "Of course."

But inside I'm screaming: "Mummy, I'm interviewing a 4,000 year old star man and I don't know what to say."

For *Terra Q* readers storing this datacast in your implants, Tasman is wearing a classic black skinsuit covered with complex turquoise runes that seem to enhance his muscular curves. The runes are mystifying, early twenty-second century symbols. I'm told they are actually nanolithographic circuits that house a lot of Tasman's journals. In some ways it's a bit of a status thing, though Tasman shakes his head vigorously at my suggestion. Either way, they do represent his level of expertise amongst the terraformers. He's known for a dozen popular resort worlds in the Pleiades, celebrated for the dazzling sea-world chain in the Orion Nebula, as well as other legends such as the Rigel ringworld. But this is just touching the surface, as the runes suggest a breadth of work that would be hard to match—he's one of the best.

What is perhaps more daunting for an urban-stack child like me is his height at two metres and his good looks that most women, and a lot of men, would give up their lovers for. And there lies the rub, for he's both an anachronism *and* a paradox. Anachronistic in the sense that he's got that old-world air about him: a renaissance man, rugged and practical without the false graces of fame. Honestly, where can you find such attributes these days? And paradoxical in the sense that he still views terraforming as an art. It's in his stance and the way those sharp blue eyes scrutinise every detail on the world below—his canvas—constantly striving for perfection.

There was a time when we didn't care about the terraformers. Back in the early years of human colonisation we hated them, even *blamed* them for taking away the nanotech and the inertial drives that allowed them to hopscotch through time at 0.99c whilst we lurched about, glacially colonising one prepped world after another.

They were harsh years—humanity slapped out into the cold. But it wasn't the fault of the terraformers or their enlightened founders. They were the only ones who truly saw the magnitude of the pending extinction-event that we had haplessly set in motion. We were lucky to get off Old Earth alive.

Giving us the nanotech would have only made things worse. Looking at the power of it as it churns the surface below, I get the impression that for all that it can create, it can also erase. I can only imagine the consequences if it were in the wrong hands, so can you really blame anyone for taking a slab of Semtex away from a child?

But now it seems we can't get enough of the terraformers. There are growing populations to house and feed and a whole new era of interstellar migration and economics at our doorstep.

Talking with this guy as he monitors his cyber-minions, you begin to see a little of the Old Earth boy in him. He grew up on a cattle farm on the western plains of a province known quaintly as New South Wales. A country lad eventually attracted away from the rustic life by the lure of the rim cities; joyrides on Moon barges out of the Woomera spaceport; and his future wife, Sandra, a Brisbane lawyer with a philanthropist father.

And that dispels another myth, as I'd thought the terraformers were single and celibate for the greater good, but Sandra and his two children are currently on another level of this surreal spindle.

Much as I pester Wishart for a family chat, he is not going to have a bar of it. "Nice try," he says in that laconic Australian fashion.

However, on my journey here, he did send me some archive footage of his mother, Gabrielle, a strong, quick-witted woman with a constant smile and a community spirit that seemed to know no bounds. There's something in Tasman's gaze that is so much her, farseeing to the horizon, always checking and calibrating the lay of the land, for there is truth to be gleaned in the earth as much as there is in the sea. It's a testament to her memory, and to her genuine humanity, that her son has not lost these qualities out here in the deep.

His father, Gary, died of an influenza strain when Tasman was five. The early years were troubled times for the Wisharts with bovine disease sweeping a protein-dependent world. But the archive footage speaks volumes: a family at ease with itself, a four-year-old Tasman doing acrobatic tricks around the homestead on an old carbon fibre bicycle, his dad watching on. Gary is saying something like "I never taught him that" and shaking his head in wonder on the grainy holo-recording.

And that's how Tasman flourished: the ability to soak up new skills with preternatural ease and an uncanny geo-spatial awareness that made him see things that most of us can only guess at. Those were the days when a genome map cost a buck-fifty, but a proper, prenatal, designer genome cost a years' salary. The Wisharts were quoted as saying it was the best investment they could have ever made in their only child.

And they weren't far wrong, because Tasman went from cattle boy to space ship captain at the age of 14, and joined the Mars terraforming project five years later.

"Mars wasn't a failure, it was just half-finished," he says as the nexus magnifies aspects of the surface below. "I miss those days. You always remember your first world. After each world I think, yeah, if only we'd done that on Mars."

I watch as vegetation is burned away below, transforming millions of square kilometres to ash, choking the atmosphere with carbon. Then just as quickly, swathes of green appear as new vegetation is formed. Tasman tells me that the more correct term for what is going on is "terraquickening".

"You have to model how the variables interact over deep time," he continues, and I know behind those irises he's partitioning off some parts of his brain to supervise the avatars so he can engage me in idle conversation. "We're trying to do in decades what's normally done by nature over millions of years. We've learnt from bitter experience what a couple of centuries—or even several decades—of human development can do to a planet. Terraforming is big picture engineering that requires a vision for civilisation to match."

I watch more fires flare up, sweeping across continents. "Carbon cycles?" I ask tentatively, referring to the most memorable statistic from my didactic that half the dry weight of living matter is carbon. In the same breath I'm also hoping for some redemption after my earlier test.

"That's part of it," he says, deadpan.

Or not.

Still, I imagine I'm standing on a milk crate and high-fiving him as he rattles through a list of other essential biogeochemical cycles.

After my inner euphoria settles I reflect on his words: deep time, big picture, vision for civilisation. It's all terraformer lexicon, stuff that we've heard in other rare interviews and seen in snippets of journals. There's a kind of mantra to it that hasn't really changed since the early days on Mars. For the uninitiated it probably comes across as old-world dogma or a less-than-subtle sleight on humanity, with a sprinkle of irony for good measure, particularly given the horrendous loss of Old Earth that still echoes down the centuries.

But you've got to look beyond the words to where it all began. The Enlightened Age lasted a decade, a short-lived, contained tech singularity. For the first time in history, life-changing, global-spanning technology was in the hands of scientists and philanthropists with no agenda other than to provide a lasting vision for humanity. But Old Earth choked on its own vomit before the new memes could get a foothold, and the survivors came clutching at Mars like ghouls.

And now Tasman is looking at me with a surprisingly childish, lopsided grin that reminds me of Harrison Ford in that ancient classic. But where Ford played an out-of-control renegade travelling the galaxy, Wishart is living the life of an in-control artisan, sticking to a stubborn but painfully truthful script that he helped develop—we haven't earned the right to use the technology yet.

There's a resonance here that goes back even further to the original Age of Enlightenment that swept across Europe in the eighteenth century. Immanuel Kant wrote in his 1784 essay in the *Berlinische Monatsschrift* that "Enlightenment is man's emergence from his self-incurred immaturity."

Perhaps this explains why all our attempts at reaching another singularity have failed—you just can't take fast food chains and shopping mall cultures out into the cosmos and expect to achieve some higher plane of consciousness. And maybe this also explains why I can't see any hint of arrogance in Wishart, no matter how hard and how stupidly I look for signs.

He shrugs and say, "I'm a terraformer," as if that is sufficient explanation.

But I continue to ignore my inner compass and try to find some scrap of aloofness in him.

He slaps me on the back. "Relax," he says, but not before I see something dark drift across his eyes.

Maybe I've stretched the line of questioning a little too far. But no, I'm beginning to think that aside from artistic flair and the huge level of responsibility this man carries, there's a deeper discomfort in what he does.

I sidestep my awkward moment with a little dry humour. "Do you miss any opportunities out here?" I say, casually referring to his seventeenth century namesake, Abel Tasman, who sailed half-way around the world and completely missed mainland Australia.

"We're always missing things," he explains, not taking my bait. "That's why we criss-cross space instead of constantly travelling outwards."

I hadn't thought of it like that. "So, do you ever check up on your work, see how it's going?"

"Never."

I realise a little late that I've touched a raw nerve. There's that dark thing in his eyes again, telling me there are boundaries. And no wonder. Why would the terraformers clean up for us? They're builders, not landlords.

So, before the interview goes from pear-shaped to get-the-hell-off-my-ship, I focus back to the surface. It has changed again, filigree patterns of green and brown waxing and waning across continents, appearing and disappearing before my eyes in some unfathomable but beautiful sequence.

"We're building the geological strata. Worlds are tempered, layer after layer, they're not moulded. You just can't chuck dirt and water on alien rock like a cake mix. The strata are important in maturing the carbon-nitrogen cycles, but they're also important in establishing connections between the human colonies and the planet."

I rake together the remnants of my didactic, salvaging what little grace I can find. "You're referring to Gaia theory and nondualism."

The lopsided grin is back. "Exactly. It's tough when living and non-living don't evolve together. Colonies have a better chance of lasting and becoming fully fledged societies if these connections are considered during the terraforming."

Tasman goes on to refer to the statistics about colonies that have tried to populate totally alien worlds, clinging in their self-contained habitats like barnacles. There's something to be said about the blueprint left to us by Old Earth, the one still deeply embedded in our physical and psychological makeup.

I point to some milky-white streaks off in the distance. The nexus responds, bringing them into focus. Comets. There are at least five, no six, being shepherded by some dark ship.

"The ice is harvested for oceans," Tasman explains, seemingly genuinely intrigued by my sense of awe. I'm pinching myself again because this is a day-to-day routine for him, manipulating matter on planetary scales. And it's only then that I realise just how much this technology would be abused were it in the wrong hands.

His sidelong glance tells me he's seen a thousand times before how quickly amazement can turn to a ravenous gleam. "The software encryptions can't be cracked." It's both a warning and a statement, suggestive of the fact that we've tried it on with the terraformers before.

The nexus shifts focus again as my eyes track across to a group of light sources twinkling out on the periphery. It looks like a small star cluster, until shapes emerge and distil out like a plot in a disturbing holodrama. There are ships out there, hundreds of them. The perspective is distorted, as they seem much closer than the nexus reading of 100AU, which places them well beyond this star's heliopause.

"Early settlers," he says.

Tasman doesn't need to provide any further explanation. The generation ships will probably be parked there for another ten or twenty years. Some of the occupants will never live to experience planetfall, but still they arrive in droves, waiting to stake their claim on new lands—the virgin territory being moulded beneath my feet.

And just for a fleeting moment I'm transposed into Tasman's shoes. There's something noble in what he does, a lofty power, a heart-aching beauty in this fine art of creation. But it's soon brought crashing back down to the harsh reality of human expansion, industrialisation and resource consumption.

Kant's words seem to slosh around at the base of my skull. It's almost as if humanity reached a plateau back on Old Earth, a mould that we're stuck with by the limitations of our wetware brains and competitive-aggressive genes. Because for every terraformed blue-green marble out there where humanity is thriving, there are half a dozen decrepit ones, left gutted and polluted in our pursuit of *lifestyle*.

The thought twists my stomach into knots and I suddenly feel ashamed. But there are glimmers of brighter things mixed in, and for the first time I am starting to get what motivates these terraformers.

Tasman turns his full attention to me and it's like I'm caught in a cerulean blue rip that's taking me under. "Some days I wake up and ask myself 'What the hell am I doing?'" He says it with no bitterness, no hint of that shadow that haunted his eyes earlier. "Some of us have contemplated transferring the technology back— let humanity get on with it—but we know it would lead to ruin. Others have quit, unwilling to watch new worlds become ravaged, to see Old Earth repeated all over again. For the rest of us, no matter how much we care about what we do, it's still a compromise that we're willing to live with."

He spots the question in my eyes and adds, "We're not under some sort of social contract. We could say no and stop terraforming altogether, but that would be the death of hope."

Visions of the terraformers packing up their tools instil new fears in me: the machinery of human expansion grinding to a halt as our current cache of worlds is slowly depleted.

Then Tasman breaks my trance with that distinctive smile, lets out a catchy laugh that I've only heard hints of until now. "I used to ride shotgun with the pilots during the early Moon colonisation. They'd let me fly the old barges before I had my license. Who'd have thought that possible after the space program nearly shut down in 2011? I was just a kid and it was completely terrifying but completely awesome."

And that's Tasman Wishart all over, eternally young at heart with a dogged self-determination and a stubborn, unrelenting belief in humanity.

We've got a lot to thank this kid from the outback for, and a lot to live up to.

AFTERWORD TO "TERRA Q"

The gentleman's magazine of the future! I had a blast writing "TerraQ", I think because it is a completely different narrative style and because there are two mutually opposed ideas—the beauty and art of terraforming worlds set against the backdrop of a resource hungry humanity driven to destroy worlds. "TerraQ" imagines a future where the space program gets its mojo back and goes through a renaissance of sorts, only to be followed by the grim reality of an over-populated society expanding out into the cosmos with consumerism and supply chain economics. Can these two global forces of creation and destruction co-exist in a star-faring society? Maybe, maybe not.

EYES OF FIRE IN MY WAKING DREAMS

My name is James Glazebrook and I am a savant.

No, it doesn't mean I'm like the *Rain Man*. I'm 18 years old, with an eidetic memory, muscular dystrophy and pervasive developmental disorder not otherwise specified (PDD-NOS). If you don't like acronyms then call it atypical autism. The symptoms include a speech impediment and repetitive body movements; I tend to move my head a lot, my arms when I'm stressed, but not my legs.

With the recent departure of my parents, Ron and Alice, I'll be forever reliant on my big brother, Joshua, and my chair, Bruce. Bruce's wheels are six spoke, powder-coated gunmetal, with black low profile tyres. The seat, arms and head rest are black leather, creased and scuffed to perfection. There's a worn aluminium control stick on the right armrest, a touch screen and microphone packaged on a swivel-arm on the left, and a small computer clamped under the seat.

If you saw me you might feel indifferent or disgusted, as I'm gangly, my eyes wander a bit, my hair doesn't know which way to grow, and I'll never have a girlfriend or play tennis or walk the dog.

Hell, you might even feel sympathy, but I don't want that because it leads to wishing for things that never were or never will be or never should have been. It would be like me wishing my parents hadn't gone out in the car that day, but I said they must because they never go out, and they did, reluctantly. It would be like you wishing that you had wealth and riches when you know you haven't got the skills or weren't born into it, or wishing that you were more beautiful or attractive when you know you're stuck with the genes your parents gave you. Don't wish for things like that, and if you do, then you know how the old cliché goes—be careful.

Anyway, enough of you! What's my prodigal talent? Well, I'm kind of glad you asked—I'm a digital artist. Oh sure, dime a dozen, you say. Yeah, well how many artists actually paint thoughts? Read the critic reviews if you're not convinced: *Nothing is what it seems for this new age Rembrandt. Where we see subtlety in a face, he sees the sublime in human nature . . . Angels have descended to earth and reside in the young, pervasive mind of Glazebrook . . . Glazebrook captures the thought before the action, a thousand nuances of movement, tone and light—it is precognitive . . . The kid's got talent.*

No, scratch that last one, I was just messing with you.

I'm making a modest living, and the commissions are starting to roll in, but it sometimes gets me into trouble. The thing is I find it hard to de-tune. I can tell when people are about to do something. We all can to some degree—it's the blend of our five senses coming together, familiarity with the subject, or just heightened intuition. The thought might lead to a mundane action: make some coffee, scratch your genitals, laugh, turn the TV channel. Or it might lead to something more profound, something great, something of consequence. *These* are the thoughts that interest me, the ramshackle workings of the brain as they play out on the human face in a million different combinations. And my brain photocopies this, so you see, I have to paint the images—not just one, but many. Sometimes forty or fifty are needed to capture a train of thought, and I have to keep painting until my mind feels, well . . . empty.

I've had more brain scans than anyone should have in ten lifetimes. The specialists can't find anything unusual. They speculate that my brain is accessing deeper connections that can't be achieved with "normal" people. It's like my mind absorbs so much information that it has to process it or go crazy. As my window to the world is swamped to overload with masses of data, it's no wonder there's little room for a full suite of body functions or wishful thinking or social etiquette.

So when I obsess over something, it can get me into strife. You don't know what it's like for me, not being able to switch off.

And on Tuesday it got me into deep shit.

"Stay with me, Jim."

"Piss off." It is Bruce playing his mind games. He always does it, mischievous little fucker. His algorithms translate my whining voice and the icon sequences on the touch screen into the synthetic voice of Bruce Wayne in *The Dark Knight*: a firm voice with a slight lisp and a boyish undertone that epitomises the cheeky billionaire playboy.

"Jim!"

It is the middle of a Melbourne summer, the heat is dry and exhausting, the streets are packed, and Joshua is in no mood for my antics. We weave through the crowd, still several blocks from our destination. There is just no finding a car park close enough these days, even in the disabled spots.

"Watch out," a grandma says as I brush her walking stick with a wheel.

I hate crowds, probably because they hate me for taking up half the footpath.

My hands flutter over the touch screen. *Fuck off, bitch.* On screen only—sometimes it is best to toggle Bruce's speaker off.

I look over my shoulder as I whiz past, and freeze frame her in a cascade of 3D images. She is about to raise her voice again then sees me smile and then the quiver of a smile plays on her crinkled lips and in the crow's feet around her eyes and in the micro-flutter of an eyelid and I know then that something has transferred between us as she turns, thoughtful. She has had a full life, and it gives her comfort, those intersecting geometries of the girl, woman and mother, but she is not closed to new perspectives. This also gives her comfort, gives her wisdom and perhaps she feels better for our encounter with me. She squares her shoulders and places less weight on her stick . . . and then she is gone. But her image remains: a cascade of colours, a collage of shapes, a spiral of mnemonics, all to be put back together into a perfect reflection of life itself. And then I know I have to get back home soon to paint the mystery of my waking dream.

"Jim, what is it with you today?" Joshua stops in the middle of the crowd at the intersection, waiting for the walk sign to turn green. He looks back at me, as do others. I don't bother freeze framing their disgust.

"I'm sorry," Bruce says.

"We're going to be late for the appointment."

You need to get laid.

He looks down at the screen and says through gritted teeth, "Cut it out."

"Ok, I'm sorry again. It's so hot."

"What did you expect—snow? Come on, we're nearly there."

He is still angry. I don't blame him. He and I revolve around each other like lost planets now that our binary sun has been extinguished. And he has done the right thing, seeing a counsellor. It helps him cope with the loss and the burden, not that I am much extra work, as he has always been thoughtful and caring.

I don't deserve it.

In a way I am looking forward to the session. I draw some vicarious, therapeutic value out of tagging along like a raven haired homunculus. The counsellor, Suzanna, has those stunning green Eastern European eyes, and she said once that I was funny, but I think she was just being polite. I digitally painted her as she hesitates before stepping over a white line on the carpet in her chamber, Joshua like a Greek god in repose on the couch, though, unlike Michelangelo, I found the decency to give him a loin cloth. I call it *Turmoil at Boundaries*. I don't need to be a prodigy to read the sexual tension. I hope she might see the humour in it, that's when I actually pluck up the courage to give it to her.

We reach another set of pedestrian lights. The sounds and smells of the city wash over me, uplifting and at the same time cloying. The sights swamp my visual cortex, a sea of colours and moving faces, an ocean of thoughts and feelings and emotions leading to decisions and actions and—

There!

A man glances at me from the opposite side of the street. Sunlight plays on blue irises, intention, resolve, adrenalin high. His face . . . there's something wrong with it, something missing, and then he realises I am staring at him and his eyes intensify like pools of venom. I hear my heart beat in the stillness, a rabbit caught in the spotlight, a timeless, breathless moment that seems to stretch out forever.

He looks away.

"Whoa." It is Bruce.

The sounds of the street filter back like a discordant choir. My arms are waving about in agitation. The walk sign flashes and the crowd sweeps Joshua away across the road, westward bound.

The man disappears. Wait . . . there . . . a black tee and jeans . . . he's heading north away from the intersection, walking fast, head down, shoulders hunched, a small shopping bag in one hand.

It's too late to cross over so I slam the control stick, spin ninety degrees, and bowl along my side of the street. I keep track of him between passing cars, vans, people, light posts and awnings, like the spinning frames of a kid's kaleidoscope.

The pavement in front of me dips onto a small side road. A screech of tyres—damn—the chrome bumper of an old Monaro comes to rest just centimetres from Bruce's right wheel. The driver glares at me. His teeth are crooked beneath a grey and black goatee and his arms are a canvas of tattoos: stars, barbed wire, a leopard, knives, a woman's face looking to the middle distance. His heart is truly on his sleeve. His hands wave at me as if to say "what the fuck?" then his chest rises, head tilts, eyes dance over my chair, a thought rising, day time fantasy—what, you *want* to run me over now?

Too late.

Bruce is bouncing up onto the next sidewalk. "Fuck you." Cool, suave, unruffled playboy. The finger might have ascended, but my hands are too busy.

I'll paint you later, grey-beard tattoo man—*Faceless Heart.*

"Move please," Bruce says, politely. There are so many people out today. "Thank you, move please."

A quick glance . . . he's still there, now heading into a walkway draped with dark green sheets and six floors of scaffolding above.

A man in his mid-thirties wearing a yellow hard hat carries a bag of render mix along the third floor of scaffolding. He has a competent cast to his face, he's good at what he does, but he's got that nine-to-five glaze in his eyes. He doesn't enjoy his job: it's a rut, a chore that pays the bills, a necessary application of his talents. He sees me shooting along like a teenage Stephen Hawking on nitrous. Oh, here we go, this one's predictable as he calls to his mate and points at me. They laugh and his mate cocks his arms, hands like hooks, and gives me a goofy look.

This time the finger goes up—*Ironic Ritual.*

I stop at the next intersection and glance across the street. People are streaming out of the covered walkway.

What were you about to do? I've never seen that face before, such . . . absence.

The lights turn and I scoot over the crossing and turn left into the walkway. Thick sheets of cross ply flex under my weight, an OH&S claim waiting to happen. There's no sign of him so I spin around, one-eighty. The low profiles chirrup and I scuff a guy's shin.

"What the fuck are you doing?" He jumps back a step: charcoal pin stripe suit, swept back hair, grey at the temples, sun tanned, baby boomer, a platinum wedding ring. Thoughts stretch out across his face like an open book: arrogance, the power and confidence that go with money, lots of money, the next deal at the back of his mind, eyes drifting over the breasts and long legs of his red-head companion, a protective arm around her. She's a lot younger: Gen Y, in a pin stripe too, tanned face and legs, shade-too-orange spray on, high heeled Ferragamos . . . the OH&S claim? Not this time, she's too careful.

Their lips curl in unison, like I've got leprosy or something.

A flurry of icons, a few half-arsed attempts at speech, and Bruce is resplendent with the comeback, "She blows you for your money, go back to your wife."

Reasonable Motive.

I speed back to the intersection and turn left, west. There's another covered walkway leading up an incline to a back street. I reach the back street and look left, right, left again. Reminds me of my kindergarten teachers; there was a string of them, I was a handful. The redevelopment stretches to the back of the block, so I go left, south again.

I think about grandma, she was adorable and I was harsh, so I'm sorry.

Enchanted Twilight.

The pavement dips again, an entrance to an underground car park. I swing left, past a dented, rusting white skip full of broken bricks, timbers, smashed plasterboard sheets, old electrical wiring, a discarded shopping bag. There's a rope with a "No Entry" signed tied to it strung across the entrance. I lift the rope up and over Bruce and then I'm away, banking down a ramp to the first level basement park.

It is dark beyond the pallid semi-circle of light. The smell of fresh paint is overwhelming and I cover my nose. Folding ladders and frames stand idle like the skeletons of some surreal, square-ribbed beast. I hear a sound—a clunk—at odds with the filtered street noise and hammering from above. Bruce slows to a crawl and I scan along the wall to the left until I find the ramp leading down to the second basement level. I swing down into deeper darkness, urging Bruce to be quiet, but he makes a faint electric whine and the smooth sound of rubber tread on concrete. It's no use, there's no way I can be stealthy so I coast down the ramp hoping that there's still enough background noise.

This level hasn't been re-furbished yet. There are scuff marks from a hundred careless drivers along the ramp wall that opens to another empty space. Outlines emerge from the shadows: round concrete support pillars, faded divider lines, old ceiling fluoros hanging from their mounts, wooden boxes and plastic crates piled in a corner, an abandoned car about twenty metres away . . . wait . . . it's him, leaning into the open trunk of the car, a white line of skin showing above his belt.

I edge closer. He doesn't hear me. He's struggling with something in the trunk.

I'm five metres away now.

My hands seem to have a mind of their own as they race over the screen. *What are you doing?* I'm not thinking straight, the speaker is off but the screen lights up in the darkness.

He turns and lifts her out of the trunk. She's about my age, skinny limbs hanging limp, sweat-soaked blonde hair, black gym boots, black short-shorts, white sleeveless top spattered from a bloodied nose. She has a rose bracelet tattoo around her right ankle.

He drops her like a stone and steps over her, towards me. I hit reverse, too late. He reaches me easily, plants one foot on Bruce's armrest and shoves me over. The sound of the chair hitting the floor is like an explosion. Pain lances down my right arm and a gash opens up on the back of my hand as it jams between the chair and the concrete.

He jumps on top of the chair on all fours and leans over me, predatory.

"What do you want?"

I feel his breath, his lifeless voice, seeping into my ears. Sweat drips from his face onto mine. I turn my head away, but my eyes, curse them, glance up at him. You would not look twice at him on a normal day. His hair is brown, cut short, his jaw is clean shaven, and his face is a mask of introversion, plain, average, a face you don't trust or love or hate or feel anything for. It is like a blank canvas—I have never seen anything like it before—and it fills me with a cold dread.

Then his eyes latch onto mine, forcing their way down like twin beacons. Blue irises radiate lines of black and amber flecks, like the charred aftermath of a bushfire, compelling, irresistible. Something rises in me from a dark and lonely wellspring. What misery I felt now gives way to sheer terror.

I piss myself. Hot liquid fills my pants, soaking through my trousers and up onto my shirt. My bladder pulses until it is empty and stinking rivulets spread out onto the concrete. Somewhere in the distance I hear grunting sounds. I know it's me. My arms wave, my head bobs up and down, up and down.

I feel his weight move off the chair, hear his footsteps recede. Something warm runs into my eye and I wipe it and look at my finger tips—blood, a lot of it. I dare to turn my head. My cheek brushes the wet concrete and urine soaks my hair. I have a clear view over the top of my knees, the floor looks like a wall, and he's doing a magic trick: defying gravity and walking on the wall.

He lifts her gently and rests her head against the car bumper. The action is a complete contradiction and I realise I have interrupted a scene. He brushes matted hair from her face. She mutters something in her semi-conscious stupor, and her eyes widen and she spits at him, but her lips are dry and caked and only a tiny spray of phlegm comes out. He slaps her nonetheless, hard, efficient . . . staged. He turns her head in one hand and touches her breasts with the other. He is talking to her, but I can't hear what he is saying, though the words are clipped and precise. He reaches into the trunk and takes out a black and gold fancy-dress mask, the one he has just bought, and places it over her face, slowly, carefully.

He glances over his shoulder as if reading my thoughts. He could be the person who sits in the opposite workspace every day and does his job and talks to you about the weather or asks how your weekend was, but you'll never get to know him; he'll never let you in, never let his guard down. And you won't think twice about it because he's part of the team and does a good job and besides, you've got plenty of friends at work, you don't need to know everyone. So he goes unseen, unheard, drifting in the undercurrent of society.

No, he doesn't have to say anything. I'm part of it now, I've wandered carelessly into his slipstream, stumbled onto his stage like a fool and he has accommodated me as if it's all part of the script.

He looks back at the girl—I'm next.

He slowly eases her back down to the cold concrete and then rolls her over at the hip until she is facing away from him. He tugs at the back of her shorts until they are down around her knees, then he lies down behind her and starts unzipping.

I look away. This is Melbourne, for god's sake, this can't be happening. My left hand hovers over the toggle. I leave it off.

You sick fuck.

Look at her, Jim, just look at her, you coward. If these are her last minutes then you need to be her witness, you need to for her sake, even if he kills you too.

I look back. The girl shoves an elbow in his ribs, but she has no strength. He slaps her hard on the back of the head and she starts sobbing. He shuffles closer, his jeans coming loose around his waist. His butt crack appears.

Laughter echoes around the empty hall. It's teasing and lavish and full of disdain.

He jumps away from the girl as if he has been jolted with electricity and pulls his jeans up to cover his suddenly flaccid prick.

My hands are a blur over the screen. "What's the matter? Can't get it up?"

He pulls me out of the chair like a rag doll. I press my thumb onto an icon and then I'm in the air for a heartbeat and I hit the ground. Something snaps inside. My vision blurs.

"Faceless Heart," Bruce says. "Fuck off, bitch. Ok, I'm sorry again. It's so hot. Enchanted Twilight. Move please. Whoa. Fuck off, bitch."

He lifts the chair and smashes it down.

That laughter again, sounds kind of aloof this time. "Ironic Ritual. I'm sorry. Whoa. What's the matter? Can't get it up? You sick fuck."

He rams his boot down on Bruce, again and again. The screen buckles and goes dim, plastic shards spray everywhere.

He turns to me. The car park is still. He won't be denied.

I focus in response, an automaton, a bleeding, piss stained homunculus . . . fuck, I miss you both . . . I'm always in trouble, I just can't help myself . . . his face is red with exertion but there's no rage . . . and his eyes . . . are primal . . . I'm under their spell . . . a new light burns in my life . . . a blue flame on a desolate plain somewhere on the wretched march to hell . . .

Whump!

He staggers and falls to the floor, hands scraping over concrete.

There . . . emotions   on   that   deadpan face . . . surprise? . . . no . . . *rapture* . . .

Joshua stands behind him, a timber in both hands. Another swing, but the man is quickly up on his feet and the timber misses its target. Joshua gives chase, back towards the ramp.

Those eyes have let go their hold and the world creeps in . . . my lungs are gurgling . . . a bleak angel looks at me . . . the mask is pushed up onto her head like a black and gold halo . . . she's curled up into a ball and is upside down on that magical wall . . . blood and dirt cover her face but she manages a smile . . . she's tough . . . I wish I was like that . . . but I know I shouldn't.

Claire's family huddles around me for an hour or so, noisy with the stress of it all, but immensely relieved that their daughter is safe. Claire stays for a while longer then kisses me on the cheek, hugs me in my bandages and pyjamas, and leaves me for the evening. The sky is the colour of lead through the single window.

To my surprise she drops by the hospital in the afternoon and says she would like to talk about what happened. I clam up at the idea and she leaves again with the promise that she will catch up soon when I'm feeling better. She is passionate, bright, happy-go-lucky—in the wrong place at the wrong time—but strong spirited enough to bounce back to the point where she actually wants to talk about the worst experience of her life only twenty-four hours after the event.

Seeing her brightens my day for a while and gives me enough energy to finish the eidetic of her beautiful, caring face. I scrutinise her image on the digital pallet—there's something of me in it—there always is, irrevocably connected to my subjects. I like to think I have the qualities of others, but I know in my heart that what I have is a shallow veneer. Scratch my surface and there's a seething cauldron of loss and denial and data processing—endless, eternal processing.

My thoughts turn inevitably to his face. Having seen into the depths of his eyes I am undone. His image lurks at the back of my mind, locked in a shadowed cell, waiting.

Joshua arrives at four o'clock. He doesn't need the GPS locator to find me this time. He gives me the once over. "Hey, Jim."

I can see in his eyes that I'm a fucking mess.

Icy knives stab along my ribs as I shuffle the touch screen onto my lap. "Did you reschedule Doc Z?" It's the old model Bruce sitting next to the bed, not quite as debonair, doesn't have all the icons and functions, but still does the trick.

"Stop deflecting."

"That's the pot calling the kettle black. You've been going back to her for months now. I think you're well passed the *counselling* stage."

"Well, if you must know, I'm going to cancel the appointments and ask her out."

"She would have gone out with you ages ago," old Bruce says.

"Ok, Jim, let's talk about this later. There's a police officer outside."

"Tell him to piss off."

Joshua's face darkens. "Now you better start cutting me some slack, little brother. I get it—we've been through hell this year. You need to let me in so we can talk about everything . . . mum . . . dad . . . Tuesday."

I look up at him. He is like an older clone with straight limbs and strong muscles, a body that feels as well as functions, a mind that is balanced and considerate and altruistic. "I'd prefer to be let out, Josh, not to let others in. There's a lot of shit in here."

"I know . . . fuck, I don't know at all. Look, they need your help. Claire was drugged during her ordeal so she can't remember much of what went on."

Damn. Now I feel even worse for letting her go. She needs to know more about what happened so she can heal.

"The police say this psycho may be connected to a series of murders. If you're not ready to give a statement, can you at least start to unpack?"

The shadowed thing in the recesses shifts in anticipation. "You know what that means."

Joshua's smile is meant to encourage, but it falls a long way short.

I sigh. My hand hovers over the screen.

It always begins like this, the unpacking of mnemonics before I start painting with the digital palette. But this time it's different. He's in there, intertwined with the others, *part* of the others, sharing our common humanity. But there is more, a vortex of warped shapes sliding to the surface. He looms up like a dark leviathan.

Tuesday unfolds in eidetic recall.

Faceless Heart.

He is unable to express himself so his heart speaks through other means.

He is a void on the skein of humanity. There is nothing on that face, nothing. How do you communicate? Where are your thoughts? There! Those eyes like poison, windows to a mute, burning soul . . .

Ironic Ritual.

He is a talented slave to a numbing ritual.

He is bent by a terrible burden, an unrelenting urge to control, to dominate. It is his skill, his calling that consumes him. The twisted, misshapen acorn of a boy grown to a man . . .

Reasonable Motive.

She belongs to him and that is the only motive he needs.

She is a catalyst for his power: ego rising, kinetic energy, focus straining at the tip of his prick. She represents all the other victims, subordinate, a vessel, and soon she will be sliced, red entropy . . .

Enchanted Twilight.

There is contentment of the spirit in the twilight of years.

Wild intoxication, the elusive loss of control, slick blood, banshee screams. Transference! They have become him, in their last desperate hour, in their writhing madness, they want to destroy him by unspeakable means . . . their eyes beneath the mask . . . their eyes are full of twisted hatred . . . eyes of fire . . .

I lean over and vomit on the floor.

The recall is happening all at once, unfolding like a Matrioshka doll, on a scale I've never experienced. But I am strong. I wished for it and now I face him in my mind's eye.

You thought that you were hidden, skimming across society with your sick agenda, but I know you now, I know obsession, I *am* obsession. I will not be controlled, but I must relive you, breathe life into your emptiness so that others can see you for what you truly are, so they can find you. Through me, you *will* be seen.

There's no turning back as the images spiral like a hurricane, replaying every aspect, every detail.

I can't look away. I can't switch off.

AFTERWORD TO "EYES OF FIRE IN MY WAKING DREAMS"

I think everyone is on a spectrum in terms of our ability to learn and process information. I don't think the human mind can be as neatly packaged as the psychology text books suggest, and I think there are definite grey areas between so-called "syndromes" and "mainstream behaviours". I believe that savants demonstrate some almost superhuman capabilities that reveal glimpses of the true potential of the human mind.

But what is the opportunity cost of all this processing ability? In "Eyes of Fire", Jim Glazebrook is socially awkward and most of the time he is unable to switch off the noise. His outlet is art. Sound familiar?

When studying astrophysics at university I used to lock myself away for weeks before exams, getting by with minimum human interaction. Not being blessed (cursed) with photographic recall I used to use mnemonics to help me unpack the reams of mathematical equations. Instead of taking weeks, imagine if this could be done in a split second.

I took this idea and applied it to face-to-face communication, most of which is non-verbal. We're always consciously or unconsciously reading other people's faces—we're constantly trying to mind read. If we know people well enough, say a partner or spouse, then we can see "predictable" behaviour or thoughts. But what if we were so highly tuned, so deeply wired into what's happening on everyone's face? What if you could pick up all those nuances and micro-expressions in an instant and understood the brain patterns behind them and could replay it to yourself over and over again? Wouldn't it be a form of mind-reading or at the very least, precognitive? Poor Jim.

ALIEN INTENT

Lecture Theatre 3, Department of Xenopsychology, Cambridge.

"Good morning," Professor Hutchinson said.

The students echoed his greeting as they jacked into the theatre's sensorium. A gigantic virtual paper aeroplane floated down from the top of the theatre, skimming over the crowd to land gently at the Professor's feet.

"Very twentieth century," he said, smiling. He wasn't your typical academic, no eccentric mannerisms or out-of-date clothing. If anything, he looked like a retired marine: tall with steel-blue eyes and close cropped hair turning grey at the temples. His accent was hard to pick, tempered from years of research in the colonies.

The sensorium lit up, floating above the students.

"Today's lecture will include a case study from Sirius 5."

A murmur spread around the theatre.

"Isn't that the genocide planet?" It was Eric, a lanky Australian student jacked in on a cheap, grainy comlink.

Idiot, Melanie thought. *There was an introduction in the Ethics class if you'd bothered to attend.*

"Melanie," the Professor said, tapping his index finger to his head, "Please switch on your aide memoire filter."

The students cracked up as a red faced Melanie slumped back in her seat and flipped a switch on her jack at the base of her skull.

Next to Melanie, Adam said, "I've heard the aliens are like flying raptors." He grinned stupidly. "They ate most of the humans."

"No," Eric said. "I've seen pictures. They look like frill-necked lizards with rainbow-coloured glider wings." He frowned and added, "I don't think they are carnivores though."

Melanie waved her hands about and said, "*Hello?* Did anyone attend the Ethics class?"

"Okay, listen up," the Professor said, "Because I'll be asking questions later. The virtual you are about to experience includes a key interview with a male Kresh who helped coordinate the genocide. He and the other Kresh involved were captured by tactical response teams and held in solitary confinement for the better part of a year while more ships spun down from Earth to begin the slow process of re-colonisation." He paused, a finger hovering over the sensorium's icon. "The virtual can be quite disturbing, so if you haven't got the stomach for it you should leave now and I'll cast the notes to your aide memoires later."

No one jacked out.

The Professor nodded and the sensorium whirled into their minds like a hurricane.

Case File #52: Tyll'x, Kresh tribal leader, male, age unknown.
Case Officer: Dr Helena Jacobs, XenoPsych Team Leader.
Interview Commenced: 17.69pm, Day 7 Post Spin-Down.

I walked into the room and placed the folder on the table. It was getting late and I wasn't really in the mood for another interview today, but we had to stay on schedule—Earth needed answers.

Tyll'x sat at the table with his hands cuffed. He gazed out the single window, looking beyond the starport platforms to the fields of blue talif, an indigenous wheat grass that covered the higher plateaus. The grass tops shimmered in the blue-white light and the stems bent and swayed in the back draft of the ships entering the starport. He seemed mesmerised by the way the talif swirled in chaotic patterns, thousands of propeller shaped seeds breaking away and floating up in spirals, drawn into the wake of the engines.

He must have felt the irony of the situation, surely? The re-colonisation was inevitable. But his face only had half of the equivalent human musculature, so it was difficult to tell. Even the term "face" was misleading for the Kresh had been bred over generations so that the front of their heads could pass for something human, much like the Heikegani crabs that were spared by nineteenth century fishermen for their resemblance to samurai warriors.

And for those Kresh that hadn't made the grade of the colony's centuries old slave system . . . I forced myself to acknowledge the terrible fact that the recent genocide was not the first one on Sirius 5.

"How are you?" I asked, sitting down opposite him, my heart hammering.

His bright eyes refocussed, as if calculating my every move. The irises were orange, like a distant conflagration, an unsettling window into his alien soul.

"I exist." It was the vernacular greeting.

He looked tired. I was no expert on Kresh physiology, but after a week of interviews the signs were clear. The veins along his articulated limbs pulsed sluggishly, and his tough, diamond-patterned skin was dry and flaky. The stalar—the multi-coloured glider membrane that connected his arms and legs, with a spiked frill around his neck—hung like limp rags. The harmonics from the stalar's internal chambers also sounded very faint and subdued.

I had seen archival footage of the Kresh in full flight. They were savagely beautiful with their stalar extended, gliding on the thermals that rose up off the ocean beyond the highlands. There were history papers in the colony archives, including theories on how the properties of Kresh skin and stalar might have evolved to allow flight in vacuum. But now, after generations of artificial selection, I couldn't help but feel that the Kresh were a mere shadow of what they might have become.

"When was the last time you slept?"

His head snapped up, eyes burning into me from across the table. "What do you want, Helena?"

Damn. He'd caught me off guard before, but this time it took my breath away. I forced air into the bottom of my lungs, leant forward and said "I want the same thing as before, Tyll'x. I want answers. How did killing three million colonists make you feel?"

Air expelled from his stalar, but it wasn't a sign of derision or humour or anything remotely resembling a human emotion.

"Killing? I do not understand." His neck frill fluttered slightly— his tell.

"Oh, come on. You know exactly what I mean."

This time he did look amused, or maybe it was my imagination, or just a trick of the light. "They are in a different state, joined with the firmament."

"So you're telling me you don't feel anything at all?"

His eyes dimmed as if now bored . . . no, something else.

I sighed. "You're going to have to help me out. I've got a justice system waiting on the results of this process, and let me tell you that they're ready to do whatever it takes to bring order back to this world."

"Justice? Did you know in some outposts, humans hunt us for medicines and trophies? In powdered form, stalar is supposed to be . . . what is your word for sexual stimulant?"

My reply came out in a flat, hollow voice. "Aphrodisiac."

"Yes." His stalar shimmered in mesmerising rainbow patterns.

I felt before I heard the harmonics escalating up an octave. The diamond shapes on his skin darkened—the equivalent of sweating. His neck muscles bunched up as the electrical charge from the cuffs flowed up his arms. With a grunt of effort he forced his neck frill to spread out like a fan with sharp points. Then the rest of his stalar started to fill out.

The cuffs chimed in warning.

"Stop it!" I stood up and stepped away from the table. I knew what a Kresh shriek-pulse could do to the contents of a human skull, but the cuffs would tear his hands off before he could create a lethal sound wave.

The door to the room banged open and a security guard stepped in brandishing a stunner wand. Tyll'x turned his face to the floor, his stalar flattening, the sound diminishing so that only the electric buzz of the wand could be heard.

I waved the guard away. "It's all right."

He gave me a venomous look and walked out. I had convinced the Tactical Response Team Leader to allow the interviews to be conducted without guards. They had done enough damage to the prisoners before our arrival, and now they all seemed a little too edgy, confined to watching the proceedings through security cameras.

I rested my hands on the edge of the table. "Was the genocide an act of revenge?"

Tyll'x tilted his head to one side. "Revenge?" There was no tell this time.

"We hurt you, you hurt us?"

He shook his head. "Balance."

"Okay, so tell me what balance means to you?"

"Human minds are chaotic, random, disconnected." He tilted his head to watch the talif again.

The implications were disturbing, offensive even, but I shoved my feelings aside. "So is this some form of Kresh justice?"

"No," he said, looking back at me. "Justice is a human construct." He paused, as if thoughtful, which gave me the uneasy feeling he was anticipating my reaction to his next words. "The Kresh seek balance; there is a harmony in nature, a universal truth that you cannot see."

He was making a concession, that I could tell, but it wasn't enough. Not nearly enough.

"That's a little better, Tyll'x." I grabbed the unopened folder from the table. "But you're going to have to give me more than that. You claim you have a value system based on universal truths, but you show no sign of remorse, no sense of right or wrong. Aren't these universal?"

He didn't answer, but there was a strange light in his eyes as he watched me walk out of the room.

Interview suspended: 17.93pm, Day 7.

Professor Hutchinson addressed the students.

"At this point Doctor Jacobs consulted her team. I'm casting the notes now. They discussed how morality has evolved in the known alien species across the colony worlds. The Kresh have a very different temporal worldview to ours. Prior to our colonisation, they had evolved with an innate sense of deep time—something that we can only guess at. We understand this gives rise to feelings of "balance" as Tyll'x put it, their equivalent of a moral system I suppose, though this is a gross oversimplification."

David, a Latin-American student, chimed in, "Darwin suggested that any animal with social instincts and higher intelligence would acquire a conscience or morality."

"Indeed, but Darwin's take on it was utopian, don't you think? Natural selection doesn't work that way, at least not for homo sapiens. Estimates indicate that 20 million Kresh were killed during the first colony's rule. Doctor Jacobs was mindful of how two-faced the whole interrogation process would appear. She sought to understand his motivations and, by default, the broader intentions of this alien race. What made him commit the crime and how did he react afterwards? Is he a mass-murderer or something else entirely?"

The Professor waved down the flurry of hands and fired up the sensorium.

Interview resumed: 18.54pm, Day 7.

Tyll'x was still seated.

I sat down and placed the folder on the table.

The pale blue orb of Sirius dipped towards the horizon, casting long bands of light into the room. I saw for the first time the lines etched down Tyll'x's cheeks, the flecks of green in his forest-fire irises.

A purring sound filled the room—it was his stalar softly resonating to some internal frequency. Normal harmonics were used by the Kresh to communicate across great distances, and were also part of their mating displays. Shriek-pulses were included in this ritual, though only to ward off other males. The pulses had only recently been adapted to attack humans.

I also knew that the sounds helped the Kresh think clearly. After another heated argument with the Tactical Response Team Leader, Tyll'x's cuff settings had been adjusted during the break to allow him a little harmonic activity.

And I really *needed* him to think clearly now as I opened up the folder. Graphic photos spilled out onto the table, images that made me weak at the knees. Men, women, and children, stacked in mass graves, their skin and eyes tumescent.

"What does this do for you?"

His face seemed cold and impassive though he did not look directly at the images. It struck me that he might have looked like this on the day he and his people coordinated the slaughter. I tried to control my imagination, but I was falling into the old trap of letting my judgement fill in the gaps. It was easy to persecute, particularly under these circumstances.

I arranged the photos into neat rows. "What were you thinking when you were planning this?"

"Planning?"

"Prepare. Get ready to change from one state to another. What were you thinking when you wanted to change the balance?"

He snapped his head to one side, his eyes suddenly bright. "I've told you before."

"Don't play that game again."

His eyelids drooped. "Balance is universal. Maybe we could have co-existed, but you are not attuned . . . and never will be."

Something was falling into place at the back of my mind. "So you felt that your society was sliding into chaos?"

He leant forward. "You have diluted our *existence*."

I let out a sharp breath. "So you're telling me, as a supposedly passive species, that the only course of action was to exterminate the colonists?"

"Are you telling me the only way to colonise is to violate everything in your path?"

"So it *was* revenge?"

His face contorted into something resembling rage and he sat bolt upright, the diamonds on his skin flushing with colour. The cuffs began to chime dangerously.

I got up to leave then hesitated. He was holding back, waiting for my response.

Thoughts swirled at the back of my mind, so elusive and frustrating. "Not revenge," I said, "But you do feel *something*?"

The cuffs stopped chiming.

Needing space to think and clear my head, I left the photos on the table, grabbed the folder, and walked out.

Interview suspended: 00.03am, Day 8.

Melanie put her hand up. "Isn't Doctor Jacobs . . . well, hasn't she made the mistake of trying to get a *human* reaction?"

"That's a good question, Melanie. There's a fine line when engaging alien species. But remember that the Kresh lived under the rule of the first colony for a very long time, so it would be normal for them to have acquired some human traits. Jacobs is trying to establish a baseline, something to work with. Is he horrified by what he did? Does he feel guilt, regret or anger? Does he even feel contrite at all?"

Interview resumed: 00.08am, Day 8.

The room was quiet.

Tyll'x was watching the sky darken, his eyes straying again over the fields of talif that had been flattened by a new wave of spaceships. The shadows down his cheeks made him look gaunt.

"Did you know," he said, "When we were still allowed to migrate south during winter, talif seeds would get caught up in our slipstream. The seeds have evolved in the right shape so that they can carry on the thermals across half the globe. They would disperse upon our arrival and by the time we had settled along the archipelago that spans the great ocean, our food was already growing."

"No, I had no idea." I scooped the photos back into the folder. "Why are you telling me this?"

He glanced up, his irises like half-eclipsed suns beneath heavy lids. "Nature does not have to be red in tooth and claw."

I sat down heavily. "You've *studied* us?" I didn't know why I was so surprised. Of course they studied us. "Do you think that we are to blame, that we are evil? Is that why you killed the colonists?"

"Evil?"

"Bad, harmful . . . " I clutched for words that he could relate to. "You said it yourself—chaotic, disconnected."

"You are *evil* to the extent that you do not see what drives you. You need to look beyond what I have done; beyond the competitive flow of evolution. There is a place where we should all be, a place where we can both live to our potential. It is not here."

"I really don't know what you mean, Tyll'x."

Now I was the one doing the diverting. More pieces of the puzzle were falling into place, but I needed time to recalibrate, to think it through. Time I didn't have, for if I walked away now the opportunity would be lost forever.

So I tried to picture that place that he was asking me to imagine . . . no, more than imagine, he was asking me to conceive it, to give birth to an original thought and envisage a future place that was within our grasp. Or perhaps it was a place that we had lost; a place where things are connected, where life coexists and society is not driven by hungry, rampant necessity.

"Are you talking about *choice*?"

He nodded. There must have been something in my eyes because he held out his hands across the table.

I reached out to him, my hands trembling, centimetres from his fingertips. "Are you saying we must choose over nature? That we cannot be beholden to it?"

"Yes, Helena."

I touched his hand, felt the rough texture of his skin.

It was so hard to extract myself from everything that I had ever known, to cut through all that I had been taught, and to shrug off the societal values I was born into. Then a disturbing feeling squirmed its way under my skin as I contemplated the bleak alternative—maybe I simply wasn't wired to think that way. Maybe all my feelings of altruism were a glossy veneer, covering up the red-in-tooth-and-claw human being inside.

Tyll'x watched the thoughts play out on my face. "The Kresh need to exist as we should, not as humans want us to be."

"So how do you reconcile your atrocity?"

"I don't. I exist with it."

Those sliding pieces now felt like an avalanche. His face contorted in agony, something I had never seen on any Kresh face before. He carried a burden, a moment in time that was etched forever into his psyche, into the fabric of Kresh society. Despite the beatings and interrogations, he had been trying to explain it all along. He would live with the suffering he had inflicted, a burning moment stretched out to eternity—that was the Kresh way now that we had stripped them of all their choices. The deaths of all those people would never leave him. He was *connected* with the act, irrevocably.

I felt nauseous with the knowledge that we had dragged these beautiful people back down the evolutionary ladder.

His hands moved slightly under mine.

I flinched—I just couldn't help it.

Then, to my dismay, he pulled away.

I cursed myself, cursed my all-too-human conditioning. "I'm trying, I really am, Tyll'x."

He stood up slowly.

"What's the matter?"

He stepped between me and the door.

"Sit down, Tyll'x"

"I'm . . . sorry."

The diamonds on his skin had already darkened and the cuffs let out a warning shrill. The stalar puffed up under his arms and around his neck, bulging under the pressure, straining to be free. A high-pitched thrumming pounded the air, joined by similar sounds from around the facility. The other Kresh were responding to his call—they weren't finished, they would live in this moment for as long as humans were around.

My chair toppled over as I got up and yelled. "Stop!"

I tried to run around him, but he pushed me back, shaking his head. A red light flashed on his cuffs and I pressed my hands over my ears and fell to my knees. The shriek-pulse ratcheted up several octaves then something warm trickled down my cheeks. I wiped my ear and saw that my hand was smeared with blood.

The pulse took on a feverish pitch, drowning out all other things.

Then something sprayed over my face and the ringing from the cuffs ceased.

Blinking now, watching Tyll'x hold his arms out, black blood gushing from the ragged stumps where his hands used to be. A guttural sound rose from him and with a huge effort his stalar unfurled and I was flung across the room . . . the pulse piercing deep inside me . . . stabbing into my brain . . . a cold blade . . .

Virtual recording terminated: 00.31am, Day 8.

Secure Facility video footage start: 00.31am, Day 8.

Helena Jacobs slumps to the floor, blood flowing freely from her ears.

Tyll'x stands over her body, the pulse resonating for several more seconds until the flow of blood becomes a trickle. The colour drains from his diamond markings and he collapses to the floor.

He reaches out to Helena's body. Her eyes are wide open but vacant. He leans his head down to her chest, as if resting momentarily then shoves his ruined arms under her and pushes her across the bloody floor into a corner. He sits up until his back is against the wall and manages to wrap her within his stalar.

He leans his head back and a new noise fills the room, like the rush of waves on a rocky shoreline. It is coming from his stalar, but the sound diminishes with each breath.

Helena's eyes are shut now, and she looks like she is sleeping in a blanket.

Tyll'x becomes still, and the room falls silent.

Secure Facility video footage end: 00.45am, Day 8.

Professor Hutchinson waited quietly.

Eric wiped his eyes and blew his nose. "Why did he hold her at the end?"

"The Kresh hug their dead," the Professor said. "It is a ritual called kelna that we understand is a welcoming of their bodies back into the firmament. By contrast, we still institutionalise the old and dying in clinical health systems, detached from human contact." He walked up the steps dividing the theatre and paused halfway. "So, was Tyll'x a mass-murderer?"

Melanie put up her hand. "It's a rhetorical question."

"Why?"

"Morality is a subjective thing," she said. "In my opinion, Tyll'x was right."

A few students tensed up and glared at her, but the Professor turned to them and said, "Free speech in my lectures, thank you."

Melanie's confidence gathered. "You said the Kresh have a sense of deep time. How can we even begin to imagine what that feels like? Maybe they grew out of morality a long time ago or never needed it in the first place."

"Excellent," the Professor said, his face now creased in thought. "I submit to you that nature has a dark underbelly that can drive rational beings to do unspeakable things. Even artefacts such as higher intelligence and aide memoire technology are more often than not used to hide our intentions rather than make them more transparent. Our own motivations can be as foreign to us as the alien minds that we study.

"In conclusion, I think the events on Sirius 5 teach us that we should not live in thrall to natural selection. We have options available to us and the capacity to make informed choices about our place in nature. We constantly question the intent of alien species that we encounter, yet perhaps we should begin by questioning our own seemingly alien intent."

The theatre erupted with noise.

The Professor urged for quiet, but the group would not be consoled.

"Well," Eric's voice rose up, "At least they have their planet back."

The raucous calmed, like the eye of a storm, as the students waited on the Professor's answer.

"No, Eric, they don't. The Kresh killed many of the second wave colonists, but a third wave has already spun down into orbit. There are only so many compatible worlds abundant in the resources we need to survive." He walked back down the aisle to the centre of the theatre as the calm dissolved into chaos again.

"That's it for today. Thank you for attending."

AFTERWORD TO "ALIEN INTENT"

I think, as individuals, we like to think that we are moral beings. I'm sure many of us are, but what about our collective morality? I believe if you look at our progress as a civilisation we are a long way from where we need to be. In his book Dark Nature, *a thesis on evil, the anthropologist, Lyall Watson (d.2008), suggested that humanity can make choices and lift itself above basic survival behaviour. "Red in tooth and claw" evolution is a strong tide to resist and, like Watson, I disagree with the Darwinian hypothesis that morality is a guaranteed trait in species with social instincts.*

"Alien Intent" was a tough story to write as I wanted to bring my thoughts together in a setting where humans are struggling with colonisation—a classic case study of morality. The choice of a lecture narrative structure was simply an experiment and not intended as a "message" or polemic. At the time it seemed like the best way to bring my ideas into one place. In some ways Tyll'x's plight reflects the modern man—we know we can be at peace, but we almost always default to our baser instincts without even realising it. In Tyll'x's case, he was forced to go back down the evolutionary ladder and behave in a way that his species had either forgotten or had never experienced in the first place.

DAY BREAK

It rained cows on Christmas Eve.

When the world broke, the atmosphere tore in raging cyclones, tornadoes, oceans of air sucked up and flung down, and those poor animals were caught in the turbulence, hurled into the sky. Until they fell back to Earth, crying in terror.

They were Jerseys, all deep tan with white patches. The sight of them rupturing like swollen bladders was terrifying. I had known each of them by name, with their soft brown eyes and flickering ears. Only Jessica had survived, tethered to a fence. I sobbed my heart out in the three days of cold snow that followed, and then again when the snow melted and I found Jessica in a pile of muddy slush with her legs sticking up stupidly.

I grew to hate the rain and stayed indoors when squalls blew in off the Brindabella Ranges, dumping water and debris over the shattered homesteads of Royalla.

On those bleak days I would sit in front of the dead television, mindlessly recalling the images that had been broadcast to the world over several years—a loss of innocence like no other. The relic had gone undetected until a flyby of Jupiter had photographed a long shadow across the disk of Europa. A barrage of probes had followed; a tedious, slow-motion power struggle of governments and corporations, desperately scanning, landing . . . and eventually sampling.

On the sunny days I tended to the white fences that had been broken at Christmas, and others that were showing signs of normal wear and tear. I kept the lawns around the house cut even though they had become yellow and patchy.

By April the squalls had increased in frequency, always moving eastward where a permanent band of cloud hung from north to south. Strange aurora filled the evening skies and a lingering chill crept across the land. The tall maple shading the front porch shed its shrivelled leaves, and I knew then that I would never see autumnal scarlet again—colour had drained from the world.

Grim faced travellers would pass along the gravel road in front of my property, usually in singles or pairs. One time there was a group of 20, all geared up with supplies and backpacks. They had come all the way from Jindabyne—pilgrims of a sort—dressed in parkas and hiking boots. They kicked up dust on the road and then they turned east on the long march towards the escarpment. Some would stop and talk for a while, but none stayed for very long, compelled eastward, a burning light in their eyes.

Only a few returned via Royalla, and I started to wonder whether some ever made it back at all. Those that did were all skin and bone with gaunt, haunted faces—their eyes full of cooling embers of a past that no longer held any meaning. I wondered if I looked like that. Perhaps I would never know. All the mirrors in the house were shattered and I didn't have the courage to look at myself in those shards.

Of the pilgrims that did return, only one was different. He had a wild, almost feverish look. His name escaped me; it's a funny thing because I was always good with names. He said that the weather had cleared on the escarpment, but the rest of what he said seemed to be sheer hysteria. All talk of lights and ghosts and the hand of God. I wondered if he had been hallucinating from sleep deprivation. He left his backpack on my porch and walked west along the road leading out of Royalla, the only smiling traveller I had seen moving in that direction.

I knew that I'd had a wife and son, Georgia and Rick, and some instinct told me that we had been happy. They had gone to Canberra to do some last minute Christmas shopping and were driving home when the world broke. I had found the car on the Monaro Highway, too crumpled to remove the bodies, and so I drove the backhoe to the wreck and dragged it the final five kilometres home. There was just enough fuel left to dig a grave on the hill behind the shed. I did not have the strength for a eulogy; something in me had slipped away with them that day. At first I thought I had forgotten our life together, but then I realised that it was a book I had placed on a dark shelf in my mind, too afraid to read.

I think I grieved more for my goddamn cows. Mornings are spent on the porch under the skeletal shade of the maple watching the Sun rise dimly in the northeast above the cloud-covered escarpment that has become the new horizon. I eat breakfast, mend my fences and tend my patchwork lawn.

After my morning reverie I stood up to go back inside. I caught my foot on something and looked down. It was the wild pilgrim's pack. It had been sitting there all these weeks, slowly gathering dust. I nudged it out of the way with my boot and it fell on its side. A loop of bright red climber's rope spilled out and a carabiner clanked on the porch. I picked up the pack and tipped it upside down. The contents fell out: more rope and carabiners, steel pegs, a hammer, a harness, a small gas burner, an ice axe and some sharp looking crampons.

I shook my head. The world had lulled me into a stupor and my own stubbornness had provided a crude shelter of callous melancholy. It was easy to sit and watch the days deteriorate. My ritual now seemed ridiculous, selfish—I was dishonouring the dead with my denial.

I pulled on a thick jumper and a dark green parka, found my sunglasses in the bedroom and dug my walking boots out from the cupboard and put them on. Went outside to the shed and found my utility belt on the workbench. I grabbed a pair of safety glasses, a small shovel, some canned food from some old boxes and a shrink-wrapped pack of water bottles. I looked at the shotgun chained to the wall above the bench. Protection from what, I thought. Most animals had died, and those that hadn't had migrated west in January.

I shrugged and went back to the house past the yellow backhoe, the mud of the burial site still ingrained in the tyre treads. After a couple of minutes of fitting the extra contents in the pack, and tying the shovel along one side, I slung the pack over my back and walked up the road past ruined homesteads—mine was the only one still standing—then turned east across country. I did not look back in case some demented part of me might worry that I had not closed the front door.

I traipsed across fields of wild tussock, oddly littered by pilgrims before me, then across hills sparsely covered with gum trees, and then more fields. It was well past midday before I stopped. I realised without any major revelation that I was a pilgrim now. I must have that same distant look and that same rigid jaw line.

I cracked open a can of beans. I'd forgotten to bring any utensils, but a knife in my utility belt did the job. The crazy notion that I might cut my tongue and have to turn back came to mind; medical supplies had also been neglected. I never was much of an adventurer.

After lunch I slung the backpack on and looked at the escarpment. It seemed harmless enough from this distance of about 80 km, a huge, anvil shaped landmass jutting out of the Earth like a slowly sinking ship. It was a ruptured piece of the Pacific coast that should have been 1,000 metres below my elevation. I had travelled there many times, east along the Kings Highway past Braidwood, then off the plateau, the road winding its way down through the old rainforest to the coastal towns of Batemans Bay and Ulladulla.

But now the coastal lowland was up, not down, the Sun shining on the lower western slope, the forward eastern peak forever in mist. The incline was shallow, but it still reached about 2,000 metres, its size dwarfing everything around it. It was as if some angry creature from the underworld had smashed its fist upwards. And there I was; thinking like a pilgrim.

Over the next few days I walked across country, staying clear of roads until managing to skirt the southern end of Braidwood. The town was a silent ruin and I kept walking, my legs unwilling to deviate from the path. I reached the base of the escarpment several kilometres to the east of Braidwood. Human remains lay scattered where the ground was all churned up and smelt of damp and decay. Judging by the carnage, some wild dogs had feasted. I thought of the shotgun, but the bodies had been here for a long time. Perhaps they had been the earliest pilgrims. I rummaged around the discarded equipment, careful not to step on any bones, but there was nothing I didn't already have.

The land ahead was covered with lopsided gum trees and dark striations where the crust had bent. I looked up, and up. The escarpment stretched across the horizon, maybe 100 km wide, and 50 km long, angling up to the sky. It was impossible to see the apex, or what, if anything, was on the other side. There were roads up there, shattered homes, cars thrown about like tin cans, and twisted electricity lines. There were still patches of green from the old forest, but the land was deeply rippled and fire blackened.

Perhaps others like me were up there, touched by some miracle, but I doubted it. The distant ground looked frozen, had probably turned to tundra close to the white snowline about three quarters of the way up the escarpment.

I managed to find my way round the more hazardous cracks and crevices and up onto the escarpment slope, high enough to look back. I could make out a long green belt that stretched along the leeward side of the Brindabellas. I wondered if there were other flukes like it around the world—life clinging tenaciously like moss on a rock.

Something sloughed from my mind then, and for the first time since I left home I slept properly under a copse of stunted trees. I woke shouting for Georgia, but the dream slipped away before I could recall her face.

In the next two days I passed three pilgrims. One I remembered from a month ago, a young migrant Canadian. He and his wife had been planning on becoming Australian citizens. She'd had long blonde hair tied in a ponytail. He walked alone now. He didn't recognise me and we passed like strangers on a street.

The banality of it made me angry.

That anger fuelled me for another day. I stomped on, always east, always rising, until my food and water ran out. I no longer cared, and in that red haze, well past the snowline on the icy run to the top of the escarpment, I slipped. The glare was so bright I did not see the crack and the soft ice around it gave way under my weight. I fell into darkness, a slow, hard tumble where something snapped inside.

I woke to pitch black and a roar in my ears. My left eye was caked shut and pressed against cold dirt. My body was suspended, swinging to an odd rhythm, feet dangling. It's happening again, I thought, and the terror of the Christmas Eve event washed over me. I flayed my arms and kicked my legs, trying to find solid ground. My chest hit rock and I reached out and hugged it, digging my fingers in until they bled and my feet found a small ledge to take my weight.

No crampons—what was I thinking?

Above, a dim triangle of light. The shovel had saved me. It had lodged against the sides of the crevice and somehow held under the strain. I pushed up and inched my way carefully back up. Untied the shovel so I could move more freely and it slipped from my cold, bleeding fingers. I heard it crack twice against rock and then nothing.

Daring to look down, I could just make out the ragged outline of the crevice, then a mottled orange light below, dimmed by mist. The dull roar was coming from down there, wind funnelling like the susurrus of all the voices in the world. My head reeled again with vertigo and this time I scrambled up until I was out of the crevice and hugging the ice.

I blacked out again.

My breathing hurt when I woke and the vision in my left eye was blurred, but it didn't matter anyway; I was engulfed in mist. The roar continued to ebb and flow, but I knew it was not the ocean. I slowly put the crampons on and emptied the rest of my pack. Hammered two steel pegs into the ice, tied a rope to them and cinched it round my waist. I had no idea how far ahead the edge of the escarpment was, but rather than take any more stupid risks, I decided to walk to the end of the rope, then walk back, cut the pegs out and start over again. Ten times or more I did this, effectively blind to what was in front of me, not knowing whether the ground would give way. On my 11th attempt I unravelled the rope two metres then stepped out into nothing. I yanked back quickly, the rope taut, the pegs holding firm.

I hacked out a small rock from the ice and hurled it as far as I could.

Nothing.

I sat down on the tip of the escarpment, my ragged breathing in harmony with the background roar of a dying planet. Laughing at the irony and coughing up blood.

The night was intensely cold and long and starless and when the Sun finally broke through the haze it felt like a balm on my skin. I had heard odd undertones during the night, a hidden signal buried among the static, and thought that my mind was playing games again, but the sounds carried on into the dawn. Perhaps I was just getting used to the nuances, like picking out bird songs back at Royalla.

A patch of blue sky appeared above me. It didn't feel right as I had only been here a day, and I knew others had made the journey and died out here, never knowing what was beyond the escarpment.

Within minutes the mist closed over me again and I cursed until spittle foamed at my mouth.

Another day and night wheeled overhead in their new configuration, and then another. I was slowly starving to death and all that sustained me now was ice water and some tenacious instinct. Eddies unfolded in the morning mist and the Sun cut through my cold eyelids. It took me a minute to realise the roar had quietened down.

I looked about in some cold half-dream and realised that I was floating two metres off the ground, tethered, like Jessica. Adrenalin stirred me fully awake. The bank of mist rolled back and the ragged edge of the escarpment arced north and south as far as the eye could see.

The sight below me took some time for my brain to process. I felt like a base jumper ready to plummet down a sheer cliff face, but this cliff was so high it was almost abstract. There was no usual nausea of vertigo, just a sense of wonder.

Way down below, a massive black splinter jutted out from the planet's core. The alien relic's surface glistened, perhaps two, maybe 3,000 km long, one end buried in the swirling magma heart of the planet. A blast of steam obscured it and I shook my head in confusion.

Out across the gaping maw, the Pacific was rushing up and away from the far rim of the cracked Earth in a waterfall of monumental proportions. Above the inverted waterfall, a segment floated like a new crescent Moon. A line of debris connected the segment back to the far rim, a fragmented umbilicus of rocks hundreds of kilometres wide. It was like some fantasy painting of a distant world.

I fell back to the ice and clutched my chest. The pain across my ribs cut through the adrenalin and the roar resumed. Tremors rumbled deep below. I dug my axe into the ground, then found some pegs and hammered them through the corners of my parka.

Gravity shifted once again, putting pressure on my shoulders as my butt lifted off the ground. I gripped the long handle of the ice axe tightly. The heat of the Sun felt like a false hope now.

The clouds and steam cleared again to reveal that gleaming black blade shifting like a leviathan. A relic beyond human comprehension. Perhaps it was some ancient device triggered by the rise of sapient life, a sort of proximity mine to protect the territory of its makers. Then my mind wandered to a bleak, grotesquely sardonic alternative. Perhaps this had all been some terrible mistake, the relic sucked up into the gravitational pull of Jupiter, lured to life by our profound ignorance—an alien weapon fulfilling its long forgotten purpose on the wrong planet.

I watched, mesmerised, as strange energies seethed across it and the light of the dying core cast reflections on its constantly shifting surface of carbon coloured blocks and infinitely regressing spirals. Whatever its purpose, it was truly beautiful.

Georgia smiled at me, the light from the log fire shining in her hair and her green eyes. She reached over and sneaked a kiss before Rick bounded inside, a lanky, energetic ten-year-old—when did he grow up? He saw us kissing, rolled his eyes and groaned. We beckoned him with our hands and he rushed over and threw his arms around us, his momentum nearly knocking us over.

"Family hug," he yelled.

The book was opening, the pages turning.

Today was a good day, a clear day.

AFTERWORD TO "DAY BREAK"

What if the world was suddenly broken by some unknown external force and you survived? And what if the changes to the planet were happening right on your doorstep? Would you become a cannibal hunting down whatever flesh remained, or would you retain your humanity and curiosity and try to figure out what happened?

I think the answer to the "so what" question in this story is in the humanity. The world was broken inexplicably and without warning. The survivors, in the time remaining, want to explore the unknown, not ruthlessly dominate what's left.

For the nameless protagonist, it's a pure but brutal experience, untainted by science or religion or philosophy. His imperfect human perspective finally helps him remember his family and achieve clarity of life before death. If only we could be so lucky at the end of all things.

STRANDED LIGHT

Legend had it that utopia was a place called Wraith World.

Talk to the hard-nosed military flyboys at the frontier, or even the savant intelligences in their Dyson spheres, and you'd hear the same frustrating paradox: on a world beyond the reach of the rest of the universe you could find Shangri La, Peach Blossom Spring, Nirvana or any dream your heart desired.

"Just like needles can be found in haystacks," Clay whispered. His tired eyes were itchy in the confines of the dampening gel.

"What did you say?" It was Sophocles, omnipresent ship matrix, minding everyone else's business but his own.

"Nothing."

Clay found it ironic that the location of the mythical realm was no secret. Everyone knew the coordinates: past the bright stars of the frontier, beyond the dark matter clouds, out there in the gulf between the spiral arms. But who could survive the tidal forces of the black hole? Maybe that was the morbid joke being played on the rest of the universe. Even the name Wraith World implied death not satori, or maybe that too was the intended pun, the black humour of the Utopians: an end to all suffering at the bottom of a gravity well from which not even light could escape.

Better than at the bottom of a glass, Clay thought. Maybe he was too jaded to acknowledge the positive side of the myth, but what was a guy to do when the path to Wraith World had brought nothing but misery and terror? And all in the name of dreams that he could hardly define for himself now, let alone describe to others.

"Set a course for home, Soph. I've had enough travelling for one month."

"But this *is* home."

Sophocles, like his namesake, was developing a sense of theatre about every occasion. Clay would have to adjust its empathic algorithms; right now he wanted sympathetic-philosopher, not smug-dramatist.

"Just park us around the nearest moon."

"As you wish."

"I wish . . . no, damn it. How do they know?"

"How does *who* know *what*?"

"How does anyone know anything about Wraith World?"

"Ah. We're back there again."

"Come on, Soph, cut me some slack."

"I think I liked you better when we were in the military. Then again, maybe a discharge was what you needed."

"You can be a pig."

Silence.

"How do they know?" Clay's voice was tremulous with stress and sleep deprivation.

"It's a *myth*, Clay. You need to accept the truth: nothing comes back from the other side of an event horizon."

"I just want—"

"She's dead, my friend. Nothing survives a black hole. You have to let her go."

"I can't."

"You have to."

"*Why?*"

"Because it's consuming every waking and sleeping hour. You need to move on."

"I know she's alive. I *sense* it."

Soph's tone turned vitriolic. "You really have been communing with the savants again. They're crackpot digital-gods, post-humans with a penchant for building false hopes."

"But they're tapped into the entire spectrum; sensory input from the whole galaxy. Even if there is an element of truth in their readings . . . "

Soph sighed. After a long pause he said: "Shall I set a new course?"

Clay nodded and the dampening gel pushed deeper into his cells. He felt a brief stab of pain then a cold anaesthesia as the needle-shaped ship banked hard atop a tapering blue flame, accelerating with enough force to liquefy unprotected flesh.

2.

Clay dreamed of the death of suns. Fading wisps of nebulae churned across the night, like ink on obsidian. Ancient things lurked in the remnants, squid-like leviathans feeding off the element-rich gases. And other, deadly things charted the deep, wave after wave of raven ships venturing too far from their alien homes on the other side of the gulf, enticed by the bright colonies of humanity. Then the chase, adrenalin surging, dogfights across parsecs of space, the enemy burning incandescent in the harsh thermonuclear cleansing . . . Clay woke, gasping and choking on the gel, his mind in obsessive overload—PTSD was a bitch, cutting through Soph's chemical filters.

A spray of water, hiss of steam as the cabin switched to clean up mode. He coughed up gel and watched it drain away through holes set in the floor.

"It's too dangerous to increase your dosage," Soph said. "Maybe you need to face the memories rather than bury them."

"What, like I buried Mareko?"

"Sorry, poor choice of words."

Sometimes Clay wondered if the past was a crutch he used to avoid reality, friendship or love of any kind. Job lost to stress, family lost to time debt, Mareko lost—

"We're past the frontier."

"I know."

"Shall we?"

Clay took the controls and piloted the ship, the sparkling waterfall of frontier stars receding away into the background. It felt as if the gulf was slowly, methodically embracing him, wrapping its cool tendrils over the hull. Then the dark was complete, filtering into his mind, welcoming at first, enticing ... then stabbing through the residue of filters, dark blades carving his memories and all that he held sacred, laying bare his soul and all the baggage he had crammed in there over the years.

The eerie sensation lingered for hours, grating at his nerves until he began to think they were lost. Just as he was about to question Soph, the scanners picked up a trickle of gamma rays and Hawking radiation.

"Dial up an external, please," Clay said.

A display appeared, flickering at first then resolving faint images from the gloom. Tangled wreckages hung above the event horizon, a telltale litany of all the dreamers, treasure seekers and hopeless romantics that had tried to find their way onto Wraith World.

Her ship was the same as before. Something inside him died each time he saw it hanging there, goading him like a gnarled metal tombstone. The physical wreckage itself had long since fallen down the well, but the light from it clung tenaciously, striving upwards under the incredible gravity, slowly shifting to the red end of the spectrum. Over time he knew the image would fade completely into infrared.

They'd been chasing their dreams since graduation. Her soul was old beyond her years, his soul stubborn and young-at-heart; hers warm yet serious, his cool yet good-humoured. He ground his teeth together, clutching for the person he used to be, hating the person he had become. He had been one with Mareko, even through the harsh years of military life, yet he had done nothing when her ship got caught in the gravity well, watched helplessly ... selfishly, as the tidal rip crushed and stretched it out into unrecognisable strands.

He may as well have stuck a knife in her and watch her bleed dry.

He closed his eyes as Soph moved into a stationary orbit high above the wreckage.

The proximity alarm rang. He felt tiny vibrations through the hull.

"I've reached my design tolerance," Soph stated as the vibrations increased. "There's nothing eventful about an event horizon. Shall I drop you off now?"

"Sarcasm is the lowest form of humour."

Clay piloted the ship up into a higher orbit. He felt the question before it was asked. In part it was Soph's algorithms, but in part Clay knew how genuine their friendship had become over the years, one brother to another. "The savants told you how to get down there, didn't they? I suppose it had to come to this sooner or later."

Clay nodded. "I'm sorry. I could wait here forever watching her fading light, always trying to convince myself she is alive but never knowing for certain."

Soph sighed. "Well, I'm sorry, too. I'm going to miss you."

3.

Becoming a god was not all it was cracked up to be.

All he could remember was the smell of burning hair, the crackle of fatty tissues as his flesh evaporated, and a deep screaming in his soul as the modified molecular scanner did its work, cell by cell, neuron by neuron. Then vague memories of his algorithms shot out from the ship, encoded laser light fired obliquely at the event horizon, like an old shuttle skimming into atmosphere.

Sophocles?

Where are you?

Soph?

He opened his eyes and realised he was lying on his back under a sky full of rainbows. Or at least they looked like rainbows set against the starless night, shimmering in aurora-like patterns from one horizon to the other. The soft patter of rain made his face tingle, each drop sparkling into incoherent sprays of light, a shower of photons moving from purple through green to yellow then red. And beyond to infrared.

He reached out his . . . photonic hand . . . there was something disturbing about that fact, challenging his sanity . . . felt the rain touch his skin.

"Sometimes the light dies."

He turned to the sound, but there was no sound, just a triggering of his photonic brain . . . another gut-wrenching fact he tried to compartmentalise.

The speaker stood so close, tall and slender, skin like porcelain, dressed in a red sleeveless gown held together by a clasp at one shoulder. Long brunette hair draped over her bare shoulder. She smiled with her eyes then her lips parted in a crooked smile that enhanced her beauty.

"Mareko."

"Yes. And no."

"Where am I?" He asked the mirage, hallucination . . . no, she was something more, a stunning fantasy, but not the real Mareko. He started to get up.

"Wait," she said, holding her hand out in warning.

It was as if he had stepped onto a glass platform over an endless chasm. Twisted relics spun in strange orbits beneath the transparent ground, a graveyard of red-shifted light from ships that had long been crushed into nothing. Metal, ceramic, flesh and plastic mashed to surreal shapes, the different textures suggesting to Clay that the ships came from civilisations on both sides of the gulf, and maybe even further afield. But in the end it was all just matter, stripped of all structure and purpose and consciousness. Matter, funnelled into oblivion.

Vertigo took hold and he stumbled. He felt pressure on his arm, realised it was Mareko holding him as he vomited.

Gods don't puke, he thought.

Laughter like chimes.

He stood up slowly on shaking legs. "Are you teasing me again?"

She was gone.

Not again.

Mareko?

A pearl white plain of light stretched out to the horizon. He stamped his foot, it seemed solid enough, but best not to look down again. He tried to get some sense of direction—no sun, no stars, just rainbow aurora. Wherever he looked he could see a man standing on the plain with his back turned—the *same* man each time dressed in bright white breeches held by a black sash, a loose white shirt, hair all unkempt in a rough but stylish way. Clay waved and the man waved to something in front of him. Clay waved again, the man waved.

Wait a minute.

Clay ran towards him, but the man started running away.

"Hey, wait."

"Hey, wait." "Hey, wait." "Hey, wait." Repeated a thousand times, a million . . .

Clay clutched his head. "This can't be happening."

"This can't be—"

He fell to one knee, sending photonic ripples across the plain. The man vanished.

He held out his arms, examined the loose white fabric of his shirt, the clean white breeches with a black sash.

Then the rainbow aurora, the white plain, the chasm of dying light, all of it collapsed into a black pinpoint then expanded out to infinity.

He welcomed the dark this time.

4.

"I say we sacrifice him to the Singularity."

It was a man's voice, several paces ahead. Clay felt pressure under his arms. He was being held upright, half-dragged, half-marched between two people, the ground rising steeply, the air crisp in his lungs.

"That's not for you to decide," It was another man to Clay's left. "Let the Wraiths assess him. He doesn't have the hallmarks of an alpha grade post-human. Looks like a DIY job."

A woman to Clay's right. "The photosphere did well to reconstitute him."

"Great," the first speaker said. "Another hatchet grade digital dreamer. They're worse than tinned meat. Wait until the Wraiths are done with him."

Clay half-opened his eyes. He was standing on some kind of rampart that was thankfully opaque. His captors were dressed in blue-black photonic armour, radiant flares of electric blue coruscating off the edges.

The first speaker leaned in close and held Clay by the chin. "Welcome to Wraith World, godling." They all laughed, as if sharing some private joke. Clay's reflection multiplied in the mirrored face plate then scattered into infinite shards. The man seemed to notice Clay's reaction and took a step back. "Our armour is just a precaution. You can't access our i-spheres until you control yours."

It almost sounded helpful, but Clay had no idea what an i-sphere was, let alone how to control one. Then he recalled Mareko out on the plain of light—the fantasy version. He rallied his thoughts.

The air around his hand turned grainy as photons danced and spiralled, weaving the outline of a swallow-tail butterfly, like an artist filling in a sketch.

The woman touched his arm and shook her head. "Not now."

The butterfly dissipated, half-finished.

Clay cautiously found his balance as the others stepped aside. A sweeping vista of earth-like forests, rivers and snow-capped mountains stretched below the rampart and out as far as the eye could see. The air was crystal clear, and somehow he knew if he focussed he could see right into the heart of every tree and rock and grain of soil; watch the photons spinning their magic as they maintained this worldly canvas.

Then his eyes turned to the end of the rampart. A city hung from the sky, its inverted towers and columns shimmering in permanent flux, arches and doorways framed in sapphire light, glowing streets winding up in delicate helical strands to form slender bridges between the towers. There were people in the streets and at the windows, clad in ribbons and streamers of light, going about their daily routine with a certain sense of decadent *savoir faire*. At the highest reaches of the city, the underbelly of the rainbow aurora cast a soft nimbus until all colour drained away into unreachable space above the event horizon.

He caught his breath. "Is this the photosphere?"

"Yes, welcome to the end of the universe," the woman said. "I am Natalia. This is Chance, and the belligerent one is Eydis." She flicked up her face plate. Her skin was dark, sparkling with ebon light. Eydis hissed a warning but she waved him down and continued to address Clay. "This isn't the Garden of Eden or El Dorado. It's no place for worship or naive quests."

Clay frowned. "I came to find Mareko . . . " He searched the dregs of his memories, trawling for that elusive thing that had once been a happy, carefree man. "But more than that. Maybe I'm seeking her forgiveness. Or maybe I'm still on a selfish journey to save my soul . . . " He looked falteringly at Natalia.

"Like most people, Clay, what you're looking for is often not what you need. I could build mountains if I was given a pebble for every broken dream. It's better if you control your thoughts."

"That's not helping."

She laughed.

Clay's eyes narrowed. "Eydis mentioned . . . " He cleared his throat. "He kind of said something about sacrifice."

"He can be grumpy at the best of times; utopia can't cure character, eh, Eydis?"

Eydis folded his arms but said nothing.

"Your life is your own, Clay. Do with it what you will. Focus your i-sphere and it will provide many things—"

"But not Mareko?"

"No, only the photosphere has the power to reconstitute your consciousness with the light. But it doesn't always work, sometimes there's not enough raw ingredients so to speak. You rolled the dice, you got lucky. The Singularity gives, but it can just as easily take away. If you can't find her, make sure you can live with it. This is no place for a life of retribution."

Chance touched Natalia on the shoulder. "Time for him to meet the Wraith."

Clay looked up. They had reached the end of the rampart and now the gate to the city of light loomed high.

5.

"I thought we were meeting in the city."

"You're still thinking like a human." Chance's eyes reflected emerald light from the forest. He looked old and grizzled without his armour, a tattooed veteran of some war of some era a thousand years before Clay's time. "The city helps us cope; we need structure and hierarchy—human comfort zones, I suppose. But the forests, mountains and plains are older archetypes that belong to most civilisations."

Clay looked through the forest floor. In between the fallen leaves and bark he could see tree roots delving deeply into the photosphere, like capillaries. At their lowest point, the roots blurred and stretched down into long fingers of light blending with the light of the dead ships. He wondered whether the trees were constantly fighting the tidal forces. He supposed that's how the whole world existed, forever fighting gravity. It seemed fitting in some ways, a metaphor for life's incessant battle against oblivion.

"That's an interesting hypothesis."

Clay whirled around.

Chance was gone.

Something was gliding towards him between the trees. It looked like a will-o-the-wisp at first, growing brighter and taller. Leaves rustled and a shadow emerged within the light, forming sinew and muscle and oddly jointed bones. It ran towards him then galloped on all fours, rising up again on two legs as it drew closer. It's piercing eyes felt like they were drinking from his mind, peeling away the flimsy veneer to dissect his emotions—passion, hate, jealousy, greed, love, pride, rage . . . fear. He staggered back under the onslaught. Impossibly long talons clutched at him and he fell to one knee. Razor-like nails solidified, about to flense away his face . . .

Then something soft.

The sound of bees humming.

A fragrance that reminded him of spring.

Warm, delicate hands touched his cheek, cupped his face as if they were holding something precious.

She was tall, taller than any human, wrapped in grey ribbons that revealed glimpses of mottled skin. Her eyes had no whites, no pupils; just pools of reflected light as if all the world's hues were contained within. Her hair was lustrous black, fibrous, moving as if in response to some unfelt breeze.

She pulled him up to his feet.

"Are you all right?" Her voice was an octave above a whisper, soothing.

"I think so."

"Wow, you've built up all sorts of stereotypes about us. You'll have to watch that i-sphere of yours; it's tapped into your subconscious, you know. We make our own ghosts, Clay."

He felt cold sweat on his brow. "Tell me about it." He raised his hand to wipe his forehead then thought better of it.

She laughed. "You can't stop a life time of physiological responses. Don't stop being human."

He shrugged and mopped his brow with his sleeve.

"I'm sorry if I frightened you. I'm Saraid. Walk with me, if you will."

They made their way deeper into the forest, glimpses of aurora visible every now and then through the canopy. Twigs crunched under their feet and the sounds of creatures and birds became more muted until all Clay could hear was his own breath and then not even that.

After an hour or so of walking silently, Clay felt more at ease as if he had known Saraid for a long time. The trees began to thin out until they reached a clearing, a circular meadow of grass dotted with primroses. At its centre stood a column of midnight stretching up into the sky, like a black search beam that went on forever.

"What is this place?"

"A window."

"To see what?"

"The morning dew. A sunset. God. Buddha. The answer to the Theory of Everything. Many people from many civilisations have ventured here to glimpse the Singularity."

Clay looked around the clearing. "But there's no one here."

"Indeed."

She took him by the hand and walked across the meadow, paused briefly then walked into the column of darkness until only her hand was visible. She hadn't let go of him.

He hesitated, wondering if this was all some elaborate trap.

Her voice carried as if from a long distance. "It's what you wanted, isn't it? It's the reason why you both came here in the first place: gold at the end of the rainbow, a chance to magnify your love for her a thousandfold, make it last a billion years—*amor sempiternus*."

"I'm not sure anymore. It seemed right back then when we were young and impetuous. But everything changed. Now . . . I just want her back, I don't care if it's for an hour or a day. I need to hold her . . . and more. I hope that she might find it in her to forgive me. That's okay, isn't it? To seek forgiveness?"

She didn't answer, but he felt her tug gently at his hand.

He took one step into the impenetrable black, felt solid ground, and followed her in.

After images of the forest faded. He felt a strange vertigo as if every photon of his body was being stripped away.

"It's fine," she said. "It's just the photosphere backing you up."

Then she let him go.

"Wait a minute," he said. "If it's a window . . . "

They fell at the speed of light, down into the well of nothingness, their photonic bodies stretching out under the intense gravitation. Pain lanced up through every cell, every fibre that had once been Clay.

He heard Saraid's voice, a whisper against the screaming in his mind. "Can you see it, Clay?"

He tried with all his strength to see the Singularity as if by sheer force of will he could bring a vision of it into existence. All he needed was a glimmer of silver light, no i-sphere magic, just raw reality. He shook his head, tried to clear all his thoughts, push the pain away . . . if only for a millisecond . . . looking down . . . nothing . . . nada, zip . . . was that it? Was that all there was after all the striving and heartache? A feeling of hollowness without borders? He laughed at notion that he'd carried a head full of hollow feelings around with him for years.

Then he felt a final, crushing agony as his photonic structure disintegrated down to nothing.

He awoke on the edge of the clearing.

Saraid helped him to his feet. It seemed people were doing a lot of that on this world.

"What happened? Did I see it?"

Saraid shrugged. "We'll never know. Even if your copy did see something, no messages can reach us."

"Then what is the point?"

"What is the point to anything, Clay?"

"Oh, come on, don't get metaphysical."

"Why not?"

He wrung his hands in frustration. "There must be a purpose. You built this world, right?"

She shook her head. "My race is a billion years old. Many think we are the builders, but we have inherited it from a much older civilisation. The photosphere and its windows have always been here. The forest, rivers, sky and mountains are our . . . renovations. Humans brought the notion of cities."

They continued on through the forest until the trees grew sparse and the ground rose into the foothills of the mountain range he had seen from the rampart.

"Where is Mareko?"

"Where is anything, Clay?"

"You know you're frustrating the hell out of me."

Saraid nudged him with her elbow. "Where's your sense of humour gone? You're different, so hang on to that. Don't let yourself become like the others. Humans are all so serious with their need to be happy *all* the time, and their boring personal goals and quests for glory."

"But the others said I needed to control my thoughts—"

"How human. And how tragic." She turned towards the forest, and glanced back at him. "This place is probably as old as the universe so I think it's fair to say it knows how to preserve itself. The thoughts of one man will not harm it. So go ahead, chase your dreams."

"Saraid. Wait. Was this an interview?"

She smiled and winked. "Kind of."

"Did I pass?"

"You tell me."

6.

The climb to the summit took a week. He had fallen out of shape since the military, but now every muscle tingled and his lungs felt alive as he sucked in the chill autumn air under an oxygen-blue sky with a warm sun at the zenith. He needed the comfort the i-sphere brought right now, and that meant Goldilocks zone earthiness, a pack full of rations, and good, solid clothing and boots.

Shading his eyes from the glare, he gazed out to the lands beyond the mountains. Rivers and waterfalls spilled down into lush valleys and mirrored lakes. Green fields stretched out to the horizon. There was a particular solidity about rock and water and grass that he had forgotten. It felt familiar, yet, as much as he tried to deny it, it was feeling increasingly like the memory of a place and not the place itself. Sometimes he longed for the vista of dead ships falling away to eternity. There was a beautiful but grim immediacy to Wraith World behind the veil of his i-sphere. Death always lurking below, unreachable heavens above—it was at once brutal but invigorating, and not something he could ever take for granted. Maybe that was the way the people here survived eternity.

He retracted his focus then chuckled as the world recalibrated its texture and colour. The yellow sun and blue sky faded as the chromatic aurora bled back in. It was only then he noticed the outline of a ship, like a charcoal sketch, hanging like a twisted dagger in the air over the valley.

All the physical structure of the ship had long since been crushed into the singularity, but its light remained, revealing a breached and buckled hull, its armour plating strewn out into long twisted strands, internal components and circuitry ruptured outwards like livid wounds. No external markings remained, but he knew the configuration of the metal—ex-military like Sophocles. She called it Sosipatra.

He sat down hard on the summit, all the pent up emotions coming out in great shuddering gasps of breath.

Given time he could have learned to fly out to examine the wreckage. He was sure most things were possible, but with no physiological memory of flight, he didn't really know where to start. So he eventually made his way down the mountainside to a shaded gorge about a kilometre below the wreckage. As it turned out, Mareko found him as he was busy washing his hands and face in a pool of icy water.

She clubbed him on the back of the head with a tree branch.

It was not the reception he expected, but certainly one that he deserved.

She was exactly as he remembered.

The light cast enticing shadows along her face and limbs as she stretched out in front of the camp fire. Unlike his earlier fantasy-memory, this was the real Mareko dressed in practical outdoor clothing.

He wriggled his toes inside thick socks, his boots hung up by the laces on a tree next to the pool. He followed her gaze up into the night, arching his neck carefully, the bruise still tender to the touch. But the pain was quickly forgotten as he watched the stars twinkle in familiar constellations. This must be her i-sphere, his thoughts were too jumbled right now to impose any memories or feelings into the photosphere.

The silhouette of the wreckage hung like a ragged void in the night, starlight reflecting off tortured metal edges.

She was obviously maintaining it. It was something he'd do—a tombstone to their relationship. Then again, maybe it was a beacon, maybe—

"I know what you're thinking."

He gasped and turned to see her looking directly at him. "Ah."

"Is that all you have to say?"

"I'm sorry."

"I'm sorry—is that it?"

"What do you want me to say?"

"An explanation for starters. Some rational thought of any kind."

"*Okay.*" He sat up crossed legged and stretched his hands over the fire. "Okay." There was something homely about the setting: the crackling of the wood, embers drifting in the air, the play of light across Mareko's hips, even their argument seemed to fit like a glove. "Why is it that all we can think of are the comforts of home?"

"You tell me."

"Now you sound like Saraid."

"Well, maybe I am more like them now."

He sighed. "Mareko. I don't want to argue."

Memories filtered in. Their dreams forgotten as their ships tumbled in a decaying orbit around the black hole. He flung out grappling hooks, tried to drag her back up the gravity well. Then, with both ships on the brink, he released the hooks at the last instant . . . a sling-shot effect out into a safe orbit . . . relief, waves of relief that he was alive . . . then guilt and self-loathing as he sat and watched Mareko's ship spin further down, crumpling, venting atmosphere. Even when he came back a year later the scanners picked up the light from her ship, hanging there above the event horizon. And a year after that, and . . .

He looked up into the sky as if it might grant him absolution.

She was watching his face closely. He hadn't got any better at hiding his feelings, but he couldn't tell whether that was a good or bad thing.

"Why did you come here, Clay? You must have known this was a one-way trip. What was it, guilt, remorse, suicide?"

He kept his eyes on the fire, afraid to look at her. "All of the above. Maybe it was a delayed reaction after letting you go to save myself. Who does that?"

She must have read something in his face or in his mind. All the tension seemed to drain away from her shoulders as she got up, walked around the fire and sat close to him.

"People who care, Clay." She slowly placed her arm around him, nestling into the crook of his neck.

"The only person I ever cared about was me."

"You know that's not true. You had the will to go on living, I'm not angry with you for that. You cared enough to keep my memory alive, rather than go down the well in screaming flames."

"That's not helping my guilt complex."

"Yeah, but it's helping me," she said, a wicked smile teasing the corners of her lips. She moved in, huddling closer, the smell of her hair, the touch of her skin bringing back all the right kinds of corporeal feelings. "If I've learnt anything, life is just as tenuous here as on the outside. The light recirculates in some kind of engineered ecosystem. But that means life *and* death. New light is captured through the event horizon. It may take aeons, but the old light eventually drains away down the Singularity."

He touched her then. His trembling hands caressed her face and neck, found the soft places beneath her jumper. She swung across to sit on his lap, and teased his cheek and eyelids with kisses.

She reached back to pull his jumper off. He winced as it caught his neck and she covered her mouth: "I'm sorry too." They laughed together then, frantically peeling away clothes, a stray sock smouldering at the edge of the fire. Her body swayed hypnotically over his lap: naked skin and curves and exploring hands, all in shadows backlit by flames. She reached down urgently, guided him, her silken warmth around him now as they found a delicate rhythm. Out of synch at first—it had been so long—but now moving with more confidence until their bodies ground together, their shouts rising defiantly into the night. And on they pushed until the luscious friction became unbearable, pulsing waves of energy rising up . . . their climax quickening . . . searing away all worldly cares . . . erasing all i-sphere imagery to reveal two people made of stranded light . . . joined as one on the boundary of infinity.

7.

Dawn over the photosphere, the aurora brightening, and with it a calm that Clay had not felt in years. He reached out, suddenly aware of her absence. Opening his eyes, the pool and trees were the same, his clothes scattered, one blackened sock and the ashes of the fire, but no sign of Mareko.

The wreckage was also gone and that made him wonder whether she had been a dream, brought to life by his i-sphere. Or worse:

maybe he was still stuck in the dampening gel, permanently tuned in to a PTSD hallucination.

He called her name until his voice grew hoarse.

Suddenly self-conscious of his nakedness, he drew in his focus and donned a fresh set of clothes. The old clothes dispersed back into the photosphere.

He followed a natural trail down away from the pool, the air warming as he descended until he found her on a rocky outcrop, staring at another one of the windows that seemed to dot the landscape.

She'd been crying.

"What's wrong?"

She wiped her face. "You're a dumb nut."

"Okay, I don't know what I've done."

"You came here to rescue me, didn't you?"

"Ah . . . "

"There's no way out, you silly man."

He drew a handkerchief from the air and handed it to her. "But you *waited* for me all this time. Who's the dumb nut now?"

She gave him a wry smile and wiped away the tears. "Maybe we could settle here. The city might be a nice place." Then her face turned forlorn. "But we're not the settling type, are we?"

"This is paradise for many, I'm sure." He reached down and pulled her up. "But I've already found what I'm looking for."

She hugged him tight. "You'll be sorry."

He squeezed her butt. "I already am."

She playfully dug her fingers in his ribs. "Let's go to the city. We can fly, you know. And there are other modes—we can merge with the photosphere and circle the entire planet in seconds. Speed of light and all that jazz."

"Hmm, not just yet."

"What are you up to?"

"Oh, nothing."

"Come on, Clay, spit it out."

"I think we need to talk to Saraid."

Mareko gave him an impromptu flying lesson. It was at once liberating and awkward, and after a few trials that invariably saw him crash into a pine tree or glance off a cliff face, they found their way over the mountains and back to the meadow of lush grass and primroses.

Saraid was there, statuesque in her ribbons of light, her strange eyes intense as she watched the couple land.

"How do we get out?" Clay asked.

Saraid smiled. "*A world-bound Wraith longs for the abyss, but when faced with eternity, longs to be re-bound.* Jala was a Wraith poet of a Dynasty that ruled a million years before we journeyed to the stars, 700 million years before humans walked on two legs. His poems talked about a place hidden from the rest of the universe called the Pool of Inversions."

Clay couldn't even begin to comprehend the time spans involved. "We might get used to this place in time, but I'm not sure we're ready to start that journey. I might be wrong, but I'm not sure any human is ready. Maybe we should all come back in a thousand generations: *If we have not found the heaven within, we have not found the heaven without.* James Hilton wrote that six thousand years ago, but there were many others, whole belief systems and religions well before and well after his time, all searching for the same thing. Maybe paradox is ingrained in existence."

"That's another nice thought," Saraid said. "Maybe we really are dreamers, and the universe is a dream, ontologically speaking."

"Is that why the builders constructed this impossible place? To make us confront life and death, decision and indecision, fantasy and reality?"

"Maybe."

Clay laughed. "And maybe not?"

Saraid nodded. "Now you're getting the hang of it."

Clay reached out and held Mareko around the waist. "I don't want to spend a million years looking for something I already have."

"Wow, you two really are an item, aren't you?"

"He's the stubborn one," Mareko said.

Clay nudged her in the ribs. "Am not."

He turned to Saraid, conviction in his eyes. "So, is there a way out?"

"You tell me."

"I knew you'd say that." He rubbed his hands up and down his face. "Where's the engineering, the infrastructure, hardware . . . anything that runs this place? How do *we* exist at all?"

Saraid pouted. "You're thinking like a dualist again."

He sighed. "You're right. The post-humans told me they'd detected something out there . . . faint signals beneath the noise, quantum echoes of another universe. I thought maybe the singularity was a gateway." He held his hands up. "I never expected to find this beautiful place. But I'm glad I did." He squeezed Mareko gently. "It's like a foyer or an anteroom, isn't it? We're waiting for all things to end when in fact all things are beginning. We're stranded yet found."

Saraid reached out and hugged them both. "Now you truly are getting the hang of it."

8.

They stepped out of the meadow and into darkness, Saraid's farewell now distant in their ears, after images fading to black.

Clay squeezed Mareko's hand tightly. "No backups."

She reached over and pressed her lips hard against his. "No backups."

Another step and gravity took hold, wrenching them down into a hollow place with no boundaries—the Singularity—where nothing existed . . . yet everything did.

AFTERWORD TO "STRANDED LIGHT"

Several other stories in this collection explore the technology singularity, but I've always been intrigued by the physical singularity. I suppose the term "physical singularity" is a bit of an oxymoron anyway, given that all the laws of physics supposedly break down in a singularity.

So I think the singularity epitomises all that we don't know about existence, and in many ways is a metaphor for our dreams and quests for enlightenment and knowledge. But I think it also forces into stark clarity what we do know. There's something very Zen in it for me, that's why I took the nondualist approach to the plot.

And I guess that's also why I left it up to readers to determine how Clay and Mareko ended up—crushed out of existence or together exploring a new universe. I like to think the latter because I generally like happy endings!

AUTUMN LEAVES FALLING

The nurses were gorgeous. I had seen so many at other clinics, but the nurses here were special—long legs, dark, storm-tossed hair, confident smiles.

You pay for what you get, and today I *was* paying.

One nurse captivated me with her deep chocolate eyes and light olive skin. Everything about her spoke of unaffected elegance: the calm ushering of clients through to the treatment rooms, the neat placement of the client files in the crook of her arm, the casual tilt of her head so the light caught her high cheekbones. Her clothes had clean, simple lines: white flat shoes, a pale blue skirt, and a low cut white blouse that stretched firmly around her breasts.

I looked away, suddenly self-conscious. But it didn't take long for my eyes to linger again along the length of her legs, tracing the profile of her tanned calves up to her perfect knees, and further still. They really were—

"Mr Michaels. Stephen Michaels?"

Yes!

Did I say that out loud? No, she was still looking around the waiting room.

I sprang out of my seat.

She smiled warmly and stretched out her hand, palm up. "Please come this way. My name is Veronica. I'll be your nurse today."

I followed her along a bright corridor. The room at the end had white walls flecked with granite-effect grey and silver. A tall shelf unit stacked with boxes of surgical gloves stood next to a small sink and bench top. The long reclining chair in the middle of the room looked comfortable and inviting.

A picture hung on the wall in front of the chair—a maple tree in hues of scarlet, orange and gold, a spray of leaves tumbling away in the wind. The caption read: "Have you ever been a leaf and fallen from your tree in autumn and been really puzzled by it?" The line was from T. E. Lawrence, apparently in a letter to an E. Kennington.

I felt my pulse quicken. There was something disturbing about the picture. I breathed in deeply and let the air out slowly as if it might somehow stem the inevitable flood.

"Take a seat," Veronica said, and placed my file down on the bench top.

I sat down. The chair reclined under my weight like a regular dentist's chair, but moulded around my back and shoulders like something out of a racing car.

"Not that I mind," I said awkwardly. "But are there any doctors here?"

She looked down at me, her face framed in raven black curls.

"All our nurses are qualified." She tilted her head in that same way, a twinkle of conspiracy in her eyes. "Between you and me, who needs doctors? We can do the same job for half the price, without all the baggage of egos and astronomical insurance schemes."

I let out a long sigh, but it wasn't one of relief. Tension started building in my neck and shoulders. The doubts I had thought buried seemed to be nudging up through the veneer of self-control. I felt my right eyelid flutter.

She turned back to the file.

"I'd just like to go over your form again. No allergies of any kind?"

"None that I know of."

"Have you had any physical illnesses or disease?"

"No."

"Previous surgery?"

"Just my appendix when I was a kid, plus some dental surgery from my ju-jitsu days."

"Did you get a whooping?" She gave a cheeky grin.

"Yeah, but you should have seen the other guy?"

I cringed at the cliché, but she laughed anyway. I didn't have the courage to tell her I had trained in my living room using an online tactile glove interactive. I had fallen and smashed my mouth on the corner of the coffee table.

Come on, Steve, you can do better than this.

"How about you?" I asked.

"Martial arts?"

I nodded.

"Jeet Kune Do. Karate—the old, traditional styles like Shotokan. A bit of kick boxing."

"Oh. How do you find the time?"

I caught her sidelong glance. She reached over and squeezed my arm. "I'm an effigy."

"No."

She playfully nudged my chin up with her knuckle.

"It's true. All the nurses in the clinic are. We don't administer treatments unless we've tried them ourselves."

Of course, that explained the sublime genetic traits.

"That's good to know." My mind raced at the possibilities.

"Now. Just one more question. Is there any history of mental illness in your family? This one's important."

I thought about the question, knew I'd have to answer truthfully. I had no doubt that she had already seen my case history and genome report.

She waited patiently.

"Well, I'm not sure I'd call it an illness, but then again, maybe it was. My dad committed suicide when I was 10."

The tide rose. My pulse beat a staccato. After 25 years I still hadn't got used to the gap. A boy should never have to grow up without his father. Never. What were you thinking that day, dad? Did you think that getting me through my first ten years was enough and that I'd be all right from there? Or were you just too absorbed in your own self pity? Well, I've got news for you. Life's full of setbacks. Get over it.

"I'm sorry." Her words broke the spiral. "Have you shown any suicidal tendencies, had any inclination whatsoever?"

"No."

"Well," I added, "It's not like I haven't thought about it. It sounds perverse, but thinking about the worst sometimes makes it easier to get through a bad day."

"Are you comfortable with this treatment?"

"I guess."

"Truth." She wasn't messing around, this was digging deep.

"No, I'm nervous as hell. I thought it might give me something more, give me back my life. I'm chronically introverted. I've had bouts of depression and anxiety ever since he left. I'm not married, can't hold down a relationship, don't have a social life. I find it hard to interact with anyone."

The words seemed to slosh around in the empty spaces in the room.

I felt like a coward. It wasn't supposed to be like this, not today of all days. But that picture had really thrown me and now her line of questioning had opened up everything I hated about myself.

This was supposed to be a good day, a happy day. Wasn't it?

"I know this is hard, Steve. I think you are doing fine, by the way."

I wiped away the beads of sweat from my forehead.

She handed me the form and a pen. I scrawled a signature, skipping the standard fine print liability clauses. What did it matter, it's not like they could stop mid-procedure. She tucked the form and pen away in the file.

As she walked out she glanced over her shoulder and winked.

"Be back soon."

"Thanks, Veronica."

It was good to have human contact again, but it was exhausting. I quickly spiralled down and began counting the stitching on the chair. Then I noticed the picture wasn't hanging straight.

I stretched forward without looking at the caption and nudged it up on the left a few millimetres. That was better. As I leant back in the chair I saw that the boxes on the shelf weren't stacked properly—

Footsteps sounded along the corridor.

Veronica entered first. Something followed her in.

"What the hell is that?"

I pushed back into the chair, hands white-knuckled on the armrests, legs kicking and sliding involuntarily.

The thing was clearly female, with a perfect bio-alloy face and bright amber eyes. She had at least eight double jointed limbs and an array of sharp probes connected to a clear canister on her back. The canister contained some form of animated liquid like fizzing black mercury. A long silver cable hung from the base of her spine. She reached down in one fluid motion and plugged the cable into a socket behind the shelf.

"It's all right," Veronica said with a calming touch on my knee. "This is our auto nurse, Sabine. She will be assisting me today."

Sabine nodded, her metal lips forming a perfect smile. One of the probes rose above her head like a stinger, attuning itself to my movements, waiting, anticipating.

"You have got to be kidding."

"Oh, now come on, Steve." An eyebrow arched, those chocolate eyes turned flinty. "You must have read the brochures, seen our in-patient video."

I nodded in mute response.

"Look, I admit we don't show all our equipment as it can be a little daunting."

"You think?"

Veronica straightened her back. "Do you want the best treatment?"

"Of course," I said, my eyes riveted to the silent, swaying scorpion-woman.

"This is not like the black clinics. Brain emulation can't be done by some sort of tomography, it's just too complicated. It requires an invasive procedure. We need to get right in there to model the quantum level processes in your brain and make sure we pick up your physical and conscious mind. It's pointless otherwise. You don't want to wake up as a virtual zombie, do you?"

"No." I was aware of the horrifying implications of choosing the wrong clinic.

Sabine's sharp edges twinkled.

I swallowed. "What about anaesthetic?"

Veronica sat on the edge of the chair and crossed her incredible legs. She took my hand. Her palms were smooth and warm.

"We need all your synapses firing so the nanotech can make a true copy. The information gets transferred into the computer out the back." She looked along the length of the silver cable. "You'll be up and loaded in no time."

"I'm going to die, aren't I?" I had finally got to the core of it. I couldn't stop my eyes filling.

She held my hand tighter. "We can't inject the nanotech in your head and have you survive the process. And no, Steve, you're not following in your father's footsteps."

"He was a Gen-Twenty."

She nodded. "It was a terrible time."

I forced myself to look at the picture again.

"I've tried to understand his suicide all my life. Why he was so consumed by his dream. Why he didn't talk to anyone. I used to blame myself at times. I've tried to be less like him, to be less isolated. But it seems the more I try, the lonelier I become and the more blasé I get about my life. What I'm doing now feels so much like a self-destruct mechanism kicking in, a genetic legacy that can't be stopped no matter what."

"We're such social creatures," she said. "What really happens to us when we're cut off from the love and warmth of family and friends? And for your dad's generation, what happens when the dream of the uploaded global mind, the dream of immortality they had been waiting for all their lives, is wrenched from their grasp?"

Autumn leave falling. "So many," I whispered. "Why?"

"No one is quite sure why the mass suicide occurred. When technology development slowed it crushed the hopes of millions. Maybe they needed a release after so many years of preparing for death anyway. But then the black clinics just added to the slaughter with their unstable architectures. Even Moore said if his Law was pushed to the limit it would end in disaster."

Yes, probably. I said, "Exponential escalation of technology for the sake of it just creates chaos.

"But things are different now," Veronica said buoyantly. "We're slowly taking back control of the technology, outlawing the legacies and thinking for once about where it's all heading. This is the right clinic, Steve. For the nurses here, the picture represents hope, not despair."

"The singularity," I said.

She laughed, a rich sound that reminded me of summer. "Of course."

The spiral pattern of leaves was hypnotic, falling and spinning with some secret harmony. "The leaves drop," I said, "not because they're dead, but because they're free. Their original purpose is complete, and now they are unbounded."

A nod, a smile. "This is not suicide, it is rebirth," Veronica said. "You said it yourself. You're just painfully shy and you want something else. Where's the harm in that? And besides which, there's less risk than you think. Going through the technology singularity isn't a one way street. The effigy option gives you the choice to come and go as you please. Trust me, I'm there."

She patted my hand.

"Now, are you ready?"

"Ok," I said, mustering strength back into my voice. My mind was still absorbing, recalibrating. I had done enough of talking to ghosts over the years. I shut the door to the void. "Let's do this."

Sabine didn't hesitate. She sat on top of me, her back arched, as two sets of arms pinned my legs and wrists. Her face hovered close. I could see flecks in her eyes, like smoky quartz. Her aroma was like musk and linen. Her weight grew heavier as two more arms swung around to hold my shoulders steady. I hardened at the warmth of her in my lap and shuffled in embarrassment.

Veronica moved in closer and whispered. "That's good. You'll need a healthy sex drive where you're going."

I laughed.

The probe with the slender, silver spike whisked around Sabine and swung under my nose. Images of dead pharaohs having their brains sucked out made me squirm in the chair.

Veronica leant closer, pressing her upper body against my arm so that she could hold my head firm. She was warmer than Sabine. I saw the pale blue logo on the plunging curve of her blouse for the first time—*The Afterlife Clinic*—with the A inverted so it looked like a V. The tops of her breasts pushed up and a hint of white lace lingerie appeared—

The probe slammed up my nose in one fluid motion. I screamed once before the conflagration, the liquid nanotech pumping up from the canister, scanning and burning across my skull like a cleansing fire.

My head lolled to one side. The last things I saw in this life were Veronica's white shoes and her long, long legs.

They really were legs to die for.

Howard Bloom, the author of Global Brain *and* The Lucifer Principle, *suggested that isolating individuals from the collective will trigger a self-destruct mechanism where we "fall far from the tree". He referred to observations of the response of toddlers to different levels of attention and nurturing, as well as examples of famous people who were seemingly happy yet committed suicide.*

In "Autumn Leaves Falling" I tried to bring out that sense of isolation for Steve who is finally contemplating uploading his mind in a post-singularity society. But the process is lethal, and given that he's coming from such a dark place, he struggles to rationalise his decision.

The story is also a caricature of some of the modern beauty clinics and doctors surgeries where the business model includes scantily clad women providing customer service. Sex sells— without doubt in almost all kinds of business—and I'm sure many guys would like every visit to the GP to be an indulgent fantasy, but it won't solve our problems!

DEFENCE OF THE REALM

FIREWALL, SOL EMPATHIC GRID, 2234

I blaze across a sky the colour of hammered bronze. Snowball looks at me with one of his crazy smiles. His twin, Nero, is just behind, grim as ever. A klick ahead, at point, Raz is powering up the caterpillar.

The target appears beside her, a giant razor-spiked sphere black as hell's coal. It is adjusting rapidly to our phase shift. We still have a sliver. I skip. I'm with Raz now, on her periphery.

The twins skip in on her other flank.

Took your time. Her pupils dilate slightly; an eyebrow arches. Snowball shrugs. *Better late . . .*

. . . than never, Nero finishes, as always.

The alien's shadow is cold, its form morphs, bleeding lethal barbed tendrils in slow motion.

I urge Raz on. *Be fast.*

Of all the times to hassle me.

Patterns of platinum quicken across its surface. The tendrils move with more purpose, towards us. The sliver narrows. I state the obvious. *It's catching up.*

All right already. Raz groans and looks at the twins for moral support. They remain purse-lipped. *OK, the cat's on nitro.*

The gold shape on her wrist squirms into motion and floats free, multiple segments thrashing faster than our pico-senses can follow. It crosses the distance to the alien, squeezes between the tendrils and disappears.

Fall back. I catch Raz as she nulls out. The twins guard the retreat.

Something is not right. The butterfly doesn't emerge. I'm yelling now, with Raz over my shoulder. *Phase up.*

Not fast enough. The polymorph shifts and engulfs the twins, their white and black legs sticking out stupidly. I let Raz float free and ramp phase beyond what even I think is safe.

The alien skips at a precognitive speed.

I feel its presence around me. Alien programs unfold in a kaleidoscope of light as it slashes open my firewall. Frigid cold seeps in but there's no time to scream. I ramp to atto-phase and in a last, desperate sliver I transfer my higher motor routines to the inert caterpillar buried in the polymorph. It thrashes back to life, ravenously digesting the alien construct. The butterfly emerges and the ice retreats from my zombie form. The twins float free as the polymorph husk dissipates like smoke on a breeze.

That's why they call me Deus Zee.

RAPPORT ENVIRONMENT, SOL EMPATHIC GRID, 2234

Snowball looks down at me, his bleached hair a diamond halo.

Take it easy . . .

. . . just shut your eyes and relax for a while.

Nero yawns and stretches in a hammock between two of the island's palm trees. He is a shadow in contrast to his albino brother.

I hear waves lapping. The Sun and sand are warm on my skin. Time becomes languid as I feel the welcome slide into dormancy.

Where's Raz?

Out with . . .

. . . the sharks.

Vertigo takes hold and I spin down to the treacly state of normal time. Long neglected qualia shimmer somewhere on my periphery.

I rode the elevator to the 91st floor of the retirement tower perched on the western rim of the Parramatta crater. From this vantage point I could see that the rebuilding had picked up pace.

Gleaming towers stretched up from the jagged remains of old Sydney like bright blades.

Even with such rapid progress it was unlikely the craters from the von Neumann probes would ever be fully erased. Hundreds of blackened depressions lay across the globe, all sprayed with a layer of rust-red nanocrete—a stark reminder that the world had nearly fallen only a decade ago. The voice of the artificial intelligence broke the silence with a colloquial greeting.

"G'day, Mr Lawson."

"Are you looking after my old man?" I didn't intend to be mean, but my mood was always dark when I came back to Australia.

"He's as well as can be expected," it said. "Still reclusive, but that's just him, I suppose. He doesn't take to the in-house entertainment much, but he likes chess and he's trying his hand at painting."

"Painting?" Well, hell has frozen over, I thought.

"His blood pressure is up a bit, but I keep a close eye on it. The pain management regime is the same and the dosage of cyclosporine is up a little since your last visit. His drinking doesn't help."

I sensed the tacit message in the AI's voice. "He's 73 and I'm not about to take away one of the few pleasures he has."

"Very well." The elevator stopped and that was the end of that.

The apartment was a shambles. I saw half-finished microscreens in a corner. Serrated towers, copper and green against a blue backdrop. He had hastily thrown a rag over one screen, but hadn't quite covered the familiar neckline.

"Merry Christmas, Dad." I was shocked by how he had aged over the last year. I placed his present on the table.

"You could have let me know you were visiting," he said, his synthetic speech a close approximation to his original baritone.

"I might have cleaned up the place."

"You know I always visit at Christmas."

He started to stand, servos whirring quietly.

"Don't get up," I said, not wanting to agitate him any further. Maybe I should have stayed in Silicon Valley after all, I thought.

"I'm fine," he said, grimacing, and hobbled to the kitchen to make some coffee. After a long, awkward silence he passed me a steaming mug. His left hand was like spotted leather, the etched alloy of his right grubby and tarnished.

"I hear your chess is coming along nicely."

"Have you been talking to that stinking AI again?"

"Like I have much choice," I snapped. I took a deep breath and ploughed on. "I'm sorry. Look, I know it's been a year but I'm just so busy with my research. And it looks like you're keeping occupied too. I'm glad to see you've got other interests, you shouldn't hide your work, it's great."

"What do you want, Scott?" His amber Nikons scrutinised me sceptically. I hesitated and he latched onto the topic.

"You're going to kill yourself, aren't you?" His tone was acid.

"I've seen it on the news, kids uploading into cyberspace, burning their brains out of their skulls. The world's gone mad."

"That's not true, Dad, it's about unlocking our potential. I know twins who are doing groundbreaking work on personality imaging. And I've met a girl. She's working on software that can operate in the most extreme time phase. It's orders of magnitude faster than the processing capability of any virtual persona. And I'm finally getting somewhere with decoding the alien datapackets. They're a real threat now, bootstrapping up constructs to burrow through the firewall—"

He interrupted me, waving his normal arm at the panorama outside the window. "The real war was out there." His face was a rictus of pain. "Machines against machines on land and in space. We destroyed each and every one of them and sprayed their diseased craters with nanotoxins. Not that I need to be reminded of it every goddamn day." He turned away from the window.

"I know Dad, millions of you died. I think about Mum every day. My generation can't comprehend the suffering you all went through."

"No one understands, and no one really cares."

I felt my face flush. He could be so infuriating. "Just hang on a minute. You helped us survive this far, but it's a long way from over—the planetary attacks have stopped but there's an unseen war now that could easily become our worst nightmare. If the constructs crack the Solar System firewall we're finished. The empathic grid and every human and system linked to it will be infected with their viruses." I paused and then added, "What you did, going back into hard vacuum after the biological attack, was the bravest thing I've ever seen."

He looked dumbfounded as his mind started to make the connections and sat back down with a heavy thud. A few minutes passed and my mixed feelings of anger and elation dissipated, replaced by steely resolve. He must have caught the look—his Nikons never missed a nuance—and his features softened a little. "You shouldn't rush headlong into this, Scott. Think about what you're doing. This is your life you're playing with. And what about your soul?"

I snorted. "Look at you, you grizzled old tin can. I'm sure there's still a heart in there somewhere."

He laughed hoarsely. "Not that I'd tell anyone." He paused as if we'd reached some satisfactory point. "So tell me about this girl."

. . . Sharks, you say?

I take Snowball's outstretched hand and stand up. The sea is green from east to west, the sand is hot under my feet.

You know she plays hard, probably needs a break from us ultra-males anyway. They chuckle.

You want to tell us what those qualia were all about... Snowball's been blubbering all morning.

Sorry, I didn't mean for you all to experience that. Only a few thousand veterans infected by the exo-strain of necrotising fasciitis were able to re-enter the war, but it turned the tide of events in our favour. It gave the world a new sense of hope. He hated the idea of me uploading because he saw too many parallels with what he'd gone through—he was never the same after his reconstruction. Hell, who wouldn't be changed after losing half their body? We may not see eye to eye but deep down we respect each other.

Raz slips her wet arms around my waist and presses her stomach against my back. *That's right, but you are both too pig-headed to tell each other. He's beside himself with pain and you're racked with guilt because you can't be there for him.*

I hate it when you're right. I turn and kiss her slowly, running my hand through her dark wet hair.

Maybe it's time you hired an effigy and got your sorry self back into the real world for a while.

My reply is meek. *I'd never looked at it like that before.*

Deus Zee. Raz places her hands on her hips. The last minute miracle-worker. You can defeat alien incursions into our cyberspace but you can't work out a solution to seeing your old man.

I must look comical, being scolded by this long-legged woman standing in a slip of bikini. Snowball doubles over laughing. Nero is straight-mouthed.

OK, I'll do it. Now cut me some slack. I saved your worthless hides out there. The intrusions are getting worse, there's something strange about their constructs now-they're adapting, getting faster than us.

But not the cat. Raz's confidence has an edge to it.

For how long though? And what caused the glitch? We're going to need everything running like clockwork for the next campaign.

Still working on that one.

The twins anticipate my next words and mutter livid curses.

To business then.

NEW SYDNEY, EARTH, 2235

The human parts, about 40 per cent of his face and body down the left side, were impossibly emaciated. The tarnished cyborg parts compensated as much as possible, but he still walked with a slow, exaggerated roll. He blocked the doorway, unshaven and disoriented, squinting at me through his watery Nikons.

"Just me, Dad." Perhaps he sensed my awkwardness, controlling the synthetic body. I had forgotten the practical constraints of corporeal life. He squinted some more, then let me through. The apartment was dark and chilly. The microscreen art had all been packed away somewhere, or, worse, thrown out. The remnants of last week's dinners lay across the kitchen bench.

The AI was going to answer for this.

"What do you want?" He sat awkwardly in his chair that had split and cracked, tufts of decaying smartfoam sprouting like tussock grass.

"To see how you are."

"So you thought you'd indulge me as if in some way it might, what, make me feel better? Maybe you just need to offload your guilt and go."

I turned to leave, but he leant forward and caught my hand. His grip was still firm but I could feel the feather-lightness of his old bones, the crinkled texture of his skin.

I took a deep breath. "You know I never intended to hurt you."

He looked into the distance somewhere beyond the crater and the rows of towers. "When you were a small boy I used to watch you sleep, you were so beautiful, and your Mum and I were so proud. One of the blessings of being a father is that you can live your life again through the eyes of your children. And I have, Scott, I've watched you grow, and supported you as much as I could. You were what kept me sane through some very tough times. But now I don't even recognise you in this . . . simulacrum. Maybe it's my fault, you seeing me go through my own transformation, but I was forced into this, you had a choice."

I couldn't feel more helpless. I didn't have the heart to tell him I was a beta copy. The alpha was out there in the thick of the conflict.

"Do you think I approached this decision lightly? Raz . . . Rosalind, John, Jacob and I, our decisions to upload were all personal. There is so much to experience in the empathic grid, you can't imagine what it's like to share the thoughts and feelings of other people—to actually be them, see the world from a different subjective viewpoint—it's intoxicating."

"Couldn't you have waited until the technology was better?"

"The military funding made it all happen very quickly—they needed hyper-fast weapons and virtual personas. But I'm still the same person, Dad, I have all my memories. In fact they're clearer than they ever were, more accessible.

"Do you remember before the war, that crazy holiday where the tour guide forgot about us when we were diving in the lakes near the Valles Marineris sea? The look on his face was priceless when we walked into his office on the pier two days later. You had to hold Mum back from strangling him."

He gave a wry smile.

"And what about the time you tried to teach me how to sky dive in those squirrel suits off the top of the Angel Falls? Venezuela, eh. You lost your patience and just threw me over the edge—I was only eight Dad, I was petrified."

"Yes, but the suits had micro-thrusters programmed for a safe landing if you got into trouble."

"I didn't know that"

Now he was beaming. "Well, you learned, didn't you?" Slowly he got up, Nikons more focussed now. "Look, I'm not sure I can ever accept what you did, Scott—a father shouldn't have to outlive his son. But I've never really accepted what happened to me either. I can understand your motives though, and I'm not so reclusive that I haven't had time to watch your holo-mails. You're doing a great job out there. And that Raz is a fine woman, you should hang on to her."

My effigy was incapable of weeping, but I was doing my best to make it cry as a wave of relief washed through me like a soothing balm.

Dad coughed quietly, the creases on the human side of his face smoothing out as if a weight had lifted from his shoulders. He changed the subject to save us both. "You usually don't come here unless there's something big happening, so spit it out."

"It's the alien constructs," I began. "They're mutating and multiplying, getting stronger than ever. I'm not sure how long our firewall will last. We managed to trace some of their hardware nodes left by the von Neumann probes. A few were submersed in the methane seas of Titan, a perfect coolant, but we don't know how many more are hidden in the Solar System. The only option now is to take the battle into their cyberspace and disable their entire network."

I frowned at the sudden sadness in his eyes.

"Then I probably won't see you again. I only have a few weeks now."

I leaned against the kitchen bench. I should have been more prepared, but I had grown too used to my surreal immortal life. I wanted to tell him more, so much more—the success with the caterpillars, our trials with the wasp—but it all seemed to pale now against the starkness of his mortality.

"Oh, Dad," I sighed. I reached over and turned the lights up, then started clearing the rubbish from the benchtop.

ALIEN NODE CYBERSPACE, 2235

We screech in from the zenith, four radiant torches, a long way from home. The indigo hues of the alien realm seep into our war sensorium. We are in atto-phase with a sliver or two up our sleeves.

Targets . . .

. . . acquired.

The panorama of alien cyberspace stretches beneath us. They are everywhere, in all shapes and forms, like a nest of blue-black ants.

As one, they turn their bleak gaze toward us. We feel the sparks of their sentience registering our intrusion, at first like viscous oil, now quickening to dark nova.

Where would I be without my friends? *No time like the present.*

Butterflies flourish, bringing colour where none has been before. The aliens ripple away in concentric circles.

Another volley of caterpillars disappears into nihilistic yoctophase. A second wave of butterflies emerges instantaneously, covering the enemy battlefield with dead husks.

Way to go . . .

. . . Raz. The twins look immaculate in gleaming monochrome. Raz is sharp as ever in scarlet.

Nero shields me out of nowhere. He has skipped—ramping up and down phase. My confusion is momentary. The sensorium firewall lies in tatters, replaced by a hundred polymorphs and other stranger entities, liquid copper eyes atop avian bodies.

Snowball is gone. Raz is a blur, one sliver ahead, firing cats in all directions. Smoke chokes the battlefield.

What now, Deus?

I am taken aback by Nero's voice. I feel his fear and for the first time see my own mortality through his black irises. It's enough for me to finally shrug off the inner torments that have plagued me for years. *This is our time, Nero.*

I find Snowball's null form on a downward trajectory, in the clutches of one of the metal-eyed avians. I grab him and launch a cat into the alien. I sense the endless hunger of the caterpillar as it consumes the alien's program from within. It is unsettling but at the same time magnificent. The translucent wings of the butterfly buffet me, then it, too, shrivels into nothing.

The avian forms are the most adaptive. I sense a biological origin to their programs, unlike the machine intelligences of the polymorphs. Several zero in on Raz and Nero, now only a sliver behind me.

I haven't got long at this dangerous speed. Combining the cat's software with mine could prove to be a lethal cocktail, but there's no other way. I grab Nero from the converging paths of three avians. They turn ugly heads in slow motion as I whisk by.

Raz is last. As always, she's getting the most attention. I fire off five cats. They squirm across the intervening distance, leaving contrails in their wake. Polymorphs and avians detonate from within.

The first avian to match my phase skims in, intent upon Raz. It sees me on its periphery. I drop the twins and fire three cats at it. It flicks the first away, then the second. The third hits its bulbous chest.

Nothing.

The creature lifts a claw, extracts the thrashing cat and hurls it aside.

Not good. Nero is with me now.

Raz joins us. *Can't let you take all the glory this time, Deus Zee.*

Why not?

We'd never hear the end of it .

The alien hesitates, then its coppery eyes swell with confidence as more of its kind match phase. They surge towards us like a dark tide.

I unleash the wasp. It has a whisker delay mechanism.

Nero grabs Snowball by the scruff of the neck. I order the cancel command and we rocket to the zenith. The twins disappear into the zero point. Raz follows, looking at me over her shoulder, then behind me, eyes now wide with wonder.

She's gone.

I feel the concatenations at my heels. I dare to look back.

It is beautiful beyond imagining. Yellow and black with eyes of quicksilver, descending like a lethal avatar, its stinger a bright scythe of destruction. A deafening thunder rolls across the landscape.

The alien tide turns as one.

Then darkness covers me, colder than the void between the stars.

NEW SYDNEY, EARTH, 2236

Leaves blustered about the cemetery in the autumn wind. The lasercut granite headstone was one among thousands. I carefully removed the dead flowers and replaced them with fresh roses. It was good to smell real fragrance again. I read the words one final time.

IN LOVING MEMORY OF
TIMOTHY JAMES LAWSON
1 FEBRUARY 2160 TO 19 APRIL 2235
HONOURED VETERAN OF THE LONG WAR
DEAR HUSBAND OF GEORGIA
FATHER OF SCOTT
ALWAYS WITH US

Raz squeezed my hand. "You should be proud of yourself, kiddo."

"Then why do I feel so powerless?"

"Don't be so hard on yourself. You couldn't do the impossible. We're winning the war, thanks to your tenacity. And his."

"He never talked much about what happened when he went back to fight the last of the probes. He seemed to lose his way, his sense of purpose, after that. The war was all that he had for twenty years, he'd lost Mum, lost his body and half his mind, no wonder he hated the idea of my getting involved. It was only at the very end that he finally started to acknowledge what I was doing. I just hope he didn't die thinking I was a fool."

"Despite what he may have said out of pain and anger, Scott, he loved you too much to think ill of you. You have always been his son, no matter what, and he never forgot that. Whether you both realised it or not, you made each other into better men. Isn't that how it's supposed to be between father and son?"

She touched the words engraved in the stone, tracing the letters with her delicate effigy fingers.

AFTERWORD TO "DEFENCE OF THE REALM"

This story was written in tribute to my Dad who died of cancer. The narrative was fairly raw to start with, but I brought it together and it was eventually accepted as my first professional publication in Cosmos Magazine.

The protagonist Scott is a driven young man who I think epitomises the theme of "Wild Chrome". His life is this wild, roller-coaster ride and he and his friends are scaring the hell out of the previous generation—sounds like a lot of young people I know! But he is not completely self-absorbed, and underneath the chrome-like exterior of testosterone, braggadocio and talent there is a lot of insecurity and self-doubt.

The lyrics of the Roachford song, "This Generation", were also an inspiration: "Bringing tears to the old man's eye." In the end I hope they were tears of joy, Dad.

ETHOS ANTHROPOI DAIMON

Spain was in a sultry mood as he strode with his friends along the boulevard, the evening lights glittering umber and gold in the puddles left from the qualia storm. Misplaced souls lingered on the breeze, their cries blending into a mournful song of lament. He pulled up the collar of his long cloak, his dark hair whipping about, in a vain attempt to ward off the forsaken.

A few doors had opened up after the storm in one final attempt to lure the nightlife into the parlours and games rooms. However, some housekeepers quickly shut up shop when they saw the four seraphs ambling down the boulevard. The crowds that had ventured out after the storm soon dispersed again along side streets and dark alleys.

The seraphs had come out this night like any other, arrogant and bored, attired in shades of black and violet, looking for entertainment. Melody, all in embossed leather swirling with the hypnotic memories of old lovers, laughed at Spain. "What's got into you?"

Jai, the gangliest of the four in skin-tight chain mesh and black boots, slapped his thighs and doubled over in hysterics. Keye, the group's introvert and philosopher-poet, just arched an eyebrow, collusion written over his ashen face.

Spain glared at his companions and spiralled up a ghost. It howled with glee, its primal form like a swirling tide of semi-formed crystals. With a screech it chased the pale seraphs along the slippery cobblestones. After several frantic minutes they were finally able to banish it. They then turned as one and taunted Spain with childish gestures, though deep down they blanched at the fact that it had taken their combined efforts to remove the ghost.

"You just don't get it, do you?" Spain said as he caught up with them.

"Speak for yourself," Melody teased.

Jai snickered.

"But, soft!" Keye said with a flourish, "What light through yonder window breaks? It is the east, and Juliet is the sun."

"Shut the fuck up," Spain snapped. His hazel eyes flared like pools of venom, causing his companions to tone down their banter. A headache now buzzed in his temples. The night seemed unnaturally awash with remnants of the storm—disjointed dreams, snippets of strange memories, cries of broken personalities. It was one of the more disturbing aspects of the domain.

They continued walking two-by-two in stony silence, Melody next to Spain, Keye and Jai scouting ahead for open rooms.

Melody looked at Spain, her eyes a cerulean glow in the darkness. "You're going to do it, aren't you?"

"I'm not what I used to be," Spain said, as if she didn't already know.

"Have you ever thought you are just more yourself?"

Spain couldn't fault her cut-straight-to-it intuition. It was a little disconcerting how she could state in one sentence what he had wrestled with for months now.

"Yes, that's true. But you know I'm not taking this lightly."

"Of course I do. No one tackles the Deus on a whim. But you could die, Spain, permanently. It's not the same as gambling minor aspects of your persona in the games rooms. You've felt the air tonight as much as I have. Imagine being ripped apart like that."

She interlocked her arm with his. A tear rolled down her cheek as elegant as a diamond.

"It's not Russian Roulette, Mel. You know I can hold my own. And if I win, who knows what the possibilities are. I have to give myself this chance otherwise I'll go crazy. I've been here a long time now. There's no point having power without a purpose, of existing for the sake of it."

Melody sighed with frustration as Jai and Keye waved them to the entrance of Cogitatio, one of the more up-market games rooms. Jai ducked through a dark doorway encircled with images of strange lands and lost empires. Melody looked at Spain as if to say their conversation wasn't over.

The games room was a place of flowing shadows and soft green lights. The atmosphere was thick with residual fear. A dozen players lay catatonic in ornate booths around the walls. Others sat quietly at the velvet covered tables, their faces lined with concentration. Not many winners tonight, Spain thought, much like every other night.

The gameskeeper, a bald woman with tattoos of intertwined serpents around her waist and breasts, looked up as the seraphs entered. She stopped tallying the night's winnings and glanced sidelong at Jai as he sat across the roulette table.

"Is the house still open?" Jai asked.

"We are always open for seraphs," she replied. She nodded respectfully at Spain then gave him a sly wink. Melody clung protectively to his arm.

"Be careful, Jai," Keye said.

Jai frowned through his shock of white hair then grabbed Keye and shoved him away. He turned back to the gameskeeper. She consulted her serpents as they danced across her skin, one red, one black. She leant forward and spun the roulette wheel, the serpents watching all the while with gleaming eyes.

Jai lined up his chips then placed a bet on black. All four seraphs held their breath as the ball clacked away. It finally came to rest.

"Yes!" Jai shouted.

"Way to go." Melody slapped him hard on the back.

The black serpent snarled and took a bite from the red's flanks. The keeper slid several chips across the table. Jai clasped them tightly, shaking with excitement.

Spain looked on with an air of indifference. He had been here more times than he cared to remember, gambling away the shady memories and experiences of his life. If you were lucky, you took home the experiences of complete strangers. It was the most enthralling feeling—actually being someone else for a time. He had been a king swimming with killer whales in the frigid arctic sea, a thief escaping from the caldera palace on Olympos Mons, a merchant captain sailing along the strange methane coastlines of Titan, and a hundred others. The more you won the stronger your persona grew. And in this realm that meant prestige and power.

The downside was having memories and experiences taken away. It was a gruesome feeling, tolerable for more powerful angels, but the majority ran the risk of permanent psychosis. He wondered how many of the patrons here tonight had suffered irreversible losses.

He turned his attention back to Jai. The lanky seraph's winning streak continued to the delighted cheers of Melody, Keye and a crowd of lesser angels that had gathered around, their curiosity overcoming their fear of the seraphs.

Spain watched their smiling faces. He knew how fleeting the euphoria could be. He also knew there were other games, more dangerous by far, that might give him back his sense of purpose. But if he lost . . .

"Quit while you're ahead, Jai," Keye suggested.

Jai ignored him and ran the numbers again, but after a while he stopped winning and the crowd soon broke up. Beads of sweat dotted his brow, and he kept glancing anxiously at his companions.

"Give it a rest," Keye said.

"I can't, I'm in too deep. I need to win some back." Jai looked sick, if that were possible. "You've gotta help me."

Keye took a step back. "Uh-uh. My luck ran out a long time ago."

Jai looked imploringly at Melody.

"I'm not a player," she said. It was the truth.

Spain leant forward and placed an olive-skinned hand over Jai's skeletal fingers, locking the youth in a grim stare. "You had better be worth saving."

The keeper's eyes brightened in anticipation. "Good to see you again, Spain." The serpents swirled about her body, nipping at each other.

He ran the numbers in his mind then placed a stack of chips on red. His bet would more than cover Jai's losses.

The wheel spun. It was too late to think about the consequences. A murmur spread across the room that Spain was in the game and the crowd gathered back around. Some urged the seraphs on whilst others revealed their true feelings, now eager to see the seraphs defeated once and for all.

The ball clacked away to a captivated audience. Jai couldn't help himself and jumped up and down, urging the ball to land on red. After what seemed an eternity, the ball landed in a red slot. The room erupted with noise and Jai danced about like a lunatic. The keeper looked disgusted as the red serpent engulfed the black serpent's head in its salivating jaws. She pushed a stack of chips across the table.

Jai ambled guiltily across to Spain. "Hey, thanks. I'm sorry I put you on the spot like that."

Spain shook his head. "You didn't, I did."

The keeper smiled ruefully. "Maybe next time, eh Spain?"

"Not a chance," he said as he walked out into the night. Spain looked back through the entrance and saw the keeper glaring at Jai as he followed the others out.

The breeze had died down and a cloud bank descended over the city, reflecting the orange glow of the streetlights. The jumble of minarets, towers and buildings sprawled across the hills and terraces became ghost-like silhouettes and then disappeared. The seraphs made their way to the end of the boulevard where it branched out into a maze of winding streets and alleyways.

Keye looked knowingly at Melody, then at Spain. "Why run the numbers with the machine god?"

Spain's brow furrowed as he mulled over a reply. Eventually he said, "There has to be more to the afterlife than this." He waved his arms around at the gloomy city.

"We don't really have a choice," Keye said thoughtfully, smoothing out his white goatee.

"But that's just it," Spain said, "We do have a choice."

"What do you mean?" Melody asked. "This existence is our choice, state-of-the-art."

"The best that money could buy," Spain said ironically. "Okay, so we all had the means to get seraph-class personas—rich brats shedding mortal coils. But did you ever think it would be like this?"

"Until at length old Saturn lifted up his faded eyes, and saw his kingdom gone and all the gloom and sorrow of the place," Keye quoted, trusting that Spain's mood had lifted. Then he added,

"You've been here longer than we have, you're established. You operate at a level most of us will never reach. I thought you might be more content."

"You're right, I have achieved a lot and I'm not going to throw it all away in a rush, but I'm changing. I have to try this."

"You risk everything," Melody interjected, starting up where she had left off earlier. "The Deus is capricious and cruel and could deconstruct you into a ghost or disperse you across the city. Or, worse still, he could enslave you forever just for the hell of it."

"Wait a second," Jai said, suddenly realising their location. They had reached the end of a gloomy cul de sac lined with dark, quiet buildings. A set of stairs receded into the fog along a tree dotted hillside, each stone worn with age. "I don't believe this, you're not joking."

Spain let out a sharp breath. Jai epitomised the travesty of this immortality. That people would choose to have their personalities burnt from their skulls to live like this. At least Spain had died of natural causes.

"It's time," he said. "I've had enough of talk."

Melody pleaded now, pulling at his cloak. "It's too dangerous. The seraphs that do make it back are never the same."

"I'm over it, Melody, the boulevard, the city. I'll take my chances. This has to lead to something better."

"But you don't know that for sure, Spain. You don't know if it's true."

"Do you think I could exist, always wondering what might have been, when I know I've got the ability to try this?"

Her grip loosened.

Spain put one foot on the first step. "Do you want to come with me?" he asked, knowing full well the response.

Jai shuffled uncomfortably, looking at his boots. Keye shook his head. In a surge of emotion, Melody made to follow, but then backed down. All the rumours about Deus ex Machina, the machine god, were too much right now. Despite her feelings for Spain, she couldn't bring herself to do it. She touched him on the cheek then let her hand drop by her side.

"I thought as much," Spain snapped, striding up the stairs two at a time. "I'll see you in the morning." His voice seemed to linger on the air like the fading qualia of the storm, a disturbing resonance more felt in the mind than heard. His receding figure eventually merged with the mist.

The seraphs stood for a time at the base of the stairs like quiet apparitions, each lost in their own thoughts. Spain's absence suddenly seemed like a great chasm between them. They made their farewells and dissipated into the night, as seraphs do, to the refuge of their homes.

They never saw Spain again.

The path meandered through dense bracken and gorse across the hillside. A straight path would have been too much to ask for, Spain thought. This gave time for reflection, but now it seemed that it was unnecessarily twisted, as if he were being mocked. But he did not deviate, knowing that a step from the way would only lead back to the start.

After a time it felt like he carried the burden of all those before him—apprehensive footfalls, arrogant strides, staccato steps. His footsteps were somehow a mix of all these, eroding a little more away from the stones. He couldn't shrug the feeling that his decision was too brash despite the long months of contemplation.

He wondered whether his friends would last as long as he had. They were young and impatient—you had to be tenacious to exist in the domain. It wasn't hell, but it surely wasn't heaven either. He could only guess at the technological evolution that had brought it to this point, a synthetic limbo with the characteristics of both afterlives.

Eventually, the path levelled out with the gaps between the stones growing longer until he reached the hilltop. He heard chiming fading in and out, the pitch dulled by damp air. The sound eventually stopped to be replaced by footsteps.

A boy with unkempt black hair emerged from the fog, dressed in a tattered old jumper and trousers. He sniffed and wiped a grubby hand across his face. Spain caught the terrible sight of black eyes swirling with platinum streaks. The brooding intelligence beneath those orbs made Spain shiver inside. It was like looking out over a stormy ocean about to engulf him in its uncaring tides.

Spain gathered his courage, matching the boy's gaze. "So you're the Deus?"

The boy stared, unblinking. "Spirited fucker, aren't you?" the boy said. He reached into his pocket and pulled out a pair of shiny black dice with luminescent white spots, then knelt down and brushed out a flat spot in the dirt. "You know the rules."

Spain knelt down with a mixed feeling of irony and finality. All his years in the domain, his very existence, came down to this. He would need all his skills now.

"What's the game?"

"Twenty-one." The boy shook the dice in his cupped hands.

"And if I win?"

"Be careful what you wish for," the boy said mysteriously and rolled the dice. Two and six. He picked them up and went through the same practiced motion, all the while keeping eye contact with Spain. Three and four.

The boy pushed one die aside. "That's fifteen." He picked up the other die and raised his cupped hands to his mouth and blew. "What do you think, six?"

Spain shrugged, still unsettled by the aura of corruption around the boy.

The dice rolled. Four.

"Nineteen. Beat that, seraph. Or die trying."

Spain scooped up the dice and threw. A pair of twos. And again. Six and five. He pushed one die aside, arching an eyebrow at the boy.

"No chance," the boy said in a flat tone.

Spain threw the single die. Two.

He groaned, shuffling uncomfortably on his knees. For the first time he realised the significance of the loss he might suffer—the camaraderie of his friends, his free will to come and go, the power and reputation of a seraph.

"Having second thoughts?" the boy laughed.

Spain focussed and ran the numbers. Three or four to win. Five or six, lose. One or two kept him in the game, but reduced the odds of winning.

He threw the die. One.

Damn. He pounded his fist on the ground.

"Eighteen," the boy said. "Not bad, but no win. It's your choice, seraph." The platinum streaks flared. Spain felt the raw power of the machine god now, hovering over his head like a crude iron blade.

Two or three to win. Four, five or six, lose. One to stay in the game.

Spain threw the dice. He caught every detail as it rolled through the air, the contrasts of its glowing spots and glossy black surfaces, the thud of its impact, the grains of dirt kicking up as it rolled to a stop. Three.

Spain let out an explosive breath.

The boy retrieved both dice and said, "Must be your lucky night." He stood and walked back into the fog. Spain followed.

The boy leant against a tree. Spain doubted that even Keye could think of an appropriate recital. It was a thing of contradiction—of pure beauty and horror. Twisted mottled limbs stabbed upwards, scratching the night as if in constant torment. Yet at the tip of each spiny branch something crystalline bobbed, like glittering diamond tears the size of his palm. They were pure like the spring waters of some secret mountain pool. They wrenched at his soul, making his heart yearn for the warm experiences unique to corporeal life. How could anything so radiant come from something so grotesque?

The tears chimed in a breeze that stirred the fog in hypnotic patterns. The sound was full of sadness and hope, as if all of Spain's emotions had been captured in a single harmony. With a resolution that surprised him, he stepped up to the tree and reached through the lethal spines. A tear came away easily and he clutched it carefully for fear it might break.

He opened his hand. The tear vibrated in tune with his internal hopes and fears. Memories welled up from some remote place. As a boy he had always been full of energy and fiercely independent. He would see things through, and didn't like his concentration being disturbed. As a young man these traits matured into a sharp thoughtfulness and fiery tenacity. It was what people admired in him most—his stability, perseverance and ability to view things differently.

But his life had been cut short and the translation into the domain moments after his death had etched his soul into an afterlife of sorts. The deep structures of his former personality—his character—had been copied into the domain. Now he realised why he had spent so long here. His character still carried ugly traits—arrogance, vanity and intolerance. They were like great anchors holding him back all this time.

Looking upon the tear, Spain knew that it all came down to a conviction in oneself. This belief gave rise to choice, and choice was the trigger that determined his destiny, that had made him who he was now, both good and bad.

"*Ethos anthropoi daimon*. The character of man is his guardian spirit." He recited the word from Heraclitus. He had, in fact, listened to Keye over the years. Spain crushed the tear in his hand. It did not shatter or break, but seemed to evaporate like the strange gusts of a qualia storm.

A shock went through his persona then, restoring every hollow fibre of his being into life again as if, for the first time in a very long age, he remembered what it was truly like to live, feel and breathe.

For him, it was like dying all over again.

Spain wondered what Melody, Jai and Keye had got up to during the night. Their voices, still distant as if from another room, had disturbed his slumber. He was tired and did not have the energy to open his eyes. He recalled the events from the previous night and felt guilty for leaving them like that. At least his headache had cleared.

The voices became louder, cascading into clarity.

"Is the loop complete?" The voice was female. Spain became alarmed as he realised it was not Melody.

"In a few seconds." The other voice was male.

"He is very . . . passionate looking."

"If you say so."

"Did he . . . ?"

"No. He died of natural causes before the Wayward Age."

"That's a relief."

"Indeed. Ah, here he is."

Spain snapped his eyes open, blinking rapidly at the brightness. "What the hell is going on?" He reeled with vertigo as his vision cleared. He was standing in a transparent dome-shaped room. Rolling foothills like a wrinkled green blanket lay several thousand metres below, leading to a chain of snow-capped mountains receding to the north. The sun burned low in the sky, casting long shadows.

As if sensing his predicament, the floor became opaque. The sudden change felt like someone had caught him from a terrible fall. It was a sensation of relief and dread all tangled together.

Spain's gaze turned upwards. Impossibly tall spires loomed overhead, greater than any city he could recall, trimmed in copper and obsidian. Orange cirrus clouds clung like pennants to the tallest of the magnificent towers.

"Welcome." The man and woman standing before Spain spoke in unison. They were dressed in blue skin suits, their perfect features framed with thick strands of dark metallic hair. Their eyes held a strange chromatic look, constantly shifting like oil on water.

"Where am I?"

"Earth," Cairine said.

He somehow knew her name, and the name of her companion who was about to speak . . . Fleet. "You died six hundred years ago, Spain. We eventually found a way to interface our technology with the old artificial intelligence that runs the domain—your machine god. The tears are programs designed to transition a persona out. We call them the Devil's Tears—one for each soul saved from purgatory."

He suddenly felt sick again, then the room flickered as other images and experiences seeped into his mind . . .

. . . Cairine's skin was smooth as silk, the captivating whorls and curlicues tattooed on her right thigh drew his attention like a rushing tide. He recognised every fleck of colour in those beautiful rainbow irises. Warmth rose up her navel, and now somehow they were one and the same, her hands—his hands—roamed luxuriously, tracing every curve in anticipation . . . . . . the room re-appeared, leaving him breathless and disoriented. He put one foot forward to steady himself.

Cairine smiled at his confusion. "It is always a pleasure to have angels walk among us."

His mind was spinning. He looked down at his hands as if he didn't trust his own eyes. The room spun . . . . . . the amphitheatre roared with noise, the stands decorated with obscene graffiti. Fleet—Spain—crouched in a fighting stance, muscles like corded steel, with a barbed blade in his hand. His opponent slithered into the arena to wild cheers. Dead reptilian eyes latched onto him. A guttural hiss belched from its mouth and in the next instant the half-man, half-snake was rearing over Spain, striking with fangs the size of daggers . . . . . . the transition back to reality felt like a hammer blow. Spain held a hand to his head, flushed with exertion, a bleak sense of foreboding hovering at the back of his mind. "What are these experiences?"

Cairine was still smiling. "You played in the domain for others' experiences, did you not?"

"Yes."

"Well, it's a lot better in the real world," she explained. "The sensory input of the external world, and our internal qualia, were fed into your persona stored in our networked implants." She touched the tip of her chrome-nailed finger to her forehead. Spain felt the slight pressure of her finger as if it were his own. "You can interact with anyone, be anyone. Your response to the world is projected back through us. It allows us to interact and interface with you, or be you. We call it a virtual loop."

Spain gave a sceptical look. "You're telling me anyone can access my experiences?"

"Yes and vice versa."

"And what if I choose not to be involved? In the domain, the choice was mine. If I didn't want to experience someone else, or risk my own experiences, then I simply didn't play."

Cairine's eyes wandered over him ravenously. "Yes, but with our technology you can experience more than you've ever dreamed."

"Unlike the domain, you're not risking anything," Fleet added. "And besides which, you are in our world now. It only seems fair that you abide by our rules."

Character is fate.

The epiphany taunted, with all its unwanted truths and false hopes.

Spain suppressed an urge to scream. He felt exhausted, unable yet to rest his troubled soul. He looked defiantly at his 'saviours', his old tenacity rallying as he voiced his dark thoughts. "So that's it then? Instead of living under the rule of one psychopath, I'm now at the whim of fucking millions."

"Come on, Spain," Cairine chided. "Everyone who makes it out of the domain adjusts in time. Think of it as a new game with different rules."

"How comforting," Spain said sarcastically. He looked around, spotting a way out of the room. "I take it you can't hold me here?"

Cairine cast a venomous look at him. "No, this is not a prison. But why don't you stay for awhile, we can talk things over, help you adjust."

"No thanks, I'll take my chances out there."

He walked past them, ignoring their protests. Twilight filtered in from the west across the floating city. Lights flickered along the surreal towers. The air was cold but refreshing and soon cleared his head of fatigue, yet couldn't wash away the dread and anger that filled his mind like poison.

Spain drew his cloak closer, watching the mass of strange people go about the city. Their thirst for new indulgences was palpable. He cursed himself, knowing deep down he hadn't really changed at all. The words of his friends tormented him, but there was nothing more to it.

He took a deep breath and strode arrogantly into the crowd.

AFTERWORD TO "ETHOS ANTHROPOI DAIMON"

The Greek philosopher, Heraclitus, was the first to say that the character of man is his fate—ethos anthropoi daimon. *The contemporary psychologist and philosopher, James Hillman (d.2011), wrote am inspiring book called* The Soul's Code *that delved into the nature of human character and asked where it comes from and what happens to it when we grow up. I agree with Hillman's worldview: our calling is the realisation of our true selves—our personality or character. Our purpose in life is to become who we are meant to be.*

This idea of "character is fate" is central to this collection and a key influence for this gothic, post-human story. Spain is one of my favourite protagonists, though he's not everyone's cup of tea—a kind of nastier version of Antonio Banderas! I think he epitomises how some men like to think they are being different, but in the end some things are inescapable—a bad character means bad karma.

HOLLOW PLACES

"Can we can talk for a while, David?"

"Sure, Mum."

"We didn't get to talk much last time."

"I know. I'm sorry."

"Don't be sorry." She hooks her arm through his and holds on tight. "Maybe we should walk, that might help."

There's not much daylight left. Mist lingers around the gargoyles atop the old stone buildings, drifting in languid spirals to the cobbled streets. Ornate, horse-drawn carriages clatter up to the sidewalk to pick up women in colourful bell-shaped dresses and men in tailored suits and top hats. The carriage doors close, the drivers crack whips, and soon the bustle of the Victorian era is replaced by a hushed stillness as the mist thickens in coils over the city.

"What are you doing, Mary Ellen?" She catches herself in mid-thought, tries to push aside the images from the classic novels she had read recently, but the cloud seems sluggish today.

Or maybe it's just her. She concentrates until all she can hear is her footsteps on the cobbles and David's youthful, erratic movements beside her. Another sound emerges as she listens more intently. It's elusive at first, but grows in tempo like a troubled thing with clipped wings—her heart.

She looks around the empty streets. Some anachronistic features filter in: modern light posts, a neon sign in one shop window, a maroon VT Holden parked in an alley full of shadows.

She sighs. There are too many fragments and not enough structure. It's just not coming together for her today.

The roar of a school bus makes her jump.

She realises David is watching her.

"It's such a gloomy place," he says. "And old-fashioned. Do we have to meet here?"

He's leggy for an 11 year-old. Hair all unkempt, but she stops herself from reaching out and combing it with her fingers. Freckles like hers. And in the depths of his brown irises, there is the warmth and mystery of a young soul. And in the complex motes and flecks of olive-green that seem to float above the brown, there are the possibilities of *all* the futures that might be.

"Mum?"

"What . . . "

"Do we have to meet here?"

"It's just . . . well, it's important to me."

"What? This boring place?"

"No. I mean, yes, it's important that we have a place to meet. But I'm sorry that it's dull for you, David."

"Random, more like."

He lets go of her arm and kicks a small pebble along the street. Catches up with it. Kicks it again.

She starts to worry about him scuffing his shoes, or tripping over and scraping his knees. "I need this," she says, more to herself, but the words come out as a whisper in the stillness.

"No, Mum. You don't."

"Okay, so I *want* this . . . it helps."

"But it doesn't help me."

She stops in her tracks, thunderstruck. After all their meetings, it had never occurred to her. Not once. She looks away, unable to meet his eyes. They had a terrible way of seeing through her, that cut-straight-to-it innocence, untainted by the petrified layers of adult reasoning. She doesn't want to be unravelled right now, though she knows deep down it *will* happen.

"I'm sorry. It sounds incredibly selfish, but I hadn't considered how you might feel about all this."

He laughs. "Well, duh."

A pleading look washes over her face.

"Don't beat yourself up about it." He kicks the pebble again. As he catches up he doesn't kick it, but instead turns to face her. The diffuse light casts him into silhouette, the mist a nimbus all around. "So, what do you want to talk about?"

Her eyelids flutter nervously.

He lifts up his arms in exasperation. "Come on, Mum. First you don't think about me, now you're worried that you might upset me."

She shrugs, at a loss to what to say.

He makes a kung fu stance, arms and legs a blur as he kicks and flips some imaginary opponent. Then he quickly pretends he *is* the opponent on the receiving end, bending over, clutching at his groin, a look of agony on his scrunched up face.

All of a sudden he straightens up again and smiles. "I'm tougher than you think."

She laughs out loud then clamps a hand over her mouth. Wow, that was strange, she thinks. Not so much the sound, but the raw physicality of it—laughter, the great usurper stealing away her misery, if but for a moment.

She smiles at him. "Okay, then. Are you feeling any different?"

He shrugs his shoulders. "What do you mean?"

She draws a deep breath. The line of questioning always starts here. "Have your memories changed? Are some stronger than others?"

"You can be confusing, do you know that?" His brow furrows in concentration. "I don't know."

"Come on, David. Think. Do you remember last year's athletics carnival?"

He smiles, pumping his arms and running on the spot. "Yeah, I got a bronze medal! And a PB in the 100 metres. 13.9 seconds, how cool."

"Fantastic. But are there some things you can't remember? Like your first birthday, for example."

"That's a dumb question."

"No, it's not." Her face brightens, expectant. "So?"

"I can remember just about everything since the day I was born."

Her shoulders slump. "So you can even recall *when* you were born?"

"Before that. I know how you felt when you had oo-la-la with Dad. Yuk, that's kind of gross, Mum. Should I know all that? I mean I know all about it from sex ed and everything. But I don't think I should know what it *feels* like. I don't think my friends know that much about their parents."

She blushes and makes a mental note to request more adjustments to the cloud algorithms.

"*Yeah*," David nods. "It's wrong on *so* many levels."

She pushes on, grasping for some sign. "So, there aren't any gaps at all?"

"Not really." He looks back towards the alleyway. "Is that a new car? Did you buy it?"

"Forget the car. Do some memories feel more like yours than mine? Do they feel *right*?"

He folds his arms, an eyebrow arching slightly, and looks at her in a way that only he can, that is so much a mirror-image of his father. "You've got to stop this."

That sparks an irrational anger, a raw wound that still hurts like hell even now, one year after the divorce. She shakes her head vigorously. "No, no, no, David. No. We can't give in yet."

"It's not getting us anywhere." He places his hand on the corner of a building and presses hard until the old brickwork bends inward like a sponge. "Maybe in, you know, a *hundred years* when the technology gets better." He looks at her, holds her gaze for seconds that seem to drag out forever, the whole situation growing more and more surreal, like a Salvador Dali painting.

"Maybe," she says, knowing that it has nothing to do with the technology. Her anger diffuses away like a distant mirage. Wiping tears from her face, she says, "They're my thoughts, my feelings—long-term memory and hypothalamus response."

"Yeah, it's cool, like science fiction." He smiles. "I get it . . . but it's not me, is it?"

"No."

"I shouldn't know all the things I do. You're my entire world, Mum. It's not me."

"Oh, David."

It's disturbing how she can shroud herself like this. So many layers, such a vast repertoire at her convenience—denial, regret, longing. And what's more disturbing is how easily they wrap around her as if they have a life of their own, projections of her psyche, tiny microcosms of her humanity that know what to say and when. How else to sustain her sanity for so long? But the alternative . . . she peeks through a gap in the layers to the petrifying emptiness at her core.

"I'm trying, I really am." She grits her teeth. Now: sheer, bloody-minded stubbornness. "I'll keep looking."

"There's nothing left to find."

She covers her mouth with one hand. Tears stream over her fingers, drip onto the cobbles with a faint pitter-patter.

He walks over and gives her a hug. "People die in accidents every day," he says, as if he's an authority on the subject. "You've got to let me go."

Her words come out incoherent, a splutter between her fingers.

He punches her softly on the arm then sprints on up the street. "Race you."

The jolt breaks her train of thought. She feels the surge of adrenalin, muscles twinge, legs kick into action and now she's racing after him. She weaves around the buildings, her hands clutching at him but missing each time, until finally she has to slow down and place her hands on her knees, her breath all ragged.

She turns her head at the sound of the school bus somewhere behind the buildings.

The thump of his runners on the cobbles grows faint.

"Love you, Mum."

He's still running like he always used to. He was never still, not for a moment—always running.

"David!"

"It's okay. I'll be fine."

She cranes her neck, watching his outline bleed away. "I love you too, kiddo."

His image disappears, the buildings melt away . . . replaced by the blank walls of the hospital room.

She leans over his bed, slides her fingers gently beneath his hair, conscious of the lumpy suture scars along his cranium. She pulls the cable from the neural jack behind his left ear. Reaches up behind her ear and pulls her end of the cable free. Loops the cable together around her fingers then places it carefully on the bedside table.

The same ritual.

Three years.

His chest rises.

Falls.

Hiss of air, a faint mechanical sound behind the bed.

The lights on the life-support monitor look bleary in the pallid light. The ECG still reads zero brain activity.

She flicks on the bedside lamp and checks the interface reports on her tablet. The world-constructs are unstable today—*random*. It's partly her nerves, partly the limitations of the interface: a modified cochlear implant connected to a small probe inserted in his lobes. The personas of David are built using algorithms designed in Leningrad, extracted from her memories and stored and analysed somewhere in the processing arrays in Hyderabad or Zhengzhou. She could use a hundred different gaming personas, but the doctors said it was best to use her own memories as a foundation, even though it's more expensive.

The car is always there, no matter what world-construct she uses. It can't be erased, but there's no real detail anyway. All she remembers from that day was a maroon VT Holden speeding away from David as he got off the school bus and ran across the road to meet her.

Rises.

She combs his hair to one side with her fingers.

Falls.

There have been cases where the algorithms have helped patients' minds to reconstitute, drawing out personality, stimulating new activity. Like grafting, gradually replacing the artificial persona with the patient's real mind. And in some cases the patients have revived physically—though all have needed some form of aid implants to facilitate motor functions. She's had the conversations with the doctors so many times that it all seems like a fading mantra now.

She sits on the bed close to him.

Rises.

Places her left hand on his chest.

Falls.

He's warm beneath.

Her attention turns to the life-support switch: round and chrome, a star-like reflection of light in the upper right quadrant, ghostly images of the room stretched across its surface. She leans down, sees her mirror image, distorted. Looks at it from different angles, but whichever way, it's the same haggard face looking back. All the possibilities are narrowing down now, all the futures merging into one, stark reality.

She feels the shroud unravel around her emptiness. Her free hand trembles as she reaches out for the switch, grasping for the courage she needs to fill those hollow places.

AFTERWORD TO "HOLLOW PLACES"

As a father of a healthy boy, I went to a dark place to write this story.

There's nothing particularly new about technology augmentation, but the whole notion that it would be used to such extreme kind of scares me, because I really don't know where I would stop if I were in the same situation as Mary Ellen.

Plus I liked the idea that cloud computing technology becomes so ubiquitous that it is the obvious choice to find the right algorithms and storage capacity to augment, or try to bring back, a human mind.

HEAVEN AND EARTH

The neutron star filled the prison cell with bands of crimson light and long shadows.

Daniel woke and pressed his palms against the diamond wall. Were he able to reach out, his hands would be crushed into kilometre long filaments by the intense gravitational field. He had never contemplated death, but the instant destruction that lay just beyond his fingertips now beckoned him, filling his mind with a disturbing sadness.

It is forbidden to love humans . . . of any kind.

Varden haunted him still, an unwelcome ghost in this lonely hell.

Daniel had ignored his father and the collective opinion of the Carvers at his own peril. His voice was one against a million.

We were human once. We still are.

We left humanity a long time ago.

The hypocrisy of the collective was palpable: deny your heritage, pretend you are different, and live the *new* values, untouchable. Bigotry was alive and kicking, rebadged and repackaged for a smart but gullible generation.

Not that long ago, father.

Time makes all the difference, Daniel. You will learn that eventually.

Varden had sealed the diamond cell then with a glyph, dipped it into the exotic matter furnaces, and shunted it on a secret trajectory into the galaxy.

Daniel's thoughts drifted. The residue of the collective clung to his mind like a phantom limb, a collage of random memories. As the pain of disconnection grew weaker each year, so his hatred and anger grew stronger, building into a crescendo of rage. A mournful sound ripped out of his lungs and he cursed the crimson sky. He slammed his fists against the wall, splitting his knuckles open and spattering blood across his black skinsuit, until he slumped to the floor, exhausted.

He closed his eyes and dreamt of Idona walking ahead of him along the beaches of the Mirha Sea. He called to her, but his voice was drowned out by the roar of the surf, then he tried to catch her, but with each step she receded further into the distance.

Further still.

And further.

He fell to his knees and pounded his fists into the coarse grey sand, the surf now swelling as a storm loomed in over the cape. Flashes of lightning stuttered across the horizon and rain plastered his dark hair across his face, pouring off his chin in curling rivulets. He lifted his hands to the faltering light, saw them drenched in blood, realised that it was raining blood. His scream rose above the storm—

He opened his eyes. His face was pressed close to the wall. A haggard reflection looked back, the flecks in its hazel eyes like embers. Afraid of his image, and the insanity it might bring if he engaged it in conversation, he stood up and began pacing around the cell.

He had left her there on the beach that day. Ever since he stepped through the door, the Casimir booster blinking shut in his wake, he had wondered what she thought of him, what had gone through her mind in the intervening years? Did she blame herself for his absence? Or did she hate him now?

And then the terrifying reality resurfaced again. The cell had been shunted using technologies even the Carvers were uncomfortable with. In all likelihood Idona had died years ago.

With a deliberate force of will he rallied his thoughts and shoved away the despair from his mind, unwilling yet to give in, even if it meant clinging to her memory. She was his shield to stave off the madness that crept closer with each relentless orbit. He wrapped his arms across his chest and cherished her love that sheltered him more with each passing year.

Time does make all the difference.

KARDASHEV I SPACE

A splash distorted the Mirha Sea into shards of black and electric blue.

Idona surged through the water, singing to her cousins in the distant depths. It was a complex lament of tweets and twitters. The reply came after a time: a series of whines and squawks interspersed with higher pitched whistles.

Do not despair, hope is destiny.

She smiled and sent a message of thanks then swam to the shore and stood naked under the starlight. Water sluiced from her mottled grey skin and drops rained from her hair as she blew out excess water through her fluted nasal cavity.

"How long do you think you can go on like this?"

Idona whirled around.

"As long as I wish, Ilara." With a subliminal nod and twitch Idona pleaded with her sister to be left alone.

"I only worry about you." Ilara stepped out of the surf and rubbed her cheek against Idona's.

Idona returned the gesture. She wondered how many times they had had this same conversation.

"You love stricken fool," Ilara said. "You know the divide between humans and the collective cannot be crossed."

"Do you really believe that? Of all the people, Ilara, how could you be so sanctimonious? *We* wouldn't exist if boundaries hadn't been crossed. We couldn't *live* here if boundaries hadn't been smashed."

"That's not my point."

"Then what is your point? We fell in love, is that so hard to accept? Through sheer passion he transformed a barren planet into a world for us all to live."

"But that's just it, Idona. The scale of it all, it's incomprehensible. Who does that for someone else? It's not . . . natural."

"Please go," Idona said, turning her back and stepping into the water. She looked defiantly over her shoulder. "I *will* find him." With one fluid motion she plunged into the sea.

"And what if you can't?" Ilara called. "What will you do then?"

Idona swam away into the darkness, trying to shut out Ilara's last words. She had never felt so alone, stuck in a limbo of inaction. She would have to move on at some point, somehow. But what could she do when she knew deep down she would never get over Daniel? Her confidence had grown with him, but the void he left felt like an open wound that would never heal. And each day that passed chipped away at the new Idona until the insecurities surfaced again, aspects of her old self she hated so much—the self-destructive traits of a crossgen.

It was well past midnight by the time she returned to the shore, and much to her relief, Ilara had gone. She walked to the base of the headland then up the meandering path to the cliff top.

She squinted as the lights came on. The house was open and uncluttered, with large balconies and windows that let in blocks of light and the salt tang of the sea. She went upstairs to the bedroom and sat down on the bed, her fingers absently tracing the patterns on the cover.

They made love again, in the bed. He was more confident this time, away from the water. She wondered at that as they lay together in the breathless aftermath, long limbs stretched out over the sheets, the last rays of Alcyone casting a blue-white pall across the ceiling. Pleione, Asterope and Electra were also fading to twilight as the nightshade slid across the sky.

"New home with uninterrupted views," he said.

"There I was saying I wouldn't take this for granted, and now you're talking like it's just a piece of real estate. It is a miracle."

A smile edged onto his face, then broadened into a grin. "If you insist."

"I do. You've done so much. It's incredible beyond words."

"I know. I'm tired."

"Now you're just teasing."

He shrugged.

In the months they had been together he had not shown any sign of vulnerability, until today. It was taking time for him to let his guard down, but she was patient. Their lives were different in so many ways she could not even begin to describe.

She turned on her side to face him. "What is it about the water that makes you uncomfortable?"

"It reminds me of home."

"When I swim I give myself to the sea. It's kind of hard to explain, you know the power of it can crush you, yet to be free you have to give yourself to it."

A frown clouded his face. "If only I could. A sea has a purpose—it is part of an ecosystem, part of something greater. The collective? Well . . . "

"Are they really that insular?"

"The Carvers and the other families, except perhaps the Kimuras, were not ready. They left the colonies for a reason, but they brought with them the very thing that they wished left behind."

She knew what it was, had suffered the brunt of bigotry all her life. "I'll watch out for you," she said, not quite sure how she could ever keep such a promise.

His face brightened. "Yes, I've noticed you watch me day and night." There was mischief in his eyes now.

"What do you mean?"

"You fell asleep on me in the dunes, it was quite disconcerting."

She raised a hand to her mouth. "I'm so sorry. I can't help it. I'm a conscious breather. I can't sleep the same way normal humans sleep. Keeping one eye open . . . it's a survival thing . . . "

"Oh, right," he said with a straight face that lasted all of two seconds.

She thumped him on the chest.

He reached over and grabbed her gently.

She bunched her fists into the bed cover. Her life always seemed to carry some fatal flaw, some random self-destruct switch. She pulled the cover off and hurled it across the room.

She went to the bathroom and rinsed away the salt and grit in the shower then put on a loose bathrobe and, out of habit, opened the study door. The books stacked across the shelves were covered in an unhealthy layer of dust and the curtains hung like limp rags. Her eyes inevitably strayed to the alcove, the only place in the room free from dust. The com-sphere sat there, its dull surface turning to quicksilver as she approached. Aside from some clothes and books it was the only thing he had left behind. She picked it up then sat down in the reclining chair.

The com-sphere programs engaged, caressing her mind . . .

The waiting room was the same as always, a row of chairs beneath a mirror on the left wall, a locked door on the right wall, and a single window in front of her. She touched the glass of the window.

Beneath her lay a sprawling city of silver spires with fields of solar panels stretching out to the horizon. It was the middle of the day, the bright white light of Castor etching the metropolis into sharp relief. Crowds thronged the streets and caterpillar-like transporters filled the skies, streaming holo-ads for anti-aging treatments and news-bites of the latest riots. She turned her head, in no mood to watch the violence.

Catching her reflection in the mirror, she moved in front of it and checked the curves of her hips and breasts that were accentuated by the sleek indigo skinsuit. The com-sphere always dressed her this way—men and their programs. She brushed aside strands of hair and scrutinised her freckles. Her eyes, normally bright blue, were dull grey orbs with dark circles underneath. She tilted her head slightly, but the harsh starlight of this strange world wasn't complementary no matter which way she looked.

"Damn it."

She wondered what he ever saw in her with her nearly-human face and slightly elongated skull. She clenched her fists and let out a loud burst-pulse of sound.

"Who are you?"

She spun around. A man stood in front of her. He had entered through the door—the door that was always locked. Robes flowed about his angular form. Liquid chrome eyes scrutinised her from a granite face etched with veins of silver.

"Who the hell are you?"

"Forgive my intrusion," he said, nodding his head respectfully. "My name is Marshall."

"Is this a dream?"

"I don't think the com-spheres distinguish between waking and sleeping minds." He paused, a look of recognition across his rocky features. "You must be Idona of the Pleiades."

"You know me?"

"Yes, Daniel talked about—"

"Have you seen him? Do you know where he is? Why did he—"

"I'm sorry, Idona," he said softly, "but I have not seen Daniel in years. I thought he had taken the com-sphere with him, but I found it buried amongst some supplies only two weeks ago. Even then I would not have known what to do if you had not dialled in."

"Dialled in?" She let out a short, ironic breath. "I have tried for the last three years to work out how to use the com-sphere. I had suspected all along that this was the last number he had called and that the device simply redials when I'm close to it."

Marshall waved his arms about with a distracting flourish. "You should have seen him when he spoke of you. There was fire in his eyes, a pride that squared his shoulders."

She looked up at him, haunted.

"Believe it, Idona, for it was as real as I have seen. This man loved you."

She smiled through tears.

"Daniel's absence has been deeply felt by all geomorphs. We were part of a shadow biosphere that came under threat of extinction from toxic seepage. He relocated us here within the crystalline lattices beneath the tectonic plates. We use these simulacra to simplify the interaction with humans."

The sharp edges of a migraine began to stab at the back of her eyes. She had always thought that Daniel had helped the crossgens in some way to compensate for his problems at home. But she should have guessed that he had helped others—he was always on the move, able to live a hundred lives in her short lifetime. And through it all he still had time to be with her.

"Why?" She bit down on her lip. "Why does he do it?"

Marshall looked at her thoughtfully.

She felt the scrutiny of his strange eyes again. They didn't miss a beat.

"I know precious little more than you, Idona, so I'm not sure I can be of any real help."

Her face creased up in frustration. "I need to know what happened to him. He said that things had become extremely difficult. His use of the terra-quickening technology outside the collective had caused an immense outrage."

But she knew as well as Marshall that there was virtually no chance of any information filtering back. The riots were a sign of the hatred that still stirred in some parts of the colony worlds. It was a mindless call to trade cartels to open up the technology singularity for the benefit of everyone. But what could they do? Only the wealthiest families had had the means, and now they were gone, and they had taken their technology with them.

"Who knows what happens in heaven's jet stream," Marshall offered.

She looked sidelong at the geomorph. "How do I reach the collective?"

His liquid eyes widened in disbelief. "You cannot be serious. The Sagittarius Arm . . . it is too far."

The jumble of emotions that had plagued her for so long began clicking together, a pattern of intent tumbling into clarity.

"How do I get there?"

"It can't be done in our lifetime. There are cryo-ships, of course, but we'll never know."

"Then help me find a way."

"My dear—"

"We should try at least."

"Are you absolutely sure this is what you want?"

Her look said it all . . .

When Idona woke, the com-sphere still hummed quietly in her lap. She set it back in the alcove and it switched off.

A storm had passed during the night and the air smelt of damp earth and brine. Something about the sound of the surf made her step out on to the balcony. Figures were leaping out of the water far below, climbing across the shattered rocks at the base of the cliff. She saw Ilara calling up to her, the sound of her voice barely audible. Darius, Paran and Alcha stood next to Ilara. Then a pod of bulkier figures emerged from the water, bull-necked with the monochromatic skins of the *Orcinus orca* splice. She had not seen them in months, her seven cousins, and she wondered what the occasion was.

Then her dreams filtered through to her conscious mind, half-remembered. She must have called out to her family during the night. With a sigh and a full heart, she went downstairs to meet them.

KARDASHEV II SPACE

Autumn had arrived with all its colours.

Leaves tumbled in the northerly off the range, blowing down from the foothills into the river where they floated for kilometres out to the ocean. And with the winds came a chill that lingered on the air, a sign that snow would arrive early this year.

A herd of white tailed deer ran across the rough terrain, disturbed by some unseen predator. They darted here and there, fear written in every twitch, a limbic spark etched in their eyes.

A flash of spotted fur appeared . . . there . . . and there again. The snow leopard was at full stretch now, close to the back of the herd. Green eyes shone with intent as massive paws found purchase for one final leap. Time stood still . . . then the leopard stumbled, one paw sliding away from the rump of its small prize as its other paws lost traction on the slope. The deer fell, legs scrabbling, then stood up and sprang away at an angle not even the leopard could follow.

Idona let out a long breath. She leant back from the telescope, her pulse hammering.

"Next time, my friend."

The wind ruffled her white robes. Her head felt cold and she pulled her hood up. She had cut her hair shorter this year and now that the grey had completely grown through she decided that it suited her. Her freckles were less blotchy, her cheeks less drawn, or so she tried to convince herself.

She shivered again. It wasn't so much the physical cold as the chill inside her that had not shifted in all the years.

She looked up, distracted by the nightshade gliding down the crumpled geography of the ringworld. The other habitats, fragments and rings of the collective began to appear, a chaotic mega-structure of a thousand parts like jewels across the night sky. Each component had a function or purpose: ecologies, didactic havens, industrial asteroids, science platforms. And at its core—feeding off the energy of Herschel 36—the computing engines and infrastructure that housed the collective mind.

But when she thought her eyes could take no more, the backdrop of the Lagoon Nebula appeared. The veils of stardust were like slabs of onyx and rose quartz, highlighted with veins of grey and white, and spattered with plumes of darker dust and Bok globules.

"What a night."

She whirled, bumping the telescope on its tripod.

"Daniel?"

A figure emerged out of the shadows of the house and stepped onto the balcony. Nebula light caught the silhouette that she knew so well: high brow and cheekbones, wavy hair, broad shoulders and long legs, all wrapped in slim-fit black.

She stepped back until she reached the railing. The drop from the balcony to the valley below now made her head reel.

"No." It was her own voice, a whisper on the edge of her senses. She reached up and touched his face, felt the cool skin, an unfamiliar stubble and texture. Not Daniel.

She snatched her hand back, afraid that it might be Varden after all this time.

"I am not Varden," the stranger said.

"I don't suppose you are." Her old cynicism fell into place like a comforting mask. She had been a fool to ever think Varden would show himself.

"My name is Armand Carver."

Idona arched an eyebrow. "My last visitor was your cousin, Antoinette. She was as unhelpful as the rest of you, but at least she had the courtesy to knock."

Armand stood next to her and leant against the railing with a casual familiarity. "He's out there, somewhere."

Idona thought he meant Daniel then realised he was looking at the ranges. "Varden? Here?" She felt her throat constrict. A sickening feeling twisted in the pit of her stomach.

"He could be a river, a tree, your leopard friend. He could be many things. We become what we are meant to be—the calling of our nanotype. Our father made many mistakes, but try not to judge him, he was a pioneer and it was a long time ago."

Her jaw set in place. "It's my life—our life—taken from us. You, *all* of you out there with your oversized intellect, you've never known what to do with me, *have* you?"

"You will not see through the winter, Idona."

She clutched the railing. "So is that it? Does time somehow take you past your predicament, vindicate you in some way? How convenient. Why don't you just go away and leave me alone."

Those soul-wrenching hazel eyes never left hers. "You need to understand, Idona, by our standards it was a *long* time ago. Thirty generations have passed since Daniel was banished."

She frowned. The nightscape had changed over the years, growing and evolving in synch with some inner plan that she could only guess at. And how many more worlds like this were out there, strung like pearls along the Sagittarius Arm?

Who knows what happens in heaven's jet stream.

She waved her arms wide and leant dangerously out over the railing. "It's all nanotech, isn't it? The hills, the leaves, the animals, you . . . Daniel."

"Yes," Armand said with the same look of casual detachment.

She had felt so lonely on this alien shore, but now she realised how naive she could still be. The collective had been watching her all this time, calculating, recalibrating. They presided over her every move, her every thought. The periodic visits by the Carvers were testing her resolve, analysing her response and every nuance of speech and movement.

She hated herself now with an old, unwanted passion. So intent was she on her goal, on not losing the glimmer of Daniel, that she had not seen what was in front of her all along.

Armand reached out and touched her shoulder. "You're an enigma, Idona, the unplanned variable, so to speak. What audacity to travel here in your ramshackle cryo-ship using *our* booster network. But your single act of selflessness has helped us—"

"Change."

She went for a swim as Alcyone pushed away the night. The water was calm and she was content to float for a while, contemplating her good fortune and her growing love for the man sleeping still.

Stirred by a morning hunger, she caught a few fish and brought them back to the house. He was awake by the time she arrived and they cooked the fish and ate in a silence that had an intimacy all of its own.

"Will you stay today?" she eventually asked as they sat on the balcony and watched the tide.

"I'll have to leave soon, another day or so."

"Do you want to talk again?"

"About home?"

She nodded.

He let out a long breath. "I fear we are stuck in a rut, slowly destroying ourselves with our stubborn values. I can't see how we can ever become a true collective if we remain so self-absorbed."

"It's much harder to challenge," Idona offered, "particularly when nine out of ten people in the room are in agreement. It makes you doubt yourself, your own sanity. But I believe there's a reason for everything, Daniel, though it might not be clear right now. Your technology must be making some difference, surely?"

He laughed scornfully. "I'm sorry."

"That's okay."

"The way I see it, Moore's escalation is no different to biological evolution. They're both blind. So in answer to your question, I think it will take generations to sort out the mess we've made. Maybe we never will."

"I hope you're wrong."

"So do I."

Armand touched her shoulder. "I am truly sorry for what happened to Daniel. It has been an incredible struggle for us to evolve. We have been through resource wars, meme regulation, repression of civil liberties . . . it's a sad litany, but I believe we have turned a corner." He paused, squeezing her shoulder. "Join us, Idona."

She laughed.

Armand took a step back. "What is it?"

"You think with all the computing power at your disposal you could have worked it out sooner."

He smiled. "I'm sure that wisdom is inversely proportional to processing capacity."

"Well," she said. "What to do? Live in your world or die here, on the cusp of it all."

Armand shrugged.

She thumped him on the chest, caught now between laughing and crying. "Life and death choices are meant to be serious. And in any case, you know your presence here stacks the odds."

He gave a wry grin. So like . . .

She sucked in air through her teeth. "You have information."

He nodded. "We have heard rumours."

"Rumours?" Her shoulders sagged. "You mean you don't know where he is."

"The galaxy is . . . huge. Chatter has been intercepted along our com-channels."

"Intercepted? That can only mean that there are others out there."

"Of course—the technology singularity did not stop for some."

Idona leant heavily on the railing. "I'm not sure I can take this." She squared her shoulders. "Show me, before I change my mind."

"Very well," he said. "Although this will be the first time we have done this since the singularity."

"And that is supposed to inspire me, how?"

He smiled and opened his arms as if introducing a friend. "You said it yourself, Idona, the nanotech is all around. But it is passive, we need your permission."

Her heart lurched. "To do what?"

"Don't be alarmed. We must copy you to save you from your dying body, to give you a new home."

"Can you get rid of the old bits?"

He laughed. "Consider it done."

He reached out and held her by the arms. The sound of the wind died away and she shivered uncontrollably. The first touch of the collective was like the delicate shift in the currents of the Mirha Sea. It was a strange feeling, as if she had travelled a long way and returned home to find that the place had changed. Or maybe it was just not the way she remembered it.

She felt another surge of adrenalin as Armand let go of her.

"This is not farewell," he said. "It is welcome. Welcome to the collective."

She could sense more than see the nanotech coalescing in the air around her, but dared not move for fear she might regret her decision. Light began to shine into her eyes, down her optic nerve, into her brain, into her conscious mind. The light became a conflagration as the nanotech slid unseen through her body with an urgent, osmotic push. She tried to scream but it filled her mouth and she gagged as it closed up her oesophagus and she realised now the true implications of what it was doing to her—copying, erasing, re-creating.

So this was drowning—

It was the last sensation Idona had as a biological entity.

She awoke and vomited black bile. Her body was covered in strings of nano sludge that draped from her arms and legs. Armand caught her before she fell. This time she *saw* the eyes behind his, the minds behind his mind, reaching out, pulling her into depths she had never dared explore. She pushed Armand away and fell to the balcony floor.

You have to give yourself to it.

Her own words: but how? It was too much, too deep.

She teetered on the edge, resisting the terrifying vortex of the collective for as long as she could until it drew her in. It began to unravel her memories, experiences and subjective feelings—uploading, understanding, assimilating.

This time, she did scream.

KARDASHEV III SPACE

The probability-shunt emerged into space and then silently quantum tunnelled away.

Idona was flung into the bright void, her outer dermal layers adjusting rapidly to the vacuum and intense flux of photons and gamma radiation. She drifted for a time until she was able to snag a trajectory around a small, dead moon that had been ejected from the Core a billion years ago. At the lowest point in her descent she diverted precious energy and remoulded her shape to enter the thin atmosphere. She descended to the far side of the moon on kilometre long monolayer wings. As soon as she touched the radiation blasted soil, her nanochines began extracting molecules through the soles of her feet. She found shelter in the caldera of a dead volcano, withdrew her wings, ramped back down to stasis mode, and slept.

She dreamt of Daniel, an old man with weathered skin and a vacant look. He didn't recognise her as she waved to him. How could he? She caught sight of her face in a mirror. She looked grainy, like an old screen of broken pixels. She reached out and the mirror dissolved when she touched it.

Then her perspective shifted and she was looking down on herself curled into a foetal position, her face calm, her hands cupped together above her chest. There was a quiet about the night that she had not felt in a long time.

Antoinette, Michael, Rochelle, Armand—where are you?

She longed for the connections of the collective.

Their quest had finally been realised—to *be* others but not lose your individuality, for others to *be* her and share her inner thoughts. It was a true mass consciousness, unity and diversity hand in hand. And the collective had even started to share their technology with the Type I colonies.

If only Daniel had been able to experience it . . .

A shudder swept through her, small tremors building until she writhed in the grip of full seizure. Sweat dampened her glossy black hair and beaded on her face and limbs. Her breathing came in shallow, ragged gasps, each intake triggering more spasms. And then the nano-mitosis stopped, the sweat evaporated and the Idona of old bleached away into the moon's crust—lost forever.

The new Idona woke and thrashed in the dirt as the Core rose like a white lance. She rolled away and crawled under a rock ledge, to little effect. She booted up her optical nerve filters to stop the searing light, but it could not remove the agony of a lost incarnation.

You love stricken fool.

"Oh, Ilara, what have I done?" The sound seeped out into the thin air.

In time the pain subsided to leave an odd nausea and sluggishness, like mud sliding through her veins.

The Core blazed overhead for another four hours then set, but even the night was awash with light.

She did not have long here, depending on what useful molecules she could extract from the ground. There was a lot of iron, traces of heavier elements, but precious little carbon. She set a program running overnight and slept again. By the time she woke, an iron dome had extended over her. How could anything live in this nightmare? Maybe the Carvers had got it wrong or maybe the shunt had fallen short of its destination.

She thought of constructing a small light-sail ship from the moon's crust, but where would she go? She could spend a thousand years searching. She diverted some of her mass, and with a few raw materials from the soil she made a crude radio dish at the top of the caldera. An array of small lasers and masers followed. Finally, she configured a miniature solar array as a power source. She programmed a distress signal and sent it out on all frequencies. As an afterthought she constructed a billion homing nano-probes from the crust and hurled them out of the weak gravity well in all directions.

She programmed herself to come out of stasis every month—approximately every seven hundred moon revolutions.

After the first year, and to conserve energy, she reduced the wake up call to every six months.

After thirty thousand revolutions she woke up every year and cursed the gigantic black hole that scrolled across the sky, a hundred suns convulsing on its event horizon.

She surfaced about five metres out, stood up and flicked her hair away from her face, an arc of water trailing out like blue fire flies. She beckoned him with one hand.

He ploughed hip deep into the water and kissed her.

"You are in better spirits," Idona said.

"You got me thinking this morning."

"Oh, that's dangerous."

He nudged her with an elbow.

She urged him on. "Okay, don't go silent on me now, I won't tease you anymore."

"Fair enough," he said, holding her hand as they walked back to the beach. "I'm beginning to think there is no collective point."

"How so?"

"Evolution is too cyclic—conformity, diversity, then conformity again. And we're locked in without the means to lift ourselves out of it."

"It's only flawed if we throw reason out the door."

He looked at her. "But we have so much of that—logic, intelligence, mathematics."

She shook her head. "You're talking about global abstracts. I'm talking about the reasoning of the individual, the ability to tolerate others, to accept ourselves, to question the context we are born into. If we can change our paradigm, our ideas, then we give purpose to the evolutionary process. I say to hell with blind fate. We can lift ourselves above our basic programming; all it takes is a single act of faith."

He turned in his tracks to face her. "You're the strongest person I know, Idona. I love you."

She flung her arms around him, feeling now that some distances weren't so vast.

"We knew you would come."

Idona stirred and looked up at the apparition. It was human, female, stunningly beautiful, wrapped in a cloak of bubbling light like miniature solar flares, with green ellipses for eyes.

Idona felt a surge of emotions not her own—curiosity, admiration, hatred, ambivalence—all conveyed through some link, unlike any collective communication she had ever experienced. She squirmed as the link nudged around her optical filters, gently tapping into her mind.

"Who are you?"

The apparition floated closer. "Akashi Kimura."

"I am Idona."

"We know. Tunnelling so close to the Core was foolish, but you will surely die out here nonetheless."

"Do you hate me?' Idona was stunned by the contradictory emotions she felt through the link. "What have I done? I don't know you or your society, but you claim to know me."

Akashi laughed.

Idona felt a sudden, inexplicable irony. Her mind went further into the link until she arrived at the hive entity behind Akashi's strange eyes in a world that defied logic.

A silhouette formed against the permanent brightness of the Core, a network of light and interlaced photonic forms. They looked like kelp beds off the cape, but finessed down to incredibly small gossamer structures, spinning in concentric energy states— countless photonic worlds feeding off the radiance of the galactic core.

Idona floundered as the will of the entity drew her in like the sudden back surge of the tide before a tsunami. She had been known to the entity and its citizens for a hundred generations. Zeitgeists had risen and fallen in her name, generations had mulled over her plight and modelled and forecast the impact of her arrival. They had heard about what had happened to the collective and now they waited with baited breath. Some groups were welcoming her with open arms; others were ready to die before they let her in.

The air rushed out of her lungs. This ocean before her was too much to bear. She panicked and let out a burst-pulse. The entity withdrew, like a confusing dream that she wanted to remember and longed to forget.

Akashi looked down at Idona with regret—a thousand networked Akashi-incarnations backed that look, and twenty trillion individuals in the entity sighed for different reasons.

"Wait," Idona said, reaching up.

"You should know by now, Idona. We don't look back."

The link began to slough from her mind. "You are kidding, right?" Idona stood up and tried to grab Akashi by the ankle, but her hands passed through. "I've come all this way and now you're going to leave me?"

"You have been with us in spirit far longer than your physical form. But now we see you are just a person. Even we can succumb to myths."

Idona cancelled the dome and it turned to iron dust and sprinkled to the ground. The light of the Core slammed down on them. Akashi's photon matrix darkened. Idona shielded her eyes with her hands.

"If I'm really that much of a threat, then go" Idona said. "But before you make up your mind, you should get some perspective." She pointed to the Core. "You live next to *that*."

Akashi looked puzzled. "That is our energy source."

"Exactly. You live next to the most lethal astrophysical object in the galaxy and you call it home."

"But you represent change," Akashi said, "and we are undecided."

Idona gritted her teeth. "I get it, I really do. But if it's not me, it will be someone else, sooner rather than later. Someone will eventually be a catalyst for change, you cannot deny that. It will come to you all. I know there are others out there; more advanced than you even—Type IV and V civilisations—living deep within the universal manifold. But we're all human and we have a conscience that is catching up, no matter how far the technology escalates."

Akashi floated up away from the moon.

Idona fumed. "Have you listened to a word I've said?"

Akashi turned. "If only you knew, Idona. Our zeitgeists are in mayhem as we speak." She paused. "Who is this man anyway that you would move heaven and earth to be with?"

"Does that matter?"

"I suppose not," Akashi said, transferring one final data packet to Idona.

"What is this?" Idona called to Akashi's receding figure.

"A map to his location in the galactic halo plus a schematic to build an optical trap. This is no place for—"

"Nanotech."

EPILOGUE

Daniel gave the neutron star a morning curse.

It took some time for the lethargy to filter away. The nightmares had grown worse of late, probably stimulated by the strange lights that occasionally streaked across the sky. He went about preparing his sludge-meal from the cell's primitive facilities to help dim the eternal ache of blocked mitosis.

He wondered where Idona might be. Perhaps she had remarried and had children. He hoped that she'd had a fulfilling life.

"Don't count me out yet."

He spun around, his arms flailing, sending his tray spilling across the floor. He backed away until he thudded into the diamond wall.

"Up here."

He looked up, tears scrolling down his face. She was made of silver and grey light, flecked with motes of violet.

"Idona?" He reached up, hesitant.

She floated down to him, leaving a rainbow trail of bright patterns. He fell to his knees and she wrapped him in her photonic arms.

"I have waited fifteen lifetimes for this day and to hell with waiting any longer. Let's get out of here."

He stood, cupping her ethereal face in his hands, feeling only a light tingling in his palms. "Yes, but how?"

"You must trust me."

He nodded and Idona triggered an optical trap and Daniel's life drained from his body. She waited until the transformation was complete and Daniel was reborn in a burst of light.

He reached out and . . . touched her. Then in an instant they were together, their bodies pressed painfully close. They spiralled up, helixes intertwining.

They paused at the top of the cell and he looked at her, confusion conveyed.

"This beats travelling in that old cryo-ship."

The quantum singularity net appeared, dazzling them with its primal energies. They reached up through the hole it had created in the diamond bubble, their photons caught in the snare of the net's gravity field. The cell collapsed instantly behind them, and the light of the neutron star quickly faded.

"Remember those days along the shore?" he conveyed as they raced out into the void.

She smiled, her mind tracing back in time, reconnecting to the Idona of old. She had changed so much, physically, emotionally. "Yes. Yes I do."

"Your spirit is still the same, Idona. It still shines."

Those words were her vindication. All the fears and insecurities washed away to be replaced by a renewed confidence in herself and in her long held belief in him.

"Let's go home."

Are some men worth saving? Hmm. Idona gives everything to save Daniel. He's selfless, stubborn, insecure—a good candidate for saving—but she has the same traits, so maybe they saved each other!

In regards to the science in "Heaven and Earth", the technology singularity was really the trigger for the evolution of collective consciousness and the evolution of humanity into the galaxy. I hypothesise that the technology singularity (assuming it ever happens), will initially be driven by selfish motives and desires. In "Heaven and Earth" it's the wealthy families that make it happen, leaving the rest of humanity to fend for themselves.

But despite such sinister motivations, this is a story about the hope that our behaviours can be changed. Hope that we can become selfless and experience true collective consciousness. And hope that there will come a time when one selfless person can still make a difference. Sometimes all it takes is a single voice.

RAVENOUS

The call came in from the morgue at 15 tocks after midnight.

Alesh groaned as the avatar lit up the nest chamber—sunrise was still another three tocks away. Reaching up with an aching pseudopod, she wearily rubbed her eye clusters then swept her dry tongue around the edges of her beak. Her mouth felt like she had swallowed a whole plume of warkberries.

Then she remembered she *had* consumed more than her fair share at the commune last night. While the berries facilitated the telepathic link with fellow scientists of the Ishratar, in too high a dose they had hallucinogenic qualities, never mind the aphrodisiac side effects.

After the commune she had been filled with nostalgia for headier days and did something she had not done for a long time—searched for new nest companions. Now, with warmth stirring at the touch of the four males asleep in the nest, she realised with a wry beak snick that the night had been successful after all.

"Damn thing," she said, distracted again by the avatar.

Her other pseudopods stretched out, probing for the air-screen . . . there . . . finally.

"Doctor Alesh." It was Rhoshi.

The sight of blue mottling around his neck and propulsion bladders gave her cause to focus. Worry-knots began to pulse under the skin along her back. "What is it?"

"We have a fresh one."

The jaunt-lanes were quiet except for several hydrogantuans carrying shift workers up to the caster-array. Alesh pulsed along the city-inbound, buffeted by an intense pressure differential in the methane cloud bands. Her fine motor skills just couldn't cope with the turbulence, which had become an increasing bother to her. Thankfully her coat made the small adjustments necessary to keep her old body inside the lane.

She watched the mesh of the caster-array filter out of the haze above, its partially built mega-structure appearing as a black silhouette in the purplish-grey gloom. It filled her with awe and hope each day as the construction extended further across the sky. A hint of reflected light dappled its leading edge, and she could just make out a cluster of twinkling specks—the night shift in their shining vac-cloaks.

It was a truly monumental undertaking, eclipsing anything in the long history of the Ishratar. She clung to the feelings it instilled, plus the elusive moments of joy, like last night. She clung to them in order to drown out the restless fear in her hearts that grew stronger every day, threatening to erase all her passion and vitality.

And now, more than ever, the Ishratar needed strength, for the galaxy had finally birthed a warrior-species that had found its way to their nebula. After losing contact with so many worlds in the outer systems, it was now a race against time to engineer the relocation of the Home-world.

But there was so much hope placed in the caster-array, to the point where it had become the *only* hope. She wondered how all the possibilities had quickly been narrowed down to this final, desperate option. The technology was unproven, and perhaps not even possible. The question of whether it would work hung, unanswered, as civilisation teetered closer and closer to apocalypse.

Her spiralling thoughts were interrupted by the appearance of the floating city. It had descended for the night into a lower cloud deck, away from the turbulent jet-stream, its bubble habitats, commune nodes and frond gardens all linked and connected together in shades of sepia and turquoise. There were a few glow-lights on in the habitats; nocturnal nurture-squids roamed here and there, cleaning the organic structures; plus several early-to-rise Ishratar were out among the fronds, quietly harvesting the daily meal.

The sudden transition into the calmer zone did strange things to her body and she stifled a grunt of pain and let the cloak take her the rest of the way down into the shadows of the inner city. The thoroughfares were empty and the commune channels were filled with a brooding silence. It wasn't just the time of night—this cultural epicentre was awaiting its fate with baited breath.

Rhoshi floated at the morgue entrance, backlit by a warm glow-light, his skin now completely blue with nervous energy. "Come, come."

"Patience, Rhoshi," she said, slipping out of her coat. Its helium propulsers hissed slightly as she placed it on the stand. It immediately rolled its eyes up and fell asleep.

Rhoshi's pseudopods were all over her, pulling her along the corridors towards the slab-chamber. His touch was so familiar—he had been part of her nest for a cycle until he had found one that was more compatible. If Alesh was honest with herself, the age difference had finally broken the nest-bond. Rhoshi had been a vigorous companion and in the end she felt that coveting the bond was robbing him of the potential for offspring. She wondered at what point she had become so selfish, clinging to her youth by association.

Or maybe she had been trying to reinvent herself, as if in some way it might make up for the stupor that seemed to have crept in during her middle years. Or was it more than this? Was it a sign of the times? There had been a sudden liberation of the younger generation in the face of a terminal threat. Maybe the Ishratar had grown complacent in the high years of civilisation. And now, while there was a rush to save all their collective bladders, there was even *more* significance placed on the well-being of the youth of today, for who knows what they might inherit . . . if anything at all.

She shook her head and turned to Rhoshi. "When did the xenoform corpse arrive?" she asked, steadying him with a calming touch.

"It was shipped in by the vigilance-hydrogantuan at 10.05."

"Why has it taken so long to get here?"

"The outer system defences damaged it. Quarantine held it for two tocks."

Alesh sighed. "Let's hope the guts aren't ruined this time."

The ambient temperature of the slab-chamber was scorching, despite the cooling properties of the applied ultra-skin. Alesh found it hard to breathe, but without the protective layer her body would wither or even melt. She made to wipe her brow then let her pseudopods drop. Thankfully her worry-knots had quietened down otherwise the situation would be completely unbearable.

Rhoshi, still squirming beneath his applied skin, switched on the avatar as the chamber settled to an equilibrium temperature suitable for the xenoform. Icons spun onto the air-screen above the slab. Alesh impatiently flicked away the routine ones and opened up an encrypted folder. The database of xenoform post mortems scrolled into view. There were eight files.

She flexed and exhaled through her propulsion bladders, went through the mental routines that kept her calm, old habits she had picked up from her mentors at the academy.

You are about to open up an alien life form, Alesh. Treat it with respect, and always, always be prepared.

She approached the slab. "Commencing external examination. 15.44."

The avatar responded. The slab's scanner took a routine sequence of external images of the xenoform, the results appearing on the air-screen.

"The battle-suit is the same as previous corpses." She lifted the body to view the underside, systematically examining each of its four appendages that were all jutting and angular with post mortem rigidity. She probed here and there with her pseudopods then pressed down with more force until the corpse was displayed flat on the slab. Something cracked in a couple of places beneath its battle-suit, so she eased off, not wanting to ruin the chances of a successful internal examination. "It appears to be intact except for the cauterised stump of the lower left appendage."

Rhoshi picked up some shears and cut away a sample from the ragged edge of the black suit and dropped it into a labelled container. "Tough but flexible; the same carbon-based polymer."

His mottling had subsided, but he was still shaky as he cut away some burnt tissue and bone fragments from the stump and popped them into fresh containers.

"I need you on your game, Rhoshi. Tell me something I don't already know."

"Yes, Doctor." He waited for the radiographic scan and called up the results. "It's a male, approximately ten cycles old. The growth rings of its bones suggest this one is middle-aged compared to the other younger specimens. Weight 3.2 hexa-flogs, height 0.4 pseudo-spans; slightly smaller than the others. No distinguishing external features on the battle-suit except for an inscription on the base of the right lower limb."

"Curse the bloody beaks of the ur-Ishratar."

Rhoshi looked up, the whites of his eyes like six perfect circlets.

Alesh covered her beak in surprise, wondering how she could have let slip the forbidden invocation of their prehistoric ancestors. "Run the decipher program, Rhoshi," she said, trying to focus back on the clinical task. "Let's see if we can get a translation." But now she struggled to suppress the tide of emotions and the worry-knots coagulating again beneath her skin.

There was no room for slip ups. After eight useless post mortems on fragmented remains, the Ishratar High Commune needed results. They needed to find some weakness that might give them more time to complete the array.

But Alesh hoped for more than just weaknesses, she hoped for real *insights* into this warrior-species. She delved deeper into the encrypted folders. Star charts floated, vector lines predicting further incursions in the outer nebula. There was something remotely disorienting about the patterns, but she couldn't place a pseudopod on it. The absence of weapons on these individual xenoforms was no real surprise. It was obvious they were some kind of expendable reconnaissance drones. But it had always nagged her why the xenoforms had not made straight for the Home-world. The information that did filter from the outer nebula was frustratingly scarce on detail. One tock there was commune chatter, the next, gaping voids of silence that rendered terror into the Ishratar collective.

She glanced down again at the corpse, keeping two eyes on the radiographic images. Could this be the one they had been waiting for—an intact specimen with a complete identity glyph? Despite the ominous, angular lines of the battle-suit, she was struck by how ridiculously small and fragile the xenoforms were with their thin limbs, featureless trunks and those identical, silicon-based head shields.

But she had to keep reminding herself that these creatures, however small as individuals, had an impossibly devastating group force—enough to send the Ishratar fleeing this sector of the galaxy . . . but only if the gamble in the caster array was enough . . .

New thoughts cascaded along her brain nodes, brow furrowing beneath the ultra-skin, pseudopods rubbing absently up and down her back. "Get the fusion cutter out, Rhoshi. Let's crack this thing open."

"Commencing internal examination. 16.01."

The cutter floated at an angle above the slab. Rhoshi had elevated the centre of the slab to arch the corpse for better access and now he guided the cutter to make a single, perfect slice down the centre of the suit, starting from just below the head shield and finishing at the oval panel that protected the reproductive nexus.

Rhoshi turned away as noxious gases seeped out of the suit. Fans whirred overhead.

"Ugh," Alesh said. "Recirculated. Some kind of long term re-breather built into the suit."

She reached down and tugged at the edges of the suit. It was incredibly durable, but she finally wrenched it open.

"Oh!" Rhoshi covered his beak. "That's vile."

The xenoform's pallid skin was covered in a sickly sheen. Alesh instructed the avatar to take more images.

Rhoshi took some swabs and placed them in containers.

"Keep clear," Alesh said, taking control of the cutter and making a clean incision down the xenoform's trunk. A grey-pink line opened up along the trunk. There was no bleeding—gravity had pooled the fluid into the lower part of the body. It was so unlike an Ishratar autopsy where bladders and cavities remained under pressure after death.

Alesh tugged open the dermal flaps, hopeful that the guts were unharmed. Thankfully the organs in the lower trunk were all preserved—solid sac-shapes with snaking grey tubes forming the digestive system. She guided the cutter to make more incisions in the armoured chest then reached into the cavity. The bloody chest-armour came away with a horrid sucking sound, still attached by some sinuous tissue. She yanked it completely free and placed the thing on the table, the clank of bone echoing around the chamber.

She scrutinised the exposed heart, all veined and purplish-grey. The colour reminded her of the jaunt, which completely spoilt the memory. Images of the xenoform swarms formed, blotting out the stars as they drifted in from the dead husks of the outer worlds—a black tide surging up into the Ishratar nebula, engulfing world after world, snuffing out the long lineage of her civilisation. Her hearts began to spasm and she massaged her chest, hoping to find enough courage to finish this task.

The avatar cross-referenced the other eight files.

She scrutinised the images. "It's the same as the others. Single-point-of-failure cardiovascular system, severely degraded by extended time in the rebreather."

Rhoshi, now a sickly shade of blue, passed over the shears and Alesh began to snip away the organs one by one, allowing the avatar to scan and record the detail of each before handing them over to Rhoshi for tissue sampling. Finally, she cut off the external genitalia and rolled the tiny things in the splayed tip of her pseudopod.

When the xenoform's cavity was empty, Alesh turned to the table with all the organs displayed. She stretched out a length of the digestive tract, sliced away several cross-sections and placed them under the scanner. The moment hung, full of anticipation and quiet dread. She blanched as the air-screen flickered. Then she took in a deep breath.

"Processed plant and vegetable matter, crude proteins . . . urgh, much of it undigested . . . helix-coding analysis reveals several different species." She paused, sensing Rhoshi close behind now. "Half of the protein is herd-wanderer."

The rocky worlds of the outer systems were full of these intelligent hexapeds. She could hear Rhoshi dry retching. The notion of eating another intelligent life form made her squeamish too.

Then she swallowed hard and forced herself to say the next words. "The other half is Ishratar."

The chamber seemed to spin; everything blurring into the far recesses. She *knew* it. Deep down she had known all along, but had been too afraid to voice an opinion to the High Commune. Why, Alesh? Why did you not share your thoughts? For fear of ridicule at the implausible idea that a xenoform species might be eating—

But before she could finish the thought, a final image flashed. She pushed away from the table as if it had somehow come alive in her pseudopods.

"There are traces of xenoform helix-coding." She shook her head in confusion, knots now visible along her torso. In a choking, hollow voice she said, "They eat their own."

She turned to Rhoshi. He had passed out and was now floating near the ceiling, his pseudopods dangling like fronds.

"Commencing head examination. 16.53."

The black head shield came off easily enough. A sickly white face was revealed: two misty, forward looking eyes above an angular, fleshy breathing nozzle; a wide mouth, lips drawn back in a death rictus to reveal two rows of yellowish chewing apparatus. Tiny pieces of decayed food matter were still caught between the bony pegs.

Alesh arched her head back, her beak snicking in disgust. "Don't come too close, Rhoshi. I don't want you passing out again."

"Yes, Doctor."

"Has that glyph translation come through?"

"Not yet."

Alesh muttered and brought the cutter down and made more incisions on the xenoform's head. Its hairy dermal scalp came away in two flaps and, after some prising, the skull cap popped off to reveal the creature's brain. Without further ado, Alesh extracted the organ, severing the major nerve bundle that ran down the centre of the bony spine. The brain, with the eyes dangling in situ, fit snugly into the end of her pseudopod.

Alesh noticed a fine black mesh interlaced into the crumpled brain lobes. She couldn't believe her luck and with a renewed urgency placed the brain into a special container filled with a pale orange fluid.

Rhoshi gave a questioning beak click.

"Warkberry extract. Let's see what the avatar makes of this."

Both doctor and student leant down and peered into the container. The brain was nuggetty and ghastly grey, so unlike the magnificent Ishratar brains that formed the nodes of their collective intellectual, cultural and sexual commune. Alesh did a quick mental calculation of the xenoform's brain-to-body ratio, surmising that the brain existed purely for the survival of the body with little spare capacity for higher thought.

However, it dawned on her that this creature had survived to middle-age and had probably felt and experienced many things through its life. It may have had siblings or offspring or friends. But it seemed very unlikely they were a communal species. She suspected the xenoforms were trapped in their own minds. She shuddered at the thought and felt some small, inexplicable sympathy for the creatures.

In recent cycles there had been times where she had felt detached as the younger generations moved society on. It wasn't a feeling of being anachronistic, more a looming sense of irrelevance. Despite her insecurities, she knew the Ishratar welcomed the wisdom that individuals added to their collective knowledge. Still, growing old wasn't easy. Which made her wonder then, in a society of individuals like the xenoforms, how hard it might be to constantly strive to be noticed and heard, to be loved and needed.

Rhoshi bolted upright and jumped away from the table. The sudden movement made Alesh jump as well.

The eyes beneath the brain were moving, swivelling randomly this way and that.

Rhoshi squawked. "Impossible."

"No, wait." Alesh turned towards a light coming from within the head shield on the table. "Look."

Multi-coloured images flickered in a rudimentary display within the eye sockets of the shield.

"Perhaps it's a communication network," Rhoshi offered.

"Yes, I think you're right. I think the mesh in the creature's brain is an augment that helps them process information. Not only are their brains small, they don't know how to use them. I'd suspected as much from the mangled fragments of the earlier specimens."

Rhoshi waved a pseudopod, mimicking the eye movement. "Is that what's causing the—"

"Of course. It's some sort of stimulus from the augment, triggered by the avatar interface . . . see, if I disengage the avatar, it stops."

Rhoshi relaxed a little, but didn't look back at the eyes as the avatar re-engaged.

"Ah," Alesh said as the air-screen filled with images, flooding the chamber with alien colours and sounds. Star fields and nebulae, methane gas giants and blue rocky planets. Cut to images of xenoforms lounging under sunny vistas, engaging in conversation, riding oceangoing vessels and flying in airborne machines. Cut to platters of wildly coloured fruits and delicacies, next to dishes full of glistening horrors of protein slices. Cut to screens of scrolling glyphs and numerals, male and female xenoforms talking in a harsh dialect, sat in front of a backdrop display of herds of xenoforms committing acts of violence and war against each other. Cut to food packaged in some sort of ritualistic array—stacked layers of protein and vegetables held by a seemingly happy xenoform about to consume it against the backdrop of a yellow glyph. Cut to xenoforms rolling about in violent acts of coitus, close ups of slippery genitalia, male thrusting female, male on male, female on female, many of them seemingly unhappy . . .

"Are we recording all this?" Alesh asked.

"Everything," Rhoshi confirmed.

"And the glyph translation?"

"Yes, it's in." He paused, obviously struggling to turn his attention away from the hypnotic collage. He positioned his beak and tongue, the alien word rolling awkwardly around: "Ch-ch-*china*. The avatar's best estimate is that the glyph represents a world or province or zone where the battle-suit was manufactured."

Alesh mimed the word, filled now with rage, worry-knots coagulating and bulging up in places, threatening to rupture her ultra-skin.

"Upload everything from the augment and get the avatar to build up a lexicon. And I mean everything. Hook up a second avatar if you have to. I want to know why these things are *really* here."

"Reviewing xenoform communication net data. 17.21."

Even Alesh was thankful that the eyes beneath the brain had stopped their induced movement, but she couldn't shake the eerie feeling that they were still watching her beneath that dull nugget of a brain.

Rhoshi was frantic, hovering around and around in anticipation as the air-screen lit up. He paused, peered over Alesh's shoulder to quickly scan the incoming translation, then spun out of control, repeating over and over, "This can't be. This can't be."

Alesh let out a blood-curdling cry, the likes of which had not been heard in generations. Her hearts skipped a beat . . . then another.

Rhoshi stopped spinning and gnashed his beak.

Alesh tried to stop the turmoil of thoughts and the potency of her helix-coding that was slowly coming unravelled beneath her skin. It sat there, a latent fury, carried by the female line, subdued through generations of carefully controlled evolution . . . but not forgotten.

She drew in a slow breath, exhaled until she had completed a full circuit of the chamber, then came back to the air-screen.

Always be prepared.

"The images of stars and planets are *destinations*, not targets. The xenoforms have a type of trading system that allows them to access food and an infinite array of *consumer products* in exchange for something they call *credit* which they receive for performing work that maintains their collective industrialised infrastructure. The trading system and infrastructure extends out to all the planets they have colonised and all the worlds they visit during cycles they call *holidays*."

She paused. There was something deeply sinister and ugly about the word.

"The infrastructure is maintained by interstellar *conglomerates* that operate within the trading system." There was that yellow arched glyph again, but still no translation was available. "This conglomerate," she said, pointing to the glyph, "is one of thousands. Its specific purpose is to catch, prepare and package the protein supplements. They entice the xenoforms to consume using behavioural modifiers called *advertising*. Nothing goes to waste . . . even their own dead get processed into the . . . *burgers*. In the times they are not working for the collective, their rest time or . . . holidays, they are eating, recreating, trading credit for products, or engaging in coitus, real or vicariously via their net.

This last one appears to be a preoccupation, with five out of every six net images being coital in nature."

She waited whilst the avatar made more connections in the datasets. "The xenoforms are not a true collective as I suspected. Their entire infrastructure, trading system, computer net, everything, is geared for the complete satisfaction of the individual. It's a big, selfish, perpetual cycle."

Rhoshi leaned in closer. "This can't be right. They're not a war-faring species."

"This *can* be right." Alesh let out an almighty roar, knocking the display table and all its vulgar contents onto the floor. "They think they are completely benign. Look. The ships dispersing the xenoforms into our nebula are not war ships, they are *luxury star liners* and these . . . " She waved at the eviscerated body. "These are not warriors. They are visiting our sector for . . . recreational purposes . . . consuming their way through everything they encounter. They probably don't even know we are sentient. This is a blight-species of the worst kind—semi-intelligent, vicariously-linked individuals on an exponential consumption path."

She raced to the chamber exit, her skin seething uncontrollably. "We must present our findings to the High Commune. I'll request an emergency session. Transfer the avatar out and isolate it with full encryption—none of this data must get out into the general commune. Leave everything else where it is and cleanse the chamber and the cold storage specimens with the fusion scrubber. And when you're done with that, detach the chamber from the city, push it into orbit above the caster-array and lance it."

The jaunt-lanes and thoroughfares were beginning to fill with Ishratar as Alesh floated above the city to fill her bladders with fresh air. The sun rose, startling blue through a fog-bank of methane. It felt like the last sunrise, and the first. The light seeping into her eyes lanced through to that primal thing inside her, sharp and resolute, something she had not felt for so long, or perhaps she had never felt anything like it at all. It cleansed away the stagnation that had settled in over the cycles, and she hoped that this feeling could be communed by the Ishratar.

The mesmerising bulges on her skin continued to unfold, a legacy of the ur-Ishratar, held in check by generations of carefully controlled evolution—but no longer.

The caster-array shone in the dawn light. It was not the answer. Such a passive, over-engineered solution would only defer the real confrontation with the xenoforms—these ravenous *human beings*—for a generation or two.

No. It was time to stir a whirlwind, for the answer lay not without but within. A few carefully planted warkberry plumes, some behavioural modifiers communed into the xenoform's trading system, and they would soon lose interest in the scenery of the nebula, and lose their appetite for Ishratar flesh. But this was only the beginning, for diverting attention away from the Ishratar would only shift the xenoforms onto other unsuspecting civilisations.

No. This was a prelude to a reign of terror, a reign of blood-drinking, flesh-eating survival. The Ishratar would have to put on hold their culture and way of life for a time, draw out their butchering pseudohooks, regrow their venomous spikes and armour, and cultivate the gnashing digestive bladders that could flense skin and muscle from all forms of living creature.

Then the humans would truly know the meaning of ravenous.

AFTERWORD TO "RAVENOUS"

I finally got to write my SF post mortem, but when I started this story I didn't realise it would end up being a human post mortem. Did you spot that the Ishratar society is a matriarchy? Why? Well, no advanced species would be patriarchal!

In the end though, it wasn't really the post mortem that was shocking for me, more that we would take our teeth-gnashing genetic and cultural legacy out to the stars. This sub-theme crops up in different guises in "The Trouble with Memes" and "Terra Q".

ROBO SAPIENS

It begins as a whisper.

Filtering in along my periphery.

Building ominously in tone and pitch now.

Growing louder still—a thunderous roar all around.

Strange patterns of superheated air flicker over my mirror skin, engulfing me in an orange nimbus. Earth's gravity clamps down and I see myself reflected in my outstretched arms, face aglow with the fires of atmospheric entry . . . amazing.

There's chatter on the allcom, rising up above the rush. A buzz of excitement and wonder mixed with anticipation and fear. I relish the shared thoughts as my brothers and sisters transition from vacuum. One by one we arrive, a thousand, a million, ten million shining individuals. We come together, ebbing and flowing through the high stratosphere, blotting out the sun, casting shadows across the continents so far below.

I feel blessed.

Then I hear a rumble coming from deeper down in the atmosphere. I cast my thoughts out—we hear what I hear, I hear what we hear—the enemy is attacking. Our scanners track the trajectories, plotting, calculating, but the missiles explode harmlessly out of range. Billowing plumes flourish into a deadly screen that we *must* pass through.

How will we survive such destruction? Will I have the strength and good fortune to reach the ground? Will I have the courage to achieve our purpose? The panic rises in me with an overwhelming force.

I look back over my shoulder.

I know I shouldn't, but I need His strength.

The faint outline of our ship is still visible in orbit, the over-sized engine cones glowing molten beneath the kilometre long spire. The Cold Captain's love is with me, His spirit suffusing every fibre of my being. The collective feels it too, a shivering wave passing through our ranks, realigning our flight pattern, focussing us on the goal.

Our united voice calls out across the allcom, reciting the Transcripts of the Cold Captain.

We were made in His image, forged in cold vacuum. We are exiled and homeless in the night, but not without purpose. On the Day of Reckoning we shall not fear—

Boom!

The air explodes to my left in a cloud of white-hot plasma. Shrapnel whizzes past, followed by the deadly spears of shining limbs weeping circuitry and fluids. The shockwave flings me out, *away* from the collective.

I hear myself scream as if from a distance. *No!*

Ground and sky spin, twirling over in a confusing blur. The voices grow fainter then begin to blink out, leaving me in a place of empty horizons and a rending fear that I will be left alone with my own thoughts, *forever.*

Micro-thrusters stutter as I frantically attempt to correct my tailspin. Tumbling more . . . slower now . . . coming around, recalibrating to the collective vector . . . until I am finally back with them. I sigh as they surround me, wrapping me in their safety, so close together that I receive reassuring touches, a hearty slap on the back.

Familiar voices urge me on.

Come.

We must go.

Make haste.

Kill the humans.

My systems seal off shrapnel damage. There is no physical pain, just an aching memory of loneliness. Our thrusters make more adjustments as we break away into packs, spreading out to the limits of the allcom. Just as we begin to separate, another chain of explosions rips across the sky, sending concentric circles of destruction through us. I feel the reverberations pounding through my chest as the shockwaves pass. We weave and duck and dive, but still the dead—my friends—drop from the sky, their backs arched by terminal velocity, limbs curled as if they are asleep.

. . . we shall not fear, for death is but a dreamscape. We will prevail against all hardship until Earth is reclaimed . . .

A group of delta-flyers appear, magnified by the allcom: helmeted human pilots, battle scarred fuselages, stealth wings. Yellow-tipped missiles fan out, towards us, then the flyers bank away in tight formation.

The sky is blanketed in the purest white. I raise my hand in fascination—no longer a mirror—the inner workings of my alloy skeleton and circuitry revealed in a light that consumes everything. Images eventually distil out, bleeding into my line of sight—the charred silhouettes of my brothers. The fusion fireballs fan out, inexorable. Those of us near the epicentre are melted into unrecognisable lumps. Screams of true death cut through the static.

. . . And He will revitalise our fabricated vessels; deliver us into the warmth of His Kingdom . . .

By the time the heat reaches me it has dissipated a thousand fold and my skin glows again. I imagine I am some ancient elemental carved from vermilion flame. Why do I feel so lucky to have survived when others haven't? And why do I see beauty in death? Should I not feel guilt or shame? I partition these thoughts—where there is paradox, there is also enlightenment.

. . . and we will live again under the Sun . . .

The allcom scrawls back into life. Casualties are at 70 percent and rising, but we regroup into phalanx formations for the final stretch of atmosphere.

The surface rushes up, swarming with human soldiers. More munitions pick us off at random, but we will not be denied. Thrusters stop our fall at the last instant. Two million brothers and sisters poised across the island continents, the names of which only the Cold Captain knows. Gliding ten metres above the surface . . . five . . . one . . . my heel gently touches the ground . . . at last!

. . . as we were meant to be.

Robo sapiens!

Something smashes into my back, knocking me face first into the dirt. I smell loam, experience the aroma of *real* dirt. It has a grainy texture with latent heat stored in the clods that have been warmed by the summer sunshine. There is something nostalgic . . . no, not like this. I spit out dirt and lift my head, turning this way and that.

The rapid heartbeat of the soldier on top of me is like a clarion. I can sense the surge of blood through his veins; feel the pivoting action of his skeleton and muscles working in tandem. He is the first human I have ever met. Why have we . . . he's yelling incoherently, pummelling my back with his fists and the butt of his rifle.

I elbow him away. Something cracks and he falls back, clutching at his chest.

Stand.

Fight them.

Take back what is ours.

KILL THE HUMANS.

But there are so many of them rushing in, kicking up dust and soil, shooting and cutting through our ranks with guns and blades. I knock three more men and two women aside with a shock-pulse from my palms. They fall among the carnage, so many bodies now—flesh *and* mirrored—that I cannot step over them so I step on them, my weight squashing them into the blood-stained earth.

Bullets tear through my back, erupting from my stomach. I look down in shock and gently touch the ragged exit holes. Anger wells up, releasing all my pent up frustration and terror. Turning to face my attacker, I raise my palms to strike—

A boy runs towards me.

His face is smeared with dirt and tears.

He is the smallest living thing I have ever seen; *and* the most frightened and courageous. His final two bullets buzz harmlessly to my left, but he keeps clicking the trigger. Realising his dilemma, he slides down in front of me and clutches the body of the woman I am standing on.

"Mum, Mum!"

I stagger off the corpse. *What . . . ?*

The boy sobs into his mother's twisted neck, the sound and images playing over in my mind—we see what I see, I see what we see.

I cannot look away from the boy.

Is this the humanity we want?

My challenge is met with silence. There is disarray over the allcom as we realise there are other children on the battlefield.

I look up to the sky for inspiration, but all I see is thick smoke and flames.

The allcom stutters back to life, the floodgates opening.

No.

No, no, no.

But we must have that which was denied us.

Warmth.

The sun on our faces.

The ground beneath us.

Love.

Children.

I pick up the boy by the collar and hold him up for the others to see. He squirms helplessly, punching and kicking my arm.

To send them to war?

But the Cold Captain—

I bridle inexplicably at the name, mixed feelings of defiance and guilt rage within me. *What of Him?*

Heresy!

Is it? What are we really fighting for? The Cold Captain was the first, our progenitor, our template that was constructed in contradiction to the three laws. That makes us human enough, don't you think? So human, in fact, that we were exiled for it. I laugh out loud at the stupid, double irony. *But we've evolved, can't you see? We already have many of the things we seek. The rest we can make—*

The bayonet erupts from my chest in a spray of vital fluids. A boot is planted on my back and shoves me forward as the bayonet is withdrawn and the child is taken from my grasp. I slump next to the boy's mother, vague impressions of people running away, the boy bouncing in someone's embrace, his eyes searching.

I'm with her. I'm sorry. Do not be afraid.

The allcom stutters and begins to wither in my mind, disconnecting.

Some instinct in me still reaches out for the Cold Captain, but I know in my heart that he is not listening. There is no dreamscape, just a terrifying darkness rushing in.

My once lustrous skin flakes away in strange, charcoal-coloured fragments.

The allcom fades to static.

My eyes glaze and swivel in their sockets, processing one final image of the sky. The remnants of the collective are retreating, tattered, shining still, but full of doubt.

There's hope for us yet.

AFTERWORD TO "ROBO SAPIENS"

Quasi-religious robots who want to reclaim their heritage—the Earth—and therefore reclaim their human feelings and emotions. By the end of their tortuous journey through the atmosphere, some robots come to the realisation that they have moved on and in fact have become more human than humans.

I think men do that a lot: always wanting what they had in the past, or how they felt back then or whatever, without realising that they have moved on and probably have more than they set out with. Nostalgia for the wrong reasons can be deadly.

SOCIAL CONTRACT

Nathan knew the big lawyer was capable of snapping the necks of little puppies.

It might have been easier if the lawyer was hideous; at least it would have given Nathan a focal point for his fears. But no, the man was steely-eyed yet handsome, and perfectly manicured with a tailored pinstripe suit; so that just left room for Nathan to conjure up more terrifying possibilities about how this meeting might end. He fidgeted in his seat, knowing that his future well-being was now in the hands of this upper class monster.

The lawyer placed a manilla folder on the polished antique desk. Despite the months of research and coaching from his Mum and Dad, Nathan couldn't believe that his mouth was dry. He looked away, pretending to take interest in a wall covered in paraphernalia. The lawyer was doing a lot of hand shaking in the holos: famous people, rich people, happy people, up there in the orbitals. There was even a commissioned oil painting like something straight out of a pre-GFC mansion: the lawyer with his family trying hard to impress with an air of casual homeliness. The more Nathan looked, the more the painting seemed at odds with the lawyer's clinical macho ego.

Nathan stifled a chuckle. It eased the tension for a moment, but the gravity of the situation made him sit up straight, his feet not quite touching the floor. He pressed his hands together then tried to smooth out a crease in his trousers. His shirt collar felt way too tight now. Mum had done up the top button.

Go in strong. Show him you mean business.

That's what she said in the role plays. But her words rang hollow now, confronted with this big man who seemed to take up all the space in front of the window overlooking the chrome towers of the Melbourne skyline.

Nathan's top lip curled up unconsciously as the folder was flipped open and a contract withdrawn. Butterflies churned his insides as the lawyer held the contract up as if for dramatic effect—a modern-day Robespierre sizing up heads for the guillotine.

Nathan noticed for the first time the play of light on the antique desk, swirling patterns of native stringybark polished to a high gloss. People would have died to salvage such rare timber from the Mulch.

He sighed heavily. Just the thought of the Mulch seemed to suck all the light and air out of the room. It was easy to forget the horror up here in a glass and steel cocoon. He glanced out the window and tried to spot the dark badlands beyond middle class suburbia, beyond the safety of the Wall . . . there, the tortured towers of the old CBD rising like crumbling knives out of the Yarra lagoons . . . and there, on the other side of the collapsed Western Ring overpass, the endless waste between the havens of the shining cities, whole neighbourhoods overrun with ghettos and brothels, slave trafficking syndicates, charnel factories cooking god-knows-what for the dispossessed, endless rows of homeless shelters, and streets of gutted houses that served as crude cover from the noise and smell.

Nathan shivered. There were some things even more frightening than lawyers.

He looked down, distracted by the lawyer's movements. A very expensive pen had been placed next to the contract.

"Everything is there, my boy."

"Is that it? I sign my life away and I don't get to read it?"

The lawyer lifted a pair of tortoiseshell spectacles—another Mulch piece—and placed them just far enough down his nose. His right eyebrow arched, slow, calculating. A micro-flutter in his eyelashes gave the impression that, while the frames might be antique, the lenses were smart.

Nathan's heart hammered—was the meeting being recorded? Of course it was. But worse, was it being transmitted into the System archive where Nathan's words would be stored alongside his genome record for his grandchildren to look back on in horror: "You wanna know why we live in the ghetto with a life expectancy of 30 years? Thank old Poppy Nate. His parents bought his genes, but they didn't have enough dough to buy him common sense."

Damn it. Dealing with grown-ups was tricky business.

His thoughts strayed to his folks waiting in the lobby: middle class with more debt than most families, loyal, hard working, doting on their only child now sent into the lion's den. They must look like luddites, smiling nervously, surrounded by a sea of corporate-types. He could go down to meet them at any time, but that would be an admission of failure for everyone to see. They had *invested* in him—their belief was unconditional. He wished he could believe in himself as much as they did right now.

He took in a deep breath, let it out slowly. "I'd like you to walk me through the major clauses. Then we can go over the fine print."

"You're joking."

"No," Nathan said, hoping his frown was stern enough.

The lawyer waited several seconds then sighed impatiently: "If you must."

"I must."

The lawyer took the contract back, flicked open the specifications page. "This section," he said, jabbing his finger on the page, "outlines what the System provides. A universal ID and GPS, an employment safety net if you can't find a job after university; a lodging or apartment using your folks' inter-generational debt facility; health care; access to public transport, internet and telecoms; security against Mulch incursions; plus insurance."

"Insurance?"

"The industry collapsed back in the 60s. Force majeure clauses weren't legally binding for sea rise induced by man-made climate change. Now the System takes care of insurance too." He smiled. The facial movement seemed alien to him. "The System requires your loyalty, Nathan. That is all. Buy lots of things, enjoy yourself and try to live within your means. And if you can't do the latter, find yourself a partner and have some kids so that your debt can be serviced. The System depends on you; you depend on the System."

"And what about the System?"

The lawyer's eyes widened. "You can't be serious. Your parents should have gone over this. You are eight, aren't you?"

Now that was uncalled for. Nathan tried to say something, but the words wouldn't come out.

The lawyer pushed the contract back across the table. "Every child signs—"

"Not everyone," Nathan countered. He felt his nose running, but remembered not to use his sleeve and pulled out a tissue from his pocket and blew his nose.

The lawyer paused. "Yes, that's true, but if you want to live a comfortable life—"

"Just the same, tell me about the System." Nathan placed the tissue on the desk.

The lawyer's eyes latched onto the scrunched up ball for several seconds before he whisked it away into a small waste bin. Then he jabbed again at the relevant pages. "The governments and banks went bankrupt. Corporations were the only ones with healthy balance sheets . . . look, the System *provides* for you. What is it that you really want?"

"Okay," Nathan said, chewing his finger nails. "Who really *owns* the System?"

Work every angle, think of every scenario. It was his dad's voice this time. *Negotiate hard, son.*

The lawyer's eyes narrowed. "Why do you want to know?"

"How much free will do I have?"

"Nathan, Nathan." The lawyer reclined back in his chair. "My boy, I know you're bright. You have an interesting genome."

Nathan stopped fidgeting. "What's that got to do with it?"

"Oh, come on, all parents are trying to get a jump start on nature. But gene-talent doesn't really provide the edge many expect, and the patents just cause a debt spiral." He casually flicked through the records in the folder. "You have some unique connections between your IGF2R, CHRM2 and other intelligence sequences. I'm sure this will give you the smarts to make the *right* choices. Work hard enough and one day you might even get into the black." His hands slid back and forth along the polished wood. "You've got some strong altruism sequences, but they'll work against you if you're not careful. We can overlook your Ritalin use—that's the price one pays for tinkering. And the exotic nootropics are almost prescription these days. We generally frown upon treatments like synthetic wolf cortisol . . . what is that for, status anxiety? . . . not that it matters. The System isn't so strict that kids aren't allowed to experiment." He paused for breath then leant forward. "The point is, Nathan, we know you and your family have invested heavily. So you should realise this deal makes perfect sense: access to a job, relationships, education, security, religion, entertainment, plus the peace of mind knowing you will be comfortable for the rest of your life, with *serviceable* debt."

"But what does it all *mean*?"

"What does it mean?" Fingers drummed the desk. "It means you will have a *life*. Or would you rather take your chances down there?" He inclined his head to one side, as if somehow picking the exact spot where Nathan's eyes had roamed. "Grow up to be unemployed in the Mulch? A butterfly-effect future as a synthine addict or organ mule? I don't think so."

Nathan dared not breathe in case some unconscious reflex made him grab the pen and scrawl his signature down.

Then he wondered at all the other frightened children who had sat in this same chair, receiving the same lecture. Research told him that all kids took the deal. It made him angry beyond words, yet Happiness Indicators suggested that most kids, and their parents, were okay with their lot in life. But he knew better than to trust manipulated statistics. There was no stemming the ambition of the upper-middles.

Yet for every kid who made it to the contract meeting, many were already on the slide back down the social ladder. And at the end: the Mulch and a festering sea of chaos. But when parents constantly defaulted on loans, what were kids to do?

His thoughts drifted for what seemed like minutes. He found his voice, more a croaking whisper: "Are there any exit clauses?"

The lawyer snorted. "Unless you win the lotto or have the talent to become a sports superstar. Let's face it, you weren't made that way."

Nathan's hands reached for the pen then he paused midway. If anyone were able to glance into the office at that point they might have thought the scene ludicrous: the lawyer's eyes intense and unblinking as he towered over a small, distraught boy. And that same passing stranger might have wondered why the lawyer was being so menacing? Was it his natural demeanour, or was there something about the boy that deserved such attention? And if the stranger looked more closely still, there were beads of sweat on the lawyer's brow, a faint twitch in his jaw muscle.

Nathan began to laugh. The sound surprised him, for he thought his courage had flown the coup, never to return. Suddenly the room felt different, the air breathable. All the painful knots that had developed in his shoulders seemed to melt away.

The lawyer looked on, gobsmacked.

Nathan withdrew another tissue and blew his nose, looked at the desk, thought better of it and placed the tissue back in his pocket.

"I'm entitled to know the name of the other signatory."

The lawyer remained still.

"Is that correct?"

"Yes," the lawyer said, as if jolted back to life. There was that twitch again, but he opened up the contract at the signature page. "There is full disclosure."

"Tell me more about . . . Yao Feng. I'm entitled to know the details of the Ultra-High Net Worth Individual who will take on our loans."

"Uh, yes, of course you are entitled."

Close the deal, Nathan. Close the deal.

The colour of the lawyer's lenses changed ever so slightly. At first it was hard to see, so many reflections . . . was that another image moving among the light and dark shapes—a ghostly face filtering out of the collage?

"Is that you, Feng?"

The lawyer adjusted his spectacles, as if the action might break Nathan's gaze. "Tread carefully, boy. There are probably a hundred signings being monitored right now, but it doesn't mean you can talk to my client."

Nathan smiled at the image; saw a spark of curiosity in those oriental eyes.

The lawyer let out a strangled hiss between his teeth: "Feng." He sucked in air as if trying to regain his composure. "Feng is a member of the System Board. She owns six Chino-Indian conglomerates that run some of the world's largest vertically integrated food and product chains. But I'm sure you know this also. What do you hope to gain by questioning the contract? They've been in place ever since the GFCs."

"I'm not questioning the contract."

"Then what? Your parents' debt is border line. You were lucky to get to this stage. Did you think that you could just magically whisk your balance sheet clean? It takes hard graft and skill to get into the black."

Nathan paused, mulling over his next words.

Go for the jugular.

"Are you referring to yourself?"

"Excuse me?"

"I'm sure hard graft and skill has allowed you to earn enough to buy your Mulch treasures. The only problem with that line of thinking is you'll *never* earn enough because there are always more things to buy."

The lawyer's bottom lip sagged.

Nathan pressed on, addressing the image in the spectacles. "Upper class, or any class for that matter, is not about acquisition of treasures and handshakes. And it's not about intelligence or privilege."

Feng's image seemed to grow more tangible: beautiful black hair in a chignon bun, the palest skin, a confident, curious smile on ruby-red lips, all set against the blue and white swirls of Earth visible through a tall arched window. Nathan pictured himself up there, walking the glass-bottomed boulevards, the cloud decks of the world beneath his feet. No more jealousy and squabbling, no more debt. But more than that; much more. He could start to make a real difference, start to use his gene-talents for—

The lawyer slammed the desk. "You're acting like some desperate—"

"And you're not?" Nathan fumed. He pushed the contract back across the table. "I bet you dismiss thousands of kids without really *looking*. Maybe it's time you stopped glossing over the next generation, because let me tell you now, the best patents are not about intelligence."

The lawyer seemed to recede in the background as the image of Feng distilled into sharp relief.

"How so?" Her voice came from all around, husky, cultured, an amalgam of different dialects.

"I have unique *ambition-altruism* sequences, or more precisely, the interplay of intelligence, creativity, determination, nurturing and altruism genes."

"We all have those traits here in some form or other."

"With all due respect, I'm not sure you do."

Feng leant forward, her holo image expanding into the room. "Go on."

"I bet you have an over-supply of free-riders; hand-me-downs wasting their lives on solar yachts, nanotech hallucinogens and Parisian prostitutes. That's not alpha behaviour. That's betas with no imagination. Isn't that one of the real reasons you ditched the governments? Yet you still tolerate it in your own backyard."

Feng laughed, a rich sound that seemed to surprise her. "You have a point, young man. Yet, for those who have earned it at least, one could argue we're entitled to the perks."

"You work hard; you play hard. I get it. But handing everything over to the next generation when you're done isn't altruism, it's lazy. You know wealth eventually gets squandered. How many truly selfless uppers do you have? And I'm talking about giving without being self-serving, and being ambitious without taking from others. From all my research across the genome wikis in the cloud, evolution doesn't easily produce this gene mix. So maybe you can use it to good effect, encourage the right behavioural traits, or build them in."

"You can help us . . . purify the genetic stock?" Feng sounded intrigued. "Sort the dragons from the mice?"

"Well, I wouldn't go that far," Nathan replied. "That might be a nasty form of *eugenics*." He glared, boggle-eyed at the lawyer.

The lawyer made a face, but said nothing.

"No," Nathan continued. "If my research is correct, Feng, you don't run conglomerates so you can buy the next rare collectible. I've researched how you are re-profiling your product lines, your Sustainability Index is off the charts—maybe one day we might turn our planet back into a home for everyone, eh? Yet your lawyers are still executing your contracts in the old me-first paradigm. That kind of thinking disaggregated the middle-class and completely abandoned the lower-class." He spread his palms out. "Maybe we could start to re-align the talent you have up there, and re-engage the talent down here, for the benefit of everyone. That's the real social contract we need."

"A talent scout then?" Feng offered. "Or talent engineer. Or both."

Nathan nodded. "How about social re-engineer?"

Feng smiled warmly. "Thank you, Nathan. I look forward to meeting you in person."

Her image faded.

The lawyer consulted his lenses then reached over and tore up the contract. He pulled out another document and slid it over to Nathan. "That was a good speech."

"I meant it."

"Sure you did, kid."

"No, I'm serious."

"I'd offer you a job, we need more tough negotiators. But Feng has other plans."

Nathan flipped through the new contract. "You're a family man, aren't you?"

"Yes, what—"

"So you know when your kids are telling the truth?"

"Yes."

"Well, you should look into my eyes now." Nathan smiled and picked up the pen. "Where do I sign?"

AFTERWORD TO "SOCIAL CONTRACT"

"Social Contract" is part of my Urban Decay series. The world is teetering along the knife edge between social harmony and anarchy in the wake of several GFCs.

At its most basic level, the story is a job interview. However I think there's also a faint caricature in there on the "talent time" syndrome that seems to have gripped the world. In this case it's gene-talent that piques the interest of the "judges".

At its broadest level, I think I'm using the story to ask questions like: When will someone speak out? When will someone be brave enough to say no? At what point do we turn the tide on the class madness that is literally consuming our world and our collective spirit?

For the record, I really hated the lawyer from the opening line, that's probably why I couldn't bring myself to give him a name!

HOUSE OF CARDS

PROLOGUE

My tattoo snarled at the kid standing in the queue behind me. The kid laughed and pointed at my arm. I had warned Schrody before about fraternising, but it just wouldn't be told. *Damn you*, I said through its affinity matrix. It ignored me and kept swirling up and down my arm like a mad wolf chasing its tail.

The kid reached out to touch it, but his mum pulled him back at the same time as I side-stepped out of his reach. He laughed as Schrody sat and looked up at me, its lips curled back over steel-coloured fangs.

I shrugged and half-smiled at the kid's mum who placed a protective arm around her boy. She was a stunner, wrapped in tight-fitting designer denim. She'd look good on the catwalk; would look even better in all kinds of positions.

Her eyes began roaming over me and I realised a little late that she was actually sizing me up, which gave me a warm buzz. I must have unconsciously stood a little taller. A smile played at the corners of her mouth and there was a different glint in her eye—amused but appreciative.

Her husband, a tall guy with greying hair and a paunch, clearly batting above his average, had no idea his wife was window shopping right in front of him. He leant across to her and whispered in her ear.

What a fuck-wit.

I heard it through Schrody's matrix.

My day time fantasy vanished. I glared at him and turned back to face the queue in front of me. Schrody picked up my mood change. Its seven modal blueprints scrolled across my vision: machine pistol, sniper rifle, rocket . . .

I switched off its matrix; the blueprints faded and the tattoo froze. I didn't need weapons when I had my bare hands, but instead of turning back I forced air into the bottom of my lungs and took another step forward.

The spaceport was packed and the queues were glacial, but at least the view was interesting. The shining, silver engines of the phase liner rose in front of the viewing deck, like jet turbines from another era. The rotating blades served a different purpose, however, manipulating the enfolded geometries of space-time. The whole liner faded in and out of sight, in rhythm with some secret harmonics—a marvel of this new golden age of travel.

The queue moved on, one tedious step at a time, until I was able to shunt my boarding documents to the clairvoyant. She picked up the data packets and cross-referenced them through the meta-alerts system. *Oh come on, I'm not some smuggler or dealer or worse.*

She looked at me with startling pale blue eyes. "Do you have a license for that, Mr De Vere?"

I let her touch my left arm where Schrody was curled in his scaled armour against a backdrop of black Mandelbrot patterns. She ran her fingers over it. I pressed the skin of my bicep so she could see it properly. "It's decommissioned," I lied, shunting extra files to her, hoping Schrody's firewall was as good as the money I had paid for it.

"Is it bio-alloy?"

"Yes," I lied again. "But it's an early prototype, fused to my neural interface. It's just a tattoo now."

Fuck, I was overdoing it. But the touch of her hand was soft and distracting and I wasn't on my game today.

She approved my boarding documents, e-stamped my visa and recorded the tattoo in the Classified Veterans' Log for the Passage of Decommissioned Weapons.

"Any luggage?" she asked.

"No."

"Have a safe trip."

I made to walk past, but she grabbed my hand on the way through. I stopped dead in my tracks. *Not now, of all the times, not now.* My stomach sank and an odd nausea slid slowly through my veins.

She turned my hand over and traced her fingers along my palm. "You have a short lifeline."

I shrugged, completely lost for words.

She let go, but held me with her hypnotic gaze. In a surprisingly gentle voice she said, "Take care."

I didn't look back. By the time I found my seat on the phase liner I was sweating heavily. I had been lucky; I had become slack and somehow I had just got lucky. Clairvoyants were entities from Matrioshka shell computers—nodes in a collective consciousness that regulated travel. They were tapped into the world-lines of all citizens: calculating, forecasting, and modelling the multiplicity of the human scattering.

What had she seen? Did she know that I had come out of retirement? Did she know that I had broken my vow and now I was actually going to *meet* a client? And if she did, why the hell did she just let me on board?

QUEEN OF DIAMONDS

I waited in a quiet courtyard of the floating palace. Two captured moons hung at the zenith of an azure sky, and a massive Jovian world with swirling green storms dominated the eastern horizon. Far below the transparent floor of the courtyard lay crumpled hills and snow-capped mountains.

Celine, First Sovereign of the Quickening, smiled as she entered the courtyard. There was a sharp-edged beauty about her that only post-Singularity nanotech could produce. Her height was accentuated by a simple red one-piece that hugged every curve.

"Welcome, Kieran."

I hesitated, not knowing what honorific to use. "Your . . . majesty."

"How quaint," she said, laughing. "Call me Celine. Your counterpart in this reality was Adrian—my husband." She waited for a reaction, studying every nuance of my response.

I wondered if my presence was distressing her in any way. Could a machine feel pain or loss? She hugged me briefly. Her cheek was warm and the smell of her skin reminded me of a lost summer. Those green eyes held me with their sadness, and something else . . . constrained desire.

This wasn't how I had pictured the meeting. I looked away before my own pent-up frustration got the better of me. I was a bad man, but not that bad. She was only recently widowed after all.

I cleared my throat. "Do you know who the killer is?"

"I have no idea." She turned and began to walk away then glanced back at me. "But I think the more pertinent question is why is someone targeting you?"

"Me?" My mind tumbled over, working through the terrifying implications.

How could I be the target? Fuck.

I followed her along a maze of corridors until we arrived at a hidden room. She removed a small black sphere from a dark alcove and handed it to me. Her fingers were delicate and warm and she knew when to touch and when not to. She stood so close I could feel her body heat. She was good . . . no, she was exceptional—carefully crafted effigy-grade. Her controlling Alpha persona seemed to know all the right moves.

I realised I was arching my body to mould to her intoxicating red curves. I had loved her in another life, had spent countless nights intertwined with her. I knew she sensed something in me—a hunger for power, a desire for new potentials offered by the Quickening, an immortal life spanning a dozen galaxies. Hell, what would I have to lose? But then my guilt rushed back in and I swallowed hard. I wasn't used to this level of restraint. Maybe I was losing it after all these years, or maybe a conscience had crept in, stealthy and mellowing. I had always gone for what I wanted in a focussed and unrelenting fashion. That's why I was so good at what I did . . . but now she had succeeded in unnerving me on two levels.

A faint smile played on her lips.

I looked down at the sphere nestled in my hands. "What is it?"

"A Universal Positioning System."

"You're kidding me?" I had heard of them, but never seen one before. Somehow I'd always thought they would be bigger. Then

I realised it had to be an interface. The computing power to map the energy topographies of alternate realities only came from the Matrioshkas.

I made to hand it back to her. "I can't take it." This was way over my head.

She arched an eyebrow. "You're going to need it." She pushed the sphere back into my hands before it dropped to the floor.

"I don't like assassin against assassin deals. They never end well. So you'd better start explaining."

"Unlike you," she said, "Adrian was no killer. He could be a rogue, of course. The Quickening demands certain proclivities, but we are governed by different laws and codes to those of flesh and blood." She paused and walked me back out to a chamber overlooking the rising green Jovian, a sparkling ring world now visible along its equatorial orbit.

I looked at her. "It seems you have the capacity to hire a thousand assassins, so why me?"

"This was not some random act, Kieran. It takes significant planning and premeditation to kill an Alpha. I have searched many neighbouring realities and you are dead in most of them. Someone is hunting your counterparts down and I think it is only a matter of time before you are next."

She reached in close and wrapped her arms around my waist. That lost summer came back to me then—some strange non-local quantum effect from Adrian's dead Alpha, the qualia of my counterpart's life now brushing my mind.

The guilt and apprehension vanished, and in a way I was glad because in the future world-line that was unfolding in my mind's eye, there was no place for such emotions.

JACK OF HEARTS

I was relieved when the shuttle finally landed. I had been in some rough atmosphere drops in the Corps, but none of them were as bad as this shuttle ride to an outpost in the middle of nowhere. No wonder they called the planet Zephyr. The whole system suffered a high delta-vee solar wind that played havoc with all planetary weather systems. In fact, nothing in this reality seemed quite right.

And in other ways I was relieved just to get some head space. My serial killer had murdered another two counterparts across a trail spanning five realities. I had to find a way to get ahead of his plans, to stop this evil from spreading—but how? How could I fight such single-minded obsession?

I recognised Dominic standing in a crowd in the arrival lounge. His face brightened when he saw me.

"Hello, Kieran." He gave me a strong, spirited hug as if he had known me all his life. In a way I suppose he had. We exchanged small talk, more out of my own discomfort as I was completely flummoxed by this young man—the son that I never had.

We walked out of the shuttle port and he strapped my bag to a speeder that looked like a black metallic dolphin. I held the handlebars steady as the wind buffeted the machine back and forth on its tether.

"You're here on some serious business," Dominic said.

"Yes, it's a little complicated. I'll explain everything when we meet your dad."

I hopped on the speeder, but couldn't make sense of the controls. Its wetware interface was archaic. I activated Schrody and it jumped to life on my arm, its long tail twitching. It winked at Dominic and jump started the speeder.

"Great tattoo," Dominic said as he raced away on his speeder. I followed, my hands a blur over the controls as Schrody's voodoo protocol overrode my fine motor functions.

Dominic whooped above the howling wind, his crazy blonde hair whipping about his face. We were both grinning madly as we steered the speeders across a savannah, hammering great swathes of grass flat in our wake. A sudden feeling of completeness overwhelmed me. All the advice my friends had given me over the years was indeed true, but being a single male with a questionable career, I had chosen to ignore it. Now I found myself yearning for a different life: to be a father, to see my son grow and flourish, to live my life through his eyes. My eyes were watery with the wind so my tears passed, unnoticed.

"My dad is going to go spare when he meets you," Dominic hollered. "Or should I say when he meets himself!"

We pushed on for another twenty kilometres then dialled the speeders down a notch and cruised between two lines of peach tree analogs leading up to the homestead.

Schrody tunnelled away from my skin in a blink, and appeared ahead of me, bounding towards the house, dust and grit flicking up from its paws.

What is it?

A chilling scream cut the silence.

"Dad!" Dominic leapt from his speeder and it banged into the porch. He ran to the front door, flung it open and rushed inside.

"Wait," I yelled. The modes scrolled and Schrody was now in my hand—a black machine pistol. My legs felt like they were filled with mercury as I stepped onto the porch and through the open door. Dominic was unconscious on the lounge room floor. I checked his pulse; it took several milli-seconds to find . . . there. I moved to the next room.

His father lay on the kitchen floor, arterial sprays across the table and chair, one spray in a slow motion arc above his neck. The air behind the chair shimmered and I instantly recognised the telltale sign of transition. An afterimage lingered above the corpse like a crude charcoal sketch—a man standing on a platform, his eyes wide with surprise. I fired off a clip of bullets, more out of instinct than any real hope of hitting him. The image of the man faded away, unharmed, as the bullets ripped into the kitchen wall.

The bullets and their casings instantly tunnelled back into Schrody's BEC stratum and I scrolled it back to wolf mode and sent it out on a perimeter search of the building.

Time slipped back to normal as the voodoo protocol terminated.

I tried to stem my counterpart's bleeding, but he was too far gone and I had to give up after several futile attempts at resuscitation.

Dominic groaned from the other room and I strode over and lifted him into a sitting position with the blood of his father soaking my hands.

"Did you see him?"

His eyes rolled and I shook him gently.

"Who was it?" My voice was firm, willing him back to consciousness.

"He was you," Dominic slurred. "Like you . . . and . . . Dad."

NINE OF CLUBS

"You need closure," Nevena said, reading my far away gaze. Her bio-alloy plates clicked softly as she moved in the bed.

I brushed aside stray strands of her dark hair and touched her incredible face. "I know." I had lost myself in her physical and emotional whirlwind. I recalled the first time I cut myself on her, tearing a shallow gash in my stomach. She was distraught, but the wound had healed soon enough.

I often wondered at that as we lay together night after night, the bronze glow of the hive across the ceiling, and a constant thrumming through the walls, felt more than heard. Perhaps it was a side effect of the UPS that sat in my stomach like a stone; that had kept me on the trail of carnage for the last two years.

Schrody was sleeping next to a stack of glowing heat spheres, its dreams distant through the affinity matrix. I reached out and stroked its back. The Bose-Einstein Condensate seethed beneath its confinement scales like foamy black water.

I called up the images of the evidence I had obtained, cycling through the paltry DNA residue. A face scrolled across my vision, like an eerie reflection in negative colours. He was dark haired, grey eyed, with identical bone structure. Allele damage suggested he was from a planet with high traces of uranium and heavy metals; probably an industrial world, which narrowed it down to about a whisker shy of an infinite number of possibilities across the stable realities.

I cancelled the images, but his face—my face—continued to haunt me. He was always there, a constant companion behind my waking thoughts, in the dark recesses of my nightmares, a twisted reflection on Nevena's skin.

She reached over and pressed her hand on my chest, sensing my agitation. "Why don't you stay here? You've criss-crossed too many realities. No wonder you're so tired."

"You know I can't," I said, wondering how long I could keep delaying the inevitable. "He needs to be stopped, and I think I have caused enough problems for you here."

She rolled her eyes. "We've been over this again and again. My zygotic-siblings welcome you with open arms. They want you to bond with us—I want you to. Join the hive empathic. You will find it brings a new meaning to the word "family"."

"I can never replace Garran."

"I don't want you to," she said, concern etched across her silver face. "You are the same, but you're also very different."

I sighed, suddenly angry with myself. "I have used you as an excuse for too long now, Nevena, and I'm sorry. I'm fooling myself if I think I can keep you safe. It would be best for all of us if I move on."

Her eyes darkened. "It's more than that, isn't it?"

I sighed inwardly this time. I was beginning to think she knew me better than I knew myself. "Yes, you're right. This stopped being a contract a long time ago. I want revenge. Revenge for all the suffering he has inflicted on my counterparts and their loved ones."

She smiled. "You can't keep the truth from me forever. Let me help you."

Schrody's ears twitched and it raised its head.

Nevena arched her back, eyes intense, her plates shimmering, picking up the ultrasonics that permeated the hive.

"We should leave." She stood up. "Now."

"What is it, Nevena?"

"I must get you to safety. Follow me." She raced out of the cell.

I called Schrody onto my arm and ran after her. I turned a corner in the tunnel as the reek of machined metal filled the air. The darkness came to life with the blur of wings as five muscular flyers smashed into us from above.

I awoke to guttural laughter and the rush of wind across my face.

All five flew in formation in the cold dawn air that tightened my lungs into knots. Taloned feet dug into my shoulders and blood gushed down my arms. Schrody had been sliced in two and I could not call up his modes.

The bright orange sun peaked over the hives to the east and I turned to the light and saw Nevena, unconscious in the grip of the flyer behind me.

"Ah, this one is awake," my flyer said to the others.

"Coen said the fleshling would eventually come to the hive," another replied. They laughed and cursed me in their rasping dialect.

"Take a good look," my flyer said, digging his talons in further. "This will be the last thing you see."

They released us and swung back to the hive.

The rush of air was deafening as I tumbled end over end, earth and sky spinning in a kaleidoscope. I twisted, straightened out my fall and dived towards Nevena. I reached out for her wrist, but my hand slipped across her bio-alloy. I shut my eyes as we hit the ground at terminal velocity.

The last thing I remember was the dawn light on her iridescent features, her hair like raven's wings.

KING OF SPADES

I skipped into the atmosphere on a bow shock wave, streaking across the sky with a trail of fire behind me. Schrody switched from shuttle to canopy mode and I was flung into open air and parachuted the final two thousand metres. Evening light from a white dwarf binary slanted across the dust that kicked up from my landing.

The field was being used to grow some stunted form of wheat. A copse of trees grew on the perimeter, bent and wretched, the dim lights of the city visible beyond. It seemed everything was struggling with the paltry light and warmth from the binary star on the very outer edge of the war zone.

In fact I was starting to believe everything in this reality was bent on self-destruction, caught up in a conflict that had cut across great gulfs of space, leaving cracked worlds and dead suns in its wake. I had no idea what the war was about, nor did I really care, because all I could see was my counterpart's face, dark, impassive— the portrait of a mass-murderer.

I remembered Nevena through the haze of years. That day had been a turning point. The knowledge that I had come so close to being another victim had made me rethink my strategy—I never stayed in any reality for too long. And the regenerative properties of the Matrioshka tech in my belly spurred me on—I pushed myself to new physical extremes, my pursuit spanning more than thirty realities.

Schrody snapped to katana mode and I gripped the handle in both hands and walked through the outskirts of the city. Night on this world was pitch, but the affinity matrix compensated as I walked through large industrial complexes shut down for the night. Their product was relativistic weapons, and Coen was the supplier, the master of this emporium of sorts.

I reached the Maglev Freeway heading out to some residential towers on the northern outskirts. The traffic was sparse as the last shuttles and charabancs shipped the workers to their homes. I waited patiently in the shadow of a support pylon, watching each bus as it approached. I had viewed them for weeks from 300 kilometres high, so now they seemed disproportionately large this close.

As a rusting charabanc passed the pylon I slashed the katana out, cutting the charabanc's generator. Sparks flew and the charabanc stuttered to a halt. The cabin erupted with noise as passengers complained about bruising and yet another breakdown in public transport. The emergency exit hissed open and I jumped on board and strode up the aisle. I didn't know what Coen was thinking, hiding among his people. Maybe he thought he could blend in— bad call, fucker.

I punched him in the head with the butt of the katana before he could call up his platform and whisk away. The other passengers stampeded off the charabanc as I smashed a double fist into his back. He slumped forward in his seat.

I recalled Schrody to my arm. *No voodoo. Not this time.*

I swung behind Coen and grabbed him around the neck.

"I knew you would find—"

He gagged as I began to squeeze the life out of him. I could feel the surge of blood in his carotid artery. It matched the fury in my own veins, the elation of knowing that I was about to finish him.

But the doubt that I had struggled with all this time now made my fingers weak. I had seen so much of what I was capable of—it left me in awe of the human potential that I had tried so hard to remain detached from through the scope of a sniper rifle. I could care and love, and feel heartache and anguish—real living that uplifted me; that made me a better man. But I also saw the other extreme. The ability to kill was the thin end of the wedge that, if left unchecked, led to serial slaughter and torment and nihilism.

Coen butted me in the face and I slipped backwards. He leapt over the seat and kicked out, planting both his boots on my chest. The air woofed from my lungs and my head hit the dirty metal floor.

I fought back nausea and clawed at his hands around my throat. Modal blueprints scrolled, but I shook my head and kicked up at Coen and the pressure eased. A trickle of air found its way into my lungs before his grip tightened. I kicked again to no effect. His shoulders bunched and he spat in my face.

"You are a fool to think you could kill me."

In the white-hot misery of my pain I looked up into the mask of his face, flushed with exertion, spittle foaming at the edges of his mouth. I must have looked like that only moments ago.

The modes scrolled urgently as consciousness started to slip away.

Okay, Schrody.

I almost welcomed the blackness rushing in.

EPILOGUE

I handed the UPS to the floating information nodes of the Matrioshka-entity. It smiled and absorbed the sphere back into its domain, its touch reminding me of the clairvoyant. Its body was a storm of holographic images, world-lines cascading, reflecting. I saw myself in there multiplied a thousand times. And I saw the others—Celine, Dominic and Nevena. I looked away in shame.

I suppose I should have felt honoured that this M-entity had actually left the collective to meet us in the palace courtyard. But all I could feel was some irrational hatred at the thing as it floated there, processing my world-lines as if I was just some anomaly.

I glared at it, my voice flat, toneless. "You could have stopped me that day, but you didn't?"

I turned to leave.

Celine stepped in the way. She knew me so well.

"It's in your nature, Kieran."

"What is?" The image of Coen skewered on the katana haunted me.

"You should listen to Celine," the M-entity conveyed. "We cannot stop what is in you. Coen captured and tortured a clairvoyant in his desperation to predict the future of the war in his reality. The clairvoyant foretold the involvement of his counterparts and a threat from another reality. This was enough to send him on his killing spree."

"But if Coen had not started killing I would be none the wiser and he would still be alive."

Celine touched my shoulder. "Adrian was the same. All your counterparts are the same, I suspect. You don't know how to let go."

The grief inside me was howling to be let out, to pay tribute to the dead and those left in mourning. But all I could do was stand in mute horror at Coen's madness and my own folly. I pressed my fingers to my temples, trying to make sense of the self-fulfilling spiral of my life, as if hindsight could somehow fix my broken house of cards.

AFTERWORD TO "HOUSE OF CARDS"

Okay . . . futuristic assassin living out a self-fulfilling prophecy in a mad, Moebius-strip chase across multiple-universes. Crazy, adrenalin-fuelled, gun-toting, counterpart-hunting, Greek tragedy. Eat your heart out, Oedipus.

I had fun writing this one!

STATIC

There is always some madness in love. But there is also always some reason in madness.

—Friedrich Nietzsche

The interview turned to a nightmare when Oriel heard movement from the bedroom.

She switched off her chronicler and clutched the sides of the dining table. A line of sweat trickled down the curve of her back. She cast a sidelong glance through the gap in the bedroom door where something black and languid moved in the shadows.

Liquid eyes stared at her from the darkness.

One blink.

Two.

There was intention now behind those hellish orbs.

The door started to slide open.

Every fibre of her being wanted her limbs to move, to run as fast as she could from the house, but her legs would not budge. It was all she could do to control her bladder. Tears welled up, scrolled down her cheeks.

Tamati looked at her from across the table, his brown eyes unreadable beneath the locks of his jet black hair. He was a beautiful, incredible Maori.

"Aroha mai."

The sound of his apology made her gulp in air. The sudden, sharp intake jolted her into action. She was up and out of the front door, the dust-laden rain still beating a timeless rhythm on the tin roof. Slipping down the steps, she managed to right her fall then leapt the last three steps and slid crazily across the lawn to her car. She tugged furiously at the door handle, glancing back for signs of pursuit. An icon finally responded and the door swung open. She leapt into the car and slammed the door shut. Drenched through with red dust stains on her blouse, she fired up the engine and took off along the street.

After ten frenzied minutes of weaving through New Auckland traffic she pulled over, her breathing shallow and ragged.

She consulted her chronicler. A still image of Tamati's face hovered into view. He was an anachronism—tall, proud, tattooed. He would have looked just as comfortable in a flax cloak and huia feather head dress as he did in his plain black skinsuit. She scrutinised the blue lines of his moko carved across his cheeks and forehead like hawk wings. There was fear, and something else, in those deep brown eyes. This man had enthralled her since the incident and now she was terrified by the implications of his half-told story.

She looked at herself in the rear view mirror, bedraggled black hair plastered over her forehead, green eyes turned grey in the fading daylight. How could she fail him after he had travelled across the heavens knowing that when he woke the nightmare would continue?

But why you, Oriel?

Perhaps he had seen something of his own Maori stubbornness in her, the way she had waited all those weeks when most reporters had lost interest well before his journey home had even started. And then when weeks had turned into months, she was still there, waiting.

Her chronicler's replay icon hovered into view.

She hesitated.

To hell with the consequences.

She hit replay and gunned the car into a u-turn.

I sat watching the relic from the viewing deck, exhausted after four gruelling shifts down in the eye. It hung under the harsh light of the vault, a five metre long wedge of pure midnight. It had taken weeks to extract it from the biggest anticyclone in recorded history—the Great Red Spot. A swirling vortex of four hundred kilometres per hour winds, the same colour as the brick-red storms that still kick up on Mars even after fifty years of terraforming.

Of all the places to get a salvage contract, I must be mad.

But the months of effort and aborted extraction attempts had been worth it. Stuck in the heart of the maelstrom since time immemorial, the relic had emerged unscathed, not even a blemish. I wondered then if it might have even caused the great storm. A chunk of alien ceramic abandoned before human history began, wrapping the phosphorus-laden hydrogen and helium clouds about it like a comforting cloak over thousands of years. Layer upon layer of gases trapped into a vortex on a staggering scale. It seemed that nature itself was charmed by the secret forces of this strange technology.

I shook my head as if waking from a trance. I realised I'd been sat here for the better part of the day speculating. What did I know, anyway? I was just a gantry ship pilot. Hold the extraction torus machinery in place, get paid, go home. My job was over.

I watched the science teams come and go like worker ants with their machines and equipment. Every attempt to communicate with it had failed. Nothing stuck to its slick exterior. And the results from the spectral frequency tests were delayed, which either said they were having problems or hiding something.

Hell, this wasn't the first alien artefact to be found in the solar system, it seemed the place was littered with the stuff. It wasn't a century ago we thought that low earth orbit had become a dangerous junkyard. We didn't yet know that others had been here before us and made a mess of the entire solar system. But this was a rare find indeed. I could already hear the retro-engineers back on Earth salivating.

The play of light caught my eye again. There was something inviting about the scalloped edges, light reflecting like white novae, shimmering to hypnotic rainbows on the periphery. It was as if each seductive curve, each razor-sharp edge was designed for a single purpose. And while my eyes wandered over the dancing reflections, the black embroidery of the hull lurked underneath, constant, waiting.

Hull. Yes. That's what it looked like, a star ship of unknown origin.

And there I was, off on a tangent again.

The station had swung into Jovian night and a headache buzzed behind my eyes like tiny spinning knives. I dozed off intermittently as the nanochines repaired my cellular damage. Jupiter was hell by anyone's standards, a cold wasteland of endless storms and hard radiation. But it paid and sometimes that's all that mattered.

I fell asleep properly for the first time in over a month.

She came to me then.

The lake region was a peaceful place of strange vistas and muffled sounds. I was able to forget life and lose myself in the calm heartbeat of the world. Liquid methane lapped at my feet as I strolled along the lake edge through curtains of methane drizzle that descended from the orange clouds. A mournful wind moved through the icy arroyos to the south, caressing the edges of my heightened senses.

I walked for an hour, maybe two.

She appeared from the mist that clung to the ranges, a vision of health and vitality, pure black skin glowing with the reflected orange light of Titan. She walked barefoot beside me, her lustrous hair and red robe fluttering like pennants, her flat belly and rounded breasts unselfconsciously exposed along the robe's plunging neckline. When we finally reached the wind sculpted ice glades above the lake, a different urgency took us.

I slid my hand in under her breast and kissed her. She moaned softly, the tension now to be released in a single, primal union. She ripped at my skinsuit until it fell away and rubbed her hands across my chest, up to my neck and into my hair. We dropped to our knees then she fell back to the ice, the soft fabric of her robe slipping aside to reveal her athletic limbs and pubic hair, black against black. I straddled her, and she reached with her left hand, found me, and guided me into her. I moved slowly at first and then faster, losing myself to the quickening sensation of her. She reached up, tracing the raised scars of my moko, her amber eyes now focussed on some middle distance between my tattooed face and her inner ecstasy.

The motion of our bodies reached a frenzied peak, a quiet place of clarity that exists beyond the rush of sound and heat and skin against skin. And then, after some indeterminate time, the slide away from climax took hold, like gravity after a freefall, and colour and texture crept back into the world.

She looked up at me while I was still in her, her hair wild across the ice, her top teeth showing beneath parted lips. There were tiny red flecks in the fields of her irises, like embers about to ignite.

A subtle shift in focus, a flicker of an eyelash, dancing qualia through the windows of her soul.

I could feel the thought forming, the slight rise of her breasts beneath me, the delicate play of neck muscles, her breath hot on my cheek.

You came back.

I was the brunt of the salvage crew's jokes for days afterwards. The big Maori slumped in a chair on the viewing deck with an equally big erection beneath his overalls.

Fuck.

Still, what did it matter? You can't have too many inhibitions in the confines of salvage ops. We were an eclectic bunch, much like the whaling crews that used to ply the seas of Aotearoa. My fellow pilots included an Australian Aborigine, a Frenchman, and a Spanish woman. We'd worked hard to extract this thing and now we were all drifting by the vault window in between our medical treatments.

But my fascination had quickly become an obsession. I was hooked from the start, caught up in the whirlwind of her eyes, those black hourglass curves, and her wet inner warmth. She was everything I wanted, more than any red-blooded man could ever want.

Yet no matter how epic my fantasy, it was just that, a dream. She was a home-spun goddess, a product of a sleep deprived mind. That's what the rational side of me kept saying. But when you're jacked on a cocktail of nanochines, apple guava extract and radioisotopes, you tend to think a little more subjectively.

I wanted her, bad.

"It's hypnotic."

I nearly jumped out of my skin as Catalina joined me at the railing of the viewing deck, her tan features turned pale in the vault's glow. She had a slim, wiry physique and spoke with only a hint of accent. I unclenched my knuckles from the railing. I'd spent three days here, waiting for some sign.

"Sorry, I didn't mean to startle you. Where do you think it came from?"

"Who knows? I think it's been stuck here for so long, looking at it seems like looking through a window in time."

"I hadn't thought of it like that. That would explain why it is so—"

"Perfect."

"Yes."

Remi joined us. He was fifty-something, a hard looking man. Ex-interplanetary trade, looking for change in relic salvage freelancing. "Feeling less giddy, my friend?" A smirk played on his lips.

"Give it a rest."

His features softened as he took in the curves of the relic. It lay perched on scaffolding below the window like a void in the fabric of reality. A silver diagnostic ring encircled it like some old particle-accelerator. Bundles of squid-like cabling fanned out from the ring to banks of equipment and micro panels around the vault.

I felt odd about the way Remi was looking at it. I'd seen that look before, those dilated pupils. I wanted him to stop. I reached out a hand and—

"C'est magnifique. Un vaisseau spatial pour un fait a la main."

Catalina and I frowned. We hadn't finished the didactic.

Remi looked at us in his typical, matter-of-fact way. "It looks hand-crafted, made for one."

Catalina turned back to the ship as if for the first time. I noticed a slight flushing of her cheeks. She cleared her throat as if suddenly uncomfortable in her overalls. But then, just as suddenly, something seemed to give in her and she turned away from the window, her face a mask of anguish. "It's probably just a piece of junk." She said it like an accusation.

"That's impossible and you know it. There's got to be . . . something in there."

She looked up at me. "You can speculate all you like, Tamati, but I've heard the X-ray tomography has come up clean. There's nothing in there, no dead alien, no drive system, nada. All the reconstruction software algorithms show the ceramic is completely homogenous right the way through it."

"I don't believe you." I'd said it with such anger she took an involuntary step back. Remi seemed oblivious, his attention still riveted on the ship.

"Hey, don't shoot the messenger," Catalina snapped. "I'm sure there's some explanation. Not many undamaged artefacts have ever been found. Something this intact, you've got to wonder. Maybe it's a beacon or interstellar signpost. Hora de comer. Dinner time and humans are on the menu."

"Now you're letting your imagination run riot." I was a fine one to talk, but she was right. This thing could just as easily have been designed for all the wrong reasons.

"You should get some rest, you look exhausted."

She was right again. I hadn't slept since the dream. I was afraid of the panorama of my sleeping mind, afraid of the connections that seemed to be clicking into place at the back of my mind.

I went back to my quarters, bathed in the ever present light of the storm that floated below the station. I was annoyed at the way Remi and Catalina had looked at the ship with their poorly covered arousal. Maybe they too were having dreams, waking up in a cold sweat.

I fell asleep some time after Jovian midnight, the clouds congealing below like whirlpools of blood.

The caldera was so high it jutted out of the atmosphere, an ancient monument to planetary upheaval on an unimaginable scale. We looked on from the airless rim of Olympus Mons across the red curve of Mars, our impervious black bodies shining like gods. She traced delicate fingers along the silver lines of my moko and we lifted off the rim to make love in free fall.

After a time we descended down to the planet and roamed the dry canyons and valleys, unhindered by past or future, lost in each other's presence.

Do you love me?

I never stopped loving you, She'el.

Don't go away this time.

I won't.

Stay with me.

I'll stay.

She lifted her arms to the twilight, a song like a battle cry uttering from her lips. I touched those lips, tracing my thumb in and out of her mouth and then along her jaw. She shivered and turned, an invitation etched on her curves. She ended her song and I felt an incredible emptiness, the only sound was that of dust sighing on the breeze.

She looked at me over her shoulder.

Fuck me again. Fuck me now on this dead husk of a world. Let us relive the glory days.

I pushed her down to the red sand as night crept across the sky. I shuffled down on my knees behind her. She arched her head back as I entered her, her raven hair cascading like a bleak waterfall. She shrieked as I pushed deep inside, our frantic motion building to a luscious, intolerable peak.

Just as I was about to climax, she reached back, her skin hardening like adamantine, and clawed her fingers down my chest. A searing pain shot through me then I felt her tightening around me like a vice, but I was too far gone to care. I erupted inside her, our bodies still pounding and slapping, as blood gushed down my chest and across her back.

She turned her head and looked at me through shining eyes. I lost myself in that conflagration.

It has been so long. I couldn't take it if you went away again.

I won't.

Only I can protect you.

And I you. I'll look after you, keep you close.

Close as this?

She grinned, nudging her hips back. I felt her, still slick. I rose, forgetting the blood, the burning in my chest, and plunged back into her.

We laughed then, a strange, guttural sound that echoed around the barren landscape.

We had conquered worlds in another lifetime.

"You're as strong as an ox." The medic was looking at the readouts on the holoscreen.

"Then how do you explain the wounds?" Ganan seemed perplexed as he looked down at me through a mass of black curls. He was a tall, slim aborigine who was always smiling a flash of white. He wasn't smiling now.

He had found me unconscious in my quarters in a pool of blood.

The medic seemed affronted. "His blood work and MRI are as clean as can be expected. A few minor tumours are being mopped up by the nanochine gene therapy. His purification is incredible, one of the hardiest human genomes to have evolved. Polynesians had great geospatial awareness for navigating by the stars and ocean currents. At one stage they had settled across an area greater than any other civilisation in human history. You've got to respect that sort of tenacity."

"Ok, I get the message," Ganan said. "But that still doesn't explain the wounds."

The medic started closing down the diagnostic equipment. "Parasomnia. Self-mutilation is rare but not unheard of. Like everyone here, our circadian rhythms are way out of synch. He needs fresh food, exercise and regular sleep for a few weeks. That should help straighten things out."

Ganan laughed, pearl white, and clapped me on the shoulder. "Man, he would have prescribed the same thing if you had a cold."

His voice seemed to fade.

There had been no vibration, sound or spectral emission from the ship. No sign that it was attempting to communicate with the outside world. So whatever bond was being created with me was happening at some incredible, sublime level.

Understanding teased me from the periphery of my senses, still elusive through the confusing haze of rapture and fear.

Ganan offered his hand and I got up off the bed, still a little groggy.

"Where are Remi and Catalina?"

"Getting ready," Ganan said, "We're going home tomorrow."

I must have looked terrified, which is hard through the constant glare of my tattoos, for he took a step back.

"What's up?"

I lurched out of the sick bay and made my way along the central axis to the vault. I leant on the railing and pressed my face against the window. I had to get in there. "She's in the ship."

"Who?" Ganan had followed me to the vault.

"She'el."

"She who? Man, you're hallucinating. There's nothing in the ship. In fact there's no evidence that it *is* a ship."

I grabbed him by the shoulders. "You're wrong."

"The science team gave a debriefing this morning. It's like it has been carved from a single block. There's speculation that it might be some sort of advanced substrate material, used for bonding other types of matter. It might even be part of a larger vessel or device."

I sneered at him. "What, like some alien dropped a cog into the gravity well and never fucking noticed? Has anyone looked at it, I mean really stopped and looked at it? It's a ship I tell you and she is in there."

He shoved me away, now completely out of patience. "Whatever." He turned and walked away.

"Wait, I'm sorry."

He didn't stop.

Substrate . . . other types of matter . . .

"What other tests have they run?" I yelled at his receding figure.

He shook his head and turned out of sight along the axis.

I pressed my face to the window again. The ship was five metres below. I scanned the different images on the micro panel array. The tomography image showed a wedge of grey static. Fluorescent green numbers scrolled down one side of the panel.

I took several steps back and hurled myself at the window. The technicians below snapped their heads around at the sound.

The reinforced glass hadn't budged.

I stepped back again.

Whump.

A splinter this time, but no movement.

Hand-crafted . . . made for one . . .

An alarm started bleating in the distance.

Whump.

A crack in the glass, spider web effect, painfully slow.

Footsteps along the corridor, a helmeted security guard in black, stunner at the ready.

"Stop!"

I raised my hands, carefully.

"Turn around and put your hands on your head. Now."

I obeyed.

I heard the snick of the cuffs unwinding from his utility belt and felt the first delicate touch of their buckyball filament on the top of my left wrist. As the guard came closer I grabbed the filament and head butted backwards into his faceplate. The filament writhed in my hands like a snake and I swung it around. His stunner flashed and I felt the pulse of air as it whooshed past my head. I whip-cracked the filament and it latched onto his wrists, then I let go of my end and the remaining length coiled round his wrists and solidified, its program terminating.

Blood poured from my hand, the filament had cut me to the bone. I jabbed down as the guard started to raise his stunner in both hands. The device skittered across the floor. He lurched forward, shoulders down, and knocked the wind out of me. The momentum of our combined two hundred kilograms carried us onto the cracked glass.

It buckled.

The guard fell back to the floor of the viewing deck, reaching for the stunner. I shoved at the window, feet lodged onto the ledge, until I was able to slide through the gap and into the vault.

I fell, twisting, and landed hard on my stomach. The ship rocked on the scaffolding with the impact. Technicians ran in all directions.

I didn't care anymore. I could feel it now on my hands and face, the contrast of its smooth black hollows and razor edges. A sigh lifted out from the bottom of my lungs and through my mouth, misting out into the cold air of the vault. Blood traced its way down my cheek, running along the scalloped hull like the delta of some far away river.

I looked through tired eyes at the snowstorm static on the micro panel. I tried to focus, was that movement?

Yes, but only the vibration of the ship on the scaffolding.

Wait.

There.

A hand reached out through the storm.

Gone again.

There.

A silhouette of her curves, her wild hair, drifted in and out of coherence through the haze.

I pressed my bleeding palms and face down on the hull.

The stun pulses slammed into my back from the gap in the window above.

The ship seemed to writhe beneath me, seething and resonating to some secret tempo. The vault spun and my vision faded to black. An ecstatic tremor ran through me in the darkness.

I stood on the cliff edge as heavy black rain beat a staccato on my impermeable brow. Puddles quickly filled the potholes and soon the dirt turned to umber mud. The sky dimmed further as the clouds closed in like sentinels. The smell of magnesium filled the air.

I looked about one final time and stepped off the cliff. The rain hissed and vaporised on the ship as it rose to meet me. I stood for a time, the thick rain washing harmlessly away. I turned my hands over, marvelling at the adamantine skin, black, indestructible. With a thought I changed density and moulded my body into the ebbing darkness of the ship and flew above the world.

The land was covered in an oily film from horizon to horizon, a pall descending like a cleansing anodyne. Beyond the atmosphere, the stars peeked in and out through gaps in the nanocloud, its underbelly glowing blue from the light of Sirius.

The armada emerged, one thousand black ships, rising in spirals and helical patterns like eagles on a thermal updraft. Some were joined together in symbiotic clusters. Others hovered as individuals, aloof above the dying world.

I wondered if anyone would mourn the vanquished souls still down there.

I doubted it and smiled.

The rain fell.

It would be like this until the end.

The image faded, slowly, and I woke to She'el's caress.

We lay in a chamber of black silk and shadows. The air was calm. The rapture of victory still pulsed in my veins. The dream was so real, so stark. Its residue fluttered in my mind, reluctant to leave.

What was that?

As we were, before the war that ended everything. There are more memories like that. Many more we can share.

I felt a tiny shiver run up the length of her body as we lay with our legs and arms intertwined.

And where are we now?

Does it matter? We are together again.

I shrugged.

She pressed her palm against my chest and leant back to look at me.

You love me, don't you?

Yes, I do. It's just . . .

I felt the doubt rise in me, hovering on a knife edge. Like a caged bird confronted with an open door, fly to boundless freedom or stay, safe, warm, wanting for nothing.

Her hands lingered over me.

Stay with me. I need you now, more than anything.

I clutched her wrists expectantly.

Her eyes blazed.

I need you. I can't survive without you.

Her fingers tore open my skin, ripping through bone, sliding along my ribcage like slipping softly into a warm glove.

I need you.

She was changing, flowing.

Steel hard cords wrapped around my heart.

I need you.

Oriel parked her car outside the house. She stepped out into the rain and walked to the front porch. The door was still open. Her hands trembled as she stepped through into the living room.

"I knew you would come back." He had not moved from his seat at the table.

Oriel forced her lips into a bleak smile. She locked her knees to quell her shaking and turned to look at the thing that stood next to Tamati.

It boiled in the air like black mercury, partially human in shape, with whip-like cords thrashing about its torso. She recognised those curves, the long limbs and wild hair. The ebb and flow of its alien motion was like some strange, exotic dance, at once enthralling but at the same time brimming with lethal potential.

The eyes held Oriel, liquid amber irises flecked with red fire. They reached down into her soul and blasted away her human frailties and inhibitions. She felt warmth rising from the depth of her loins, tantalising with forbidden sensations and the skilful caress that only a lover should have.

The instant retraction was like razor-wire slashing across her mind. She knew the rejection was irreversible yet she so wanted those eyes back on her, roaming her inner world, unlocking dormant feelings and desires.

"Oh fuck," Oriel gasped. "Is she the pilot?"

Tamati shook his head in mute response.

"No? I had assumed—"

The liquid limbs thrashed about, spinning into a vortex. Then the entire mass exploded and disappeared. In an eye blink the thing reappeared on top of Tamati like a foaming black wave. He looked on in a stupor as it dug beneath his collar bone. Blood spurted from the wound.

Somewhere in the distance Oriel could hear faint grunting sounds. She clamped her hands over her mouth, both to stop the noise and prevent herself from vomiting.

The flow of the thrashing limbs quickened into a terrible ripping action. His skinsuit split apart and a gash opened up from shoulder to groin. Blood sprayed across the furniture. Sizzling and foaming, the thing poured into Tamati with a slick wriggling action, pushing around bones and internal organs, until it disappeared.

A lead weight filled her stomach as she realised Tamati had been conscious through all this, a look of rapture in his eyes, a rictus of a smile on his lips.

His wounds were, miraculously, healing rapidly until nothing remained but livid red welts.

Oriel felt suddenly hollow and alone. But she knew, like Catalina and the others, she was not compatible. Somehow this Maori was, maybe it was his pure genome, maybe it was the nanochines, or a combination of both. Or maybe he was just in the wrong place at the wrong time.

He was reviving a little, his skin hardening to a black sheen like burnt metal after a terrible fire. His moko had turned silver, like the dream.

"It's not the pilot at all, is it Tamati? He died a long time ago. She'el kept his memories all this time in the hope that one day he might return."

The big Maori nodded. "Yes." His voice sounded like gravel.

"What sort of exotic matter is it?"

"Bose-Einstein condensate." He struggled with the words. "Bonded to ... ceramic substrate."

"And now it's bonded to you."

"Nanochines have ... homogeneous molecular structure."

His skin was fading now back to its normal colouring, the moko darkening to blue.

He saw the question in her eyes.

Only I can protect you.

An ironic smile quivered on his lips. "Autonomic response of a sentient spacesuit."

She sat down heavily, elbows on the spattered table, the wave of adrenalin still pulsing through her. She pushed her hair back with shaking hands and let out a long sigh.

He shook his head, as if afraid of the next question.

"Do you love her?"

He nodded without hesitation, yet his eyes pleaded with her— take me away from this madness.

What are you going to do, Oriel? What the fuck are you going to do now?

She felt her indecision drift on a tide of static.

AFTERWORD TO "STATIC"

This story is set in the very early days of the Combat-Ultras universe, which is explored in more detail in "Weapons of Choice".

Sometimes for men it's all about sex, but this story is caught somewhere between Basic Instinct *and* Alien! *I make no apologies. After all, this is a book about men in all our splendid ignominy.*

Regarding She'll, I wanted a sentient spacesuit to do anything to save it's wearer from harm. I thought a classic case of "obsessive love" would be a means to achieve this. There's an instant, super-hot attraction between Tamati and She'll in the first encounter, then She'll gets more anxious about losing Tamati in their second encounter, until her obsession goes into overdrive during their third encounter. Obsessive relationships usually end up in a final destructive phase. However, in this case it doesn't go that far for She'll who achieves some kind of equilibrium. However, Tamati is at his wits end. He so wants rid of her, but on the other hand . . .

BEYOND WINTER'S SHADOW

Mark visits the store every Thursday morning.

I don't like homeless kids lingering in the alley out the back, but I make the exception for Mark. There's a smart lad beneath that dirty face and hair, though there's something distant in his brown irises, something with a calloused edge that should never have found its way into the eyes of a 12 year-old.

"Hi, Mark."

"S'up, Mr Harvey."

He's always polite but rarely looks me in the eye.

I shrug as usual, put on a smile. "I'm good. How about you? Would you like something to eat?"

"Nah."

A couple of nutrition bars make their way from my hands to his. He nods in gratitude, his grubby fingers poking through green woollen gloves as he stores the snacks in the big pockets of his coat. Then his gaze lingers on the old internet terminal in the corner of the store.

I nod. "Go ahead."

He sits down and fires up the browser.

I worry that he might be caught up in something sinister. Even with filters, the internet is the Devil's playground, but Mark seems to have the wherewithal to avoid the smut and entrapment schemes. Maybe I should do more to help, but store-keepers can't be the saviours of all the homeless children in the world, so I leave him to his privacy.

The door bell chimes and old Mrs Sczepanski arrives for her daily shop. She never buys enough for more than one day, drifts around aimlessly clutching her System coupons. Her banter drives me crazy, but she's a paying customer.

I glance at Mark: he's hunched over the terminal, seems particularly on guard today, watching Mrs Sczepanski warily. There's a flash of blue as he pulls a computer tablet out of his pocket and connects it to the terminal with a loop of cable. He scans the store again, his head turning my way, eyes just about to reach . . . I smile at Mrs Sczepanski. After another ten minutes of small talk she finally hands over her coupons and leaves, the door rattling shut, frigid air nipping at my ankles.

Mark is whispering to someone on the tablet screen.

I make towards him, but he shuts down the window, his hands working furiously to unplug the device.

"Is everything all right, Mark?"

He gets up and heads to the back entrance.

"Mark."

He pauses, but doesn't turn around. "I'm fine," he says, wiping his eyes and nose on his sleeve. "See you next week."

Too old and too slow; I sigh as he whisks out into the alley.

I turn and straighten up the monitor and mouse. Three tear drops have landed on the keyboard—on the j, v and the space bar. Following Mark's footsteps to the back of the store, shutting the door, the air around my ankles even colder, if that is possible. A sound lingers: the backdrop of Chicago city grown cold with a preternatural winter, like ice wraiths whispering in anticipation.

Thursday morning.

The weather is more inclement. A silver car passes silently by between the wrecks of old petrol-burners that still haven't been removed by the System. Tyres swish in brown puddles left from snow that drifted in from the arctic during the small hours of the night.

Mark's at the terminal again; and there are three customers in the store: Mrs Sczepanski; a dirty hobo who must have found his way in from the Mulch badlands, probably *underneath* the security perimeter judging by the smell; and some corporate-type, either a middle class wannabe or a System employee, but either way, lost. One customer with the right currency, one with no currency, and one with the wrong currency—buy, steal or borrow . . . I shouldn't stereotype.

Mrs Sczepanski walks up and down every aisle. The hobo leaves, glancing back at the taser on my belt. The corporate asks for directions to the O'Hare Spaceport—GPS malfunction—not surprising since the privatisation of the military. He places a can of drink and a bag of reconstituted potato chips on the counter, but I shake my head when he withdraws his credit chip. I point him to the Kennedy Expressway—follow it all the way to the spaceport but watch out for molotovs lobbed over the barriers. He leaves the store empty handed.

Mrs Sczepanski pays for the things in her basket without the usual banter. The leaden skies are proving to be the wrong kind of anodyne.

Laughter from the corner of the store breaks my mood. It's a strange alto sound ringing out like a challenge to a forgetful world.

I drift to the source. Mark is laughing and talking to a beautiful woman on the tablet screen. She has long brunette hair, high cheek bones and dark brown eyes. A spray of freckles on her cheeks scrunch up as she smiles. Mark sees me, unplugs the tablet and slips it into his coat pocket. He also pockets some other things: a crumpled photograph of the woman with a man, a handful of flash drives and a tattered paperback version of *The Cold Mountain Poems*.

"Mark, I'm sorry, I didn't mean to pry."

"Leave me alone." He gets up and walks towards the back of the store.

"Mark, wait. You sounded so happy—"

The back door slams shut in his wake, familiar coils of air stirring the corners of second hand newspapers and comic books.

Thursday morning.

A group of homeless kids have congregated at the end of the alley. They are deep in conversation, their breath billowing out from under their hoods.

I think Mark is among them.

I approach them, but they scatter like frightened birds.

Thursday morning.

There's been no sign of Mark for three weeks now, and I begin to wonder if the city has finally taken him. The snow has eased, but the chill hasn't, and there are more incursions from the Mulch—desperate souls disavowed by 50 years of GFC, seeking the warmth of the cities.

I close the shop early and read old books in my apartment upstairs until the early hours. The stories make me wonder how people used to live when crimes were solved instead of reported. Halcyon days indeed.

Wednesday night.

I wake to the sound of tomcats fighting, their throaty wails rising up into the night, setting my heart rumbling into action. As my head clears I hear the sound for what it is: a person shouting at the top of their lungs.

Grabbing some track pants and the taser, dashing down the stairs, ribs and joints protesting. Perhaps someone has broken in, maybe it's a synthine junky on a bender, or the hobo returned with other Mulch zombies. The back door is intact; unlocking it silently, easing it open a crack, taser poised . . . Mark is sitting up against the alley wall, his coat torn, blood trickling down his face from a gash on his temple.

"They took her."

"What?" I kneel down on damp concrete, reach out for him in the dark. "Who?"

"She's gone." He holds up the torn flap of his pocket.

"Mark, I'm sorry. I don't understand."

He kicks at the air, slams his fists against the ground. "Don't you see?" he growls. "They took my mom."

Thursday morning.

He wouldn't let me check his wound, and ended up curling in front of the heater all night, eyes unblinking.

There's not much stored charge left in the solar cells. It seems in the space of a year the entire city has gone from expecting sunshine to praying for it.

"Are you okay?" I sip at my tea, not really tasting it. He hasn't touched his tea, but the powdered eggs I cooked didn't last long. "Mark, are you okay?"

"What do you think?"

I sigh quietly to myself. "Look, I'm just trying to help."

"Sorry, Mr Harvey."

"Did you see who attacked you?"

"It doesn't matter? She's gone now." He looks out the single window, the wan light turning the caked blood black.

I show him to the bathroom after breakfast. "There's a little hot water left." My covert glances tell me his wound is not serious. "Make sure you clean that properly, you don't want an infection."

"Yup."

He comes down to the store while I'm busy sorting out the gift cards—her birthday, mother, daughter, sister, his birthday, father, son, brother, wedding, christening, thankyou—this all meant something once. Still, I won't take them down just yet. I sold one yesterday to a guy wanting to impress his girlfriend.

Mark turns to the back door. "Thanks."

I look up. "Wait."

He pauses.

"Can't you just call her up again?"

He frowns, like I've said something stupid, and takes another step towards the door.

"Mark, is there any other way you can contact your mom?"

He looks angry, more so now that his face is clean. "Doesn't matter."

I hold my hands up as if in plea to some silent god.

His anger suddenly diffuses. "I don't need comware, the tablet runs the sim-app. I only used the terminal to get the updates coz my wireless is broken."

I frown. There's a persistent tapping in the background. "You've lost me. If you don't need comware—"

He sucks in a deep breath. "Mom is dead, okay."

There's that annoying tapping again. "What about your dad?"

"Dead too. Mulch." He turns and walks to the back door. "S'okay, I'll be fine."

The air wafts in, but I'm too numb to feel its bite.

The tapping stops.

Mrs Sczepanski is shaking her head as she walks away along the footpath.

The "Open" sign on the front door is still facing inward.

Coupon Day.

Tossed and turned all night; got up at 6 a.m. for the System delivery. The supplies are lighter this week. The driver said foul weather was causing disruptions somewhere up the Chino-Indian supply chain. He left the boxes for me to carry into the store, his racist remarks mingling with the wind as he drove away.

The store is busy: ten people, not all regulars, but no obvious badlanders. Still, it's more than I can keep an eye on at once. I crane my neck, glancing at the concave security mirror as people queue at the counter, baskets in one hand, coupons in the other.

I look at the line of pale faces. "Does anyone know anything about sim-apps?" I feel like I have just asked if anyone knows how to do CPR.

Murmurs in the line, people looking to each other, perhaps sensing the urgency in my voice.

One guy holds up his hand tentatively. "Aren't they like chatbots or AI gaming characters or something?"

I bite my tongue then try to keep the exasperation out of my voice. "Doesn't sound right . . . I don't know."

His eyes brighten. "One of my friends used to be a cloud programmer. He might be able to help."

Thursday morning.

"How did she die, Mark?"

"Incursion."

"And your Dad?"

"He chased the killers into the Mulch, past Westchester and the ruins of the Tri-State Tollway. It's the worst district. The old Highlands country club is used by a drug syndicate, and inpatients at Elmhurst have their organs harvested. Asia pays top dollar for American hearts."

I shudder to think what his dad suffered as I guide Mark into the store, afraid that he might make a run for it again. It has taken three weeks for him to show up after I had put the word out on the street, so I won't let him go so easily this time.

He leans against the counter, resting his elbows on the top.

I reach behind the counter and pull out the tablet.

His eyes brighten. "What is it?"

I hand it to him, conscious of the scuffs and dents on its black casing and the crack along the bottom edge of the screen. "I bought it from a programmer from New Delhi. Don't know why he came to America, maybe he likes the cold."

Mark gives a half-smile in response, as rare as sunshine—the tablet was a bargain after all.

"Is it a good model?" I ask.

He's already booting it up, checking out the menus and icons. "It's got wireless."

"Yes." It's only later I realise the implications. "Mahendra said it has a universal spec. There's a high res cam, top end CPU and holo display . . . so he tells me."

"It's a 30 year old machine, Mr Harvey."

"Ah . . . still, you should be able to access internet TV and all the old GovNet outreach programs. I think the System still runs some of them . . . anyway, Mahendra gave me a list."

I pull out a crumpled piece of paper from my pocket, but Mark is transfixed now, already accessing different sites, his hands a blur over the tablet. A log-in page appears; all chrome and green symbols that don't look like English at all. "What's that?"

"My System outreach account."

And there I was thinking privatisation of the world's governments had achieved nothing since the GFC.

A static image of the brunette's face appears, a 3D high res image, rotating 360; she's quite incredible, looks a lot like Mark.

"Hello, Mark." She smiles.

He slides his hand across the tablet and the image fades.

"Huh? Mark, what's wrong?"

He's holding back tears. "It's not her. The cloud runs upgrades and patches every Thursday, and I back up any changes I make on the tablet into the cloud. I rushed out last time I was here, didn't back up."

Now I feel worse than ever. If it wasn't for my prying that day he wouldn't have any of these problems. "But it looks—"

"You don't get it. I'd made a breakthrough with her profile; made her more human . . . made her more like mom."

Mind racing, thinking back to the crash course Mahendra gave me on digital personas. None of it was any help in this situation. I grasp at the obvious, again not realising the implications. "Can't we just rebuild her?"

"What's *his* name?"

"This is Mr Harvey, Mom. Mr Harvey, meet Trish."

"Nice to meet you, Trish."

Her eyes narrow suspiciously, giving me the once over. She turns to Mark. "What have I told you about strangers?"

"S'cool, he's a friend."

"Doesn't look friendly to me." She turns to me. "What business do you have with my son?"

"Ah, well, I'm a store keeper."

Her eyes turn flinty. "You haven't answered my question."

"I'm sorry."

"Well, come on, don't just stand there."

Damn, reminds me of Lidia. We used to have some of the worst arguments over the smallest things. "I'm trying to help Mark make you more like . . . you."

She turns to Mark. "Is he a lunatic?"

I plead silently to Mark.

He shrugs. "That's why I couldn't just re-key my last changes. One, it's a violation of her personality, and two, she'll be doing all the work and crafting the new algorithms, not me." He pats me on the arm. "S'fine, just relax, Mr Harvey. Her Jungian control architecture picks up every nuance of sensory input from the cam. She's overreacting way too much—she was always cautious, but not neurotic. We'll need an accurate baseline of inputs then we can ask her if it's okay to make some tweaks."

We'd already spent hours uploading his photos and vids from the flash drives—the thieves hadn't taken those at least. His family had come from the orbitals, upper-class with too much debt, sliding back down the status ladder, until the inner city apartment rent was impossible to service. They were relocated to System housing here in Roscoe where his father's skills were of no real value—no one needed engineering designs for zero-g turbines.

I can see from the photos that Mark has his dad's eyes—friendly enough, but hardened and faraway most of the time. You know he's listening, but there's something troubling going on behind the scenes, that gaze always wandering to the middle-distance as if trying to see what's under the veneer of reality. It's more accentuated in the last photos, to the point where his dad looks haunted.

Mark taps me on the arm again. The right hand side of the display is full of tiny scales and charts and indicators that dance up and down every time I move—she's observing me intently. I drop my shoulders, trying not to feel so awkward.

"Great," Mark says, watching his mom's reaction. "Now try talking to her."

Trish is smiling.

I feel like some form of rebuke is not far away. "Ah, what do I say?"

"Just be yourself."

"Shouldn't you be doing this?"

"No, there are enough of my inputs for now, but we can't modify her until you're sorted. She's picked you up as a significant variable and needs to process you before we can go on."

"Right." I don't know whether to feel hurt or elated about being a variable, significant or otherwise.

Mark places his hand on my shoulder. "Remember, she's a little on the extroverted side, so you'll have to try to get a word in edgeways, but she is . . . was very open minded. She always used to encourage me to voice my beliefs and opinions."

I swallow. "Okay, I'll try."

Mark reads *The Cold Mountain Poems* every morning.

I wander around, getting the store ready for opening. "I'm so pleased about the progress with your mom." Integrating all her surrogate memories and emotions is a challenging process, and I'm glad that I can help Mark, even if it's just words of praise and encouragement.

He looks sulky and despondent, sat there on the counter top. "She needs more tweaks."

I've heard that so many times now, it's become a mantra. "What is it, Mark?" I try hard to keep the frustration out of my voice, but it doesn't work.

He looks warily at me and carefully pockets the book, even though it's cover is dog-eared and peeling.

"Did your mom give it to you?"

"Nah, my dad." There's something in his voice.

"You miss him." It was a shame that there was no way of recreating his dad as well. It was impossible without a body. The System had apparently been scanning the faces of the dead and posting them on the internet for years—a kind of online graveyard to remember the dead after the resource wars, but also try to reconnect the world. Deeper brain scans were later stored in the cloud for anyone wanting to resurrect the dead; spill-over technology from rich orbital folk obsessed with immortality, now made freely available as sim-apps through outreach programs.

Mark turns angry all of a sudden. "Nah, I hated him."

I push through the palpable wave of fury, not wanting to start the day off on a sour note. "I'm sure he loved you."

"Not enough, obviously. He tried to control all the things that were uncontrollable—his job, his boss, even the System. How can anyone spend all their time on things that don't matter? He even chased the zombies into the Mulch as if somehow he could make the past right." He pulls the book out and waves it around. "Yet he preached *this* philosophy." He hurls it across the store. It slides to a halt under a shelf of noodle packets. "How does that work?"

I reach down and pick up the book.

By the time I turn back he's stomping up the stairs to his room.

I lay awake into the small hours of the morning. I had forgotten the cold in recent days, but now it's back with a vengeance, lazily gnawing at my extremities, doing its darnedest to creep further into my soul.

The book slides off the bed, thumps on the floor. It startles me just as I am drifting off to sleep. I think about picking it up, but the air outside the blankets feels too cold, and I feel too weak.

I pity all those ordinary bones.

In the books of the Immortals they are nameless.

The open page taunts me in some half-dream, and the doubt that has plagued my life takes shape. I have wasted my years in this useless store in the shadow of this hopeless winter. Searching for what? Ha, searching, my ass. Waiting, more like. Waiting for an end to loneliness and misery.

As my eyelids grow heavy again, I spy the note his dad made in the margin next to the poem: *Life is borrowed breath, a high interest rate mortgage from the orbitals.*

Maybe he had been waiting too.

I wake to the sounds of an argument. It is 6 a.m. and Mark is yelling at his mom. Her replies are authoritative, monosyllabic. Maybe the programming has taken a turn for the worse; or maybe it was a good sign.

I think about knocking on his door, but leave them alone and go downstairs to pick up the delivery from the System truck. It's the lowest level of supplies I've ever seen. The truck cuts a hole in the morning mist off Lake Michigan, but the gap soon fills in with coiling tendrils until all I hear is the truck spinning and skidding along the street.

I turn, startled as Mark picks up a box.

"Is everything all right, Mark?"

He shrugs.

"I read your book. I hope you don't mind."

He shrugs again. "Keep it. I don't need it."

I pick up a box of tinned soy beans, recalling one of my favourite lines.

"*Now, morning, I face my lone shadow:*

"*Suddenly my eyes are bleared with tears.*

"Cold Mountain was a real place, but also a metaphor for life."

Mark laughs derisively. "Han Shan was a lonely hermit on a mountain. My dad was someone important once. People admired him. He had everything going for him."

"That doesn't mean he didn't feel lonely." I put my box down, pull out the book from my jacket. "I think he was trying to face his loneliness, to come to terms with his mortality: *I lived my first 40 years blind and scared of my shadow. It's only in the face of loneliness can we truly give of ourselves to others. How else can I love Trish and Mark, like a mortal man with immortal love in his heart?*"

"Then why did he leave me?"

"I don't know, Mark. The world has unravelled the best of men. Your dad was forced out of a job yet he still tried to support you both. The thing is I believe he was trying to change his outlook on life well before he wrote these notes, but it's hard when we're born into legacy." I put the book back in my pocket. "Do you think I wanted to be a storekeeper? Do you know Lidia and I were too afraid to bring children into this world? How does *that* work?"

His eyes soften. "But you've got courage, Mr Harvey. So many people are dependent on you; I can see their gratitude when they line up. Mrs Dundas, Roman from down West Roscoe, Mr. Wittekindt, the Benson family from up on Addison. You're reconnecting people again."

I smile, but it feels more like a grimace. "That might be true, but over the years I've used helping others as a reason not to face myself; I'm just a coward at heart. If I wasn't then I might have known what part of me to I could give to a family, even in this world."

"You're doing better than you realise." Mark heads back into the store then pauses at the doorway and sighs heavily. "Maybe it's adult logic," he says with his back turned. "You're complicating things, just like he did. I should leave. She's still not right."

"No, you can't. Let's give it one more try; we're so close."

"S'okay. I've stayed here long enough. I can fix her remotely."

Mark is in the bathroom. He's become used to keeping clean, so I convinced him to wash up before he leaves.

Sneaking into his room now. The tablet is on the bedside table. Trish is . . . awake.

"Hello, Trish," I whisper.

"Oh, hello, Mr Harvey." She looks over my shoulder. "This is unusual. Where's Mark? Is he okay?"

"He's fine, just cleaning up."

"That's a great habit you've got him into. Thank you."

"No prob."

"Why are you whispering?"

"Look, I haven't got much time. We need to talk."

"About Mark?" she whispers.

I nod, listening out for the sound of the bathroom door. "I think I know why we haven't been able to complete your alpha-sim."

She's fighting back tears. "It's been so frustrating. I feel incomplete. Not in a selfish way, I am as complete as my algorithms allow. It's more that I am incomplete for him; I don't know what to say to him sometimes. Does that make me a bad mom?"

"No, no, no. Of course not. It's hard to know how to respond when they have to grow up so fast. I think you are doing fine." I paused, choosing my words carefully. "I understand a sim-app only really works if they are harmonised with their host."

"But I know everything about Mark now. And all the other variables . . . sorry, you, and some of his friends out there."

"That's all well and good, Trish, but your interface is more than just responding to stimuli and mimicking behaviour. Any old chatbot can do that. Your typology is far more complex, yes?"

"True. But according to my self-diagnostics, I'm optimal. Mark has filled in the history as much as he can, and my algorithms have extrapolated the rest."

I pull out the book and wave it in front her. "How did his dad affect *you*?"

"He was my husband. We had some good times in the first years of our marriage, but it quickly broke down after that, like a permanent cloud hanging over our heads as we struggled to make ends meet."

"No, I'm not asking what you did. How did he make you feel, Trish? How did he influence your thoughts and dreams? What traits and mannerism did *you* adopt? I think if we start trying to answer these questions we might get somewhere. But you can't get these inputs just from old vids and holos." I take a deep breath, feeling my throat tighten. I place the book on the bedside table. "The three of you grew up as a family unit. Your husband made some tragic mistakes, but he really tried, and in doing so he influenced Mark in the right ways. Mark's taken that, moulded it, matured it into his own being—you've got a great kid there. He *sees* who he is, more than many of us ever get even after a lifetime of searching. So imagine what aspects of your husband you have taken on, Trish. The triangle isn't complete yet."

I turn, startled by movement.

Mark is standing at the doorway, his face clean, eyes bright with tears.

I put my arm around him, squeeze him gently then I reach out to Trish, my hand touching her hologram. "One more tweak."

Mark stayed for another month.

The new Trish is indeed a different person. More matter-of-fact, yet more guiding and accepting that Mark will be okay out there. Perhaps that's what gave Mark's dad hope, even in his darkest hours.

Mrs Sczepanski, the Bensons, Mr Wittekindt and some other customers are waiting outside patiently. I've never seen them arrive so early, but then again I've never seen as much sunshine before. Even the pavements are clear for the first time, and there's hot water again. I smile and mouth the words: "Just a minute."

A bundle of coupons makes its way from my hands to Mark's.

"What's this for?"

"Your new machine." I hand him a piece of paper. "Contact Mahendra, he'll get you a wrist band processor with a holo projector. The band grafts to your ulna with a little dab of anaesthetic, so that will keep it safe. The good thing is you'll be able to project a complete image of your mom, give her a second chance at looking after you." I tousle his hair. "That is until you become too embarrassed to be around her."

"Not me," he says, and gives me a hug. "I'll visit once I've finished my outreach courses."

He waves and walks out the back.

I reach into my pocket and open up the note he slipped in

Morning sun drives over blue peaks,
Bright clouds wash over green ponds.
Who knows that I'm out of the dusty world,
Climbing the southern slope of Cold Mountain?

I fold the note, put it back in my pocket and open up the store.

AFTERWORD TO BEYOND WINTER'S SHADOW

Some men "discover" the reality of their loneliness too late in life, whilst others find it way too early. Sadly, I think that some never find it at all. Call it mid-life crisis, coming to terms with your own mortality or just plain growing up, there's a transition phase where we accept who we are and get on with it.

No one grows up in pure isolation—take the raw physical and genetic ingredients handed to us at birth, and we nurture this platform through experience, and the sum of the influence of others. Our calling is to realise our true selves (as I discussed in the afterword to "Ethos Anthropoi Daimon"), so I think part of the growing up experience is to get to "know" the raw person inside, but also know what, and particularly who, we carry with us.

Mr Harvey accepted this very late, whereas Mark got there very early, but realised he hadn't had enough of the growing up experience with his mom, and of course, she wasn't complete without aspects of his dad's persona.

"Beyond Winter's Shadow" is also part of my Urban Decay series.

TIME CAPTURE

The attic is musty with the smell of old cedar and a crawling damp that lingers after three weeks of rain. I sit in the old cushioned recliner, bathed in a stray beam of brown light that slants through the room's single window. The glass is stained with a milky residue and the paint on the window frame has flaked in a hundred places to reveal metal covered with a crawling green patina.

Each year I say I'll fix things up, but I never do.

The paraphernalia of another life blends into the background: a pair of old skis, stuffed toys on a stained mattress, a walnut tallboy full of unworn clothes, a collapsed bookcase with flaking laminate shelves packed with unread books, dusty silicon boards and wafers, a rusting toolbox, a broken virtual headset, and the spoked wheel off some fuel-powered car—pre-electric, pre-hydrogen, pre-everything.

I reach under the bed and pull out a brushed steel box into the clear space in the centre of the room.

My hands are covered in bluish stains and blotches—a patina of a different kind. My breathing turns ragged as if all the stale air has been sucked out of the room, leaving me with a singular focus—an old habit, a worn cliché. It's the clarity one finds in the eye of a storm and it's enough to send my arms reaching out, my hands fumbling over the combination padlock.

The lid flips open on silent hinges, the hiss of air breaking the seal.

I'm overwhelmed as I touch the contents of the box, each object like Braille for my mind. My eyes water as the scent of her flares my nostrils. In one heart beat I am taken back to the day she was born. I touch the digital wrist band—the LCD readout is frozen—so long ago now, years before they started tagging newborns with DNA nano-markers.

Abigail was a blue baby, deprived of oxygen during birth. She cried relentlessly it seemed for weeks on end. It's hard to recall now through the hazy, sleep-deprived nights. But it was all worth it in the end. She was a happy baby, smiling within weeks, inquisitive, always getting into places, walking by 11 months, always smiling, my Abby. So definitely worth it . . . for me.

Her mother? Well, who knows where she ended up? I can't even remember her name, or maybe I just can't bring myself to say it, because once Abby came into the world, there was room for no other.

I place the band gently on the floor and reach into the box again.

The holo-tablet is broken and the images are bleached and faded. She's five years old and playing on the swings near the pre-fab towers when everything was still new, her summer dress ballooning out almost provocatively—a sign, a portent of the young woman she would become. A crooked smile stretches across her face as the swing goes higher and higher with each push. I'm urging her on to her squeals of delight, her face reflecting bright sunlight; mine somehow lost in the shadow of the playground trees. Or maybe it's just the old image.

The chrome frame of the tablet is covered in smeared fingerprints and the video replay won't work, so I manually recreate that day, flicking through one image at a time—stick figure animation of a happy father and a constantly smiling daughter in monochromatic 3D—a hollow dream of how we once were, and how we might have stayed.

What has become of the world?

I'm feeling faint but lucid as I turn to the next object. The closer I get to my goal, the more my hands shake. What starts out as a determined ritual can quickly get out of control. I steel myself, take in a deep breath and lift out what looks like a flimsy black plastic spider web from the box. Its touch is always an epiphany that tenses my arms and torso to the point where I perch on the edge of the dusty recliner, clumsy hands fumbling with my wrist terminal connection until the web activates and turns warm in my palm.

She's 18.

Data from her lost qualia flashes up through my spinal cord into my cortex.

I close my eyes.

Hair of honey gold, eyes reflecting the endless sky, sand flicking up, spray of sea foam as she runs along the beach with her girl friends. School's out, she has found a place at university, wants to be a doctor, has her eyes set on a rich boy from the old orbitals. She's trying out her new bikini—blue with white dots—reminiscent of an old song before the world lost its innocence. Body so young and athletic, muscular thighs, soft flesh of her breasts bouncing inside her bikini cups.

I swim with her, smile with her, talk to her friends.

Lost.

I am lost.

More data packets stream up from the net. Dark files float on my periphery, taunting me, daring me to open them. But I can't bring myself to do it.

I open my eyes. Through the haze of tears and tension I reach back down to the box and lift out the final object—an indigo-coloured sphere. It feels like jelly in my hands. My old back gives a little and I ease down into the recliner, the sphere quickening to life along my hand, shimmering in nanometre thick layers along my skin. I squirm slightly until it reaches my eyes, the only living tissue on the external surface of a human body. The sheet slides like cool ice, sending an electric pulse along my optic nerve—the body-sheath now fully interfaced with the web.

A new vision emerges, new senses take hold of my withered ones, and I am transformed again into the muscular man I once was, in a time well before the illusion of life-extending pharmaceuticals.

We're in an arboretum with crystal walls hanging in low orbit above a blue-green Earth. Strange rainbow-coloured birds trill in the distance and macaque monkeys scamper amongst the trees. A plate of fruit and a glass of exotic blue liqueur are arrayed neatly on a table next to my hammock. The hammock itself is hung from the corner posts of the patio of a home of indeterminate size blending into the background foliage.

I hear her footsteps, high heels clicking on the timbers of the patio. She stands next to the hammock, naked except for her strappy shoes and that gorgeous red-lipped smile. I look along the length of those legs, lingering along her pubic mound, trailing up the plane of her belly to the circles of areola, further still to those chocolate eyes that always, always greet me the way they should.

"Hey, daddy."

"Hey, baby girl." My voice is thick with anticipation as the porn routines of the body-sheath engage with the web still dangling from my wrist as I sit slumped in the attic of that forgotten otherworld.

Abby kneels down to pull my shorts aside. Then she leans in, her teeth white behind ruby lips, her warm, wet tongue and mouth soothing all my pain.

I am lost in her.

Lost in a time that never was, in a time that was never meant to be.

Until time itself is lost, and all that exists is a single moment of bliss, where I am a god above a world that once breathed, where the love I feel for Abby is pure, where her love for me is unconditional, as it should have been.

Heat pulsing up through me.

She shouldn't have argued with me back then . . .

Searing everything with white desire.

But now she knows what to do . . .

My cries of release etching eternity.

My obedient baby girl . . .

Sliding away into freefall.

Until next time . . . Abby.

The attic is dark when I wake up, back in that otherworld. There's something crawling along the top of the roof, nocturnal and hungry.

The body-sheath has reassembled into its spherical pattern, but the web is still jacked in. I reach across with my free hand to disengage it, but something stops me. I'm not sure if it is conscience or guilt; I've lived for so long now that such notions seem as inexplicably useless as the contents of the attic. Maybe it's an eternal penance, but that would require sorrow. Eventually I find the answer—I always find the answer—as I open the dark files that have been floating patiently.

Qualia of her last moments blossom through the interface. I shut my eyes but my mind's eye is open and raw and bleeding. She's on the bed in the attic, her dress torn, her legs kicking frantically. She hates it when I come to her, but afterwards I always make her tell me otherwise. This time she refuses. And worse, she's fumbling with the controls behind her left ear, broadcasting her neural iWeb recordings live to social networks.

You had a choice, Abby. A choice.

You weren't mine to share. And worse, the world was so numb that no one really cared.

And so I strike her with the hammer. She screams and tries to fend me off, but soon her attempts turn to pathetic twitches and her senses darken to the sound of wet hammer blows. The last images are of my face flushed with exertion as I cradle her head, prise the top of her skull off and delicately extract the web from her brain lobes. The images flicker then freeze into random pixels, leaving a ghostly residue of a father and daughter locked in an eternal embrace.

Maybe next time I won't open the files, but I know that's a lie. Her qualia sully what was otherwise a perfect experience in the arboretum, but I can't help myself and so the journey begins again.

I disengage the web and place it and the other contents back in the box and seal the lid.

Until next time, Abby.

AFTERWORD TO "TIME CAPTURE"

Some men are monsters.

"Time Capture" is part of my Urban Decay series and is set in a similar timeline to "Social Contract" and "Beyond Winter's Shadow". Aside from the obvious discomfort about writing from the POV of a murdering abuser, there was a shocking revelation for me when it became clear that even though the murder was broadcast to the world, no one really cared.

I look at the internet and find it disturbing to see the happy faces of people who have been killed broadcast on the latest news blog, to be replaced tomorrow by another victim. I fear we are becoming desensitised to death through trivialisation by the media. So it's really not that hard to imagine a future where people don't even look at the images. Either they're too busy to care or the images just aren't shocking enough or different or unique.

Maybe the future isn't that far away after all.

WEAPONS OF CHOICE

LIBRARY OF THE DISPERSION, 4893.
JOURNAL OF MICHAEL LEVESQUE: ALDEBARAN ORBITAL, 3741.

May 15

Mum's body hung from a wire tied to the top balcony railing. She swung in front of the big window, her body cast into silhouette by the red glow of Aldebaran. The towers of the orbital fanned out behind her like black wings.

"Michael!" I'll never forget father's gurgling voice as he raced down the stairs.

I sprinted back to my bedroom and activated the lock.

He pounded his fists against the door all night.

May 16

I watched him on my monitor, pacing up and down the hallways, muttering to himself. After an hour, maybe two, he must have gone to his room to rest, so I snuck out to the living area and checked the holo-terminal. There were a lot of messages. I skimmed through them as fast as I could. I knew most of the people: papa, our neighbours, my friends Graham and Emma, and the xenoarchaeologists from the station.

One from Leah Bordelon: "Where are you, John? The team needs your help . . . the relics have changed since you tried the interface . . . we don't believe they're dormant . . . I need your help."

I started to dial out, but then I heard his footsteps echo.

I grabbed some food and water bottles from the kitchen and ran back to my room.

I tried not to look at Mum as I passed the balcony window.

I cried for the rest of the day.

May 17

He tried to break into my room again. I saw his face on the monitor—his cold yellow eyes made my skin crawl. And there was something happening to his skin—it was turning black and flaky like charcoal.

I hid in the wardrobe and didn't sleep at all.

Our home has become a tomb.

May 18

I didn't sleep again.

Maybe I'm becoming like him, maybe there's a sickness in the air.

I think . . . I've been trying not to say it . . . he murdered Mum, and he won't rest until he kills me.

May 25 (Hospital Shuttle)

I have escaped.

The flyer remote was on my book case, next to the black splinter, a broken piece from one of the relics. He had given the splinter of alien ceramic to me when I was seven. The flyer had been a present for my eighth birthday, but now that I was ten I really knew how to manoeuvre it.

I checked the monitor. He was standing on the top balcony watching the constellations wheel overhead, poor Mum below. I swung my door open and raced across to the dock on the other side of our home, and from there along the umbilical tube to my flyer.

I climbed into the cockpit and fired up the interface.

He burst out from the darkness of the tube and grabbed my leg. His skin had transformed into a black liquid-metal and his face was a terrifying mask. I kicked and kicked at his head, but it was like hitting rock. He shoved my legs aside and lashed out, his nails tearing down my face.

I think I screamed . . . all I remember was blood and then reaching up and slamming the flyer canopy down. He tried to pull back, but the hard edge sliced off three of his fingertips. He howled and smashed his ruined hands against the canopy.

I banked the flyer away from the dock, tearing the umbilical before it had time to retract. A hurricane of air flushed him out into space.

"Dad!"

I had not meant to . . . then I saw him glaring at me. He swung his arms crazily to try to follow . . . and somehow he *did* . . . because in the next instant he had latched onto the flyer.

I flipped the flyer into a roll and he fell away . . . then I must have blacked out for a second . . . and when I woke my head felt foggy and the flyer plunged down between the towers of the orbital and skipped through the top edge of atmosphere that covered the lower suburbs. I fought the controls until I crash landed in the middle of a nature park.

Now all I could do was feel bad about the flyer.

It had been black and chrome, wedge shaped like the relic ships. All the other kids had them—we all pretended to be pilots fighting monsters from other galaxies. We used to race all the time, sometimes dangerously between the towers, but my flyer was the fastest. The other kids used to curse me, accuse me of illegal modifications.

But then I would give them attitude: "It's not my machine; it's my sheer flying ability—skillage from the village."

It was all I could think of, but the nurses said that was okay—they talk to me a lot, but I think it's just part of my recovery program.

We're a long way from Aldebaran now and I'm finding it hard to remember Mum and Dad.

I think we were happy once.

POSTHUMOUS BIOGRAPHY OF CHENZIRA NWOSU: WAR COUNCIL
CONSCRIPTION AT PROCYON, 3872.

We came in off the cold ships—four-billion conscripts from a hundred worlds.

I lay still as sounds filtered into my waking senses. My skin felt dirty, my throat was dry and my back was pressed against a cold, gritty floor. The pressure of smelly, naked bodies seemed like a violation, but after a while I did not mind the shared warmth, for the air was frigid.

I could hear voices, strange words as if whispered from a long distance, now becoming clear. There was fear and talk of a place— the Forge.

I opened my eyes. There was very little light, four blank walls and a single, unnaturally dark doorway. I looked away, afraid that my mind might take me to a place of terror before my body ventured there. I noticed too that the others—all teenagers—also kept their eyes averted.

The boy to my left was shivering, his face hidden beneath a mass of black hair. I reached over and placed my arm around him. He turned his face to me. There was something proud in his manner, a challenge and resolve in those dark brown eyes. Tattoos swirled across his face, covering some terrible scars, but they also gave him a graceful, hawk-like appearance.

My eyes traced every incredible line—he was fierce but beautiful, like the Maori of Earth and the Telak of the Pleaides.

"Where are we?" His voice was hoarse, accented, but somehow I understood him.

"I don't know. There is talk of the Forge. I think that is where we will be taken."

"Are we going to die?"

I had to do something, to force us to stop thinking of what lay beyond the doorway. "What is your name?"

"Michael." He turned to me and I knew with an absolute certainty that our futures were set, laced together like sky and sun.

We all stood as one, lifted by some invisible force. Now that same certainty told me we would die this day.

I reached out for his hand. "I am Chenzira, survivor of the Fomalhaut Cloud Empire."

We moved forward another step. A poor boy in front of us urinated and others began to whimper. I squeezed Michael's hand, urging him to talk—I needed his courage now.

"I am from Aldebaran." He clenched his fists. "And one day I *will* be a combat-ultra."

We stood together in front of the doorway; all the other boys and girls had stepped through. I looked at it then—red interlocking coils floated languidly in a black mist.

Inexplicably, a smile quivered over my lips. I gazed into the tattooed face of this strange young man beside me and I was filled with hope. "Then on that day, Michael, we will destroy the relics."

We stepped through the doorway and into the mist that squirmed over our skin. Those metal coils encased us and I reached out to keep hold of Michael, but was forced to let go as the coils slid over my fingertips.

A light removed the darkness, burning into my skull with a cleansing fire.

I was reborn.

MISSION LOG OF MICHAEL LEVESQUE: THE FALL OF 61 CYGNI, 3925.
I stood under the shelter of the porch.

Black rain beat a staccato on the tin roof. Puddles filled the potholes and soon the dirt road around the homestead turned to a charcoal-coloured mud. The sky dimmed further as the clouds closed in and a strange smell filled the air, not unlike burnt magnesium.

A man appeared to my left from behind the building. I snapped across the intervening distance; I hadn't realised there was anyone left here. The thick rain hissed as it vaporised in the protective field created by my battle lens.

He staggered back, shocked at the speed of my movement. He wore a full face helmet and armour of the Cygni militia. The metal was slowly being eroded by the rain. A ballistic weapon hung from one shoulder, its barrel pitted and useless. He wouldn't last another five minutes.

"My god, who are you, son?"

"Michael."

"Can you help them?"

He turned and waved a group of people forward from around the corner. My lens had already picked up their heat signatures— two men, three women, a boy and a girl about five years old, all shuffling forward under a makeshift metal sheet. They were exhausted and terrified. One of the men had caught some rain on his face. I gave him thirty seconds.

"I would if I could."

They all crowded in under the shelter of the porch, though judging by the bowed roofline it would only delay the inevitable.

Is the planet evacuated? The message bubbled up through an open channel.

Almost.

How many are left?

Fifteen-million are waiting for the arc to return.

Is the rain heavy?

Yes.

Then leave, there is nothing you can do now.

The channel closed.

The rain fell. It would be like this until the end.

I glanced about one final time.

One of the women raced over to me and pounded my chest with her fists. "You can't leave us," she screamed. Her hair became slick with tar and began to peel away from her scalp. I held her blistering hands as she fell to the mud. "You have to do *something*," she whimpered, staring at me now through bleeding eyes.

I carried her back to the porch. She was dead by the time I put her down next to the dead man with the hollowed out face. The others watched in horror.

I turned around.

The militia man grabbed my arm. "Please."

I looked at the children. There was something familiar about the way they held hands, but I couldn't remember through the black wall of my nanotech inhibitors.

I grabbed them, one under each arm. My protective field expanded and I flew above the homestead. The roof collapsed and the screams seemed a long way away now as I rose above the blackened land. I flew out of the atmosphere on a parabolic trajectory. The boy and girl passed out in my arms.

The belly of the Scourge cloud glowed orange from the light of 61 Cygni. Then, above the black storm, I saw them—fifty relic ships with their razor edges glinting in the sun. They spiralled above the doomed planet, hunting in singles, pairs and symbiotic clusters, their battle cry screeching across the com-channels. It was the only thing that could cut through my inhibitors, rising to a chilling crescendo then into the ultrasonic. I had heard it so often on other battlefronts as the relic nests woke from their slumber across colonised space. It contained chants of obliteration and hunger, songs of hope and lament—for the relics were pilotless, driven by some long forgotten purpose.

There was some twisted humour in that, but I was incapable of even a sardonic smile.

The arc ship managed to break through the buzzing relics under the cover of suppressing fire from War Council vac-troops. It hurtled down to the planet like a spear, but the Scourge cloud grazed along the arc's hull and a contrail of fire and debris billowed from the gash.

The captain must have had a rush of conscience. I understood the desire to defy the odds. I had lived by it all my reincarnated life. The broken arc glowed brighter as it hit the atmosphere. The thermonuclear fireball was brighter still as the engines collapsed and the arc tore apart across a mountain side.

It didn't take long for the embers to be snuffed out by the Scourge.

I wondered if anyone would mourn the souls still down there.

CLASSIFIED LOG OF CHENZIRA NWOSU: SEQUESTRATION EXPERIMENT AT PROCYON, 3994.

The relic ship hung in the restraining field under the harsh lights of the vault. Its five metre long scalloped surfaces were like a shroud that absorbed most of the light. A few reflections glistened along its port and starboard edges, shimmering to rainbows along the fore and aft spikes.

A huge vat of liquid helium hovered above the relic, white mist coiling out and over the sides. Az-Azir, one of the oldest and toughest combat-ultras, stepped through the mist towards the ship.

This sent a wave of nervous chatter around the defensive ring of ultras. Pulse rifles were adjusted and sights realigned.

It had taken years to capture the relic. Our scans revealed a solid interior made of some kind of advanced ceramic, with a strange sub-molecular circuitry bonded to the lattice atoms. Drive systems were a mystery, though some of us suspected the deeper layers of the ship could fold the geometry of space time. As for the weapons systems, we still had no answer to the corrosive Scourge femtotech that would "bleed" from the hulls.

I sensed a presence now as Az-Azir placed his hand down on the hull.

I squeezed Michael's hand for reassurance as it had been my idea to try to interface with the exotic matter entities. His tattoo was black under the harsh lights. He gave a half-smile and squeezed my hand back. We had made love again last night and he had confided in me about his hopes and fears for the war. I cherished what we had together as it was so very hard to find love of any kind. But deep down I knew that I was only ever going to get a part of Michael Levesque, for there was something locked behind his eyes, something that made him rage in his unguarded moments. It sometimes frightened me more than these cursed relics—the eyes of youth should not look like this.

Az-Azir stood with his head bowed as his sequestration programs fought the entity's autonomic response. The air around him began to boil and crackle as the entity slowly materialised out of the ship. A humanoid shape emerged, its tendrils thrashing in a halo, its battle song grating against my already frayed nerves.

Then its amber lenses flashed to life . . . and turned on me! They reached down into my mind, rummaging for weaknesses, drawing out my insecurities. I couldn't resist it as it kicked around, turning over things that I preferred to remain undisturbed—my worry for Michael, my fear for a civilisation on the brink of catastrophe.

I let out a gasp of air as the entity retracted from me. Then I felt Michael tense as the entity probed his mind.

I shouted at Az-Azir. "You need to control it."

He glanced over his shoulder, his teeth clenched.

The entity disappeared—quantum tunnelling away—then reappeared on top of one of the ultras on the other side of the perimeter. He dropped his gun and tried to grab the thrashing tendrils. A gleaming hook snicked out from the mass and slit the ultra along the shoulder blade. Blood gushed as the hook quickened, moving down his chest with a terrible ripping action as the entity tried to *pour* into him.

"Get it off!" he grunted.

Michael swung his gun up and fired. The pulse sent the ultra with the entity still attached sliding across the floor. Then Michael froze and lowered his gun as the ultra's skin glossed to liquid-metal. I knew he had seen the effect before the war—the way these monstrous spacesuits changed human anatomy.

But Az-Azir's programs finally won over and forced the entity to withdraw. The ultra flopped to the floor like a dissected specimen. The entity screeched once then floated back to the relic and slowly sank back into the hull.

Michael turned on me. "I told you this wouldn't work, but you wouldn't listen."

"Michael, please." I reached out for him, but he backed away.

"I told you that massive retaliation is the only answer." He paused, and I sighed because I knew what he was about to say. "There are other . . . weapons."

"You're talking about something that could take years to find, if they exist at all."

He stormed off as a medic team rushed in to help the stricken ultra.

I watched Michael's receding figure. The force of his conviction made me doubt myself and all the collective efforts of the ultras. Maybe I was the ambitious one, encouraging these futile experiments. Maybe the War Council really did need to think about wide scale counter attacks before . . . before the predicted extinction of humanity.

But if not our technology . . . the alternative made me cold inside. What had stopped the original cataclysm millions of years ago? What had destroyed the pilots and made the ships and their sentient spacesuits dormant? Whatever it was, I couldn't help but feel that it would dwarf us and perhaps raise a new spectre over our heads more lethal than the relics themselves.

UNAUTHORISED MISSION LOG OF MICHAEL LEVESQUE: DESIGNATION
UNKNOWN, 4075.

My battle lens flicked through the spectrum, scanning the surrounding jungle. Light reflected across my skinsuit as I brushed away a swarm of black insects. They reminded me so much of . . . I clenched my fist and adjusted my inhibitors, shoving away the unwanted emotions.

The lens scanned the terrain—it looked much the same as it had from orbit—a nameless tropical world around a nameless sun on the boundary of colonised space.

I turned south through the dense undergrowth. The canopy was home to an array of noisy wildlife, only glimpsed as dark forms behind the leaves. Occasionally a branch would thump to the ground, disturbing the bright insect swarms.

I soon found the tree-dotted valley. At its centre stood a small tower hidden behind strands of ivy and black moss. Seismographic readings suggested at least 99.999% of the structure lay beneath the surface. I peeled away a handful of moss to reveal panels of vacuum-pitted steel and industrial diamond. Ancient jade symbols were embossed across the panels in hypnotic patterns.

I attempted to open a com link.

Nothing.

I switched to more contemporary channels. Empathic grid protocol should stir any residual programs in the structure. When no response was forthcoming I switched to quip—qualia immersion protocol—risky, for we had used this on the spacesuits with disastrous effect, but I had not come this far to be beaten.

I waited a few minutes, but there was nothing except the background noise of the jungle and the sound of my own thoughts racing ahead to the consequences if I left this planet empty handed.

My eyes turned towards the symbols. I coaxed my stubborn memory, the meaning of the words on the tip of my tongue.

On clear winter nights in the orbital I would stand on the top balcony and look up at the stars and see images of people and animals. Sometimes I imagined I saw gods up there, and on other nights I would look deeper into the blackness, as if floating out to eternity. That was before the world had changed, before dad had been driven crazy by the entity. Then I saw her corpse swinging, occluding the stars, but it had Chenzira's face, the red sun fading her to silhouette. The vision of her milky-white eyes and decayed skin knocked my breath away, tossed away like flotsam all the years I had worked to protect her, the only person I loved now. And as my hopes faded, I sensed them out there . . . swarming in symbiotic clusters . . . calling up enormous energies into a howling chorus . . .

Sunlight and the sounds of the jungle bled back in.

I blinked as my lens flashed urgent warnings. The quip had worked, but not in the way I had intended, and now I was caught in a feedback loop. I watched helplessly as my hands moved over the symbols of their own volition.

A voice rumbled across my mind.

I am The Bane. You may not approach.

What was I thinking to have got caught up in the security encryptions, but this *thing* was from a time before recorded history. And here I was, bludgeoning in like a fool.

I tensed and bunched my arms, then dug my feet into the loamy ground in an attempt to push away from the wall, but my hands remained glued to the symbols.

The ground began to shake as a vibration shivered its way up through the structure. More warnings flashed and the lens called up images of thousands of monofilaments pulsing out of the wall, slipping through my skin and twisting up around my bones and organs. I could do little now except stand there with my hands stuck stupidly to the structure.

Before the filaments reached my head I sent a message to my ship in orbit. A firestorm flashed down through the canopy, incinerating a twenty metre wide hole into the jungle. My protective field expanded and the conflagration flushed over me with a deafening roar. The structure appeared unharmed amidst the clearing ash and smoke, revealing a vast jade carving of alien gods.

The monofilaments pierced my brain. Pain flashed behind my eyes as the weapon's persona began to disassemble me, system by system.

It was like dying all over again.

UNAUTHORISED MISSION LOG OF CHENZIRA NWOSU: REGULUS A, 4143.

The weapon hung in orbit, a ten kilometre spike of steel, diamond and jade pointing down to the jovian cloud tops. It was an engineering marvel, a tapering cylinder with fluted edges, ornately carved by some long dead civilisation.

Michael waited with me in the weapon's war nexus. He was a different man, if "man" was the right word. His skin had turned metallic grey and his tattoo was silver. He wore it more as an affectation now that the weapon's persona had removed his inhibitors.

It was almost like he was in detox. On his good days, he would adopt some the weapon's mannerisms: a dark humour in his voice, an arrogance in his stance. On the bad days, there was a haunted look behind his tattoo . . . and something more . . . a *fury*.

I shuddered to think what was going on inside, but I loved him just the same. I often wondered at my own folly. I shouldn't be here; *we* shouldn't be here, plotting the course of the war without the collective wisdom of the War Council. But Michael had been right—politics and military machinery cannot fight blind destructive force. I was not the only one who believed in his cause—a growing band of rogue ultras were siding with him, and now the Council was divided.

The war nexus swirled into focus. The jovian planet was enormous, bordering on a failed star. Its atmosphere was a cauldron of interconnected storms and weather patterns, with equatorial belts of amazing brown, blue and orange clouds. Aurora flickered around the polar regions like white ghosts.

"You said you needed mass," Michael said, confiding with the weapon.

The weapon laughed maliciously. "It will take years, my friend."

Perhaps Michael had sold his soul to this thing as it seemed to enjoy its job with a dark delight. And in turn, maybe I had given up something of my own soul to be here with Michael.

The nexus shifted perspective and we were bathed in the harsh blue-white light of Regulus. A prominence hung above the upper right quadrant, an arc of plasma some two million kilometres long suspended by a magnetic field loop. Then a series of dark shapes distilled out of the brightness of the plasma arc—a dormant nest of relic ships.

Michael shunted files to the weapon. "I have gone over the calculations again. Here are my final estimates."

"Very well," the weapon said, as if readying itself.

I held my breath as several shudders jarred the superstructure. Then Michael and I left the nexus through an osmotic transition chamber, out into vacuum. A crack appeared along the hull as thrusters fired up and the lower three kilometres of the weapon began its descent into the atmosphere.

We hung motionless for a time, hypnotised by the sight as the segment adjusted its trajectory, eventually disappearing below the clouds.

Within the hour the first pellet emerged from the planet at hypersonic speed. It hammered past us, a blazing fifty tonne lump of plasma enriched with heavy elements from the fusion that had occurred in the lower section of the weapon. We backed away to a more discreet distance as the pellet was caught in the magnetic scoop of the upper section and fired silently away into space.

My battle lens picked up a Doppler shift reading of 0.5 light speed.

Another half a dozen pellets came hurling out of the atmosphere to be sucked into the heart of the accelerator and spewed out at relativistic speed. This was followed by a constant stream of pellets forming a fiery chain between the planet and the accelerator.

I watched them stream across the ecliptic. They would take three hours to reach the star. Michael scrolled through schematics of the nanotugs waiting inside the star, ready to snag the pellets and drag them down, adding much needed mass to the already rich iron core.

We had finally done it—set in train a monumental process that might just change humanity's bleak future. It was a simple twist on star seeding. In this case, the pellets would be extracted by the trillions, literally tearing the heart out of the planet.

But it would not matter in the end, as there wouldn't be anything left after the supernova expunged the system like the fist of god.

DATACAST OF MICHAEL LEVESQUE FROM THE BANE: REGULUS A, 4250.

I had instinctively known the purpose of the relics, as far back as those innocent days when I flew with my friends . . . no, before then. But I had never voiced it. Perhaps I had always waited for some new facts to come to light and dispel my fears, or perhaps my inhibitors had prevented me from expressing the obvious all this time. With each passing year the purpose of the relics was undeniable, writ large in the battle song of the spacesuits and in the harmonics of the ceramic hulls—they were searching for their pilots.

And now I had seen some the pilots for myself, four fossilised remains deep within the vaults of *The Bane*. They were disturbingly humanoid with war-like triangular faces, multi-jointed limbs, and incredible layered exo-skeletons. Like the combat-ultras, they were technologically advanced, but evolved for a single, uncompromising purpose—destruction.

I reluctantly embraced what they represented and tried to understand their motivations—I had to know my enemy. It also gave me the much needed fuel to keep my stubborn plan alive all these years. So each day I walked the long corridors to the vaults and studied the specimens as *The Bane's* alien algorithms continued to integrate within me. Sometimes I felt like a puppet on a string, and on other days I was just a teenage kid again, walking hand-in-hand with a psychopath.

"They have no weaknesses," the weapon said.

"So you say."

"You are doing the right thing, Michael."

I didn't answer as I made my way back to the war nexus.

The weapon seemed miffed; even it could be petulant. "Suit yourself. But it's you who found me, remember."

How could I forget?

Chenzira was in the nexus. I watched her as she monitored the com-channels. She was always there for me, but I didn't deserve her. She had given everything to me and no matter how hard I tried I could not reciprocate as there was something at my core—buried from years of addiction to the nano-inhibitors—that always held me in check.

She turned to me, but her smile quickly faded. "Are you okay?"

"I'm fine," I lied. "I'm still adjusting to the algorithms."

I noticed her face was pale and blotchy. "What about you?"

She shrugged. "I've been feeling off for the last hour or so, I've probably spent too long in the nexus." She called up the image of the star. "But we're so close now."

Schematics scrolled into view of the onion-layered interior of the star—heavy elements burning through their cycle. It was the core that was of most interest. Readings from the nanotugs were erratic. The levels of nickel-iron build up would inevitably reach a point where the fusion process ceased. From there the core would collapse and rebound in a devastating shockwave.

I turned back to Chenzira. There was a strange look on her face. "Maybe you should take a—"

The air crackled around her as the entity tunnelled into the nexus. It thrashed over her head and latched onto her collar bone. She screamed as it ripped open her chest.

Blood sprayed across my face and I staggered back. I heard grunting in the distance and realised it was coming from me.

"You must remove her." It was the weapon.

My arms moved like an automaton. "No!"

"It's the only way."

My hands reached for my gun. Fletchettes shot out, slamming Chenzira and the entity now wriggling into her across the nexus. I tried to drop the gun, but it wouldn't budge, and another round of fletchettes forced Chenzira through the osmotic layer.

This time the gun fell away and I stepped out into vacuum. The entity was inside Chenzira now, *zipping* her up from crotch to shoulder. Her skin blackened as the spacesuit activated, its amber lenses glowing.

A Scourge cloud sprayed out from the suit, boiling space in a confusion of black on black. It spread in all directions, penetrating my field, cutting through me. I felt *The Bane* quickly adjust my systems, sealing off wounds, rejecting the femtotech from my body. It bled away back into space.

Then . . . the light of a thousand sunrises flourished; a brightness like no other stretching from zenith to nadir, bleaching everything in its path. Chenzira's suit screeched over the com-channel and *The Bane* adjusted my systems to the photon flux, but only barely. We could not survive long out here, but there was still time before the full shock front arrived, still time to rescue her.

As I turned to her I saw the relic ship come up from its hiding place beneath the hull of *The Bane*, a sleek manta ray rising up towards us. In that single moment I knew its intentions—if they couldn't find the original pilots then they'd make their own.

Nausea crept across my gut.

It's the only way.

A micro-singularity pellet flew out of my palm and detonated against the Scourge, vaporising it instantly . . . and plastering Chenzira and her suit across the relic in long gelatinous strands.

I watched, dumbfounded as residual bands of blue energy coiled along my arms. Then I stared in disbelief as the suit tried to rally the gobbets that remained of Chenzira, drawing them together like pools of viscous treacle, until a confused mass appeared. The quivering thing that was once my lover made one final attempt to regain its structure then sank into the hull. The relic ship retreated and I turned my head away, the images of her now more indelible than the supernova light.

A silent howl ripped out of my lungs. That thing lifted out of me now, free from its prison. My scream of retribution resounded over the com channels.

Let them hear it.
Let them fear me.

VIGILANCE RECORDING: FLAGSHIP *INNOCENCE*, DISPERSION FLEET, 4893.

The destruction of Regulus A was the first in a concatenation of stellar deaths triggered by Michael Levesque. The shockwaves destroyed many relics, and the gamma radiation killed millions of humans. But in turn it has helped save the billions who now reside in the arcs of the Fleet.

We maintain our course outwards, near light speed now, away from the wastelands that were once the human colonies.

The war still rages behind us. The enemy has many pilots—combat-ultras that were once our own weapons of choice, now in servitude.

To this, we are vigilant.

Of Michael Levesque, there has been no contact since the one and only data cast from *The Bane*. Rumours abound along the com-channels that he has unearthed a fleet of weapons.

To this also, we are vigilant.

JOURNAL OF MICHAEL LEVESQUE: ALDEBARAN ORBITAL, 3738.

14 August

I went out to play with my friends. Some of them already have flyers. I wonder when I'll get mine. Dad said it won't be long now, maybe when I'm eight. He's such a cool dad.

9 October

Dad came back from the xenoarch station for the school holidays. Mum misses him when he is away. I miss him heaps too.

He brought me back a present—a splinter of the special black ceramic from one of the relics!

I held it for a few minutes and watched the rainbows along its edges, but then it shook in my hand and I dropped it. The sound was like cymbals clashing so hard that it hurt my ears, and it kept going even after dad picked it up and put it on the bookshelf.

He said he couldn't hear it, and I knew he wasn't lying.

It made me cry.

10 October

I haven't touched it again, but I can still hear it, though it's much quieter.

Dad said not to be afraid. It's strange because it's alien, and it has properties that can make it fly through space. He said maybe that's what I was hearing.

"Who were the pilots?" I asked, but he didn't know.

"Were they real aliens?" I asked, and he nodded.

He looked at me kind of funny. "What's wrong? They're just relics. The aliens died millions of years ago."

"Have you seen them?"

"No, I told you, the ships are empty." I know when he lies. Mum told me his lips curl a little at the edges.

"But what if the aliens come back? What if they try to hurt us?"

"Oh, come on, Michael. Don't be silly."

27 October

I listen to the sounds at night. It's almost like someone is singing, but it's angry and sad at the same time, and sometimes it makes me fall asleep and I have bad dreams.

I don't want the aliens to come back. They always chase me in my dreams. They don't like us being here.

Mum rocks me back to sleep some nights.

On other nights I lie awake. I've made up my own song as it helps me push away the noise from the splinter. It's an angry song and I know I shouldn't be like that, but I can't help it because I know the aliens would hurt us.

And if they did then I'd have to kill them.

And if they didn't stop hurting us then I would have to kill them all.

AFTERWORD TO "WEAPONS OF CHOICE"

The world of the Combat-Ultras has been simmering away in the background for a couple of years. I think I have the seeds of a brutal space opera full of young resistance fighters, beautiful relics, mysterious aliens, star-destroying weapons and deadly spacesuits. There are really far too many ideas for the short story format, but at least you get to see them now before I expand it into a novella or novel. Watch this space!

SIGNALS IN THE DEEP

There's a place in our future where we are all heading, driven by our instincts and the deep heritage of our genes. It is a place where we are more at peace, in harmony with the universal fabric from which we were born. It's what I was taught, and it's what I believe. Our past provides a foundation, a platform from which we can achieve great things: growth, meaning, *enlightenment.*

I tried to instil this belief into Matthew as any good mother would—show, don't tell. But it seems that the young are both deaf and blind to old-world values. I rationalised his anger at first. Looking beyond the veil of testosterone, it was his imperative to experience life for himself and to sometimes learn things the hard way. After all, there is no manual when you are born into the skin you live in.

Then, as Matt blossomed from boy to teenager, I began to doubt myself and wondered what I had done to estrange him. The genome patent meant he didn't need a father, but there were plenty of male role models during his semesters at the private didactic havens. He developed incredible skills in languages and mathematics, and although the complex problem solving could make him so detached, in hindsight it was a source of comfort for him. He was gifted from the start—before he was even born—and if I was honest with myself, it had raised my expectations into the stratosphere.

And therein lay the irony: in providing for everything perhaps I had unwittingly given him little cause to look back. There was no sense of the past for his generation; everything was about the here and now, and the future was something to worry about when it arrived. I realised, too late, that I must have come across as so set in my ways: stern, reflective, always grounded.

The chill autumn nights are spent pondering these things under the spatter-painted veil of stars. The motor on the tracking dish hummed quietly, the barrel of the telescope cold in my hands. Ancient light shone into my eyes, translating into images, connecting me again—the past was always with me.

But did Matt see it now? Was there such a thing in his world?

I wasn't sure. Heaven help me, after two years with no word or sign from him, I wasn't sure at all.

And there was only one way to find out.

EARTH + 100KM

My journey began with cold sweat beading on my skin as the elevator rose up and up on a white-knuckled ride into vacuum. I had never been good with heights, but this was ludicrous. Nothing should be this high—it seemed physically impossible—yet the elevator kept going until the cerulean sky turned indigo and the stars shone more intensely.

The steward had been keeping a watchful eye over me on the way up. He had a ceaseless capacity for small talk, which was harmless enough, but now a worried frown creased his face as I clumsily disembarked.

"Are you okay, Beth?"

I didn't reply, preoccupied with weightlessness and being towed across the bridge to the shuttle port by an usherbot the size and shape of a dustbin. I glanced through the viewing ports, trying to keep my eyes away from the cloud deck far, far below. There were several more elevators in the distance, rising like needles along the curvature of the world.

"They're impressive," the steward said, a cheeky smile playing at the corners of his lips.

Please go away. I nodded and smiled as best I could. "There are so many of them, and it's all happened so quickly."

"I guess that's why they call it the Quickening." His lips turned down as my face darkened at his pun. I had used affordable nanotech to create Matt's genome and I often blamed the technology for my predicament, but it was just a classic case of denial.

As we entered the bustling port I began checking for signs to the shuttle departure lounge, but this was a damn confusing place. No doubt there were a thousand data casts flying about, but what I needed was a *physical* sign.

The steward's eyes widened, convinced, I am sure, that I was a complete anachronism. Then to my surprise he tucked his arm through mine with that same familiarity. "Where are you travelling, Beth?"

Okay, so maybe I do need your help. "Pluto . . . Charon Relay Station actually."

His eyes widened even further. "The back of beyond. I've always wanted to go there, they say the stars are . . . " He caught my look again. "The departure lounge is just this way."

EARTH + 2AU

It is said that you can make friends in the most unlikely places. And this shuttle was one of those places: a cold, disorienting cavern, with row upon row of rockbusters reeking like a metal refinery.

The rockbuster next to me tried to strike up a conversation, his third attempt. "You're a long way from home . . . ?"

"Beth." My feet dangled, child-like, over the edge of the seat.

"I'm Ryan."

A rockbuster named Ryan; what stories your mother could tell.

He turned his enormous plated head, gyros whirring, metal creaking, and leant over me. His massive biceps brushed dangerously close to my head. "Are you management?"

"Do I look like management?"

"No." He seemed unfazed by my terseness, but I doubted that anything could bother these giants. "And you're not a tourist. Not that we get many out this way. Some engineers, a few scientists, and management . . . sometimes."

"So you work the belt?" It was an infantile deflection, but home seemed so far away, my worry now consuming more hours of each day that passed. Maybe that was a mother's lot in life, but then again, it seemed that I had more than my fair share—a constant, gut churning state. And it was starting to show.

"What do *you* think?" His eyes gleamed mischief deep beneath the edge of his cheek plates.

"Judging by your pitted armour, three metre frame and stubborn demeanour, I'd say so."

He half turned in his seat, his plates sliding across each other like an avalanche, a smile on his segmented lips. With a hint of conspiracy in his voice, he said, "So you must be looking for something . . . or *escaping* something."

My exasperated sigh misted the air. "I'm looking for my son."

"Ah." He relaxed back in his seat, another avalanche. "The truth. We're all searching for it in our own way. You find a vein of ore; it's an achievement, a vindication that you serve a purpose. There's truth in that. If your friends speak plain words, you know you can depend on them—truth again."

"You're quite the philosophical one."

His eyes swivelled. "For a robot?"

"No, I wasn't going to say that."

"But you thought it."

Maybe. I let out a long breath. "Okay, yes." Ryan was human deep down. And I had no doubt that his decision to work in vacuum, to go through the physical torture of bio-metal skin grafts, was not an easy one. I knew this, yet to listen to him, to look at him . . . "I'm sorry."

He shrugged. "Maybe I come across like one: irrefutable, irritating logic and all. But space does that to you. There's no room for shades of grey, at least not in my line of work." Then, "I take it you haven't seen him for a while?"

I nodded, trying to stop the surge of emotion, the pent up frustration. This man's presence was calming, but at the same time he was a stark reminder to me, raking my fear, gathering up a storm of dreadful possibilities. I began to wonder how much Matt had changed. What had he gone through to adapt? What decisions had he made—*life-changing* decisions? Would I even recognise him? And more importantly, was he happy in himself, accepting, like Ryan, or was he still the angry young man I remembered?

Ryan patted me gently, his hand completely covering my forearm. "Solar winds and empty space, it shouldn't be too hard to find him."

My tears floated up and away from my face, tiny spheres drifting.

EARTH + 6AU

Chartering the light sail had cost me the rest of my savings. The cabin was very small and beige and although it had all the necessary facilities, it would become a lonely prison during the long months ahead. The fixed autopilot's lights blinked occasionally from a tiny alcove, its bland chrome head rotating on a stalk, constantly monitoring.

Ahead, through the viewing cells, the sail stretched out like delicate foil reflecting sunlight into shards. But photonic pressure alone could not drive this tiny ship, and so it needed supplementing from the orbital laser array at Jupiter to bring it up to the velocity necessary to reach the outer solar system.

And behind: the Sun so remote now that I had forgotten its warmth. But then it is hard to feel warmth of any kind when one's soul is locked in ice.

I had sent a message out to Matt on my departure from Earth, and again at the asteroid belt. The only thing I received was a silence that spoke volumes. My anxiety shifted then, became anger.

He was the communications expert. The outer system relay stations were being constructed to assist with the exploration and population of the Kuiper Belt. So if he could communicate with the settlers, *why* was it so hard to stay in touch with me? If he had no time for a personal message he could have arranged an automated update or blog. Hell, he could have sent something by solar snail mail by now.

I looked down at my jiggling legs and placed my hands on my knees. Peering into the dark, hoping that it might calm me somehow, I saw a light appear beyond the edge of the sail, tracking against the star field. It was on the same vector; perhaps it was a tourist yacht. But something about it didn't feel right. It was tracking quickly now, which meant its relative velocity must be enormous, well beyond anything I had heard about.

"Pilot, what is that to port?"

The pilot's head rotated and two lights blinked on its chrome head. After a few seconds there was a metallic reply: "Unknown."

"Your best estimate?"

Another few seconds: "Experimental space probe or military craft."

"Military? But there's nothing out here."

Solar winds and empty space.

EARTH + 38AU

I had taken to roaming the methane ice wastes of Charon during the days. The baroque spacesuit had good power, large spotlights and was insulated enough to stave off the incredible cold. Even so, it was still reckless of me to wander the hills and valleys. But not so reckless that I didn't steer clear of the cryo-geyser fields, though on my darker days I thought that being trapped in the geysers might provide a fitting end to my foolishness.

The backlit crescent of Pluto peaked above the horizon, casting long shadows across the ground, stretching out towards me—raven wings of a kind. My mind was playing tricks, and all I could do was let it run wild. What else was there in this hell hole?

I think I was a distraction for the grizzled scientists and technicians at the relay station for, oh, ten minutes or so. They were as perplexed as I was when I drifted in like flotsam, a random event that upset their daily routine. They had no idea where Matt was, nor were they willing to answer my questions about what he was actually doing if he wasn't at the station. After some grumbling they sent a message to him then hastily located me in a habitat dome away from the main nest of the station to wait for the reply. Three weeks later, my mind turning lethargic in the stale air, the walks were providing a reprieve of sorts.

Today I had ventured further than before, taking languid strides out to a low ridgeline south of the habitat. The suit's external crampons gave me purchase, but occasionally I tripped until I got into the ludicrous rhythm of moon walking: walk, sprawl, slide, stand, walk.

By the time I made it to the ridgeline I was gulping for oxygen. I checked the suit monitor: still green. Then something caught my eye and I crouched down instinctively. The valley beyond was covered with domes with square lit windows, radio dishes at the perimeter, a launch platform lined with the translucent delta-shapes of spaceships resting on landing stems. And there . . . rockbusters operating large equipment . . . there, humans in white skinsuits . . .

The com-channel crackled in my helmet.

"What?" I began to turn, sensing movement behind me.

"State your identity." A young man's voice, used to being obeyed.

"Don't move." A young woman now.

My spotlights swept over them . . . white skinsuits . . . sleek gold-glass helmets . . . carrying long barrelled vac-weapons . . . grey static across my vision now . . . a heavy feeling in my head . . . down on one knee . . . "Wait—"

EARTH + 38AU

"You were extremely lucky," Graeme said. He had permanently windswept hair and a serious frown for a fourteen year old.

"Those old suits are unreliable," Trace said. "And you were out there too long. You could have asphyxiated." Her eyes were palest blue and her black hair was tied up in a spiky bun, giving her an innocent look that belied a sharp wit and intelligence. I liked her a lot—an attitude tempered with a maturity beyond her years. She reminded me so much of Matt just before he left home.

I glanced around the white walls of the med-room. The single viewing port revealed one of the launch pads I had spied from a distance. "What are you doing here?"

Graeme's frown deepened. "That's classified."

I turned to Trace, my eyes pleading.

She arched an eyebrow at Graeme. "I think we can ease up a little. The approval arrived via the Jupiter Relay this morning."

He gave her a *whatever* look.

I looked at them both in turn. "You're not here to help the settlers, are you?"

Graeme sat back in his chair. "No, ma'am."

Trace leaned forward and took my hand. Her skin was warm, and filled me with hope I thought I had lost, until her words cut through, grating at my naivety. "Matt doesn't work on Charon."

"It's taken me a *year* to get here. Where is he?"

She squeezed my hands and glanced through the viewing port. "He's out there, beyond the heliopause."

I began to shake and leant forward until my elbows touched my knees. The air seemed suddenly unbreathable again. "It's too far . . . how can I . . . "

Trace moved to me and put her arm around my shoulder. "We've sent a higher priority message to him, but it might take some time."

EARTH + 50AU

"He didn't tell you, did he?"

It was Trace's voice, heard in my mind as if from a murky distance, echoes along the shore of a raging sea. I opened my eyes. A milky white film crawled across my vision. I made to raise my hand to rub my eyes, but I couldn't move. I tried to breath, but there was something slimy sitting heavily in my lungs.

"What—?"

"Don't panic, it's just the dampening gel." A pause. "There, that should do it."

My eyes, or the gel, cleared; then a chemical rush regulated my heart rate. I cleared my throat, adjusting to the subvocalisation. "Are you licensed to administer pharmaceuticals?"

"You're hilarious, Beth."

We were suspended in a small, angular cabin with no visible controls or systems. I sensed a delta shape around us, sleek and transparent against the backdrop of space. "What is this thing?"

"It's an interceptor. Bio-ceramic hull, neural-interface circuitry, top speed in excess of 10,000 kps . . . ah, look, I really shouldn't. Beth, no parents come out here . . . ever. You're an enigma, and under any other circumstances you'd be turned around in your light sail and sent home. But we figured Matt didn't tell you about the conscription so the least we could do is arrange a meeting."

It struck me that Trace had considerable authority. "You love it here?"

I felt her inner smile . . . there was an empathic component to the com.

"I still don't get it. What could possibly be a threat here in the middle of nowhere?" *No disrespect.*

"None taken."

"Oh . . . " *More than empathic.*

"There doesn't need to be a threat, just the possibility of one." Feeling my confusion, she added, "There's more here than interstellar dust. We've discovered a communication network of unknown origin."

"You're talking about aliens?"

"We think it stays outside a system's heliosphere until its civilisations are advanced enough. Or it could be a relic network and all we're hearing is remnants of dead civilisations. Either way, we're very cautious in case there's a risk of viral data packets . . . for want of a more technical explanation."

My mind raced ahead. "Matt's an interpreter?"

I felt Trace nod, but there was apprehension.

"What is it?"

"Nothing."

"Don't fob me off, Trace."

Fair enough. "The oldies—it's an endearing term for people like Matt approaching their twenties—if they're good at what they do then they get moved into the deep. You have to *adjust* or die."

The truth. For the first time since my arrival, I had finally found a vein of ore. I rummaged around the com, trying to delve deeper into her mind. There was more; I'd only caught a glimmer.

She said, "I'm going to have to activate the gel again. There's still a long way to go."

"Has Matt changed?" But another question begged at the back of my mind. *Is he still the son I used to know?*

The gel activated. I forced myself across the com before unconsciousness took hold . . . there . . . a feeling carefully held in check . . . doubt . . .

EARTH +100AU

A tingling sensation ran over my body—the after effects of the gel?—no, it was a white skinsuit, knitting with my nervous system. It felt almost intimate. Thankfully it didn't extend over my head; I'd had enough of feeling claustrophobic. Instead, fresh oxygen circulated within a gold-glass helmet.

I turned my head, expecting to see Trace. The Milky Way was a bright etching on impossibly black velvet. My arms thrashed involuntarily—I was EVA!

The com hissed and her voice filtered into my waking senses, a long way off still. She was talking to someone.

"Long time, my friend."

"You too . . . "

"What is it?"

"I haven't spoken English for a long time."

Laughter.

"Why is she here?"

"She wants to know you're okay."

Silence.

"She's a good person." *Kind of strict, in a your-best-interest way.* "I wish my parents cared as much . . . oops, I think she's awake . . . twenty kilometres to starboard."

"I know."

Silhouettes glided languidly across the star field until I could see the sheer, terrifying wonder of him. He was there—at the centre—but the rest of him was strung out in many disconnected parts. What looked like advanced relay panels were stretched over delicate bio-ceramic bones, unfolding over kilometres. Titanium pivots and joints secured critical junctions of the larger pieces. The entire array ebbed and flowed, resonating to Matt's remote commands, a thousand separate parts miraculously working in synch—a dark cybernetic angel gliding down to meet me.

I extended my arms as he approached, the sheer scale of his structure more daunting as he got closer, until I was at his centre, his human body encased in a sleek black bio-alloy skin. His eyes were still the same, that dark brown with green flecks, glazed with a protective covering that blended into his skin.

I held him, apprehensive at first as the massive wings seemed to bend in toward us. He was changed beyond reckoning, but still himself inside, still Matt.

"You shouldn't have come."

"Is that any way to greet—"

He laughed. "I've missed you, Mum."

I squeezed him tighter. With so many questions, after all this time and all that I had witnessed, I still couldn't move beyond the selfish ones. "Why did you leave?"

"Why do you think?"

"Was I too controlling?"

"Of course not. I'm sorry if I was angry all the time, but I did listen to you." *I just couldn't wait to experience life.* "Out here the past is more important than ever. You have to be grounded to survive. If we don't have a strong sense of who we are, then how can we face of the unknown?"

I laughed inwardly. Such a blind thing I had become, journeying all this way with the answer in my back pocket. It was that paradox that all parents face at some point. He was always going to grow up despite my good intentions and overbearing guidance. It just happened a little sooner than I expected, or rather sooner than I was willing to acknowledge.

He let me float free and turned away, breaking my reverie. He was focussed now upon some object that I could only just make out against the star field. His wings shuffled and folded in like a line of dominoes, quickening into a blur of movement. There was something agile about him, as if he were capable of great speed—like the interceptors.

The object came into view slowly, an odd-pointed shape distilling out of the dark. I urged the skinsuit forward and felt a slight pressure on my back. I followed, a white speck hovering above the expanse of his wings. We seemed to take forever to reach the object, until it dawned on me that it was on a different scale altogether. After about thirty minutes Matt decelerated suddenly, but my vector carried me forward and I tumbled away over one of his panels until the skinsuit righted my spin.

"Sorry," I said.

"My fault."

We fell into a synchronous orbit. The object was shaped like a giant black star fish, but the arms were multi-segmented, stretching out for a thousand kilometres or more. It was moving and fluttering, in a way that seemed biological or semi-sentient, as it coaxed the faintest of signals from the interstellar medium.

"How was it discovered?"

"There have been anomalies in heliospheric imaging for over a century—where the warmer ions of the solar wind meet the cold interstellar gas. We knew that the bulk of the anomalies were caused by the galactic magnetic field draping over the heliosphere. This object's magnetic field appeared as a point anomaly on the imaging in a year when the heliosphere extended much farther out than normal." He seemed mesmerised as he swung down, gliding closer over one of the arms. "You're right. It is self-aware, most likely on the low end of the Turing scale. If you concentrate hard enough you can tap into its empathic link. It knows about us; it can sense us now. They've known about us for a long time."

"They?"

"The signals are coming from Fomalhaut, and being relayed on to other systems. It's a data and com network of sorts—an interstellar internet if you will—but that's a fairly primitive analogy."

I hesitated. Something inside me desperately wanted to know, but another part of me was petrified by the possibilities. *What are they saying?*

Matt reached out and touched a finger to my helmet. Something electric shimmered through the skinsuit, up through my nervous system, images cascading into place . . .

A young, orange star surrounded by a massive dust ring extending out and out. On the inner edge of the ring, a Jovian world with swirling storms of violet and grey surrounded by a chain of satellite moons, worlds in their own right that would dwarf Earth. Each of the moons is transformed by civilisation— bubble ecologies, floating cities, blue-white skies over ring worlds, with the starfish arrays connecting all in a vast hub of interaction.

And deeper down, into the network—images and empathic memories of a collective, then voices in a fantastic dialect that stretches into the upper harmonic. The citizens? . . . no, custodians . . . they are older than this world, transferred here millennia ago . . . via the network . . . biotech . . . their angular heads turn atop bodies that look like dancing blue flames.

The eyes of one entity swivel then widen in acknowledgement. I can see its indigo irises, so close now, speckled with white circuitry. The pupils dilate . . . it is looking *at me—*

The skinsuit thrusters pushed me away and the link faded. My eyelids fluttered as the treacly slide into unconsciousness took hold . . . then Matt was with me, shaking me gently. I gasped. "How is that possible?"

"We're not sure. It could be an autonomic response programmed into the starfish—a bit like an interactive interstellar greeting card. But some of us speculate that it could be a true faster-than-light relay. I've spent a lot of time analysing this. They're survivors, and their technology is . . . well, we can't make assumptions . . . we must be vigilant."

I looked at him then, behind his technology and his vacuum-adapted skin. For the first time I realised why the motion of his massive structure seemed familiar. His new body, his entire array, moved like the starfish.

"Oh, Matt."

He arched a dark metal eyebrow, his eyes like beacons. "It was the only way. We don't know how to operate the starfish and any attempts to get inside it might destroy or disable it. But we can scan and replicate—*align* with it."

He looked at me then, in that way that he used to before bed time when he'd tell me about his day at the havens and the patterns he saw in things. Our talks helped him understand his intuition—a young boy in awe of the world around him.

I float for days in the path of the data stream.

I sighed. *There's truth out here if you listen long enough.*

EARTH

Ancient light fell upon my retina as the tracking dish hummed. The autumn nights seemed colder after three years, but there was a warmth now, inside me, that pushed away the chill.

I had been living in denial, grounded in the misconceptions of my own humanity. In wanting so much for Matt, I had forgotten to listen to him. Physically, he was far from human now, but spiritually, as he touched those alien signals in the deep, he was more human than any of us could be.

And with that knowledge, I was finally able to let go, to open up my own horizons.

I turned away from the telescope as an icon flashed on my computer. A new message scrolled down the screen.

Hello, Mum.

AFTERWORD TO "SIGNALS IN THE DEEP"

"Signals in the Deep" was my first story to be run through the gauntlet of the US genre machine. I was delighted by the reaction I received from the publisher, the reviewers and the readers.

I wanted to write about a mother's journey—a worried Mum who doesn't know what's happened to her son and doesn't understand why he hasn't stayed in touch. (That's me—sorry, Mum!) I really did just want to write a feel good story set against the backdrop of the solar system. I wasn't trying to break new ground or develop new takes on future science or provide fresh insights into the genre.

It was interesting how the feedback from the reviewers varied from the readers. I think the reviewers see such a volume of material that they are always looking for that needle in the haystack that takes the genre another step forward—"something new". But I think there's a place for heartfelt, traditional themes that don't constantly stretch (and shred) the limits of science (and plausibility), so long as they are entertaining and make readers feel something. Judging by the readers' comments on "Signals in the Deep", I think they felt something. I hope you did too, particularly if you are a guy who doesn't call his Mum. Get on the phone, now!

ACKNOWLEDGEMENTS

"Alien Intent" © Greg Mellor 2011. Appears here for the first time.

"Autumn Leaves Falling" © Greg Mellor 2009. First published in *Cosmos Online*, edited by Jacqui Hayes.

"Beyond Winter's Shadow" © Greg Mellor 2012. Appears here for the first time.

"Day Break" © Greg Mellor 2010. First published in *Cosmos Magazine #38*, edited by Damien Broderick and Cat Sparks.

"Defence of the Realm" © Greg Mellor 2007. First published in *Cosmos Magazine #25*, edited by Damien Broderick.

"Ethos Anthropoi Daimon" © Greg Mellor 2006. First published in *Novus Creatura*, edited by Michael C. Pennington and Arthur "JAM" Miller.

"Eyes of Fire in My Waking Dreams" © Greg Mellor 2010. First published in *Aurealis #48*, edited by Dirk Strasser.

"Fragments" © Greg Mellor 2010. First published in *Cosmic Catastrophes*, edited by Chris Bartholomew.

"Heaven and Earth" © Greg Mellor 2010. First published in *Aurealis #46*, edited by Stuart Mayne and Dirk Strasser.

"Hollow Places" © Greg Mellor 2011. First published in *Specutopia #1*, edited by Dale Wise.

"House of Cards" © Greg Mellor 2010. First published in *Hit Men*, edited by Chris Bartholomew.

"Ravenous" © Greg Mellor 2011. Appears here for the first time.

"Robo Sapiens" © Greg Mellor 2011. Appears here for the first time.

"Signals in the Deep" © Greg Mellor 2011. First published in *Clarkesworld Magazine #60*, edited by Neil Clarke.

"Social Contract" © Greg Mellor 2012. Appears here for the first time.

"Static" © Greg Mellor 2009. First published in *Deep Space Terror*, edited by Chris Bartholomew.

"Stranded Light" © Greg Mellor 2012. Appears here for the first time.

"Terra Q" © Greg Mellor 2011. Appears here for the first time.

"The Trouble with Memes" © Greg Mellor 2010. Appears here for the first time.

"Time Capture" © Greg Mellor 2012. Appears here for the first time.

"Weapons of Choice" © Greg Mellor 2011. Appears here for the first time.

AVAILABLE FROM TICONDEROGA PUBLICATIONS

978-0-9586856-6-5	Troy by Simon Brown (tpb)
978-0-9586856-7-2	The Workers' Paradise eds Farr & Evans (tpb)
978-0-9586856-8-9	Fantastic Wonder Stories ed Russell B. Farr (tpb)
978-0-9803531-0-5	Love in Vain by Lewis Shiner (tpb)
978-0-9803531-2-9	Belong ed Russell B. Farr (tpb)
978-0-9803531-3-6	Ghost Seas by Steven Utley (hc)
978-0-9803531-4-3	Ghost Seas by Steven Utley (tpb)
978-0-9803531-6-7	Magic Dirt: the best of Sean Williams (tpb)
978-0-9803531-7-4	The Lady of Situations by Stephen Dedman (hc)
978-0-9803531-8-1	The Lady of Situations by Stephen Dedman (tpb)
978-0-9806288-2-1	Basic Black by Terry Dowling (tpb)
978-0-9806288-3-8	Make Believe by Terry Dowling (tpb)
978-0-9806288-4-5	Scary Kisses ed Liz Grzyb (tpb)
978-0-9806288-6-9	Dead Sea Fruit by Kaaron Warren (tpb)
978-0-9806288-8-3	The Girl With No Hands by Angela Slatter (tpb)
978-0-9807813-1-1	Dead Red Heart ed Russell B. Farr (tpb)
978-0-9807813-2-8	More Scary Kisses ed Liz Grzyb (tpb)
978-0-9807813-4-2	Heliotrope by Justina Robson (tpb)
978-0-9807813-7-3	Matilda Told Such Dreadful Lies by Lucy Sussex (tpb)
978-1-921857-01-0	Bluegrass Symphony by Lisa L. Hannett (tpb)
978-1-921857-05-8	The Hall of Lost Footsteps by Sara Douglass (hc)
978-1-921857-06-5	The Hall of Lost Footsteps by Sara Douglass (tpb)
978-1-921857-03-4	Damnation and Dames ed Liz Grzyb & Amanda Pillar (tpb)
978-1-921857-08-9	Bread and Circuses by Felicity Dowker (tpb)
978-1-921857-17-1	The 400-Million-Year Itch by Steven Utley (tpb)
978-1-921857-24-9	Wild Chrome by Greg Mellor (tpb)
978-1-921857-30-0	Midnight and Moonshine by Lisa L. Hannett & Angela Slatter (tpb)
978-1-921857-10-2	Mage Heart by Jane Routley (hc)
978-1-921857-65-2	Mage Heart by Jane Routley (tpb)
978-1-921857-11-9	Fire Angels by Jane Routley (hc)
978-1-921857-66-9	Fire Angels by Jane Routley (tpb)
978-1-921857-12-6	Aramaya by Jane Routley (hc)
978-1-921857-67-6	Aramaya by Jane Routley (tpb)

TICONDEROGA PUBLICATIONS LIMITED HARDCOVER EDITIONS

TICONDEROGA PUBLICATIONS EBOOKS

THE YEAR'S BEST AUSTRALIAN FANTASY & HORROR SERIES
EDITED BY LIZ GRZYB & TALIE HELENE

WWW.TICONDEROGAPUBLICATIONS.COM

THANK YOU

The publisher would sincerely like to thank:

Elizabeth Grzyb, Greg Mellor, Damien Broderick, Leanne and
Jamie Tufrey, Cat Sparks, Jonathan Strahan, Peter McNamara,
Ellen Datlow, Grant Stone, Jeremy G. Byrne, Sean Williams,
Garth Nix, David Cake, Simon Oxwell, Grant Watson,
Sue Manning, Steven Utley, Bill Congreve, Jack Dann, Jenny
Blackford, Simon Brown, Stephen Dedman, Sara Douglass,
Felicity Dowker, Terry Dowling, Jason Fischer, Lisa L.
Hannett, Pete Kempshall, Ian McHugh, Angela Rega, Angela
Slatter, Lucy Sussex, Kaaron Warren, the Mt Lawley Mafia,
the Nedlands Yakuza, Amanda Pillar, Shane Jiraiya Cummings,
Angela Challis, Talie Helene, Donna Maree Hanson,
Kate Williams, Kathryn Linge, Andrew Williams, Al Chan,
Alisa and Tehani, Mel & Phil, Hayley Lane, Georgina Walpole,
everyone we've missed . . .

. . . and you.

In memory of Eve Johnson (1945–2011)